Bruce B

Murder in our Midst

Detective Inspector Skelgill Investigates

LUCiUS

Text copyright 2021 Bruce Beckham

All rights reserved. Bruce Beckham asserts his right always to be identified as the author of this work. No part may be copied or transmitted without written permission from the publisher.

This is a work of fiction. Names, characters, places and incidents either are the product of the author's imagination or are used fictitiously. Any resemblance to actual persons, living or dead, events and locales is entirely coincidental.

Kindle edition first published by Lucius 2021

Paperback edition first published by Lucius 2021

For more details and Rights enquiries contact:
Lucius-ebooks@live.com

Cover design by Moira Kay Nicol
United States editor Janet Colter

Editor's Note

Murder in our Midst is a stand-alone crime mystery, the seventeenth in the series 'Detective Inspector Skelgill Investigates'. It is set in the vicinity of Grasmere and Rydal Water, an area famed for its romantic beauty and associations with William Wordsworth, at the heart of the English Lake District – a rugged National Park of 885 square miles.

The DI Skelgill Series

Murder in Adland
Murder in School
Murder on the Edge
Murder on the Lake
Murder by Magic
Murder in the Mind
Murder at the Wake
Murder in the Woods
Murder at the Flood
Murder at Dead Crags
Murder Mystery Weekend
Murder on the Run
Murder at Shake Holes
Murder at the Meet
Murder on the Moor
Murder Unseen
Murder in our Midst
Murder Unsolved
Murder in the Fells

Glossary

Some of the Cumbrian dialect words, abbreviations, British slang and local usage appearing in *Murder in our Midst* are as follows:

Arl – old
Beck – mountain stream
Blow the gaff – reveal a secret
Bob – shilling
Boot – trunk (of car)
Boozer – pub, heavy drinker
Brass monkeys – freezing cold
Brummie – from Birmingham, England's second city
BTO – British Trust for Ornithology
Burner – cheap disposable cell phone
Butcher's – look ('butcher's hook' – Cockney)
Carr – sparse marshy woodland
Cha – tea
Chippy – fish and chip shop
Chuffed – pleased
Cleg – biting horsefly
Clemmed – thirsty
Clarty – muddy
Cob – bread roll (Midlands)
Conk – nose
CPS – Crown Prosecution Service
Cur dog – hardy fell sheepdog
Currant bun – sun (Cockney)
Deek – look/look at
Dinner – commonly refers to lunch
Donnat – idiot
Earwigging – secretly listening
Ecky thump – expression of surprise
EPOS – electronic point of sale
Fell – hill, mountain
Fettle – health
Forsythe Saga – lager (Cockney)

Gill – small ravine
Griff – inside information
Happen – possibly, maybe, thus
Helm-wind – fierce local wind that blows from Cross Fell
Hotch – shuffle
How! – cry used for driving cattle
Howay – come on
In't – isn't (Midlands)
Int' – in the
Jock – a Scot
Kiss and cuddle – muddle (Cockney)
Loo – toilet
Marra – mate (friend)
Mash – tea/brew tea
Me duck – friendly form of address in East Midlands ('my duke', from Saxon *ducas)*
MO – modus operandi (criminal method)
Nan – grandmother
Nickt int' head – having extravagant fancies
North and south – mouth (Cockney)
Nowt – nothing
Old Bill – police
Owt – anything
Pash – sudden heavy shower of rain
Pike – peak
Prat – someone stupid or foolish
Reet – right
Rosie – tea (Cockney, 'Rosie Lee')
Rozzers – police
RSPB – Royal Society for the Protection of Birds
Scrow – mess
Snap – packed lunch/sandwiches (Midlands)
Sozzled – drunk
Stoke – place (Old English)
Stotting – raining heavily
T' – the (often silent)
Ticker – heart

Tod Sloan – alone (Cockney)
Us – me
Wersh – sour and dry taste
While – until
Yon – that

List of Characters

Members of the house party:

Daisy Mills* (nee Lux) 61 – former PA; lives in Shenton Magna

Simon Mills 58 – husband of Daisy; business owner; Shenton Magna

Karl Eastwood ('Clint') 54 – business partner of Simon Mills; Nuneaton

Kenneth Dalbrae* 61 – impresario; Soho, London

Ben Lomond 47 – fund manager; civil partner of Kenneth Dalbrae; Soho, London

Sarah Rice† 57 – younger sister of Charles; yachtie; Cowes, Isle of Wight;

Rik Hannay* 61 – actor ('resting'); Kilburn, London

Hugo Grant* 60 – entrepreneur; Milngavie, Glasgow

Jane Grant 61 – wife of Hugo; physics lecturer; Milngavie, Glasgow

Harry Badger* 61 – sales manager ('retired'); Burton Magna

Poppy Lux† 57 – younger sister of Daisy Mills; medical receptionist; Shenton Parva

Dr Charles Rice* ('Spike') 61 – television presenter; Stoke Dry, Rutland

Gail Melia 55 – partner of Dr Charles Rice; conservationist; Stoke Dry, Rutland

* Class of '79, Middlemarch High School
† Class of '82, Middlemarch High School

1. RYDAL WATER

Sunday, 7.00 a.m. – early May

'It's hard to imagine a more beautiful place than this.'

DS Jones's somewhat wistful delivery makes her statement sound rhetorical, but Skelgill looks up from his knot tying. His eyes appear olive green in the deep shadow of a Tilley hat, one that might be another of his heirlooms, judging by its aged condition and somewhat baggy fit.

'It's chocolate box country.'

Beauty being in the eye of the beholder, his tone hints that he might disagree.

Nonetheless, he casts about discerningly. And perhaps he admits some new appreciation into his critique. But DS Jones can guess he would choose a more rugged alternative. The view from the lunar rubble of Haystacks upon Buttermere and Crummock Water, or his beloved Bassenthwaite Lake with the brindled flanks of Skiddaw as a steepling backdrop. And he would probably pick angry weather.

Yet her case is strong; just about any vista would do it, whether photographed or drawn or painted from their present locus on the water, or looking down upon them from the sun-dappled fells to the diminutive oak-fringed pool that is Rydal Water; imagery that must have graced the lids of countless confectionery productions down the years; its real and romantic association with Wordsworth icing the cake. Thus Skelgill's assessment of their surroundings is accurate, if a backhanded compliment of sorts.

She anticipates perhaps what would be one of his objections.

'It's quiet at the moment, though.'

Skelgill is back at biting nylon line. He nods, head bowed. She hears the snap of his teeth. He spits away the loose end and inspects his handiwork.

'Aye. While Whitsun.'

He uses the vernacular – he means until the English holiday week, when the schools are off and accommodation prices double.

'I've heard the Lakes are sold out this year.'

Skelgill squints pensively across the water; a gentle ripple corrugates its surface and defeats the brim of his hat with shimmering reflection.

'They'll be fly-camping again – nightmare for the rangers. Let's hope it's stotting down.'

DS Jones gives an ironic chuckle. She understands his point – that rain might deter those casual visitors who disrespect the national park and tarnish the lake shores with a tideline of charred jetsam: festival tents, cheap folding chairs, disposable barbecues, plastic food packaging and, inevitably, worse. But wishing for rain in Cumbria, home to England's wettest spot is the tempting of hair-trigger meteorological fate. Even Skelgill, raised in the fells and seemingly inured to the harshest climes, has a salutary warning for those who will listen.

Clouds int' sky – rain by and by.
Sun int' sky – rain by and by.

More McGonagall than Wordsworth, Skelgill claims the aphorism is handed down through shepherds in his clan; and it does have a ring of authenticity in its terse cynicism. Undiminished, DS Jones brightens and stretches like a spring flower unfurling its petals to the sun; she notices his attention.

'The forecast says blue skies all weekend.'

Skelgill shrugs as though unconvinced. With a whip and a whirr he casts out a length of line onto the water.

'Here – try that – just a single mayfly – it should stop the wind knots.'

DS Jones reaches to accept the rod; he is teaching her to fly fish.

'I get wind knots and there's no wind!'

'They're worse in the wind – even accomplished anglers suffer them.'

'Even you, Guv?'

'How do you think I learnt to swear properly?'

She regards him with a look of amusement; she can conceive of plenty of other ways. But she turns her attention to the task in hand.

'Tell me again.'

'Do what I say – exactly when I say it.'

'Okay. Ready.'

'Lift – *flick* – pause – *flick*.'

'Oh.'

'Not bad.'

'You're humouring me.'

'You know us better than that, lass. Hold steady.'

Skelgill, taking care not to unbalance the small boat, shifts to straddle the rear thwart on which she sits sidesaddle. He reaches around and takes hold where her hand grips the cork butt of the rod.

'Listen to the rhythm.' He guides her movements, as a technician might programme a factory robot. 'Lift – *flick* – pause – *flick*.'

'Ah.'

Her intonation conveys understanding, though she seems momentarily dazed by his partial embrace. He, too, lingers for a second – then he retreats to give her space.

'Try again – this time don't bend your wrist – keep it stiff like you're using a hammer.'

She does as bidden, whispering his little mantra under her breath.

'Hey! It worked.'

'Nice line.'

Indeed the line goes out straight and drops lightly upon the water, turning over the leader and presenting the artificial mayfly with a little flourish.

'But how do I cast further? How do you keep it in mid air?'

'Run when you can walk. It's more important to be stealthy than to overreach – you'll end up in a right old scrow and spook the fish.'

'Hmm.' She sounds unconvinced; but Skelgill would recognise her ambitious nature seeking the next challenge.

'Keep your eyes peeled – if you see a rise, cast at it.'

'What would it be?'

Skelgill does not answer immediately; his own gaze is constantly scanning the surface.

'This is a coarse fishery – that's why it's open, out of season. That said, flowing from here you've got the Rothay; it's part of the Leven system – salmon's not out of the question. Sea trout. Arctic char, at a push.'

'Wow – and there's me just planning to take home some Grasmere gingerbread.'

Skelgill tuts.

'That's not the attitude.'

DS Jones simpers.

'True – but you know about my Mum and her baking. Fish is not really her cup of tea.'

Skelgill, as a self-proclaimed sweet-toothed *and* savoury-toothed person, allows the argument to fall.

'How's the arl feller?'

His companion looks surprised; not necessarily that he feels such solicitude, but that he expresses it.

'Oh, well – he's been quite good lately, actually. The doctor has put him on a new drug that seems to have improved his mobility.' She looks up and blinks at the bright sky. 'And this weather helps – it just makes you want to be outdoors.'

Skelgill reflects for a moment; he appears content to be diverted by this thread. He reaches over the gunwale and dips up a sample of water. He lets it slip slowly between his long fingers as if he is gauging the temperature.

'Aye. Although like the Scots say, there's no such thing as bad weather, only the wrong clothes.'

DS Jones smiles amenably; this is another of his favourite adages; she is only slightly surprised that he has not appropriated it entirely from their neighbours across the border, fifty miles north. She watches as he wipes his palm on his jeans. For her part, she is wearing very little – just a vest top and shorts that prompted him to ask if she was going for a jog. But as he has progressively stripped off layers of waxed cotton, down to shirtsleeves, her choice of outfit has been vindicated.

When he might be expected to hog the angling opportunities, Skelgill seems content to manoeuvre the boat; he makes occasional adjustments with an oar while DS Jones continues to perfect her technique. It is clear to Skelgill that she has quickly mastered the feeling, the principle that in order to 'push' out a line it can only be pulled. Perhaps she reads his thoughts.

'At what point can I move on to running?'

Skelgill glances at the position of the sun, still relatively low over the shoulder of Loughrigg Fell; then he calibrates his estimate against his wristwatch.

'Happen we could stop for a mash.' He nods in the direction of a wooded islet. 'Heron Island.'

'Does it have a heronry?'

Skelgill screws up his features. Now he gazes to the northern horizon.

'There's a fell about a mile yonder – it's called Heron Pike. The name origin's probably nowt to do with the bird.'

But he does not offer an alternative, and instead begins pulling at the oars, perhaps since she has known better than to demur at the suggestion of tea.

'Shall I reel in?'

'Aye. Hook the fly into the keeper above the cork.'

DS Jones diligently follows his instructions. Still holding the rod, now she trails her fingers into the water.

'This feels like *Swallows and Amazons*, Guv. I don't know why, but I always wanted to be an Amazon.'

'What, packing or delivering?'

She laughs.

'I take it you never read it.'

'It's Windermere, aye?' He says this as though it might be a justification.

'Well – it's fictionalised – but a blend of Windermere and Coniston Water, reputedly.'

Skelgill remains doubtful.

'Can't see why you'd go to all that fuss on the water and not fish.'

DS Jones reads this as a supplementary excuse for his specific illiteracy; she knows of others more general. But they are running up towards the shoreline, and now she takes the initiative. She kicks off her trainers and nimbly clambers past Skelgill and hops over the bow into the shallows, drawing the painter and thus the boat onto the shingle.

'You've done that before, lass.'

'I seem to remember you complained at me last time, for waiting to be told.'

Skelgill appears a little sheepish and busies himself with stowing the oars.

'Aye, well – I probably went a bit overboard with captain's orders. Happen it were the weather.'

'It was blowing a gale.'

Skelgill picks up a wooden crate and makes a rather ill advised leap for the bank. In over-stretching to stay dry he stumbles and is forced to stagger several paces to keep his feet. DS Jones regards him with a reproachful frown; all he needed to do was to hand it to her in the shallows.

'If you used a plastic box you could have floated it to me.'

Skelgill is down on one knee, emptying out the contents – most notably his battered and soot-blackened Kelly kettle. He looks up with a twinkle in his eye.

'Aye – but you can make a mash with an orange box.'

For a moment she is perplexed.

'Do you mean, burn it?'

'When there's no dry twigs.' He casts a hand towards the woodland fringe. 'Not a problem today.'

'I'm on it.'

When DS Emma Jones was first assigned to work with Skelgill – suspicious as he was – he soon realised she did not have to be asked twice to do something; frequently she does not have to be asked at all.

'You'll be relieved to know I filled the Kelly from the tap.'

DS Jones gives a small involuntary laugh.

Skelgill normally champions the charging of the vessel from the adjacent lake or stream, revelling in the self-sufficiency of fuel and water coming naturally to hand. She quickly supplies him with a small bundle of dry twigs, some of which he stuffs into the base of the kettle and douses with methylated spirits; he is not such a purist as to insist upon flint and tinder.

His storm kettle might be antediluvian in appearance, with smoke billowing from its chimney like some relic of the industrial revolution, but it is extraordinarily efficient, and in hardly two minutes they are sitting facing the lake cradling tin mugs of tea. Skelgill has even brought actual milk, so DS Jones has achieved a drinkable temperature. For a few moments they contemplate the view in silence, until a vigorous rise just twenty feet from the shore causes Skelgill to start.

'That just took a mayfly.'

'Oh – did you see it land?'

Skelgill glances at her sharply.

'It was a dun.'

'Guv, I read English literature – biology was never my strong suit. And definitely not after the lesson about leeches.'

Skelgill grins happily.

'The nymph swims up to the surface to hatch, in a manner of speaking. Then it's called a dun. It's the last-but-one stage before the full adult. That's when they're most vulnerable. Then, and when the females are laying.'

'Poor females.'

Skelgill makes a scornful sound in his throat.

'The males don't last much longer.'

'It's just a day, isn't it – or is that folklore?'

'A day or so – as adults. But the life cycle's a full year. Obviously.'

He casts an illustrative hand towards the lake. She nods – the logic does not defeat her.

15

'Three hundred and sixty four days as a juvenile; one day grown up.' She notices that he raises his eyebrows. 'I can see it has a certain appeal.'

Skelgill can think of a drawback of such prolonged adolescence; but before he can contrive a witticism she diverts him with practical curiosity.

'So the artificial mayfly – that's a representation of the adult female, landing on the surface to lay its eggs?'

'Aye – as you cast. If you let it lie it's more like one that's died – but you can still induce a take.'

'It's quite a cunning trap.'

Skelgill narrows his eyes as he stares across the lake.

'I'd say the fish are ahead.'

DS Jones inhales to respond but she holds the breath as a Morse-code-like alert emanates from the boat. She changes tack accordingly.

'Is that not the mountain rescue?'

Skelgill rubs a knuckle against the stubble of his chin. Slowly he turns to her with a look that is perhaps more inquiring than it ought to be. There is the suggestion that he could easily be swayed to ignore his phone.

'I'll get it.'

DS Jones rolls halfway back and then springs up. Still barefooted, Skelgill notices for the first time that her toenails are painted in a somewhat bohemian purple. It appears she intends to wade once again.

She splashes out to the craft and rummages for his mobile phone; it is in the pocket of his creased and threadbare Barbour gilet. She glances at the screen as she returns.

'Talk of adult female. It says "Casualty – Rydale – Buckstones Jump" – Rydale?'

'That's us.'

She squats back beside Skelgill and passes him the handset. But the complete message is no more forthcoming. He addresses her query.

'Rydal – Rydale – same word. But Rydale itself is the actual dale – beyond this fellside. Nab Scar.'

He points to the northeast, a little to the left of the way they face. The immediate slope rises steeply, covered in bracken and scattered oaks, but there is the suggestion that running around behind the bluff is a valley.

'I doubt Buckstones Jump's above a mile as the crow flies.'

'What is it – an abseiling spot?'

Skelgill glances at her with surprise.

'It's a plunge pool – on Rydal Beck. There's waterfalls all the way down Rydal Fell. It's popular with sightseers – when you've got Ambleside just down the road.' He scowls. 'Folk get high on mint cake and then hike in their flip-flops and high heels.'

Ordinarily DS Jones would be amused by his suggestion. But it is a serious matter and he does not joke. She indicates to the handset.

'Does the description "casualty" tell you anything?'

He understands she is asking if this is code, such as the police employ when subject to eavesdroppers. He looks again at the message on his screen and shakes his head.

'Most likely a report from a member of the public – status uncertain. There'll be a team on standby that'll be talking by radio. This text is just in case anyone's nearby.'

'Which, as you say, we are, Guv.'

There is the suggestion in DS Jones's tone that it is not something they can ignore – but in any event Skelgill is rising, albeit stiffly.

'I can be there and back within the hour. I'll probably be first on the scene. I'll hand over to the team when they arrive.'

'What – you'd abandon me on an island? What if there are Amazons?'

That she uses an unfair tactic seems to jolt his plan. But he begins to respond in kind. He makes a sweep of his arm, indicating the sandy stretch they have occupied.

'You can improve your suntan.'

'Guv – I'll be swimming after your boat if you leave without me!'

She is smiling but Skelgill knows determination when he sees it. And she adds a more pragmatic rider.

17

'I've just passed my Level 3 first aid.' She knows this is in advance of her superior's qualification. 'And I can help carry your kit.'

Skelgill grimaces and reluctantly offers a hand.

'Probably hadn't better leave you to outswim the leeches.'

2. DAISY

Five months earlier – English Midlands

Daisy Mills is pleased with herself. The party is swinging and her 'Audrey Hepburn' has received bouquets in abundance. Not bad for a now sixty-something who has kept her figure on a diet of champagne and chocolate. She flutters her lashes at Rik Hannay as she sashays into the candlelit kitchen – why can't she help herself? He winks over the shoulder of Sarah Rice; they are in very close conversation, Sarah leaning in to whisper – though they always were close, and Daisy suspects that down the years they have kept in touch (in more ways than one). Despite the meagre comb-over where once there was a blond shock, Rik looks hardly any different, a bit of a paunch, and a little careworn perhaps; and Sarah still has her auburn tresses – although she was three forms below them, with her sister, Poppy. Daisy finds it hard to compute, but – for the former Middlemarch High pupils, at least – it must be over forty years since they've all been under the same roof; probably Prize Day, in the summer term of 1979. And Hugo sweeping the board, for one last time.

Where is he?

He, too, has shed his mane, of brown hair; but he seems as fit and firm as back then. Pretty much everyone is in good shape. This is not what they would have foreseen; they're now nearer the age of what would have been their own grandparents. Sitting around sipping sherry – not mingling promiscuously like one of those teenage parties when someone had an 'empty'. Earlier, a succession of 'old' people had arrived – fleetingly unfamiliar – and then a curious refocusing occurred; the wrinkles and the hair loss became blurred leaving just the familiar bright eyes of their youth.

The theme has gone down well – 'Stars of the Seventies' – music and movies, the sensory backdrop to their coming of age. Sweaty discotheques and fumbling clinches on the back row at the Gaumont. She wonders if Hugo is sending her a covert message, coming as '007' – the Sean Connery version, he says. He can do the accent, and he carries off the tuxedo. She enjoyed asking him if that were a pistol in his pocket. He said wasn't that Mae West's line? But Karl Eastwood overheard them and made a lewd attempt to hijack the joke – something about "feeling lucky". Rather predictably he has come as his namesake, Clint.

She'd sensed Simon watching her when she greeted Hugo. She tried to act as though she were unaware. But it's so hard to hide anything from Simon; he's like a mind reader. Even when she's telling him the truth he makes her feel like she's deceiving him, that he knows the truth is just there to paper over the cracks of what lies beneath. Hugo behaved more naturally than she could ever do – he acted awkward, embarrassed. But his wife didn't like the moment – maybe he was thinking of her feelings, heaven knows why.

Jane Grant has never seemed much fun to her; whatever did Hugo see in her? Plain Jane with her man's haircut. Even he had once admitted she was dour – she smiles to herself – he'd pronounced it the Scottish way, *doo-err*, rolling the 'r'. But they've been together long enough now. He says he's avoided talking about his past, but she's not so sure; a woman can tell these things. And she wishes now she hadn't said as much to Simon. But – with the company she keeps – these things were always going to come out; Harry Badger can't keep his big mouth shut, and Kenneth is ever quick to gossip, and he and Ben enjoy winding up Simon; they call him 'Simon Says' behind his back.

She wonders where Jane Grant is. She went on Simon's tour earlier with a couple of the others. Last time she saw her she was in earnest conversation with Spike – *hah!* – "Dr Charles Rice" as he is always referred to on the television, as though the 'doctor' means he knows best – even though he's not an actual doctor, just a boring academic, like Jane Grant. When he was plain Spike, drunk and high and throwing up back in their heyday he was much more fun – though he probably resented that they ribbed him for his gangling ineptitude and inability to hold his drink. Now he is too serious; supercilious at times, she feels, towards his kid sister, Sarah.

Daisy empties into the sink the cocktail glass that has been pressed upon her and lifts a magnum of champagne dripping from the oversized ice bucket; Simon has been casually keeping it going; that it's a mere trifle. Champagne for her – she prefers it to cocktails – they go to your head – after a couple you can be flat on your back. *Hmm.* But most guests are opting for cocktails. Perhaps they're humouring Simon as host, letting him show off his moves and politely not pointing out that his 'Tom Cruise' is the best part of a decade too late. When he had announced he would make cocktails she had suggested their teenage repertoire, for the girls rum and black, vodka and orange, snowballs – and lager and lime for the boys. But Simon had turned up his nose. Gin, apparently, is 'in'. So the invitations were drafted accordingly. At his command, a battalion of white spirits and coloured liqueurs stands to attention – the guests have brought more, but he makes clear he doesn't need to rely on them – he has placed the gifted bottles to one side, like a table of trophies for an awards ceremony. She'd heard him quip to Hugo, asking had he come to take over as bartender – as if the dinner suit made him look like a butler – but before Hugo could answer Harry Badger, first to arrive and already drunk, had barged in, insisting that 'Bond' should have a martini and it must be stirred and not shaken. Then Gail had slipped between them, hooking an arm through Hugo's and insisting, no, it was the other way around.

Where *is* Gail? In her scarlet Sophia Loren dress she has been popping eyes; she fills it well enough, she's so voluptuous. She's a good laugh, Gail – what she sees in dreary old Spike, Daisy can't imagine – but they have their wildlife studies in common. Who'd have thought a nymphomaniac would breed rare bees? But even nymphomaniacs need their distractions. Of course, Gail hasn't passed the venerable sixty-mark like a lot of them. In fact if it weren't for Spike she would never have met

Gail. He made a TV programme about her beekeeping – Daisy and Simon were invited to the press screening in London. She had dressed up like Audrey Hepburn that day, too. When you've spent your adult life as her double why not make the most of it? A photo of her on the arm of "Dr Charles Rice" had appeared in the Daily Mail. She knew it had annoyed Gail – it should have been she, but for an artful switch of partners on the red carpet. Gail had to make do with Simon. But Gail had hardly known Spike any length of time, compared to her. Why shouldn't Daisy have basked in the limelight?

Where is Gail? Daisy decides to look for her. Now that she's had a few drinks she feels like exchanging gossip – to get Gail's view on all the men, all these blasts from her past; Gail has not met Hugo before tonight; Daisy has made sure of that!

She saunters into the flickering candlelight of the wide, beamed hallway and finds herself before the great flaking antique mirror. Talk about the eyes being a window to the soul – so what is a mirror? A window to the conscience? She sips demurely as she faces her reflection. She realises she is recreating the scene, 'Holly Golightly' drinking her coffee outside Tiffany's in New York. The long black dress, the bare shoulders, the dark hair piled up. And the eyebrows; still she pulls it off. She's the same height – 5' 7" – perfect for a woman. She can wear heels without making most men feel inadequate, although it bothers Simon when she looks taller than him. She can wear flats and still look elegant. Her diamonds are glittering. Simon's diamonds; he had insisted she wear all of them tonight – flaunt them. And Simon had to have an old manor house. "Lord of Mills' Manor", he calls himself. Sometimes she thinks he takes it seriously; the idea of the status. And he likes to give a casual tour of the stables. "Oh, wow, Simon – you have a Ferrari!"

From the doorway she looks into the "Great Hall", as Simon refers to it, with its cavernous hearth and crackling log fire and ten-foot fir tree that exudes the scent of Christmas. She wonders if he chose to set up his cocktail bar in there so as not to be left alone in the kitchen (that Jona Lewie song tarred some people for years). So he has made himself the centre of attention in a subtle way, not being one of them. He doesn't really get on with her friends. He doesn't really get on with anyone. She positions herself as though she is not intending to enter, so it's easier to reverse away from unwanted attention. As she suspected, Jane Grant is still talking shop with Spike. She seems to be a little awed by his celebrity status. Hugo is nearby – listening keenly to Poppy. She wonders if he ever secretly fancied Poppy. But she was never as good looking – and, besides, when they were seventeen Poppy was still a kid, fourteen. Jailbait, Harry Badger used to call her – he had his crass chat-up lines even back then (for such a remark was really aimed at her, she knew). She was never going to go out with Harry Badger – not even to get back at Hugo. She wouldn't even do anything now – would she?

They are all talking loudly because of the volume of the music. Simon had wanted his boring jazz to go with the cocktails, but she had insisted it had to be pop: soul and Motown, Barry White and Diana Ross, the opium of their formative years; Friday nights blaring from the jukebox in the back room of The Knitters Arms, and Wednesday discos at the rugby club on Ashby Road. She and Hugo, always it seemed going out with the wrong person, eyeing one another forlornly across the smoke haze that shrouded the dance floor, staccato figures beneath the pulsating strobe lights, until the flashing UV picked out her trademark blouse like she was Snow White.

Karl Eastwood and Harry Badger are having some heated discussion about global warming. Discussion, debate, argument – that's all Harry has got to show for the years. Harry is a loser, and she can see that Karl is at once revelling in it and despising him. For a moment she feels a pang of sympathy for Harry, despite everything. Harry is one of their own; Karl is an outsider – in fact Daisy doesn't know much about where Karl came from. He was already Simon's business partner when she and Simon started going out. Simon never talks much about him – she's not even sure if they like one other. When she has asked Simon about that, he answers obliquely. He always names two Manchester United footballers who apparently never spoke but who formed the most deadly striking partnership in the league. *Huh*, football. Flip side, she can do as she pleases when it's on.

A stifled squeal attracts Daisy's attention. She turns to glance up over her shoulder. Above one end of the hallway is the minstrels' gallery, with rooms and corridors off it. Daisy abandons her shoes on the first step and begins to ascend; her dress is so long she has to be careful not to trip on the hem. She always thinks of Daphne du Maurier's *Rebecca* when she goes up – but at least it's her own portrait that graces the head of the staircase – imagine, if Simon had insisted upon keeping the one of his ex. Incredible, really, that he'd thought he could still hang it somewhere in the house; originally in his study, like some men display certificates of their qualifications and photographs of their bold exploits, trophies perhaps, pretending it's a private sanctum and that they're not actually showing off, when of course they know visitors sooner or later will venture inside or be invited within on some pretence.

Now there is a rather depraved laugh and she recognises it as Gail, for sure. And it has not escaped her notice that there's no trace of Kenneth and Ben. She homes in on successive exclamations that emanate from the main public bathroom behind the minstrels' gallery. She rounds the rectangular landing, running a hand along the oak banister strung with fairy lights, and passing brooding landscapes that Simon pontificates upon. Barefooted, she glides silently over the Axminster carpet. Now she hears Kenneth's voice. He shrieks something like, "There's always a first time!" and laughs hysterically. Daisy doesn't think of knocking – not in her home – and these are her best friends. The landing, too, is candlelit, and there are more candles – scented ones – burning in the various loos, so when she pulls open the door shadows and exotic aromas confront her.

Kenneth and Ben have come as a typically eccentric pairing, Dr Jekyll and Mr Hyde – Daisy can't remember which one is which, nor can she quite figure which '70s movie star they are meant to be (maybe *two* movie stars?) – but their flamboyant period outfits are marvellous nonetheless and as usual no expense has been spared to achieve perfection.

Kenneth steps forward and blocks her entry.

'Darling, join our little breakaway party.' His delivery is suave, like an actor's. There was always a repressed hint of it at school, but he really let it loose once he 'escaped' to London, as he put it.

He holds his arms out wide and embraces her extravagantly. He is not much taller than she and over his shoulder she senses Gail and Ben moving apart.

Gail seems to rise and turn to the basin and run the tap, but then just as quickly she checks her face close up in the mirror, though she must hardly be able to see in the gloom. Ben is facing away and it takes him a moment to turn and smile winningly; he is very good looking, and a mere stripling in his late forties. Gail lifts two cocktail glasses from a vanity shelf and hands one to Ben; carefully they clink them together, as if conscious that a lack of concentration will result in a catastrophic collision.

Daisy pouts. Maybe she ought never to have introduced them; but since she has got to know Gail these last few years and enjoyed spending time with her, it was just a matter of time before Gail became acquainted with Kenneth and, inevitably, Ben.

What Kenneth and Ben get up to is not something she likes to think about, and Simon flatly refuses to discuss it – she senses he can only tolerate them to the extent that Kenneth is her lifelong friend; he does not let his thoughts dwell beyond their relationship. But it's a double-edged sword for Simon – the fact that Kenneth is gay almost certainly means he sees him as no threat, like a pharaoh delegating a trusted eunuch to chaperone his queen; in Ben's case it's a little more complicated – but *she* doesn't dwell on that.

'I need you downstairs – there should be more dancing. They're all being boring and arguing about politics and boasting about their jobs.'

Daisy suddenly realises that Gail may be offended, that she might assume she's referring to Spike – she can't think of him as Charles, no matter how hard she tries. And she feels a little

25

shocked; she's not sure quite what she has just interrupted – but also doesn't want to know. Kenneth wiped his nose in a peculiar fashion, as though it were a signal. But now he comes round to her point. It seems his opening remark was simply a gambit.

'My Daisyship is right – the night is yet young – as are we!'

They traipse downstairs, Kenneth arm-in-arm with Daisy and Ben likewise with Gail. The other three keep giggling and Daisy is in no mood to resist, despite her reservations. She has ever been capricious, an amalgam of prude and hedonist – a butterfly, Hugo calls her – one minute hidden in the long grass, hanging on to a stem, wings folded, sheltering from the rain, the next, when the sun bursts out, flying up and up, spinning with some other butterfly, a handsome stranger, no matter it was the wrong species; oblivious and ascending like Icarus until she burns off her wings! And so she joins with their laughter, content in not knowing what really lies behind it. Who needs a reason – it's a party, after all, and Christmas is coming.

They crowd through the wide doorway into the main room. "You Can't Hurry Love" is playing loudly and Kenneth swings her into a dance, holding her close. He has stayed slim and agile and she follows him easily, tossing back her head as she pirouettes. She catches Hugo's eye; he *could* be James Bond, so inscrutable is the gaze he returns. Round and round goes the room. There's Harry, watching her hungrily, but like a dog that knows its station; the taller Karl beside him feigning indifference, but cold in the eyes, more like a vampire sizing up his next victim. Simon doesn't know whether to watch her or her admirers – she can see that – he's got that fake smile that she has come to know; he's not adept at smiling at the best of times; he's looking flushed; he knocks back a drink, another telltale sign – but then Gail and Ben approach and distract him with demands of "Gin Fizz" and "Gin Rummy" respectively; even Daisy knows that Ben is taking the mickey.

Jane and Poppy are watching, too. Even though they're pretending to carry on their conversations. Funny how people's eyes give so much away; yes, those windows again.

The track ends and with a wicked cackle Kenneth slingshots her into a sofa – though she collapses willingly while he lurches towards Simon's cocktail bar. But immediately a new song strikes up and it's "Where Did Our Love Go" and Daisy sees Hugo detach himself from Poppy – and she sees the alarm in Poppy's face at his abrupt move. But hardly have the four opening clacks of the drumsticks played out before Harry, primed liked a greyhound in a trap, is skidding across the floor on one knee to ask for her hand. His breath reeks of ketones. Hugo pretends he's not coming – perhaps that he's going to the bathroom; she plies him with longing eyes, not caring who sees; he returns her gaze philosophically and exits the room. She hopes he'll stay late. The night *is* young. Things might happen. Things she can't imagine or hope for.

3. RUM GIN

Four months earlier – articles in the Middlemarch Mercury

Edition Friday 8th January:

CHRISTMAS POISONING OUTBREAK LINKED TO RUTLAND GIN

South Mercia Public Health Authority yesterday announced that the much-publicised spate of poisonings in late December has been traced to the manufacturer of Rutland Gin-Trap Gin, specifically the firm's *Nice 'n' Sloe* line.

Readers will recall that twenty-nine people required medical attention over the festive period, five were admitted to hospital, and one person died, it is believed as a direct result of the poisoning.

According to public health superintendent Kevin Ricketts the outbreak affected five unrelated households in the Middlemarch district – all of which had purchased *Nice 'n' Sloe* gin from an off licence in the town.

Mr Ricketts was at pains to play down the risk to the public. "The retailer had stocked a single case of six bottles, five of which have been accounted for. If there was a silver lining it was that gin is rarely drunk neat but instead mixed in cocktails or with tonic water, which means that it was consumed at a more dilute and therefore less harmful concentration. Our laboratory is conducting further tests to establish the precise nature of the contamination."

Approached by the *Mercury*, The Rutland Gin-Trap Gin Co. declined to comment. However their solicitors, Bishop & Rook of Uppingham provided a written statement. "Our client is a small artisan distiller, producing high-quality naturally flavoured gins for the discerning buyer. The company is devastated by the Middlemarch poisoning, and is taking all available steps to cooperate with the investigation. Until further information is forthcoming, it is not possible to speculate on the cause of the incident. It cannot be ruled out that contamination occurred at some stage in the supply chain AFTER leaving the distillery. As a precaution, however, the *Nice 'n' Sloe* line has been withdrawn from sale, and a nationwide product recall implemented. The company wishes to convey its heartfelt condolences to victims of the poisoning and their connections."

Edition Friday 15th January:

DRUG IDENTIFIED IN GIN POISONINGS

In a new development, South Mercia Public Health Authority says that the Rutland sloe gin at the centre of the Christmas poisonings was contaminated with a compound called atropine, which is used in various medical and research capacities. It is highly toxic and in only small doses may result in death from respiratory depression and heart failure. Paradoxically it is an effective antidote to synthetic nerve agents, and has recently been employed in high-profile poisonings involving the deadly chemical weapon known as 'Novichok'. Dangerous drugs such as atropine are subject to strict distribution and storage protocols, which adds to the mystery of how gin sold in a local independent off licence became contaminated.

Edition Friday 22nd January:

EXPERT DIFFERS IN OPINION

Following our article in last week's edition ('Drug Identified In Gin Poisonings') the *Mercury* have been contacted by a local expert, Dr Gemma Amanita of Daventry University Department of Botanical Sciences. We publish the main text of her letter in full, for the benefit of our readers:

"The chemical atropine occurs naturally in the plant Deadly Nightshade, *Atropa belladonna*. Fruits of this plant, and those of common blackthorn, known as sloes, are of similar size and appearance – juicy black berries about half an inch in diameter; equally bitter in taste. Like blackthorn, the nightshade favours chalk soils and can grow to a height of seven feet, preferring shade, and thus the two plants can intermingle in hedgerows. Under such circumstances an inexperienced forager or occasional fruit picker might easily mistake one for the other.

"Atropine can be found in a range of plants. I have a recent study from the United States that reports an average of 500 accidental poisonings a year, usually from the inadvertent incorporation of atropine-containing leaves into something else. There was a notable case of Paraguay tea imported by a New York herbalist when several people fell gravely ill, but fortunately no one died. Even honey from bees that have fed on Deadly Nightshade can give rise to poisoning. Honey would be especially problematic since its sweetness would mask the bitter warning taste of atropine. However, in the case of sloe gin, in which the sloes are pricked and steeped in alcohol, large amounts of sugar are added – as anyone who has made the liqueur at home will know.

"Recent reports of the 'Gin Poisoning' imply that the contamination was from a commercial source, but as you can see, there could just as well be a 'natural' explanation. Although not widespread throughout the UK, Deadly Nightshade is locally common in East Leicestershire and neighbouring Rutland, where it favours the well-drained Jurassic limestone soils."

We thank Dr Amanita for her perspicacious contribution. Clearly, the mysterious poisoning episode may have its roots running more deeply than the authorities would care to admit. Inquiries by the *Mercury* have established that a provisional report has been lodged with the Coroner's office. However, at South Mercia Constabulary no individual officer was available for comment; instead a written statement was supplied:

"There is no reason to believe this was anything other than an unfortunate accidental incident. It is standard procedure in the case of an unexpected or unexplained death for the Coroner to be notified. Due to the possibility of civil legal proceedings, it would not be appropriate for the police to fuel speculation. It is understood that the public health authorities have the necessary technical resources to complete their investigation into the precise origins of the contamination."

4. BUCKSTONES JUMP

Sunday, 7.55 a.m. – Rydale

'Will I be okay in trainers?'

Skelgill does not answer immediately. He is squinting to read the small text of his Wainwright guide. Little could the great Lakeland biographer have foreseen what a service he would provide to generations of mountain rescuers, with his detailed if at times acerbic descriptions of obscure ascents; twenty-six pages, Skelgill notes, for nearby Helvellyn. Now he is scrutinising the route up to Hart Crag, the more modest fell at the head of Rydale.

'He says it's a pleasant place for a picnic.' Skelgill snaps shut the book and glances searchingly at his colleague. 'Happen that's all you need to know.'

DS Jones nods and purposefully lifts onto her shoulder a black rucksack labelled "Oxygen". Skelgill watches for a second; it is not a large bag, but it weighs twenty-five pounds and defeats most unsuspecting porters at the first attempt. But DS Jones does not flinch, and shrugs it into place and simultaneously tightens the side straps.

'Hold fire.'

Skelgill reaches to assist with the chest clip – it seems an unnecessary adjustment; however she complies with his interference and affects a coy smile. A flush perhaps colours his cheekbones and he turns away to slam down the tailgate of his shooting brake and haul on a larger backpack, the first aid kit and survival gear. He has not deviated from his initial plan – he does not aspire to extract the casualty, merely to administer what emergency treatment is within their capabilities. "Until the cavalry arrives."

As he rowed Skelgill had dictated a text reply typed by DS Jones to the effect that they were within easy reach of Buckstones Jump. Having hastily moored at the jetty on Rydal Water and sprinted to the car, they sped the short distance to a narrow lane beside Rydal church; Church Lane, in fact, a short dead-end for traffic. Skelgill had directed DS Jones which bags to extricate from the congested rear compartment while he consulted his guide and Ordnance Survey map. As it stands, of the cavalry there is no sign.

'It's down to us, lass.'

DS Jones begins to move off in an uphill direction.

'This way?'

'Aye, just follow your nose. I find it works.'

DS Jones glances back as though she is expecting a pun, but none is forthcoming.

'Is it far – I mean, much of a climb?'

'About six hundred foot of ascent.'

'Is that a lot?'

'A small slice of gingerbread.'

They pass from Church Lane through a gate onto a woodland path. It would be a glorious morning walk, were it not for the gravity of their mission.

The still air beneath the canopy is resonant with birdsong; there is the indecisive whistle of the spectacular but elusive redstart, and a cascade of liquid notes from a more modestly plumed willow warbler. Dappled green light filters down to mingle with the electric shimmer of bluebells, an undulating carpet starred with white stitchwort. Orange tip butterflies flatter to deceive, feigning to settle but never quite obliging the onlooker; hoverflies, too, invite a snatch and grab, but shift position faster than the blink of an eye. The crashing rush of water ebbs and flows as the pair stalk determinedly uphill, sometimes closer to the beck, sometimes driven into a detour by a mossy outcrop.

They emerge from the woodland first into an alder carr, where the trees thin out and moorland takes over. Despite the dry weather the ground is boggy in places, and Skelgill picks a path that uses logs to preserve DS Jones's stylish footwear. He stoops momentarily to point out a blood-red patch of sundew, tiny carnivores that meet his approval for their war on midges. But DS Jones is distracted; she gazes up into the widening dale.

'Guv, what's that noise?'

'I hear a buzzard.'

'No, stop – listen – much lower in pitch.'

'Waterfall?'

She puts hand on Skelgill's shoulder like a parent intent upon silencing a truculent child, to quell further protest. Sure enough, from somewhere up ahead comes a low moaning.

'She must be alive.'

Now Skelgill hears it.

'That sounds like a bloke to me.'

He rises and without warning moves off, quickening what has been already a brisk pace, a mountain goat-like burst over the rocky rising path that even the devilishly fit DS Jones cannot live with.

They leave the main path and follow the uneven bank beside the beck, now a winding succession of rapids and small waterfalls precariously overhung by shrubs of gnarled holly and hawthorn. They climb a final grassy bank to reach an abrupt levelling out, a small plateau within the broader valley. There is a flat expanse of grey shingle, a beach almost; beyond this a roughly triangular pool some forty feet across; on either side the banks rise steeply as exposed smooth pinkish-grey rocks; at the back of the pool a waterfall of about ten feet tumbles from a narrow spout.

The human-like sound has stopped but as DS Jones takes in the view it begins again and now there is no doubt: plainly it is the anguished keening of a man – indeed she spies him immediately on the rocks to their right; though he is unmissable anyway, clad in a striking cerise shirt of the formal type with the glint of gold cufflinks, smart skinny black jeans and polished black ankle boots – he looks entirely out of place, and seems oblivious of their approach. To her eye he must be in his late fifties or early sixties. He is slim and suntanned, largely bald with an otherwise very short-cropped almost shaven head and the designer stubble of a beard. Equally incongruous is his pose. Squatting on his haunches on the rocks, his hands hold his head like a representation of Edvard Munch's *The Scream* – indeed, the skull-like cranium and tortured expression and even the wild surroundings combine to reinforce the image. It is almost as if they have stumbled on some outdoor performance and this is an actor delivering a contemporary interpretation of a Shakespearean tragedy.

But the man is not acting; he is crying woefully.

And now their arrival into his peripheral vision draws his attention. He stares, for some reason fixing his grief-stricken gaze upon DS Jones. She is naturally drawn towards him. Despite her heavy pack she clambers with alacrity up the rocky slope and kneels at his side.

'Sir – we are from –' She hesitates to make a false claim, despite that the branding on her rucksack would lend authenticity, and reaches out an arm to indicate behind her. 'My colleague is in the mountain rescue – we are also both off-duty police officers. What has happened?'

He opens his mouth but no words initially come out. His eyes are filled with tears. He makes her think of a child that has dropped and broken a precious toy.

'You're too late.' Indeed, there is petulance in his voice. Then he seems to realise and reproach himself. He turns his palms to her in an apologetic gesture. 'It's too late.'

'What do you mean, sir – it's too late?'

But, even as the man extends an arm to point with a crooked finger like a sorcerer casting a spell, DS Jones senses that Skelgill's path has diverged from hers. She turns. Some fifteen yards away he is crouched at the edge of the pool. As she watches Skelgill rises, but he remains standing on the spot, head bowed.

He overlooks the stranded slender body of a woman clad in a sodden clinging dress of vivid blue-violet that recalls the bright

35

bluebells she admired in the woods below. She can see a fan of damp, dark hair floating in the shallow water.

Skelgill is unmoving. The body is unmoving. She knows if there were anything that could be done, Skelgill would be doing it.

Skelgill shakes his head and she sees that he gathers himself. DS Jones does not need to shout, to ask.

Her professional training kicks in. She turns back to the man.

'Sir – what is your name? Did you telephone for assistance?'

Now he looks at her nonplussed once again, as if the questions do not compute. She finds her warrant card and presents it decisively before him. Perhaps the blatant formality will do the trick.

'Sir – we need your help.'

'Kenneth Dalbrae. And, no, I did not.'

'Where do you live?'

Mechanically he recites an address in Soho, London.

DS Jones tries to find a pitch that is somewhere between competent and compassionate.

'Do you know this woman?'

Still there is hesitation, as though the question is beyond him, another language.

But now he steels himself for a second time. Clearly he is experiencing alternate waves of shock and anguish. He gives a sob and rubs his eyes with ivory knuckles as if to pre-empt further tears.

'I have known her virtually all of my life.' He seems to understand he should elaborate. 'She is called Daisy Mills.'

'Is she your wife – your partner?'

'We are a party of friends. We have hired a house. Rydal Grange.'

There is something about the way he looks at her, his demeanour, that tells DS Jones the answer to her question is no; but confirmation of this and other such facts can wait until later.

'Can you tell me what happened, sir?'

He swallows. 'I followed her.' He makes a sound of contrition. *'I was too late.'*

DS Jones waits.

'I don't mean I followed her, exactly – not clandestinely – but I knew she would come to the waterfalls. She said as much. She couldn't wait. She loves waterfalls.' He speaks with more control; his voice is rich and his accent refined. Again he indicates towards Skelgill. 'That's where I found her.'

'Sir – did you try to help her? Did you move her?'

He regards DS Jones helplessly.

'What? I don't think – that's how I – I don't know – *I don't know –*'

And now there is a relapse. He bows his head and pulls it down with his long-fingered hands as though he is trying to roll up in a defensive ball. To hold the squatting pose for so long must be uncomfortable, but it does not seem to bother him. DS Jones touches him lightly on the shoulder and rises.

'Okay. Please just give me a moment.'

She slithers down the rocky bank and crosses the shingle. Skelgill turns and takes a few paces towards her. It seems he cannot help being protective – that he does not want her to look. DS Jones does not attempt to thwart him.

'Her name is Daisy Mills. He says he's an old friend – a companion – Kenneth Dalbrae. There is a group of them staying at a holiday rental property called Rydal Grange.' (Skelgill nods in recognition.) 'He says he came up to look for her – and that he found her like this – though he's in shock and struggling to give an account.'

Skelgill glares suspiciously at the mournful figure crouched on the rocks. Then he gazes hard at DS Jones – but she knows he is not so much interrogating her thoughts as analysing his own feelings.

'Bit of a fancy dress she's wearing.'

DS Jones takes the opportunity to step to one side and look at what he had inexplicably (and perhaps subconsciously) tried to conceal. She understands his point. If not so much fancy – for the dress is very simple, little more than a long slip – it is almost certainly expensive silk. It adds to the incongruity. And she notes there are no shoes, nor a pair neatly laid at the water's edge, as there might be if the woman had gone for a paddle.

'Did he raise the alarm?'

DS Jones shakes her head.

Skelgill pulls his phone from his shirt pocket. He glances at it briefly and scowls.

'Have you got a signal?'

She slides her own handset from the back pocket of her shorts.

'No – nothing.'

Skelgill is already swinging off his rucksack.

'I'm going to radio for the chopper – I want them to pick up Herdwick.'

DS Jones compresses her lips. He means he intends to call in the police pathologist.

Skelgill inclines his head in the direction of the woman's body as he wrestles with the straps and clips of his pack.

'She looks like she's drowned. But I'd like to know for sure. And I'd like to know when.'

DS Jones has not before attended an actual mountain rescue incident with Skelgill, though she has oftentimes heard him bemoan the self-inflicted troubles that foolhardy members of the public bring upon themselves. That said he will not complain about a genuine fellwalker or climber who has met with the kind of bad luck that can strike the best prepared; a sudden illness, a turned ankle, or an unheralded change in the weather. But the scene which they stand amidst seems to her to fall into neither category, despite that the victim and her companion could be accused of being inappropriately dressed, on such a fine spring morning and only a short distance from civilisation theirs is hardly a cardinal sin. Nevertheless, she understands that Skelgill desires a certain peace of mind.

He waits for his walkie-talkie to fire up; he sees that his colleague is studying the cowering figure of Kenneth Dalbrae with some concern.

'Why don't you take him down?' It sounds like a question but DS Jones knows otherwise. 'There should be an ambulance at Rydal by now. If you meet the paramedics coming up, turn them back. There's nowt they can do here. Tell them it's a police incident. Get him something for the shock – and get him checked over.'

DS Jones appreciates the significance of what he says – that the man may be injured or marked in some way.

'What about your mountain rescue crew?'

'Let them come up.' Skelgill casts about. 'I doubt the chopper will want to land here, or hang about. It might be simpler to stretcher the body down once Herdwick's done.' He allows himself a sardonic grin. 'He won't mind walking downhill. We can get him a lift to Penrith before the Queen's Arms opens.'

'Should I place a patrol to stop walkers from coming up the path?'

Skelgill considers for a moment. In the Lakes ramblers appear from all points of the compass. Complete exclusion is simply not possible.

'Aye – it'll keep the majority away.'

'I'll take him back to their accommodation – establish who else is there, and their relationships.'

Now Skelgill nods. She is right to prioritise the contacting of next of kin. But his mind is still troubled by the unexplained circumstances.

'See if you can raise Leyton. If he's anywhere near a landline he'll be better placed to find out who rang 999. Where and when the call was put through. Why they didn't do anything or stay around.'

'Sure, Guv.' DS Jones might reply that she had, of course, thought of this – but she guesses they both know it.

Now Skelgill regards her somewhat ruefully.

'Happen salmon's off the menu for the time being.'

DS Jones grins.

'Grasmere gingerbread it is, then.'

Skelgill watches as she chaperones the man away. Within a minute they disappear from sight over the rim of the little plateau from which Rydal Beck descends. He turns to look – not so

39

much at the body centre stage – but at the backdrop to the tragedy.

To his mind drowning seems improbable. The surrounding rocks are smooth and dry and pose no real threat of damage or injury. A fall of some kind seems unlikely. Yes, this is a natural plunge pool, but it shelves up gently from beneath the modest waterfall. There is insufficient current to trouble a non-swimmer; that is why the place is popular. Though he admits there is the possibility of cold shock, which can strike randomly and incapacitate its victim, even on a warm day; the water that pours down the fells is rarely better than a cool fifty degrees Fahrenheit.

While jumping to conclusions is anathema to Skelgill, he has witnessed his share of such accidents – in the mountain rescue for two decades (and police incidents to boot). A characteristic is trauma – physical trauma – a disfiguring fall, a bloody assault – but here they have come upon a scene untroubled by violence; the attractive woman in the long blue dress might almost have been at repose; the man, smart and well groomed, contemplating her presence; only his inarticulate lamentations shattered the tranquillity. Skelgill wonders if they will turn out to be lovers; he wonders if the man arranged her body 'at peace'.

5. REUNION

One day earlier, Saturday night – Rydal Grange

Hugo can sense that Jane is regarding him censoriously. Which is the more likely cause – that he has taken the seat close beside Daisy, or that he has joined in the séance? The latter provides cover for disapproval of the former. It hasn't helped that Daisy has immediately laid a hand upon his thigh – not that anyone can see, they are close around the table, those seven of them press-ganged, plus foreman Kenneth to complete the octet; besides, the drawing room has been put into darkness, save an ambient glow from half a dozen candles, and the hearth, where the non-participants sip their digestifs.

Hugo isn't really listening to what is going on. Daisy's palm is distracting, and he slides his hand over hers – she responds by intertwining fingers and squeezing hard – suddenly he wonders if she is scared. The others seem oblivious – most present have had plenty to drink – there were preprandial beers and bubbly, red and white wine with dinner, port and liqueurs to follow – all scrambled with the excitement of meeting up; it is often the first night of these events that turns out the most boozy, the most spontaneous, charged with nervous energy.

Kenneth is in his element. He's never happier than when he's the centre of attention. Right now he is expounding upon the rules. He pays particular heed to Daisy. Towards Daisy he behaves like clown and ringmaster rolled into one. No, that is too crude an analogy – Kenneth is more sophisticated than that – his manner more nuanced. Rasputin springs to mind. Now he thinks about it, Hugo recognises how he misread Kenneth during their teens – he saw him as a rival for Daisy – a love rival, really – and yet with hindsight it ought to have been obvious that Kenneth was gay. Yes, he was a rival – but purely for Daisy's attention; openly being gay an untenable condition in that era, in their blue-collar society; Kenneth had no playmates – but Daisy was the perfect foil. And, for her, time spent with Kenneth produced the fun and frolics about town of a boyfriend, without the complications. Only recently has Daisy confided that she knew at school about Kenneth, but that he had sworn her to secrecy.

Hugo ponders how much his peers might have wanted Daisy. He allows his gaze to drift around the table. Of the male Middlemarchers in their cohort, in their clique – there's Rik, Harry and Spike. As far as he can recall Daisy never went out with any of them. But he guesses they all did fancy her – would have liked the chance. But out of a kind of respect for him, as unofficial ringleader (best at sport, best at exams, the dux by default – an unsought-after station) they kept their distance; they all knew there was something special between Daisy and he, even though it rarely came to fruition.

Do kids today enter into relationships with such short shelf-lives? A kind of dating merry-go-round where you hopped on and off, taking an empty saddle beside someone who was available – next day finding the whole school knew you and so-and-so were now 'going out', all because of a snog on the dance floor. These adolescent flings meant about as much as the weather does to the climate or the waves to the tide, superficial encounters that were a rite of passage, a coming of age; a working-class town where couples engaged young and settled down to drudgery in the dye works or the hosiery, and their rabbit-hutch modern semis and their Mk II Ford Escorts.

But their crowd were different. Being brainier, the top stream at Middlemarch High, most of them went away to university. An anticlimactic splintering that propelled them to the four corners of Britain. He north to Glasgow; Rik to acting college at Dartington in the deep south; Harry west to Lampeter in dankest Wales; Spike to Norwich and the East Anglian fens for his birds; Kenneth to London – although that was for an alternative kind of education. So they were saved from the routine of the semi-detached and the Sunday roast. At eighteen their game of musical chairs was sundered. Very few couples in that snapshot survived. So much so that when he came back briefly to Middlemarch a two-times graduate with a Master's in IT Daisy was married for the first time – to the privately educated son of the town's biggest manufacturer of women's tights, a grandee in gussets. But subliminal bonds formed in their passionate youth would prove resilient. (He gets a sudden flash of Jane pontificating upon the weak but insidious force of atomic nuclei.) *Oh, Daisy.* And here they all are. Okay, Jane aside, there's a trio of outsiders – the too-cool Karl character, who was Simon's business partner (of course, Simon was an outsider); and Gail, who keeps making alluring passes – Spike has done alright for himself there, he was such a wimp at school (he's done alright for himself in total – a minor celebrity – probably better than all of them); and Kenneth's partner, Ben – Hugo is not sure about Ben, he has a hidden agenda, he never seems like he's really listening. And there's a couple of the Middlemarch girls, younger – Daisy's sister, Poppy (now divorced, he understands), and Spike's sister, dedicated spinster Sarah. Hugo feels a pang of awkwardness – he knew back then they both had a crush on him – purely, he was sure, by virtue of his three years' seniority. He is glad now at least he never took advantage of that.

    Jane determinedly eschewed the offer of a seat at the séance. He suspects it was some kind of passive-aggressive protest aimed at him – he knows she doesn't want to be here. She made the excuse to Kenneth that it did not befit a physicist. Harry had quipped that she must surely be "psychic" – but his play on words rather floundered, a characteristic of his attempts at humour. Ben had refused, on grounds that they might discover something from his dark past – he asked whether the collective noun for skeletons was a 'closet' – and had plied Kenneth with an arch look; Kenneth had declined to rise to the bait, if such were intended. And Rik and Sarah could not be dislodged from their tête-à-tête beside the fire – they don't appear to have let up since last time he saw them, at Daisy's place.

    The memory recalls the shock of that night and he questions, not for the first time, the merits of this reconstituted reunion –

he understands Kenneth's idea that it is for Daisy's benefit – part of her recuperation – perhaps even to slay the ghosts – but he is sailing close to the wind. That said, Daisy has seemed as carefree as he can remember; though she has secretly confessed still to be taking the Valium that her doctor prescribed to get her through the worst of the trauma, the flashbacks, the insomnia.

Kenneth is trying to get them to pay attention. Clockwise from Hugo's left around the circular table there is Daisy, Kenneth, Gail, Karl, Poppy, Spike (aka Charles) and finally Harry, on his right. Harry, very well oiled, has already attempted the joke that they should be arranged 'girl-boy' – no doubt miffed that he alone is between two males. And when Karl rather superciliously pointed out that there are only three females Harry had insisted four – and proceeded to name them, pointing at each:

"Poppy ... Gail ... Daisy ... *Kenneth!*" He alone howled at his unfashionable wisecrack.

Gail had shifted the subject, stating as far as she was concerned, the more men the merrier, seizing simultaneously the wrists of Kenneth and Karl, and drawing a look of disquiet from Spike. Hugo had speculated what exactly is their relationship like; Gail has hinted – more than hinted – that she would hustle him into a broom cupboard at the drop of a hat. He feels his pulse rate shift as he looks at her now; what was it she had said when they by chance converged at the top of the stairs before dinner? The tight dress with the plunging neckline and a glinting silver insect pendant. "Don't you just want to admire my cuckoo bee – it's parasitic?"

He sighs involuntarily and tunes back in to what Kenneth is saying. Kenneth revels in the role of master of ceremonies – something to do with his job, behind the scenes in show business, some kind of fixer, Hugo gathers. Organising this trip must seem like small beer. But to his credit he delivers vim and verve and has come up with an itinerary of excursions themed around school subjects – English literature, history, geography, biology – that means they won't just sit around and drink Pimm's all day long. And after-dinner games for the evenings – though these are certainly more compatible with alcohol, a sensitive subject, he would have thought – although Daisy does not seem to be holding back.

He wonders from where Kenneth procured the Ouija board. With its burnt archaic lettering and demonic horned Baphomet image and menacing pentagrams it looks like an original Victorian edition, designed to strike fear into credulous participants. And, while these holiday properties usually supply games, owners tend to draw the line at Monopoly and backgammon; he has never come across a Ouija board before. In the flickering candlelight the arcane contraption takes on an even more foreboding quality. The atmosphere in the room is heavy with incense and now Hugo notices that the hypnotic strains of Wuthering Heights begin to emanate from the sound system. He feels a twitch from Daisy – she was his Cathy – literally tapping on his window like branches in a storm and he letting her in – she stepping down from his Kate Bush poster to smother him with her sorcery.

Kenneth's raised voice rouses him from his reminiscences.

'Now nobody – *absolutely nobody* – must push or pull the planchette.' He indicates with a sweep of his delicate hand a heart-shaped sliver of dark wood with a disc excised from its centre. 'It will move of its own accord – if and when a spirit gets in touch. Each of us must lay a forefinger lightly and think of someone we might like to contact. The most important rule is never to taunt or goad a spirit to communicate with you. Let the spirit come in its own time – with good intent and without malevolence. Here before us is a telephone to the afterlife.'

'How do you know all this, Kenneth? You're so clever.'

It is Poppy that speaks; Hugo remembers she always was charmed by Kenneth's guile.

'He makes it up.' Harry is evidently still peeved, and perhaps envious of the adulation. 'It's well known to be the ideomotor effect, a common symptom of a dissociative state. One person starts, and the group becomes consumed by emotional contagion.'

It seems he attempts to put down Kenneth and Poppy in one, Kenneth by denouncing him as a purveyor of snake oil, a charlatan; Poppy by battering her with big words. Hugo is reminded, however, that Harry was never dumb – he always had an inquiring mind for the likes of genetics, evolution, the debunking of religion. And he did take a psychology degree before his life and career gradually veered off the rails (from what grains of hearsay Hugo has gleaned). Though he always could be a bit of a prat.

'Let us begin.'

Tentatively, fingers are rested upon the perimeter of the planchette. Hugo wonders if it is obvious that he and Daisy have their adjacent hands beneath the table. Being left-handed he would naturally have extended that arm. But perhaps they are all too drunk to notice – or maybe too engrossed with the prospect of the game.

'Is there anybody there?'

It is the cliché from the movies – hey, why not? But Hugo hears a scornful snort from Rik behind him.

Silence.

Hugo has not taken part in a séance before. With just one finger he can't imagine he could easily manipulate the planchette. Press and push it maybe, but to direct it accurately about the board would seem impossible.

But it begins to move.

There is a gasp from Poppy. Hugo sees a gleam of triumph in Kenneth's eyes (surely more than a trick of the candlelight); but an expression of annoyance crosses Harry's swarthy features. Other pairs of eyes are darting about suspiciously as if to catch out whoever is deliberately manipulating the planchette.

'M.'

Kenneth's tone takes on a melodramatic note.

'M – A – R – Y –'

Sure enough, it has spelled out the name.

'Mary Queen of Scots. Ask her if she really did sleep with Rizzio.'

'Rik – be quiet.'

The reprimand from Sarah, like the quip from Rik, comes from the darkness beyond the circle. Indeed, Rik's contribution, though flippant in its intent, adds to the tension. And Rik really was an actor for a decent time; his rich voice carries a curious sense of authenticity; a disembodied narrator.

'Which Mary?' This is Kenneth.

The planchette responds.

'L – I – N.'

'Mary Lin? Never heard of you.'

'It's *Marilyn*.'

'Well, she's illiterate.'

But there comes another gasp from Poppy and everyone looks at her.

'I thought of Marilyn Monroe. I did! I thought of Audrey Hepburn –' (she looks at her sister a little guiltily, for intruding upon her province) '– but I also thought of Marilyn.'

Kenneth pre-empts any further debate.

'Are you Marilyn Monroe?'

They wait with bated breath.

The planchette jerks and moves to 'Yes'.

Suddenly everyone is engrossed – even those of a cynical disposition. Anticipation is palpable. There is the suggestion that they have one chance – like one last command to the genie – and any moment Rik will supply some trite and wasteful question. But none of them, not even Rik, seems able to tender a proposition – until Gail grasps the nettle.

'Who was the best lover, Kennedy or Sinatra?'

She looks at Hugo with a rebellious gleam in her eye. He feels a tightening of Daisy's grip. But the planchette seems stubborn, as if uncertain – or there are competing forces (surely there are), though he is not pushing or pulling.

Then, slowly, it moves to 'F' and stops.

'Good old Frank!' With his free hand Harry reaches for his glass and performs a drinker's salute to accompany his remark.

'Fitzgerald.'

The voice is that of the ethereal Rik. There is a baffled silence before he elaborates.

'Don't forget the 'F' in JFK. She might have had a pet name for him.'

The intervention does not attract any gainsayers – though Hugo might have expected Harry to contest Rik's assertion just for the hell of it.

They wait, but the planchette seems to have run out of steam.

As one, and without discussion, they withdraw their hands and exhale and drink, and gather themselves. There is a collective impression of elation combined with nervous exhaustion – like the crew of an eight they need a breather before they can go again. It is Rik that prompts them.

'I predict Elvis. Ask him about his job in the chip shop.'

He is shushed by Sarah, and as Hugo turns to look he notices Ben rise and so does Jane and they tiptoe down steps into what is a partially open adjoining garden room that runs along the back of the house, presumably to be able to converse more freely. Hugo is wondering what they have to talk about; though Ben, he has noticed, likes to turn on the charm with the older women, flattering them with his attention. He feels a sudden pang of what really ought to be jealousy but is forced to admit to humiliation; that someone can slope off to a more intimate space with his wife.

'Is there anybody there?'

Kenneth's entreaty brings his mind back to the table. He hurriedly reaches out to touch the planchette.

There is nothing. It becomes a pregnant pause; though they all seem determined to see out its term. Kenneth, acting midwife, restates his petition.

With a jerk the planchette moves decisively and settles over the letter 'S'. Kenneth narrates.

Then, 'I'.

'Here comes the real Sinatra – he begs to differ!'

Once more it is Rik. And again Sarah chastises him. Perhaps he senses they are tiring of his interjections – Hugo hears him whisper to Sarah, "Okay, okay – I'm just saying, Ol' Blue Eyes Is Back".

But the next letter is not 'N' but 'M'.

And now the planchette spells out the name: S – I – M – O – N. And stops.

Hugo feels his ears burning – but as he glances about he realises that everyone is staring wide-eyed not at him but at Daisy. He becomes vaguely aware that in the background Bohemian Rhapsody is playing. The great anthem of their generation. It sends a shiver down his spine.

Then Poppy, Daisy's sister, breaks the silence.

'Ask him something.'

When Daisy might flinch or recoil, sound unwilling or even desperate to avoid the suggestion, her voice comes back clear.

'What should I ask?'

Her question is challenging, her tone unfamiliar to Hugo. She looks defiantly around the table, all the way, clockwise, from Kenneth on her left – through Gail, Karl, Poppy, Spike and Harry, to Hugo on her right. But as her gaze reaches him, their attention is diverted; Hugo suddenly feels the planchette move.

Now, as if it has a will of its own, sliding at a speed hitherto unseen, it shifts to 'M' on the far right of the upper line of characters and swiftly to 'U' near the middle of the lower line – and then four quick jerks around a little triangle of letters that are adjacent to one another: 'R' of the lower line, 'D' and 'E' of the top line and back to 'R' – almost so quick as to defeat the eye.

There is silence; and then Poppy's voice, naïve.

'What did it say?'

'MURDER.'

Harry sounds like he is salivating. He gladly translates what they have just witnessed, even though they must all, for confirmation, be replaying in their minds the route traced by the planchette.

Bohemian Rhapsody is reaching its crescendo; the volume seems to have risen by several decibels of its own accord; Hugo is enveloped by a great roaring avalanche, the thunder and lightning of drums and electric guitars. *A devil put aside for me.* Daisy's nails dig into the back of his hand and he is forced to suppress a cry. But just as quickly the grip weakens and the next thing he knows her chair goes over backwards and she is fleeing the room. Hugo begins to rise to go after her – but Kenneth is far quicker and is striding away before Hugo is half out of his seat.

'That's put the cat among the pigeons.' Harry is triumphant. As if to celebrate, he downs his drink. Could it be his practical joke?

The others sit in stunned silence, not knowing how to react.

It is Spike, serious Spike, with his Dr Charles Rice hat on that speaks.

'Whoever did that – it was in bad taste. They ought to be ashamed of themselves. She's still not over it.'

Hugo sees that Spike is squaring up to Harry – he must suspect him, too. Spike is angry – but he was never a fighter – it upsets him now to be aggressive – Hugo would not be surprised if he burst into tears. And Harry is likely to goad him.

But Rik pipes up from the fireside.

'What if it *were* the spirit of Simon? What if he *were* murdered?'

Spike takes advantage of the diversion. He rises and crosses to where his sister and Rik recline in the glow of the fire.

'You don't seriously believe this nonsense? You realise there is zero evidence for the existence of a spirit world? Nothing has ever been replicated under laboratory conditions. There's a million dollar prize still unclaimed after fifty years.'

Rik waves a languid hand.

'Come on, Spike – you know you boffins have tunnel vision. Give your brain a break and let your intuition have a say.'

'Spike was a dedicated occultist, once.' This is Harry. He casts a Machiavellian glance at Gail. 'As I recall, there were a couple of American spirits he worshipped. Jack Daniel's and Jim Beam!'

Hugo thinks that Spike might be embarrassed, his partner hearing this – but he seems prepared to stand as butt of the joke in order to defuse the conflict with Harry. And now Rik picks it up.

'Not forgetting the late great Scots spirit, Johnnie Walker!'

They'll be starting on Monty Python next – they (Hugo included) used to know all the skits and sketches off by heart. But he is torn by a preoccupation for Daisy. He is desperate to follow but Jane and Ben have now appeared from the conservatory and are loitering inquiringly, perhaps wondering why half of them have abandoned their posts.

'Is it Scots or Scotch?'

Hugo realises Harry is asking him, as the honorary Caledonian in their ranks. Harry's tone is pompous and Hugo understands he wants to correct Rik. Hugo defaults into mediating mode. Harry and Rik can be like a pair of duelling banjos once they get started. Rik is liable to outwit Harry and they'll come to blows as of old. Hugo finds himself answering rather woodenly.

'You can probably take your pick. Scots means from Scotland – same thing as saying Scottish. Scotch is an antiquated adjective. But it's also whisky and so is Johnnie Walker.'

'Very witty, Wilde!'

Hugo recognises the Pythonism from Harry.

Rik is more perceptive.

'Ever the diplomat, Hugo – that's why you were our leader.'

'That was because he beat us at everything.'

Hugo does not want to go down this road. He reluctantly takes a more drastic course of action. He gestures at Daisy's upended chair – then he restores it to an upright position.

'Look – Spike's right. One of us must have done that. It might be better if they admitted it. It's not really fair to Daisy. She's highly strung at the best of times.'

He senses that his wife is scrutinising him; that he is thinking about Daisy's feelings, that he has an opinion on her personality. It is the risk of bringing Jane to something like this – that one of them will say something flippantly, about him and Daisy back in the day.

'I'll admit to it.'

All eyes fall on Harry. He must have refilled his glass, for now he drains it again. He laughs a little hysterically.

'I don't mean it was me – but, if you need a scapegoat. Why don't I have a chat with her now? I'll give Kenneth his marching orders.'

He shifts from one foot to the other, as if granted approval he will seek out and interrupt Daisy and Kenneth. Hugo finds himself dissenting at this prospect – that Harry is using it as a ruse – it's not about Daisy's feelings, it's opportunism. But Hugo also realises that this is like old times: they are all looking to him for leadership – his word here will carry the day; he still has the authority that came to him naturally and modestly and they still bow to it.

He looks around. At the fireside Sarah and Rik are crushed into the same large armchair. Meanwhile Ben has casually linked an arm through Jane's – an intimate gesture that a gay man can get away with (though he's not just gay, is he?). Spike stands alone, and at the table remain Harry, Poppy, Gail and – looking completely detached – Karl Eastwood.

Hugo waits. No one is forthcoming with an admission.

He nods to Harry.

'Give it a try.'

Despite his reservations, he thinks Harry will carry it off. It is the sort of immature stunt he would have pulled and Daisy will believe that. Harry grins and exits the room with unashamed haste.

But Rik has a last cynical essay.

'You lot should have carried on – you might have found the murderer's name.'

Spike, perhaps re-emboldened now Harry is gone, rails against this suggestion.

'Great. Put the idea in Daisy's head that Simon was deliberately poisoned – and tar one of us with the brush.'

Rik affects a nonchalant shrug.

'It could have been Daisy. They say it's a woman's crime.'

There is some nervous laughter, but Rik gets a sharp elbow in the ribs from Sarah for his trouble. He puts up his hands, an admission that he is playing pied piper. He laments, employing his hammed actor's voice.

'Who's for a game of charades? Something I might win.'
'Who's for bed?'

Hugo almost falls prey to the predatory musky perfume before he processes the honeyed whisper as coming from Gail; then there is her hot and subtle presence against the side of his body. If it is a serious question it is intended for his ears only. He experiences the sudden vertiginous rush of a cliff edge, before his conscience drags him back – where would that leave him with Daisy? And alternative salvation takes shape as he sees Jane detach herself from the company of Ben with a nod of finality that is familiar to him. She strides purposefully across, plying Gail with a polite but perfunctory glance of acknowledgement.

'I think I should go to my bed. The weather forecast is good and it would be a shame to waste the morning.'

Sensibly, Kenneth's itinerary, like that of a cruise has the morning 'at leisure'. There follows a Wordsworth-themed minibus tour setting off at noon, to Cockermouth for lunch and the bard's birthplace, thence returning via Glencoyne Bay on Ullswater to take in the last golden flush of the daffodils, Dove Cottage at Grasmere, and lastly his longstanding home, nearby Rydal Mount for cream tea.

Hugo's expression becomes conflicted; but he reads the loosely coded imperative.

'Okay – I'll just be a couple of minutes.'

He shapes to dip for a token kiss but Jane has vacated the space and is striding away. He hears a faint whistle, ironic commentary from Gail.

6. RYDAL GRANGE

Sunday, 9.35 a.m. – Rydal Grange

Skelgill has many times admired the property that is Rydal Grange. In his wildest dreams it is the house he would own. Nestling in the rich oak woodland that cloaks the rising fellside, its land descends through a wildflower meadow to the lakeshore. Its aspect and elevation afford a commanding view of the picturesque locality. But most striking is the architecture, an eye-catching blend of traditional angular Lakeland stone and slate in fifty subtle shades of grey, jutting eaves and thrusting chimneystacks, with a colonial style veranda – a porch, the Americans would call it. This, too, has a mottled slate-tiled roof, supported by a good dozen timber uprights painted white to match the sash windows and external doors. Most significantly it skirts three sides to provide outdoor living space to suit every time of day and every foible of the weather. Viewing from his boat he has imagined tying flies of an evening in the light of an oil lamp, to an accompaniment of the calls of water birds and tawny owls, and sustained by a steaming mug of tea and a family packet of chocolate digestives.

A shady driveway of slate chippings approaches the secluded mansion, where its formal front façade offers a different perspective. Here five cars are lined up, two to the left of what the English would call the porch, and three to the right. Skelgill slows and makes an assessment. There is a newish silver Mini with a monochrome Union Jack roof design; a two-year-old white Range Rover; a green diesel-electric hybrid that Skelgill does not recognise; a sleek black-metallic BMW with its subtle factory badge and personalised plate; and a shabby yellow Volvo that is long overdue for a wash and a new silencer, which Skelgill chooses to park alongside. Though irked at his prejudice, he contemplates what the little fashion parade might tell him about the CVs of their owners.

As he clambers from his shooting brake to stare penetratingly into the timbered garden, anyone glimpsing him from a window might guess he is a local woodsman come to fell a dangerous tree. He is still clad in the outdoor attire to which he had stripped down in the boat and in turn hiked up to Buckstones Jump. For a better view, he drags the fingers of one hand through his hair, revealing craggy features that contribute to the misleading image.

In fact Skelgill has spotted a red squirrel on a feeder. It is a while since he has seen this elfin native and now he approaches stealthily for a better look. The little creature watches him until he stops, then carries on with its meal. Skelgill has reached the fringe of a lawn that extends between the garden oaks; at their bases magenta herb robert and delicate white pignut mingle with longer grasses. He notices a neat pile of roe deer droppings, small shiny homogeneous pellets that look almost edible (his bullboxer would certainly think so). Somewhere overhead a nuthatch is trilling loudly, a call that has fooled him more than once into thinking he is being shadowed by a persistently whistling dog walker.

He turns back towards the house, but instead of making for the front door he mounts the shallow ramp that takes him onto the veranda on the east side. There is a mobile barbecue with a sack of charcoal and the means of chopping kindling – a small yellow-handled axe embedded in a hardwood block – and an arrangement of wicker chairs engineered to catch the morning sun. He passes rooms with French doors that open directly onto the balcony. The veranda is not a raised wooden construction but built with slate flags on the solid ground that falls away towards the lake. This aspect has been artificially enhanced as a ha-ha, a steep grassy slope populated rather randomly by ferns. A dogleg flight of weathered stone steps leads to a gate in an iron fence that surrounds a small grazed paddock (although nothing grazes at present). Beyond the paddock descends the meadow, abundant with wildflowers, to the shore, a distance of maybe a hundred yards. It is beyond Skelgill's comprehension why anyone would own this place and then rent it out.

'Hello.'

Skelgill swivels to his left. His subconscious is just acknowledging the sight of a freshly forged trail through the long grass – and, thus caught unawares, there is a flash of vexation in his expression. If this were a cowboy movie he would be reaching for his six-shooter.

But the husky voice is far from threatening; intrigued if anything – and he is obliged to adjust with haste. His first impression is of a pink satiny dressing gown that reveals a good deal of suntanned flesh, long shapely legs and bare feet – and then a mass of healthily unadulterated straw-coloured hair that glows in the morning sun. As his focus settles he sees a woman, moderately tall, who is aged perhaps in her early fifties. There is a welcoming wide mouth with full lips, and prominent cheekbones that cup bright chestnut eyes. What are cruelly called crow's feet add warmth to her somewhat coy smile. She approaches to within a few feet and sips demurely from a long glass of fresh orange juice that is covered with condensation, but when he does not immediately reply, she continues.

'You must be the handyman.'

Her tone is distinctly flattering. Skelgill finds himself unable to correct the misapprehension in its entirety.

'There's plenty of folk would disagree.'

'I telephoned the number in the folder. I can't get my shower to work.'

With one hand she has been clasping together the lapels of the gown over her breastbone. Now she lets go and bends an index finger back over her shoulder.

'There's a way in through the kitchen – around this side.'

It must be from where she has appeared. Skelgill is just allowing himself to think he can probably fix it when he hears swift footsteps approaching.

'Guv? I saw your car, we're at the – oh, sorry –'

DS Jones rounds the corner, the same way Skelgill has come, beginning to address him before realising he has company. She grasps to her shoulder an unfamiliar reporter's notepad and a pen that she must have borrowed.

Skelgill vaguely detects an interchange in a language that is beyond him as the women size up both one another and the situation to which they are each unexpectedly introduced. From one perspective Skelgill appears to be interviewing a near-naked older woman; from the other an attractive young female clad in a skimpy sporty outfit accosts him. They each stand their ground – but DS Jones is not prepared to relinquish the initiative. She addresses Skelgill squarely.

'Guv – we're in a room at the front.'

She is plainly disinclined to elaborate within earshot of a stranger – despite that she might reasonably assume that her superior has introduced himself as a police officer. However, perhaps that she has twice implied some relationship of formal rank enables the woman to understand enough of the unspoken dynamics. She takes a half step back, which becomes a curtsey.

'Do not let me detain you.' She offers her hand to Skelgill. 'Gail Melia.'

Involuntarily, Skelgill reciprocates, but does not provide his name or title.

'Excuse us, madam.'

She smiles gracefully and watches as Skelgill falls in with his colleague. When they have gone from her sight she reaches into the pocket of her robe and produces a gold-coloured mobile phone. With a narrowing of her eyes – perhaps to mitigate the sun's reflection, or the condition of hyperopia – she begins to manipulate the screen. Somehow, she does not give the impression that she is trying once again for a plumber.

Once they have reached the front of the house DS Jones stops and turns to Skelgill.

'There are eleven people staying, excluding Daisy Mills. It seems it's more of a school reunion than a clique of regular friends. So they've come from different parts of the country. A few of them have gone out for walks, but the majority are still in bed – or just getting up.' She pauses, but then perhaps has second thoughts about referencing Skelgill's experience along

57

these lines. 'I'm working on the principle that we should find out what we can about Daisy Mills' movements. One thing to know is that she was not a strong swimmer. And then there's her state of mind. She was a widow – her younger sister is her only close relative, and she's here. Her name is Poppy Lux. She's shocked; I'm not sure she's in a fit state to talk to us. She's waiting now with Kenneth Dalbrae. Would you like to hear what he told me, or do you want to see them first?'

'I take it he's not admitting to shoving her sister off the rocks?'

A blitheness about Skelgill suggests he is still unsettled by his encounter with the bathrobe.

'In that respect, just what you already know, Guv.'

'Happen it'll keep.'

Rather than move on, DS Jones regards him expectantly.

'Did Dr Herdwick shed any light on events?'

'You know what he's like. Wait for the lab tests.' Skelgill screws up his features, producing an unbecoming shrewish effect. 'He didn't identify any injuries. No indication she was attacked. He's estimating time of death between six and eight.'

'But we arrived at eight, Guv – and Kenneth Dalbrae thinks he had been there for a quarter of an hour.'

Skelgill has a query of his own in this regard.

'What joy with Leyton – the SOS call?'

'I got hold of him – he's working on it.'

Skelgill nods, and now they proceed.

The front porch is probably three yards in width and of a similar construction to the veranda. On the left against the wall is a neat rank of expensive green wellingtons, like domestic staff lined up to greet the householder's return after an absence. They are ranged in increasing size order; Skelgill notices a couple of gaps. He follows DS Jones into a large square stone-flagged hallway with a broad oak staircase curving up on the right. Opposite the staircase stand a pair of mahogany wardrobes and covering much of the floor area is a rectangular Turkish rug. Directly ahead a life-size Chinese emperor statue regards them inscrutably from an alcove. The décor is plain white; the beams of the ceiling and the woodwork of internal doors newly stained; indeed there is the impression of a recent refurbishment.

Skelgill gets the idea that this is what the holiday rental company would call a 'premium' property; little expense spared, a designer's eye engaged, fine touches that create the ambiance of a boutique hotel. He reflects that he would prefer shabby, authentic, a lived-in feel. In a real country house the adornments would actually be useful – a shovel, a yard brush, dogs' leads and old coats. Though the wellies he approves of, assuming these were not for show but provided with practical intent.

The square entrance area branches left and right as a corridor, to the full extent of the building, with doors facing at each end. DS Jones now leads the way to the left, and a second staircase comes into partial view, narrower, the sort the maids would have used in days gone by. Of various doors on either side DS Jones pushes open the first on the left, which is ajar.

It gives on to a room that continues the interior-designed theme, but which is immediately more appealing to Skelgill for the presence of Trout & Salmon magazine, along with, in order of decreasing utility, Cumbria Life, Condé Nast Traveller and Tatler, arranged upon a coffee table before a Georgian-style hearth. The log fire is made up, but although it is not lit the room, with just a single sash window on the shady side of the house offers a sense of seclusion, and he could imagine escaping to peruse glossy advertisements for outrageously priced game-fishing tackle.

A three-piece suite surrounds the fire, and two figures occupy the sofa. As the detectives enter the pair sitting release hands – as if they feel their contact inappropriate, despite that it must surely be comforting in purpose. Skelgill only vaguely registers the presence of Kenneth Dalbrae; instead the woman captures his attention. Fleetingly there is the small shock of resurrection, of the female recently deceased. She is correspondingly slim – skinny, almost angular – and has the same long dark hair and well-formed eyebrows, and something about the mouth, too, speaks of their sorority, although here it is downturned in grief, when previously it was in death. But the moment passes and

59

other facets come to the fore that distinguish the pair. The nose is more bulbous, the features less well defined, and the skin, it seems, less pale, and wrinkled as if with overexposure to ultraviolet light. It strikes him that the body by the pool had acquired an ageless quality; when here is a younger sister, who must herself be approaching her sixties.

DS Jones is about to perform introductions when Skelgill swings away to scrutinise a fire escape notice on the back of the door. It is hardly decorative, but nevertheless commands his interest. There is a black-and-white plan of the building, ground and first floors. Added in handwritten red ink is a cross to indicate the sitting room, and arrows showing alternative means of egress in the event of an emergency. He scowls: why not just the window?

DS Jones, accustomed to this type of digression, resumes what must have been her seat. Skelgill, however, shows no inclination to sit in the remaining armchair. Instead he moves halfway towards the window; he is like a hound stalled on the trail of a fox – it has the scent but not the direction.

To the couple on the settee his behaviour must seem eccentric, if not a little disconcerting – and indeed it is perhaps the cause of what Poppy Lux now blurts out.

'It must have been the séance.'

Kenneth Dalbrae looks like he wishes she had not said this. Skelgill and DS Jones exchange a casual glance – but before either of them can pick up the point, the door unceremoniously opens and in it is framed a man of about Skelgill's height, though more thickset. And, for the second time in barely a minute, Skelgill experiences the same sense of déjà vu – the person is familiar to him. Aged around sixty he has thinning fair hair, an oval doughy face with a weak unshaven jaw, but distinctive pale blue eyes; he wears deck shoes, loose fitting washed-out jeans and a creased Black Sabbath t-shirt over a moderate paunch.

He does not seem to have noticed Skelgill, who stands against the light of the window. He directs his gaze upon Kenneth Dalbrae.

'What the Dickens is going on? I've just received a text from Gail saying the Old Bill are here.'

Kenneth Dalbrae indicates with a limp gesture.

'These are the police. Daisy has been found – up by the waterfalls. She's dead.'

'What!'

DS Jones rises from her seat and brandishes her warrant card. She is conscious that neither she nor Skelgill look at all like police officers.

'Sir – I am Detective Sergeant Jones of Cumbria CID and this is Detective Inspector Skelgill.'

She indicates with an outstretched arm. The man flashes a brief glance at Skelgill. But he reverts to Kenneth Dalbrae.

'What happened to her?'

DS Jones steps between them.

'We are not sure yet, sir. We were off duty in the area and picked up a distress call from the mountain rescue. It does not appear that she was the victim of any violence.'

The man is frowning, clearly struggling to process the information.

'You mean – she had an accident?'

'We are hoping to establish the cause of death as soon as possible. The relevant procedure has been activated. I'm sorry you have had to learn about your friend this way.'

He looks bewildered – and then perplexed, as if he might be wondering what is a better way – but then he cranes around her. His malleable features first seem to express concern for the bereaved sister – and then perhaps a look of reproach for Kenneth Dalbrae.

'Have you told them about last night?'

There is a silence. Poppy Lux inhales to speak but cannot manage it. Kenneth Dalbrae now responds.

'We were literally just about to when you came in.'

Skelgill, who has so far held his peace, now steps around the furniture to join the conversation. He addresses the couple on the sofa, and rather more bluntly amplifies his colleague's statement.

'There is no easy way to do this – but I suggest that together you speak to the rest of your friends. I reckon it would be better coming from you than from us. Perhaps we can have a word with this gentleman, and then any of the others as required.'

Kenneth Dalbrae reacts with a look of alarm. It is impossible to determine if this is due to the imposition of an unwelcome burden, or – a subtler and perhaps even subconscious sentiment – that there is a suggestion in Skelgill's words of an interrogation to follow. And perhaps DS Jones detects this nuance, for now she intercedes.

'We realise this has been a shock. I shall arrange for a bereavement counsellor to attend as soon as possible. Even just to understand the practicalities can help in a situation like this.' She reaches to put a hand on the shoulder of Poppy Lux. 'Your sister may have said something that will explain what happened. Often it's as simple as that.'

The woman seems reassured by DS Jones's sympathetic platitudes. Skelgill, meanwhile, is unwittingly pulling the sort of face that tells of introspection.

Poppy Lux accepts Kenneth Dalbrae's arm and together they rise and leave the sitting room.

The newcomer now steps forward and thrusts out a hand to Skelgill.

'Rik Hannay?' The inflexion invites recognition.

Skelgill is racking his brains. Could he be a former policeman – someone from the best part of two decades ago when Skelgill was apprenticed to the force? But he is no local – to Skelgill's ear the man has a neutral southern accent, actually quite posh – and yet above all it is the voice that strikes a chord. And he seems alert to Skelgill's perplexity.

'The tables turned, Inspector.'

'I'm sorry, sir?'

'I played Ladbroke – a detective with a gambling habit and a penchant for the ladies. Filmed on the Isle of Wight – that hotbed of organised crime! I was much younger then, thirty-seven – it was in the late nineties. The BBC made a pilot series, but cut it after that. I was up against John Thaw – remember, that pompous beer-swilling prig, Morse?'

A memory is dawning upon Skelgill. As a schoolboy viewer, the programme ignited his interest in police work – that a British detective could get away with being so loose a cannon.

'Aye – I remember.'

'I must say, compared to yours, my sidekick left something to be desired.' The man glances admiringly at DS Jones. 'Plenty of scope for a backstory, hey what?'

In his 'sidekick' Skelgill observes a small compression of the lips, an inconspicuous tic that he has come to know through his own indiscretions. He is reminded that she punches well above her weight – and perhaps he just has an inkling that the hornet's nest that is her temperament was prodded a few minutes earlier on the veranda. He steps across in front of the hearth and extends an arm towards the settee.

'Take a seat, please, sir.'

For his part, Skelgill is inclined to give the fellow the benefit of the doubt; a generation stretches between them, and a fish does not know it swims in water. He gestures to DS Jones – a suggestion that she resume her information gathering. She flashes him a forced grin.

Skelgill listens from the opposing armchair as she rather tersely clears the formalities. She establishes that Rik Hannay – actor, resting – is sixty-one years of age and lives alone at an address in Kilburn, London. He grew up in the Midlands and, like the majority of the party staying at Rydal Grange, attended Middlemarch High School, the Class of '79, as he puts it. They have remained in touch over the years, enjoying varying degrees of intimacy, and their provenance is the basis for them coming together.

There is a thespian's self-assurance about the man's bearing. He demonstrated this the moment he entered; he is unfazed by an audience. Even so, in Skelgill's judgement he seems overly relaxed – certainly for one met with the sudden death of a friend. But it would be premature to leap to any conclusion, when shock can engender irrational euphoria, perhaps an ancient instinct of self-preservation, to facilitate an escape from danger before the magnitude of a loss sinks in – yes, my brother *was* just eaten by a crocodile.

Meanwhile, DS Jones presses on with the simple matter of fact: that it is necessary to establish what happened to Daisy Mills; and that some among the guests may be able to shed light on her behaviour. In this regard Skelgill of course has a burning question – but he should be unsurprised that DS Jones is on the same page.

'Mr Hannay, when you came into the room – you asked Mr Dalbrae if he had told us about last night?'

Rik Hannay shifts into a more upright position and inhales with his diaphragm as if to suggest a soliloquy is imminent.

'If I may take something of a narrative liberty, it will place my answer into its proper context. What you need to know is that Daisy's husband Simon died in December – he was poisoned.'

He checks either side; he seems pleased to have the floor – indeed he begins to recite in a positively Shakespearean idiom.

'It was a gathering of this same group.

'At the Mills' place in the Midlands.

'Shenton Magna Manor House.

'A cocktail party.

'There was contaminated gin.

'A tragedy in waiting.

'It affected five homes in the neighbourhood – customers of the same shop.

'Several of us suffered mild symptoms – not I – can't stand Mother's Ruin.

'Nothing deadly serious – in all cases, except Simon's.

'Bad luck.

'He was playing mixologist.

'Must have drunk half a bottle or more of the stuff.

'Overweight, stressed businessman – dodgy ticker.

'So this reunion –' (he waves vaguely to indicate the present arrangement) ' – was to put things right – for Daisy.'

He pauses to reflect.

'For all of us, in a way.'

And now he gives another flowery hand gesture, towards the door.

'Kenneth – he's a great organiser – it's his line of work.

'Last night he had us doing a séance.

'As with the gin – I did not participate – but I was in the room.

'Daisy was among eight at the Ouija board.

'I do not know what Kenneth intended – or whether someone was up to their tricks – but following a visit from the spirit of Marilyn Monroe ... came a spirit called Simon.'

He clears his throat portentously.

'Simon spelled out the word MURDER.'

Now his gaze falls to his hands, which he folds upon his lap; he sits in silent contemplation.

DS Jones offers a prompt.

'And, sir?'

He starts and looks up as if surprised to find them there. The actor's mantle seems to be cast off. He blinks a couple of times and gives an absent-minded shake of his head.

'What? Oh – that was it – the game broke up. Daisy dashed away. Kenneth went after her, and then Harry – he was delegated to tell her he'd done it – a bad joke. I understand she was initially upset – but she seemed to recover her wits. I saw her mingling shortly afterwards.'

'Did you speak with her?'

'To be honest, the hullabaloo – it was a bit of a showstopper. And it had been a tiring journey, a long day – with more than enough to drink. At that juncture several others and I turned in. Jane and Hugo; Poppy and Sarah. I am afraid there is nothing I can add. This morning I was in bed until – what – ten minutes ago?'

There can be a time shortly before a summer cloudburst when rogue raindrops precede the storm, few in number and widespread, their trajectories invisible. Fishing in such conditions, it is possible to be fooled that these heaven-sent missiles are the rises of feeding trout, so similar is the effect upon the surface of the water. The angler, *willing* there to be fish, readily joins in with the illusion. Before now, Skelgill has found himself tilting at such windmills until, removing his hat in exasperation, he receives a splosh on the forehead. Listening to Rik Hannay's account has him waiting for the splosh on the forehead. But none arrives. And now his colleague asks a curious though intriguing question.

'Mr Hannay – what is your opinion of the séance?'

The man inhales through clenched teeth, in the fashion of a reformed smoker who has not quite shed the habit of that first satisfying drag upon the cigarette. He looks from one detective to the other, and despite the melancholic circumstances there is surely an ironic twinkle in his eye.

'If I were reading about it – if it were a scene in a script, I would say yes, it is significant – otherwise what's the point, why else would the screenwriter include it?' Then, however, he grins resignedly. 'But this is real life.'

7. GRASMERE GINGERBREAD

Sunday, 11.15 a.m. – village café

'What made you ask Rik Hannay if he drove a Volvo, Guv?'

'Hey?' Skelgill has to wrestle his attention away from some distraction. 'I were just testing a theory.'

DS Jones seems to comprehend.

'Like to guess which was Kenneth Dalbrae's?'

'Cooper S.' Skelgill's answer is immediate.

'Correct!'

She leans forward in her seat to extract from her hip pocket the folded pages she has torn from the borrowed notepad. She presses them flat on the tablecloth and slides the top sheet alongside Skelgill's cup and saucer.

'The other drivers we've not met – but I did take the vehicle details and I asked Kenneth Dalbrae which belonged to whom. He also supplied some contact details. This is a list of everyone – who travelled with whom – co-habiting couples marked with a plus sign where appropriate.'

Range Rover – Hugo Grant + Jane Grant
Mini Cooper – Kenneth Dalbrae + Ben Lomond
Volvo – Rik Hannay; Harry Badger
BMW – Karl Eastwood; Daisy Mills; Poppy Lux
Toyota Prius – Dr Charles Rice (Spike) + Gail Melia; Sarah Rice

Skelgill peruses the page. He is not so familiar with her handwriting. She normally takes notes in shorthand and transcribes them to a digital format later. However, compared to DS Leyton – who writes with surprising neatness but at a miniscule size, as though paper is being rationed – her letters are large and well formed, and easily legible. Some item causes him to frown – but then another entry wins precedence.

'*Dr Charles Rice* – the weird birder bloke off the telly?'

'I believe so, Guv.'

Skelgill hesitates, as if he does not know what he thinks about this – a minor celebrity – possibly more than minor, if one is into that kind of thing.

'So, what – he's got a live-in girlfriend?' Skelgill suddenly seems to realise that he has said this in the mildly intrigued way of a fan – that the little revelation is a window onto a star's personal life. He backtracks. 'Why does it say "Spike" in brackets?'

He looks up to see his colleague regarding him with amusement.

'Apparently it was his nickname at school. I just made a note because Kenneth Dalbrae used it a few times.'

This prompts another diversion for Skelgill. In his youth he passed through a couple of sobriquets with which he was not exactly enamoured. But despite their cruelty, to be so christened was to gain peer group acceptance. Now he leans back in his seat.

'You were going to fill me in on what the Dalbrae character told you.'

DS Jones nods reflectively.

'Actually, I see it in a slightly different light since our conversation with Rik Hannay. He did say that Daisy Mills was widowed shortly before Christmas. That he'd organised the trip as a nice thing to do. But he didn't put it as explicitly as Rik Hannay – that it was some sort of psychological recuperation. Nor did he mention that Simon Mills died in unusual circumstances – in fact he didn't mention the first party at all.'

Skelgill is looking irritated.

'Why did they come here?'

The suggestion in his tone is why has this landed in their lap?

'Kenneth Dalbrae says he's been visiting the Sharrow Bay annually since the late eighties – that he knew the founders.'

Skelgill gives a reluctant inclination of the head to confirm his understanding. His colleague refers to what was Lakeland's if not England's original and most famous gourmet country house hotel. It stands literally on the eastern shoreline of Ullswater, not so far from their present location – ten miles, he would guess, as the crow flies, but three times that and an hour's drive by road. Notorious in its time, it will remain renowned as the birthplace of sticky toffee pudding.

'What was he doing at Buckstones Jump?'

DS Jones is about to bite on a finger of gingerbread. Skelgill indicates she should eat. He takes the opportunity to dunk one of his own and consume it whole. She interprets his question to refer specifically to the time of their arrival at the mountain pool. She makes a little rewind sign and licks fine golden crumbs from her top lip.

'Since he has some knowledge of the Lakes, he put together a programme for their trip. They've taken Rydal Grange until next Sunday. They were supposed to be on a Wordsworth-themed tour this afternoon. Apparently Daisy Mills had a thing about waterfalls – she'd asked him if they could visit one. Tomorrow's outing was to be a hike from Rydal Grange – a picnic and wild swimming.' (Skelgill begins to raise a hand but she continues quickly, anticipating his question.) 'The itinerary was circulated in advance – so any of them may have been aware of Buckstones Jump. And they discussed it as a group when they arrived, and apparently Daisy Mills said she couldn't wait.

'As for this morning, Kenneth Dalbrae said he woke at about seven and saw that Daisy Mills' door was open and her room empty. The front door had been unlocked and he noticed that a pair of wellingtons was missing. He guessed she had gone on a whim to see the waterfalls. He went after her.'

Skelgill has stopped eating.

'What is it, Guv?'

He has the Ordnance Survey map from his car. With quick hands he opens and refolds it to a size convenient for their table and orientates it for her benefit. He taps with the tip of an index finger.

'You can go round by the lane from Rydal Grange – to where we parked near the church.'

DS Jones pores over the map. It is easily walkable, maybe half a mile – and plainly Kenneth Dalbrae had gone on foot, given that his car was at the property when they returned.

Now Skelgill points again.

'There's a shortcut past the end of the lake. There's a footbridge over the Rothay tucked away in the wood.' He folds his arms and glares at the map. 'I'm surprised I didn't spot anyone.'

She detects the note of self-reproach in his voice.

'Surely neither of them would have known to take that route, Guv? They don't strike me as rambling types.'

Skelgill fixes her with a steady gaze.

'Except there's a fresh track in the dew, in the long grass – directly from the house through the meadow down to the shore of Rydal Water, where it meets the trees. Someone went that way this morning.'

DS Jones is obliged to re-evaluate Skelgill's visit to the veranda. The times quite likely correspond. They were on the lake for the best part of an hour, from before seven a.m. She looks again at the map.

'I suppose we were concentrating on my casting.' She indicates with a double movement of her hand, her palm held sideways. 'Also, I feel that we were mainly facing away from Rydal Grange and the village. It would only take a minute for someone to walk down and disappear into the trees.'

But she can see that Skelgill's pride is bruised – more so that he has missed such a blatant piece of information than any significance it can hold. She shifts the discussion back to what she sees as the more pertinent aspect of Kenneth Dalbrae's account.

'Guv – I'm sure Kenneth Dalbrae believes Daisy Mills met with – let's call it a tragedy – and that he holds himself responsible. Given what we now know about her husband, and the séance last night – I think he feels he's made a serious misjudgement. He was obviously already worried about her state of mind – why else check her room this morning? At the rock pool he kept talking about being "too late" – as if he had feared what would become of her.'

Skelgill is frowning.

'Hannay didn't reckon there was much in that business with the Ouija board.'

Quite vigorously DS Jones shakes her head and has to restore strands of fair hair that fall across her face.

'I took that to mean he doesn't believe in hocus-pocus. If you recall, when he came into the room, he asked whether they'd told us about last night. What if Daisy Mills had thought one of the group was taunting her?'

Skelgill does not respond immediately. He finds his mind overwhelmed by images of the pool at Buckstones Jump; a face beneath the swirling surface of his subconscious; lips that mouth words he cannot read. But he is discharged of the burden of an imminent declaration, for there is a sudden commotion; an unruly family arrives in the small café – children clatter headlong in competition for the best seats; a father's voice reprimands them in vain. It is the Leyton clan.

DS Jones makes empathetic eye contact with Mrs Leyton, who steers with some difficulty a buggy bearing the dissenting youngest child. With a dummy and a judicious word the mother seems to have more success in quietening her brood; the two elder children flash respectful glances at Skelgill, before submitting to the distraction of crayons. DS Leyton looks quite different out of his regulation grey suit; instead he sports an aquamarine Hawaiian shirt decorated with pink flamingos. As he squeezes between furniture he performs a brief shimmy and whistles a burst of Cliff Richard's "Summer Holiday".

'Emma, Guv.'

'Leyton – what are you doing here?' Skelgill sounds rather put out.

'Promised to take the nippers on the Windermere steamer – I couldn't see any point sitting round the house waiting for

Control to get back to me.' He jerks a thumb over his shoulder. 'I'd have a flippin' mutiny on me hands.'

Skelgill continues to glower. But – true enough – the direct route to Windermere from his sergeant's home in Keswick is through Grasmere, Rydal and Ambleside.

'Is this a coincidence?'

'I am a detective, Guv.'

He grins widely, and continues before Skelgill can answer.

'Guv – there's no missing your motor – plus the creative parking. *Hah-ha!* Besides, with my lot there's always scope for a pit stop. Looks like you had the same idea.'

Now Skelgill shrugs reluctantly. However he makes a correct deduction about his sergeant's stopping off.

'I take it you've heard back?'

DS Leyton pats his shirt pocket.

'Perfect timing – they rang when I was a couple of minutes up the road.' He lowers himself onto the edge of a spare seat, and leans forward to speak with more circumspection. 'The original 999 call was made from the phone box in Rydal village at just before seven-thirty.'

'Phone box?'

Skelgill's outburst is one of incredulity. The hamlet's traditional red public telephone kiosk stands at a slight tilt just beside the small church.

'That's right, Guv – the message was relayed immediately to the mountain rescue emergency line.'

Skelgill falls silent. Naturally he assumed the contact came from a mobile in the fells, and he has since mulled over why the caller did not go to the aid of Daisy Mills. But he has a precedent of his own that could excuse the absence of the person raising the alarm. During a solo training exercise in Scotland, in the deep Cairngorm pass that is the Lairig Ghru a distressed elderly man whose trekking partner had suffered a stroke and was unconscious in their tent two miles ahead flagged him down. Rather than go to the tent, Skelgill had sent the man back with first aid advice and instead he had scrambled sixteen hundred feet up through snow to the Devil's Point, whereupon his phone got a signal. Before he was halfway down a Sea King helicopter was hammering through the valley below. As he and DS Jones had discovered, there was no service at Buckstones Jump, so the notion of a similar occurrence was a credible explanation.

'So, who made the call?'

Skelgill intones slowly, as if he is anticipating another inconvenient answer.

'Anonymous. They hung up without giving their name.'

Skelgill mutters something that may be a local expletive.

'Male? Female?'

Now DS Leyton begins to appear slightly uneasy.

'Well – here's the weird thing, Guv – apparently the operator couldn't tell. The person whispered.' He runs the fingers of one hand through his mop of dark hair. 'I mean, in a phone box – it's not like anyone's earwigging – why would you whisper?'

'To hide your identity?'

It is DS Jones – they both look at her for an explanation.

'A whisper doesn't produce a distinctive sound spectrum like normal speech. It's the best way to disguise your voice. It was covered in one of the modules on the last forensics course I took.'

While her colleagues have a rudimentary appreciation of this principle, she puts it more compellingly.

Skelgill has regained his composure.

'Leyton, what was the message?'

'Just that someone was in trouble at the mountain pool called Buckstones Jump.'

'That it?'

DS Leyton raises his hands apologetically.

'I've requested that an audio file of the recording be sent to Emma's inbox. I mean – you might get more out of it – I'm just going by what's been relayed to me, Guv.'

He glances nervously across at his family; the noise level is rising and there is the impression that it might provide a convenient excuse before he is shot as the messenger. Notwithstanding, he reverts to Skelgill.

'Does this queer your pitch, Guv? I've been wondering why you were involved – it sounded like a straight case of a mishap in the mountains.'

Perhaps to the surprise of both of his colleagues, Skelgill's expression becomes decidedly philosophical.

'That's what I'd thought, Leyton. But every time I round a corner it gets a little queerer. All I need now is Herdwick to tell us he smells a rat.'

Skelgill looks at his phone on the table and they all do, but nothing happens.

*

Clutching two drawings of fish and without what an onlooker would describe as any great enthusiasm Skelgill waves off DS Leyton and family. He is left to consider his male colleague's remark about his "creative" parking. On reflection, his car probably is in someone's front garden. There had been plenty of parking spaces when he and DS Jones rendezvoused here at shortly after six-thirty a.m.

Despite his earlier assertion tourists are queuing out of the door for their gingerbread souvenirs. He waits beside the low wall of the churchyard, and gazes reflectively upon the crumbling gravestones, their inscriptions obscured by erosion and lichen. Ancient yews deposit deep shadows; their roots must intermingle with the bones of those laid to rest beneath. He wheels slowly around. More cheerful, if unwelcome as invaders, across the road a garden hosts a pyrotechnic display of rhododendrons in great clusters of red, purple, white and yellow.

His colleague is taking longer in the ladies' washroom than he anticipated. Following their brief interview with Rik Hannay (and perhaps prompted by the resting actor's "sidekick" remark) she had made a request to return the short distance to Grasmere for the change of clothes in her overnight bag, to which he had acceded. This and other factors had contributed to the decision to take a temporary sojourn from Rydal Grange.

That it is beneficial to allow the house party to acclimatise to the news of Daisy Mills' death is a point on which they concur. This also enables those members out walking before breakfast to return. For their part, the detectives can take stock. As DS Leyton has queried – what are they doing investigating an accident in the fells?

Skelgill revisits this conundrum. Of course, in the main this was happenstance. A mission of assistance not investigation – but there has been a seemingly inexorable drift towards the latter. And this drift would become a tidal surge if the evidence of Dr Herdwick points to any suggestion of foul play. Acting on instinct Skelgill had put his neck on the block in rousing the police pathologist (the rescue helicopter he can get away with – a quiet month, long days, good conditions – they're always okay with a training exercise; and he has credit in the bank with the crew). But to call in the pathologist is asking for trouble.

And, now – just as DS Jones emerges from the gingerbread emporium, a holdall over her shoulder, and clad in hoodie, jeans and trainers – Skelgill's phone finally does ring. It is the number of the police path lab.

DS Jones comes to stand alongside her taller colleague – she seems to get the idea of who is calling, albeit Skelgill only listens. His sole question finally comes.

'Are you saying she was held under?'

He waits for the reply. Then he thanks the caller. He grimaces; he looks dissatisfied.

DS Jones raises her face inquiringly; her skin is smooth and bronzed and seems almost to glow. For once, Skelgill is forthcoming.

'It's the worst of both worlds. They've still got blood and tissue tests to run, mind.' He puts his hands on his hips and stares into the distance; his gaze drifts higher; there is a glimpse of green fellside marked by charcoal lines, the walls in shadow, and the little rocky summit above Silver How. 'She drowned. Impossible to tell if that were by accident or design.'

'And the other world?'

75

It is a moment before Skelgill responds, and he starts slightly, jerked back from the daze he was beginning to enter. As he makes eye contact she sees that his grey-green irises appear dominated by the emerald component, perhaps a function of the intense spring sunlight and their verdant surroundings.

'No bang on the head from the rocks. No grazed fingertips from trying to scramble to safety. But slight bruising around both wrists. Quite recent – probably not this morning. Would likely conceal any subsequent bruising.'

DS Jones holds his gaze. A middle-aged couple exit from the café and pass close by. She waits for them to retreat from earshot before she speaks.

'It sounds like we shouldn't let it drop, Guv.'

Skelgill turns away; he mimes a cast. DS Jones recognises the sequence: lift – *flick* – pause – *flick*.

It might be the calmest of days, but there are too many straws in the wind.

8. THE MIDDLEMARCHERS

Sunday, 12 noon – Rydal Grange

'Ahoy, there!'

Skelgill is just thinking that those absent must be back – for as he and DS Jones begin to mount the steps of the porch he notes that the line of wellingtons is now intact. He turns to locate the source of the hearty salutation. At a picnic bench in the shade of the oaks, not far from the squirrel feeder that had caught his eye earlier sits a man whom he does not recognise.

'Harry Badger.'

The man raises one hand like a schoolboy supplying his name for the class register – albeit in the other he holds a tumbler of clear reddish liquid. The detectives exchange glances. Harry Badger is first on the list of those to whom they wish to talk. Skelgill mutters from the side of his mouth.

'Might as well see him out here.'

DS Jones replies with equal circumspection.

'It's probably just as private, Guv.'

They approach purposefully. Despite his initial animation the man makes no further effort in the way of a greeting. Indeed, he remains seated and tops up his drink from a glass jug in which float slices of cucumber and fruit. Skelgill knows from his colleague's notes that he is sixty-one, yet in most respects he looks younger. The thick head of wavy black waxy hair that he wears in an out-of-date style shows no sign of greying. His complexion is either tanned from exposure or naturally swarthy. Very dark brown eyes, a prominent nose and thick sensuous lips complete what is an almost feminine, Mediterranean appearance.

Conversely, Harry Badger could hardly be a more down-to-earth English bloke's name.

DS Jones makes brief introductions and confirms the man is willing to 'have a word'. The detectives settle on the opposite side of the bench. Skelgill notices that the man's eyes follow DS Jones's movements as she clambers into position. They have agreed that she will continue to make the running – he is coming to appreciate her forensic approach to interviewing; and he is largely happy to ride shotgun, albeit there can be times, like this, when he has to restrain a proprietorial instinct. He finds himself perusing the bench-maker's mark, a riveted tin plate claiming sustainable hardwood. But perhaps even this act is intimidating; the man, first unshy and seemingly loquacious, is now clearly holding back, waiting to be asked – when surely it would be more natural to inquire whether they have any news. He seems to harbour the expectation of suspicion being held against him.

DS Jones confirms his name and date of birth, and establishes that his marital status is divorced and his address to be Jericho Park, Burton Magna, a village a few miles from the town of Middlemarch. He gives his occupation as sales manager, retired. To Skelgill's ear there is a curious resentful emphasis on the word 'retired' as though this were not his choice; at sixty-one and looking in decent fettle it begs a follow-up question. But instead DS Jones asks who was his last employer. His features contort.

'Look – what's this got to do with Daisy?'

Skelgill, though outwardly disinterested is attending minutely – but in the man's tone he detects more than anything a note of boredom – and he realises that he might be drunk. After all, the jug of whatever it is – Pimm's perhaps – is two-thirds empty, and what's to say it's his first jug of the day? It would explain his bonhomie upon their arrival and his subsequent mood swing now that they are getting down to nuts and bolts. DS Jones responds patiently.

'Sir – it's just standard procedure – when we interview a possible witness we record these basic details – name, age, address, occupation, et cetera. In part it's because we may need to get in touch again. But someone's occupation could significantly impact their ability to interpret a situation – and thus the reliability of their evidence. An orthopaedic surgeon seeing a football injury occur will provide a more informed diagnosis than the average fan in the crowd.'

Now Harry Badger gives a casual wave of his glass and takes a gulp.

'The bulk of my career I was with Glaxo – from graduate trainee. More latterly AstraZeneca.'

'When did you leave there, sir?'

'Oh – I don't know – must be – five years ago?'

The vague response reinforces Skelgill's opinion of his condition. But there is the usual challenge – when you meet a person for the first time, you have a limited idea of what might be their normal behaviour.

'So if I put pharmaceutical sales, would that be correct?'

'Sounds better than drug rep, what? I'll have you know I dealt with senior hospital consultants – none of your backstreet quacks.'

He takes another swig. To Skelgill's mind he seems to be defending his ego against a charge not made.

But now DS Jones pauses to check her page and then quite abruptly changes tack.

'Sir, I'd just like to understand your relationship to Mrs Mills.'

'No relationship! Not I. You've got the wrong man.'

Harry Badger flashes a glance at Skelgill; what is it he sees in the dark eyes – is it covetousness? Or is he just trying to make some macho connection – that this young woman has put him on the spot, embarrassed him? But it is a fleeting impression.

He mutters, almost as if to himself.

'Besides, I'm not rich enough.'

Skelgill wonders if his colleague will be tempted by these possible diversions; but she remains steadfast.

'Sir, I mean how you knew her – and the extent of your contact with her of late.'

He appears to relax a little. He takes a small sip of his drink; his glass is almost empty; he eyes the jug.

'As I'm sure you have deduced – most of us were in the same year group at school. And, like the Lux sisters I've lived in the Middlemarch area ever since – apart from university. It's a small town in a small world – occasional encounters can't be avoided. The high street. The supermarket. Country walks. Events held by mutual friends and acquaintances. Christenings, marriages – funerals – Facebook.'

DS Jones momentarily glances up from her note taking, but perhaps it is just the unexpected juxtaposition of nouns. She admits a moment's silence, as if in a small mark of respect for his mention of funerals.

'And how about since the death of Mr Mills?'

Harry Badger pulls absently at his shirt at the back of his neck; it is blue check cotton and the movement draws attention to the fact that the points of the collars are frayed. He gives a shrug of the shoulders.

'The same thing – I've crossed paths with her once or twice, passed the time of day.'

DS Jones nods.

'And yesterday – last night – how would you say she was?'

'Bright and breezy, as usual.'

'I understand she was disturbed by the outcome of the board game you played.'

Harry Badger seems content to take advantage of her level inflexion; he merely nods in response to the statement. DS Jones is obliged to press him.

'Could you explain what happened?'

He inhales and closes his eyes and makes a clockwise circling motion with his glass.

'At the table were Hugo, Daisy, Kenneth – then Gail, Clint, Poppy – Spike – and myself.'

'Sir – *Clint?*'

He opens his eyes.

'It's what we call Karl – Rik and I.' He sniggers; he seems undeterred that the laugh is not reciprocated. 'His surname is Eastwood. He even came dressed as Dirty Harry to Daisy's Seventies party. I should have had first claim on that.'

Skelgill is thinking it would not be a good choice; apart from the disparity in looks, he doubts if Harry Badger stands any more than five-seven. It would be like casting Tom Cruise as Jack Reacher.

There is a momentary hiatus, which the man seems to interpret in his own peculiar way.

'Freddie Mercury.' He holds out his arms as if to ask what could be a more natural choice? His expression suddenly becomes conspiratorial. 'Which is a coincidence – because Bohemian Rhapsody was playing last night when the words 'Simon' and 'murder' were spelled out.'

'Did you do that, sir?'

He rolls his dark eyes, exposing the bloodshot whites.

'You're joking!'

'Do you believe in it?'

'Come off it, Sergeant Jones.'

He drains his glass and leans across the table towards her. She does not move, and regards him evenly.

'Who do you think did it?'

Now he flops back, and there is the small suggestion that he would not be willing to shop one of his mates. He turns out his plump bottom lip.

'No idea. No one's admitting to it. I think you'll find that ship has sailed.'

DS Jones stares at him; it is a challenging assertion that he makes, perhaps a little unsettling; but all the same, an interesting perception on his behalf.

'What made you agree to be the fall guy – if I can put it that way, sir?'

'I suggested it.'

He does not immediately elaborate.

'For a particular reason?'

'No reason – it just came to me – Daisy was obviously upset and I thought of a way to nip it in the bud.'

'And did it?'

'I should say so.'

'What exactly happened?'

'Kenneth was through in the kitchen with her – trying to get her to drink water. I asked to have a word in private.'

The dark eyes narrow and as they hold her gaze the irises seem to DS Jones to merge disconcertingly with the enlarged pupils to form coal-black holes.

'Did you or Mr Dalbrae have to restrain her in any way?'

'No.'

The answer is hurried and, to the sceptical ear, rings of a denial.

'How long were you together?'

'A couple of minutes. I gave her a brandy – that soon did the trick.'

'What was your explanation? I mean, for interfering with the Ouija board.'

'You might call it the 'Pimm's Defence', Your Honour.'

Again he thinks he is being funny. He raises his empty glass and then stares at it rather forlornly.

'Do you think Mrs Mills believed you?'

Harry Badger seems to relax once more. He touches his chest over his heart with his left hand.

'She always had a soft spot for me. And she was quick to forgive indiscretions. I coaxed her back through – and a group of us chatted by the fire.'

'What about?'

Harry Badger looks surprised that she has asked.

'Spike was pontificating about the Lake District being an artificially maintained environment and devoid of proper wildlife. He wants to ban sheep farming and grouse shooting. He's the figurehead of some public campaign. He reckoned he got shot at, last week in North Yorkshire. Daisy was very sympathetic.'

Skelgill shifts in his seat and DS Jones can sense that he might well be tempted to stick his oar in on this matter. Briskly, she continues.

'You didn't discuss the séance?'

Harry Badger puts down his glass and folds his arms.

'Nope – I got the feeling the others had decided it was off limits.'

'Did Mrs Mills say anything about what she might do this morning?'

Harry Badger shakes his head.

'What about you, sir – did you see her this morning?'

As if inadvertently, his eyes shift briefly to the jug.

'The last I saw, everyone was heading to their rooms. Clint and I had a nightcap. I didn't get up this morning until around ten – Kenneth came banging on my door. With the news.'

DS Jones has her head down, writing in shorthand – Skelgill suspects she is doodling and using the time to think. She looks up.

'Well – that's just about all for now, sir. Thank you for your help. If anything else springs to mind, please let us know.'

Harry Badger begins to rise. The bench seat is an awkward arrangement and he takes a moment to extricate himself. DS Jones is much quicker to her feet, and to Skelgill's surprise and Harry Badger's apparent consternation she reaches to claim the Pimm's jug.

'By the way, sir – when you said we'd got the wrong man, what did you mean by that?'

'Oh – I merely meant – you know, old times? I never quite managed a romantic liaison with Daisy – I was otherwise engaged. She and Hugo had a bit of thing at school. It was rather Romeo and Juliet – but don't quote me on that – given what's just happened – *hah!*'

He seems pleased with his joke – despite its bad taste, and that the police are not amused. (DS Jones, an English graduate, wonders if her superior sees the dark side of it.) Harry Badger is looking thirstily at the jug – as though he has fulfilled his part of the bargain and that now she should hand it over.

'Like me to send him out?'

DS Jones appears perplexed.

'It's alright, thank you, sir. It's unlikely we will need to speak with everyone – given you were together as a group. I'll come along, if required.'

To his evident relief she parts with the jug. He bows his head and grins sheepishly and walks away unsteadily, filling his glass as he goes. They wait until he rounds the corner of the house, by way of the veranda.

Skelgill produces a growl of exasperation.

'What do you reckon to him?'

DS Jones appears for a moment as though she will exercise restraint.

'If I were being cruel, Guv, I'd say sleazy and sly.'

'That's just being honest. You could add sozzled. Though most folk recover from that.'

DS Jones remains standing; she stares at the point from which Harry Badger disappeared from sight.

'But no real alarm bells.'

Rather pensively, she resumes her seat beside Skelgill. He leans his elbows on the surface of the picnic table and supports his chin with the backs of his hands. He is watching the feeder, where the squirrel has quietly returned, unafraid of their close proximity.

'This is beginning to feel like a fishing expedition. Sooner or later we'll trawl up a problem to fit our solution – and find it's a red herring.'

DS Jones tries not to show she is disconcerted. Quite reasonably, he is probably thinking that they ought to be frying Cumberland sausages on Heron Island. And she understands that what some may read as capriciousness is his inherent aversion to the no-man's land that lies between conjecture and connection – or, more accurately, admitting that treading there can be an uncomfortable necessity. Not for the first time this morning, she sticks to her guns.

'It's not quite right, though, is it, Guv?'

Skelgill turns to her and now he grins.

'You're getting the hang of this detective lark.'

In the corner of his eye Skelgill notices that the squirrel suddenly darts away.

'Excuse me?'

The detectives turn to look over their inside shoulders. Across the soft turf a man has silently approached to within ten feet. Now he has at least halted to announce his presence.

'Yes, sir?' It is DS Jones that responds.

Skelgill is no fashion guru, but he recognises that the dark outfit of fine woollen sweater, slim jeans and ankle boots might be considered stylish – though perhaps inappropriate for someone of this age. He is of medium height, lean build, and facially unremarkable, with a domed mainly balding head which is otherwise shorn of its hair. He appears superficially calm, but there is something about his unblinking sky-blue eyes that suggests an underlying tension. He presses onto the bridge of his nose a pair of rimless spectacles; they may have slipped or it might be a nervous action.

'I'm sorry to intrude. My name is Hugo Grant. I don't mean to interfere – but the debate in there has taken a rather unhealthy turn – speculation, really – about what happened to Daisy.'

The man's accent shares common vowel sounds with others Skelgill has heard this morning, alien to his ear – neither the Brummie twang of Birmingham nor the northern burr of Nottingham.

'Are you feeling responsible in some way, Mr Grant?'

DS Jones's question causes a flash of unease to grip the man's features.

'I'm sorry?'

She clarifies her meaning.

'Responsible for your friends – for the group.'

'Oh – well, yes – I said I would come and have a word – as spokesperson. I run a company – I suppose I'm used to handling crises, managing people under pressure.' He takes a couple of paces forward, more resolutely now – and indeed he looks irked in the way of one about to share a confidence with business associates. 'To be frank, Harry has just come back in and relished stirring the pot with talk of third degree – as though you – well – suspect someone of triggering what occurred. Surely this is a terrible accident?'

Skelgill beckons loosely.

'Why don't you have a seat, Mr Grant?'

The man complies, and settles opposite the detectives. Skelgill glances at DS Jones. She seems to understand what she should say.

'Sir – as you may be aware, we became involved purely by chance – we happened to be nearby. However, in the circumstances of a sudden or unexplained death, particularly in the absence of a medical practitioner, it is required that a report is made to the Coroner – this is a procedure that protects the public – all of us. In most such cases there is a verdict of misadventure – but all available facts must be presented in order to reach that point. From our perspective we have to keep an open mind. Clearly the events of last night were traumatic to Mrs Mills.'

The abrupt contradiction of her final sentence prompts a defiant riposte.

'Look – I appreciate this is the elephant in the room – but I can tell you – there's absolutely no way that Daisy would have taken her own life – offended or frightened by someone or not.'

There is a tremor of emotion in his voice – and perhaps a moistening of his pale eyes. DS Jones regards him evenly.

'How well did you know her, Mr Grant?'

Her tone is laced with doubt – and this appears further to galvanise his spirit. He responds in a patently controlled fashion.

'I have a sister that lives in the States. I've barely seen her in the last four decades. But when we get together it's like we've never been apart.' He gestures towards the house. 'It's the same with the Middlemarch crowd. Most of us survived school together. We know each other inside out. Character is immutable.'

Skelgill is conscious that DS Jones looks at him briefly. He does not try too hard to construe what might be her motivation; he keeps his gaze fixed on Hugo Grant. A little to his surprise DS Jones seems to accept the man's proposition.

'Then do you think it was out of character for Mrs Mills to have set off to the waterfalls on her own, early in the morning?'

He shakes his head.

'Not at all – it's exactly the sort of thing she would do. She was dedicated to making the most of life. And she had a lot to live for. She was always the optimist. She liked socialising, travel, walks, animals, local charities, good causes – to Simon's horror she invited homeless people to Christmas dinner every year.'

'In your opinion was she adversely affected by the death of her husband?'

He looks alarmed.

'Well – yes – I mean, who wouldn't be? But in the greater scheme of things she wasn't the kind to wear widow's weeds.'

'How would you describe your relationship with Mrs Mills, sir?'

For a moment his expression suggests that he feels double-crossed – that Harry Badger was right – the police are putting everyone through the third degree. But he doubles down on his original standpoint.

'A close friend.'

DS Jones checks her notes.

'But you live in Glasgow – and you're married.'

She says it non-judgementally, but the content is provocative.

'Like I said – we formed kindred bonds – among our entire peer group. Subliminal bonds. Don't I know it.' Now he sighs and rubs the top of his head with both hands, his fingers intertwined. There are darker patches of perspiration beneath the armpits of his close-fitting navy sweater. 'But – yes – I went to Scotland to university and met my wife-to-be, and settled up there. My parents moved to London during my first year, so I barely ever returned to the Midlands. But that scenario applies to most of us. On the whole we've maintained only sporadic contact. Our generation have lived most of our lives without social media.' He forces a wry grin. 'Obviously, Poppy Lux lives close to her sister's house – they still have an elderly father in care. I'm aware that Kenneth and Daisy have seen a lot of each other down the years – I met them and Sarah for lunch once or twice in London. Kenneth helped me with a property contact when I was looking for office space in the early 2000s. Rik and

Harry get together occasionally – I believe they go to the test matches and Twickenham. Sarah Rice was in the same year as Poppy, but she has always been friendly with Daisy. Though I think Daisy spent more time with Gail in the last couple of years, since she got to know her through Spike – Charles Rice.'

He folds his arms and looks from one to the other of the detectives; he seems to be hoping that his monologue will satisfy them.

'Is it possible that Mrs Mills had money worries?'

DS Jones's persistence appears to frustrate him – he inhales sharply as if to rebut the continued implication. But then he appears to reflect, and accept that, having put his head above the parapet as spokesman, he must resign himself to such questioning.

'Far from it, I should think.'

'Why would that be?'

'Look – I don't go around asking about this kind of thing – I couldn't even tell you about my wife's personal finances. But Daisy has been married to a succession of wealthy men. And I believe Simon Mills' business was very lucrative. No doubt Karl Eastwood could tell you more about that. I think if she had inherited some debt from Simon, it would be common knowledge – she wore her heart on her sleeve.'

'Does anyone in your group know if she announced her intentions to go to the waterfalls – or did anyone actually see her leave this morning?'

He shakes his head rather ruefully.

'Naturally we've been discussing this – holding our own inquest.' He makes a face of disquiet, realising his unfortunate use of the word. 'She'd talked about the waterfalls – but from what I can gather she went to bed without mention of it – and was up and gone before the rest of us. As you are obviously aware Kenneth later followed, on some instinct.'

He glances hopefully at DS Jones – as if perhaps she might have learned something from Kenneth Dalbrae that he has not shared with the group; but he is met by a look of studied contemplation.

'What about you, Mr Grant – you've been out this morning, is that correct?'

His senses seem to sharpen.

'Actually, that was planned. Jane was keen that we made the most of the free morning.' He raises his hands to indicate the spring-green canopy above, the dappled sunlight filtering through. 'It was a good forecast and this is a new area for us. She was more circumspect with the booze – she brought up some tea – we must have been out by eight a.m. – in fact, it was – I had switched on the bedside radio and I had to forego the news headlines because Jane was champing at the bit.'

'Where did you go?'

He looks across to his left and indicates with an index finger.

'We turned right out of the drive and followed the lane. We struck off on a footpath that took us down to a river in woodland. We followed that to a lake. I thought it was Rydal Water but we realised after a while it was Grasmere. We walked along the shore but in the end we came back the same way – the full loop looked a bit too far and Jane was experiencing some discomfort with her feet. Actually, I recorded it on my cycling app. Jane wanted to know the calories. I can show you.'

He produces his mobile phone and finds the information and places the handset in front of DS Jones. She dutifully slides it across so Skelgill can see. He scowls – the caption reads "6.4 kilometres" – but the start time corresponds to Hugo Grant's account, at 07:58 and today's date. The red line marking the route travels perpendicular to that taken by Daisy Mills and, later, Kenneth Dalbrae. As Skelgill returns the phone DS Jones glances at him – he gives a minute shake of his head. She addresses Hugo Grant.

'Well, thank you for coming to speak with us. We're sorry for your loss.' She pauses, as if to convey that her words are heartfelt. 'We're not sure yet how we'll conclude matters today, but we will of course keep you all informed. However, I would ask you to stress to your friends that we are not pursuing any particular agenda.'

The man nods, now perhaps a little reluctantly. DS Jones, who is using one of her own notebooks, turns to a clean page and presses it flat. She proffers it, along with the pen.

'Could I ask, for completeness, that you write your address and phone number?'

'Sure. It's one of the few numbers I do know – I've had it since I started my company in 1989 – we were just about first in Scotland to own mobiles. The service was abysmal, you could hardly ever get a signal.'

Skelgill raises an eyebrow, though he is more struck by the fact that the man is left-handed, and writes in a curious upside-down fashion. DS Jones seems also to be watching with eagle eyes. Hugo Grant hands back the notebook and pen.

'Sir, how did you get those marks on your hand?'

His colleague's unexpected question causes Skelgill to stiffen. He feels himself reining in an expression of surprise, whereas Hugo Grant regards her with a look of confusion.

'I'm sorry?'

'On the back of your left hand – there are fresh marks.'

He turns over both hands and looks at them, apparently bewildered. His skin, wrinkled to a degree and heavily veined, is lightly tanned and what small amount of hair present is blond. He wears a white-gold wedding band on his left ring finger. More or less alternating with his knuckles are four small crescent-shaped weals, slightly red, although the flesh is not broken. He seems to swallow.

'It must have been Daisy.'

DS Jones nods in a way that suggests he should elaborate.

'She was sitting next to me at the Ouija board table. When Simon's name was spelled out she grabbed my hand.' Perhaps involuntarily, as if reliving the moment, he moves his hand to touch the bench seat. 'She was this side, on my left. Then came the word – *murder* – and she reacted quite violently. It must have been just then.'

'You didn't notice at the time?'

He looks puzzled. He rubs at the marks with the fingers of his right hand.

'It's not actually sore. I mean – her chair flew back and she broke away – at that moment there were other things to think about – I was more concerned for her. I'd had plenty to drink – I'm not sure I would have felt much, anyway.'

'But you didn't go after her?'

'Well – Kenneth did. You see – he's always been more of a confidante. I figured he'd do a better job.'

DS Jones seems satisfied with this explanation. She closes her notebook. There is the clear suggestion that they have now finished, and Hugo Grant begins to clamber free of the bench.

'Could it have been Mrs Mills that moved the pointer?'

The man hesitates – though he is perhaps relieved that she has changed the subject.

'To be honest, it beats me how anyone could have moved the pointer. Harry took the rap and if I had to guess, I'd say it was he. I don't suppose anyone will want to admit it, now.'

'But someone must have done it?'

'They must.'

When he is gone Skelgill is quick to quip.

'Miss Marple strikes again.'

DS Jones chuckles.

'I'm sure you noticed the marks, too, Guv.'

Skelgill shifts position, as if the wooden bench seat is suddenly uncomfortable.

'We all know you're the expert on this kind of thing.'

'For obvious reasons, I confess I am a bit hypersensitive. I noticed them right away – but I cooked up an excuse to make it seem more casual. I already have his contact details, from Kenneth Dalbrae.'

She looks at Skelgill a little apologetically, but he shrugs.

'Fairy snuff – the woman's wrists were bruised.'

But now she rows back.

'Actually, I think they're innocent marks.'

'Come again?'

DS Jones lays her right forearm on the surface of the picnic table, palm upward.

'Hold my hand.'

'What?'

'I'll show you – go on.'

Skelgill rests his left hand upon that of his colleague. She contracts her slender fingers, intertwining them through his longer, more gnarled specimens.

'See – the only way you could get marks like that is with a grip like this. They were holding hands. My nails are not long enough, but if they were – and I squeezed hard, like this –'

'Aargh, ya!' Skelgill protests. 'They're long enough, lass.'

'Oh – I seem to have picked an inopportune moment.'

The husky female voice comes from just behind them, and despite its apologetic words its tone is one of satisfaction. They disentangle their grip – it is impossible not to appear sheepish in such circumstances. The owner of the voice – immediately recognisable – is the bathrobe woman from the veranda – Gail Melia, as she had introduced herself, current partner of Dr Charles Rice. Now she wears a figure-hugging mustard-coloured beach dress that is almost as revealing as the inadequate dressing gown. She bears a tray. She beams at them ingenuously.

'With our compliments. Tea – and local gingerbread! I bought it yesterday afternoon.'

9. SLEEPING QUARTERS

Sunday, 1 p.m. – Rydal Grange

'Reckon she even kipped here?'

DS Jones does not answer, but moves purposefully around the large timber-framed divan to the side where a glass of water rests upon an oak nightstand. With a practised sweep she pulls back the duvet, exposing a good two-thirds of the mattress, across the full width of the bed. While the pillows are neatly plumped, where a person would repose there is a faint depression and small creases in the bottom sheet. The adjacent lie is untouched. She lifts the nearest pillow to reveal navy blue cotton pyjamas decorated with pink tiger motifs. She raises the top by the shoulders as though she were inspecting a garment in a store.

'I'd say this has been worn, Guv.' She brings it close to her face. 'There's a faint smell of perfume.' She holds it out again, admiringly. 'Expensive brand.'

Skelgill, despite his question, has entirely ignored DS Jones and, upon entering an unfamiliar room has made his usual beeline for the window. Daisy Mills certainly got a prime vista. The view down over the meadow to Rydal Water, its mirror surface inverting the greens and browns and blues and whites of fells and sky, is like something from a holiday brochure; it would sell the property in its own right. To part the curtains of an early morning would confront him with an irresistible force, to be out there on the lake. A woodpigeon, displaying bold white flashes, wings across his line of sight, evidence that this is not some elaborate illusion.

The bird breaks his trance and, further to his habit he checks the window as a means of egress. The woodwork is painted in fresh white gloss and the brass fastener is new and well oiled. It unscrews with light fingertip pressure. He raises the lower sash and leans over the pitted stone sill. He frowns in an evaluative manner. He could get out of here if he needed to, but for the average person it would not be the preferred option. A couple of feet below, the top of the pitched roof of the veranda meets the wall and slopes away, more steeply than it appears from ground level. If one were to step out unprepared, the mossy slates would precipitate a slip, a slide, a short flight and an unceremonious roll down the ha-ha – perfectly survivable but highly ignominious.

He pulls down the sash but decides to leave an air gap of a couple of inches. The five-note coo of (perhaps the same) woodpigeon drifts in on a light, cool zephyr. Skelgill snatches a last longing look at the lake and a movement away to his left draws his eye. A figure has appeared on the shoreline and now has stopped and raised a pair of binoculars. It is a man – though he is too distant to discern any detail – he appears to be wearing an olive-green jacket in the style of a birdwatcher, although that must be too warm – he appears tall, spindly, and there is the impression of fair or gingery hair. As Skelgill watches he lowers the binoculars and begins to move towards Rydal Grange, but quickly disappears into the fringe of oaks that dips at a tangent from the corner of the building, eventually to intersect with the water's edge.

'Guv.' DS Jones's voice is insistent. 'Here's her phone.'

Skelgill turns to see she has investigated the jewellery drawer of the nightstand and is opening the powder-blue protective case of a smartphone. He glances back and watches for a moment, but there is no further sign of the man. Dr Charles Rice has been absent all morning. He had also left without announcement, apparently early. The others have been unable to contact him. The consensus is that he would have gone birdwatching and quite likely would have his phone switched off.

Unaware of developments, this could be him returning for lunch and the scheduled Wordsworth tour, now cancelled.

'The screen's locked.'

'Do you know her date of birth?'

DS Jones does not answer, but lowers herself to rest on the edge of the bed. As Skelgill approaches she taps in a code, confidently, as if it were her own phone. He can see from her reaction it works. She looks up with a smile, but does not disabuse him of his minor triumph, for she has simply tried 123456. It seems she reads something of Daisy Mills already.

'There are quite a few new alerts.'

'I'm surprised there's a signal.'

'It's connected to the Wi-Fi.'

She narrows her eyes as she begins to navigate her way around the home screen. Skelgill observes for a few moments before he runs out of patience.

'Have you got that room list?'

DS Jones, quickly engrossed, looks up after a short delay.

'Sorry? Oh – sure. It's here.'

She reaches for her notebook and extracts a loose sheaf of paper. In addressing the group, following their supplementary snack of tea and gingerbread, she had explained it would be helpful if the detectives could look over Daisy Mills' room, and also make a brief check of the property. No one had demurred and Kenneth Dalbrae had supplied the room allocation that formed part of his preparations.

Skelgill peruses what is in fact a diagram. In his experience there are several popular nomenclatures that Cumbrian hoteliers and holiday-home owners rather unimaginatively apply to keep track of their guests' accommodation. Commonest, not surprisingly, are rooms named after lakes, followed – probably – by the names of villages. Even his friend Charlie up at The Partridge beside Bassenthwaite Lake has fallen for this latter system; Skelgill's favourite suite is called 'Applethwaite', not that he can ordinarily afford it. Perhaps to save on key fob engraving, the proprietors of Rydal Grange have opted for a hybrid system of well-known fells supplemented by numbers. Thus Daisy Mills has 'Scafell – 3', and her immediate neighbours on one side are Kenneth Dalbrae and Ben Lomond in 'Skiddaw – 2' and on the other Hugo and Jane Grant in 'Catstycam – 4'. The list includes 'Helvellyn – 6', 'Blencathra – 7' and 'Glaramara – 9' – good choices, though Skelgill is slightly irked by the omission of Scafell Pike, England's Everest.

Notwithstanding, as he leaves DS Jones to interrogate Daisy Mills' digital correspondence, it is to the room called 'Haystacks' that he gravitates. The layout of the upper floor is linear; the central staircase curves up to meet a fairly broad landing that runs for the full width of the building, to a tall window at each end. On the left – the west – is the smaller staircase he had noticed earlier. As with the ground floor, rooms are arranged in two rows on either side of the corridor. 'Haystacks', Room 10, he finds last on the left before the head of the second staircase and opposite Room 1, a position that means its windows will give on to the front of the property, a woodland rather than lake aspect.

As far as he knows, everyone is still downstairs, but the door of 'Haystacks' is closed and he knocks and waits a moment before entering. The décor is much the same as elsewhere, the same 'designer feel' with carefully chosen but impractical accessories that look good in the brochure as close-ups. There is a turned walnut bowl brimming with oversized pine cones, an assortment of rusty cowbells dangling from a row of wooden pegs and, bookended by carved Herdwick sheep, a collection of Lakeland whodunits that he can't imagine anyone would ever want to read – indeed their unbroken spines appear to bear testimony to his theory.

The occupants have left scant traces of their presence. The counterpane is smooth – though taking a leaf from DS Jones's book he spies corners of nightwear protruding from beneath the pillows, and there is a half-full glass of water on one nightstand and a jar of moisturiser on the other. But clothes and suitcases appear to have been tidily filed away. He opens one half of a freestanding dark oak wardrobe. On a rail hang six identical blue shirts and three identical pairs of black trousers, and – beneath – two identical pairs of size eleven shoes.

The sight raises an eyebrow, but nothing more, and Skelgill makes a brief visit to the window to check the view. The cars are parked below – he notices that the roof of his shooting brake could do with a clean some time this year. Otherwise the room does not appear to hold any great interest for him. He crosses to the ensuite bathroom.

Here it would take DS Jones to infer any significance from the expensive toiletries that have been meticulously arrayed on the vanity unit – and Skelgill does not waste his time. Instead, he slides open the curving glass door of the shower. It is a spacious cubicle, as is the bathroom itself, indeed the entire property has this desirable quality, and he has to step right inside to reach the chrome taps that project from the wall. Quite clearly, one is marked for flow and the other for temperature – as two levers they could hardly be simpler. Overhead, a large stainless steel rose operates by gravity, so he is able to avoid the deluge when he turns it on. He feels for the temperature, experimenting with the lower lever. In just twenty seconds steam begins to rise up around him.

'*Oh, my hero! Silly me – always the dumb blonde!*'

Skelgill is becoming sufficiently accustomed to people creeping up on him that he does not start, but merely reprises under his breath another from his repertoire of curses.

He turns off the noisy splashing and clambers out of the shower.

He might move with outward composure but he glimpses in the mirror a pink flush on his high cheekbones; he has been caught red-handed.

Smiling, Gail Melia leans nonchalantly against the jamb of the door.

'You're welcome to avail yourself – if you feel in need of rejuvenation – you must have had a stressful morning. Charles hasn't used his towel – I expect he didn't want to disturb my beauty sleep.'

Quite a few thoughts are passing through Skelgill's mind. That the woman looks a lot younger than her stated age of fifty-five. That the mustard-coloured dress is even skimpier than he had previously noticed. That if she closed the door they would be in complete darkness. And, that, when he had stepped into the shower, the base of the unit was already wet.

There is a brisk knock from the bedroom – followed by the sound of the outer door opening. Now Skelgill sees a crease form in the brow of his lookalike. He had left it ajar.

'Guv?'

Before Skelgill can respond, Gail Melia takes a pace towards him. She lowers her voice.

'Your little admirer.'

But Skelgill calls out.

'Jones – in here.'

He forces a grin; but Gail Melia holds his gaze for a moment before she moves aside to casually check her hair in the mirror.

DS Jones, framed in the landing doorway, looks a little bewildered – and even more so when Gail Melia emerges from the bathroom behind Skelgill.

He detects that she is carefully choosing her words.

'There's something I need to discuss with you.'

Skelgill makes a kind of awkward bow to Gail Melia and stalks across the room to follow his colleague; he closes the door without looking back.

As they head along the corridor DS Jones musters an innocent inquiry.

'Guv, what were you looking for?'

Skelgill glances over his shoulder – they are alone, but he waits until they have regained the comparative sanctuary of Room 3, Daisy Mills' accommodation.

'This morning – she said her shower was on the blink.'

DS Jones looks bemused.

'And?'

'Aye – I got it working.'

The tone of his answer suggests concern for the shower and not for anything else – and certainly not some remarkable clue.

But DS Jones has her own remarkable clue, and she cannot dwell any longer on Skelgill's oblique coyness.

'Look at this, Guv.'

She raises Daisy Mills' pale blue mobile phone in front of his face.

Skelgill begins to recoil simply because she moves the handset too close, but the reaction gains force and he shies away as violently as if she had tricked him with smelling salts, his respiratory passages invaded by the burn of ammonia. He resorts again to his Anglo-Saxon lexicon, this time without concern for his audience.

'Just as well I've only had gingerbread for me dinner.'

DS Jones decides her superior has seen enough for her purposes. She folds over the cover of the phone and lowers it at her side. Skelgill waves a hand at the device.

'Who does that belong to?'

DS Jones shakes her head.

'Darth Vader.' She pauses to let the words sink in, but before Skelgill can object she continues quickly. 'It has been sent using a messaging app. It is set to automatically delete posts in this conversation after seven days – I've turned that off. It's the only item. But these messages are encrypted at both ends. There's no way of telling who sent something if they hide behind an avatar.'

Skelgill is glaring at her.

'Who would call himself Darth Vader?'

'I've looked up Star Wars – it started in 1977. Which kind of fits with this age group.'

'When did he send it?'

'Just after one a.m. this morning.'

Skelgill nods, as if this might be what he would expect. His confidence in referring to the gender of the sender as male is because the subject of the photograph leaves no doubt – it is a striking example of the nowadays bewilderingly commonplace pastime known as 'sexting'.

'Can you tell if she saw it?'

DS Jones nods.

'I think she did, Guv – unread messages appear in a section at the bottom of a conversation. There was nothing of that sort.'

Skelgill pauses for thought. His eyes rove around the bedroom as though he might be trying to imagine the scenario.

'Did you read the caption, Guv?'

Skelgill scowls disapprovingly – as though he is worried she will make him look again. She understands she should elaborate.

'That's even more puzzling. It says, "I can tell you all about Simon" – which surely confirms it's from someone connected to them.'

But Skelgill now steels himself.

'Let's see.'

He grimaces like a person afraid of needles knowing he must brave a vaccination – but he needs to see the words written, in order properly to absorb them. He glances briefly, very briefly.

'It's enough to make me jump into a freezing beck.'

DS Jones regards him charitably – indeed, there is a mischievous twinkle in her eye.

'I'll say it before someone else does, Guv – it would be a novel identity parade.'

Skelgill wheels away, perhaps to hide his expression.

'Good one – I'll mention that to the Chief.'

He stalks across to the window and presses his forehead against the cool glass. A man – the same person as a few minutes earlier – is making his way through the little paddock towards the steps that climb the ha-ha.

'Hey up – I reckon that's the TV naturalist bloke come back.'

Skelgill observes as the man ascends the steps. He has his gingery head down, watching his footing, and one hand holding the binoculars that dangle on a strap around his neck. But he looks up sharply just before he passes from sight beneath the veranda roof, directly at where Skelgill stands. 'Aye, that's him alright – I recognise him. Even with his trousers on.'

*

'Dr Rice – thank you for seeing us at such short notice. I'm afraid it hasn't given you very long to get used to the distressing news.'

The detectives are back at their al fresco office, the picnic bench, where they have waited for Dr Charles Rice to be apprised by his friends of the situation. This time they have seated themselves facing Rydal Grange. On emerging from the front door the man had paused halfway across the shady lawn to look at a bird overhead. And upon reaching them he had merely announced, "*Dendrocopos major* – great spotted woodpecker, juvenile". He had seemed unconcerned about introductions, perhaps accustomed to people knowing who he is. He had simply seated himself and looked up expectantly as though this were one of many interviews in his schedule, that he is a busy man.

'It only takes a second to understand that Daisy is dead.'

While DS Jones seems taken aback, Skelgill does not feel disquieted by the man's brusque response. After all, he is merely stating the obvious. His on-screen persona is assertive; he is an articulate presenter, his delivery rapid if robotic. His habit is to expound in staccato bullet points, and to Skelgill's satisfaction does so to completion, unlike many commentators who rudely abandon their sentence structure and leave him waiting for the 'B' that never comes. Perhaps off screen Dr Charles Rice is no different.

Meanwhile DS Jones adjusts her understanding of how she ought to proceed. She shifts from abstract feelings to more concrete facts.

'Dr Rice, we know that Mrs Mills drowned but not under what circumstances. There is no indication that she was attacked or robbed and the most likely explanation is that she met with an accident. As yet we have found no one who knew of her intentions or witnessed her movements. Can you help us in either respect, sir?'

The man regards her keenly through hazel eyes shaded by long gingery lashes that match unkempt eyebrows and hair – something of a trademark look – and there is the familiar long-jawed face, pasty freckled complexion, narrow nose and thin-lipped mouth.

'I rose at just before five-thirty a.m. and left a couple of minutes later. The house was silent. I used the back-stair so as not to disturb anyone. I filled my canteen at the sink and exited through the kitchen door. The first living soul I saw was a farmer driving a Land Rover; split screen, bronze green with a beige canopy and a border collie in the passenger seat.'

'Where was that, sir?'

He seems unfazed by the suggestion that she may wish to corroborate his movements.

'Along a stretch of the lane that runs south to Loughrigg Tarn. I used it to reach Intake Wood. Otherwise I was mainly off road.'

'Where did you go, sir?'

'As far as Colwith Force.'

DS Jones snatches a glance at Skelgill; he appears to respond with a barely perceptible nod, which she takes as confirmation that this might be a plausible answer. That the man has named a waterfall without flinching is notable but perhaps irrelevant. And, while Skelgill harbours a detailed map of the Lake District in his head, she knows enough to determine that Dr Charles Rice describes a trajectory opposite to that leading to Buckstones Jump.

'What was the purpose of your expedition?'

'I investigated a succession of fragments of deciduous woodland. There are several species of passerines of local importance in Cumbria: wood warbler, pied flycatcher, redstart and tree pipit.'

'I see.'

Her unenthusiastic response does not deter him. He continues, unprompted.

'They are more likely to display early in the morning – it is possible to estimate the number of breeding territories. I located three, two, three and four singing males, respectively. I shall submit my records to the BTO.' (It seems she is expected to remember the sequence of names, and understand the abbreviation.) 'Like the majority of British species they are in long-term decline. Modern farming practices pay little heed to biodiversity. You know we have lost forty million birds in my lifetime? For North America the estimate is three billion. Worldwide the figure is incalculable.'

DS Jones has to resist being drawn out of politeness into his a lecture on avian extermination. Apart from the digression there is the chance he will get onto something that will turn Skelgill hot under the collar. Quite likely the man is anti-fishing. She reverts to the other main strand that can be construed as relevant to their interview.

'We have heard from your friends that Mrs Mills was upset by the parlour game that was played last night.'

His keen expression remains unchanged – he shows no sign of offence that she has changed the subject – indeed, he answers without hesitation.

'An inane idea – but most of them had overindulged with alcohol. I should not have participated. But my inner scientist piqued my curiosity.'

She notes that the content of his reply is a little oblique.

'Did you form any theory about how the Ouija board spelled out the various words?'

His features sharpen; there is a flash of incredulity in his eyes.

'Clearly it was one of our number. Harry Badger was prepared to claim responsibility. But I expect there was an ulterior motive.'

'Ulterior motive, sir?'

'To curry favour with Daisy.'

There is a note of impatience in his tone, as though this ought to be obvious.

'Do you mean that he might have done the whole thing deliberately?'

Now he smiles, revealing a regular dentition marked by longer, pointed incisors.

'You're the detective, young lady.'

103

He consults his wristwatch and turns at the waist to look back at the house. There is the suggestion that he has given them enough of his valuable time.

Skelgill clears his throat.

'Dr Rice – you seem to have a good knowledge of the lie of the land hereabouts – it's not the most obvious route that you took.'

He stares at Skelgill – again the keen eyes – and, yet, again he is unfazed by the interrogative nature of the question.

'I'm sure you've seen small children trying to catch the feral pigeons in Trafalgar Square.' He does not wait for an answer. 'They instinctively move away. Wild birds are no different. Therefore, A) it is essential to stay off the beaten track and, B) you must stop at regular intervals and remain motionless for a good ten minutes. Otherwise you will see very little. You could get an entirely false impression of a situation.'

*

Skelgill has been squatting motionless for a good ten minutes when Hugo Grant struggles into sight. He has on the same dark outfit but now a pair of black trainers with fluorescent lime-green piping. He looks a little troubled by the heat. He pauses for a moment having gained the plateau; behind him in a direct line is the far distant smudge of Windermere, lying like mist in the dale. He crunches across the shingle to stand at the edge of the pool. In one hand he grasps a small bouquet of bluebells, their heads already drooping. He is close to the spot where Daisy Mills' body lay. One at a time, mechanically, he throws the wildflowers onto the surface of the water. Then suddenly he seems to sense he is being observed. He looks up, directly at Skelgill, some thirty yards off, above the waterfall at the back of Buckstones Jump. Hugo Grant raises a hand and begins to circle around. Skelgill watches as he picks his way over the rocks. He clambers up a little uncertainly, although he moves easily enough; he did mention that he cycles.

Skelgill has left DS Jones to wrap up the missing interviews – more of a formality, given the collective nature of events, and the increasingly repetitive accounts they have received thus far. For his part, he knew what he wanted to do, without particularly knowing why – not a contradiction that generally troubles him. He has come on foot from Rydal Hall, taking the shortcut through the meadow, surprised to find that the footpath emerges directly opposite Church Lane. He dwelt for a moment at the phone box, without entering, and continued, timing the entire walk to Buckstones Jump at twenty-four minutes.

This morning a search had been conducted of the immediate vicinity, though not of the forensic fingertip type that would accompany a murder investigation, more of an inspection for anything salient, of the order of a purse or garment. He has repeated this process in his own way, but has merely noted the intact nature of the surrounding vegetation, the regular weave of heather, bracken and mat grass, sprinkled with patches of yellow tormentil and pink lousewort; he had even found a meadow pipit's nest with four young that had gaped at his fingers, anticipating caterpillars when he parted the stems. He was surprised by the absence of picnic detritus, though it is still a little early in the season for the Lancashire litter louts.

He has been absently studying what must be trout fry feeding – small but vigorous rises, as if someone were throwing tiny pebbles into the water. He has been unable to discern what they might be eating – perhaps it is simply juvenile exuberance. But now another question strikes him – Daisy Mills was in the shallows, more or less on the shingle. There is no great current in the pool. Though Kenneth Dalbrae was vague-to-incoherent, he exhibited no obvious signs of having waded in. Skelgill wants to double-check this point – he should have brought the radio from the mountain rescue kit. Could it be this little irregularity that caused him to summon the pathologist?

'Anything, Inspector?'

Hugo Grant wipes his brow of perspiration. In the windless valley of Rydale the spring sun has the heat of summer. There is the constant rumble and rush of the waterfall, and more distant

105

versions of the same, as if loudspeakers are planted up and down the fellside. The man realises he will need to come close for them each to be properly heard.

Skelgill shakes his head; he grimaces reflectively.

'You?'

Hugo Grant appears surprised that he is asked. He stops a couple of yards short and turns to look down into the plunge pool.

'I just thought I would do something that Daisy would appreciate.' He indicates loosely to where a few of the stems still drift like fairy flotsam. 'In case she has gone to the great Ouija board in the sky.'

Skelgill looks up sharply – but the man's features are blank and it is hard to judge to what degree if any he is being flippant. Skelgill gives a heave and pushes himself to his feet, and then flexes his spine with his knuckles pressed into the small of his back, his head tilted skywards. The man regards him knowingly, and is about to comment when Skelgill pre-empts him.

'I have to be getting back to my colleague.'

'Mind if I walk down with you?'

'Aye.'

Skelgill's intonation conveys acceptance, rather than a literal rejection of the question. He leads the way – there is a gentler gradient across the rocks available to the trained eye.

Hugo Grant offers an explanation for his wish to go with Skelgill.

'We're packing up to leave. All of us. Jane's particularly keen. She isn't really assimilated into this group – which is perfectly understandable. I think it's even more difficult to be an outsider at a time of mourning.'

Skelgill gives an exaggerated nod. In an official capacity he has attended numerous funerals where he has felt very much an intruder – not least when he has suspected one of the other members of the congregation of being responsible for the death. Hugo Grant continues.

'She also gets a bit irked by Harry's constant references to Scotland as *Jockland.*'

Skelgill raises an eyebrow, though he does not respond directly. These days the boundaries between banter and criminal offence are so blurred that he steers well clear unless he is sure of his company.

'Is Grant *your* name?'

'Yes. Or perhaps I should say "och aye". Scots paternal grandfather – moved to the Midlands for work in the hosiery after the war – though I never really knew him. His grandfather was supposedly a distant cousin of President Ulysses S. Grant. Jane's a Dalmellington – they're a sept of Clan Campbell, did much of their dirty work. Never trust a Campbell.' He gives an ironic laugh. Then he sees that Skelgill looks perplexed. 'It's an internecine Scottish joke – a hangover from the Glencoe Massacre, you know? She was delighted to become a Grant. I'm sure that's half the reason she married me.'

Skelgill, half of whose family are descended from the notorious Border Grahams (in fact, living relatives more like nine-tenths), has a certain sympathy with this tarring by association. He continues, conversationally.

'You've not picked up the accent.'

Hugo Grant gives a choked exclamation.

'This lot would never let me live it down. May as well support Scotland.'

Skelgill nods approvingly.

'I can't say I know your home town.'

'It straddles the county boundary between Leicestershire and Warwickshire. Leicester and Coventry are the main football teams. Though most people support the Foxes.'

'That's Leicester City, aye?'

'Yes.'

'They've done alright for themselves.'

Hugo Grant smiles sardonically.

'My dad and my uncle took me to my first match at Filbert Street in 1968. It was against Man U. Like most kids, I thought I supported them. They had just become the first English club to win the European Cup. They had Best, Law and Charlton in the team.' He casts a wide-eyed glance at Skelgill. 'Imagine that

107

– my first match. The three greatest players Britain has produced. And Leicester won 2-1. So I switched allegiance.'

'Got to support your local team.' Skelgill's tone seems to endorse the decision.

'That season Leicester were relegated and lost in the Cup Final against Man City. A harsh early lesson in what it meant to be a true fan. But I stuck with them. Only had to wait fifty-odd years – good things eventually come along.'

Skelgill sees the man's smile fade, as though the anecdote has led to an unhappy association. Indeed, they now enter the final wooded stretch of path, and between the trees like a low-lying mist a haze of bluebells carpets the ground and their delicate scent pierces the cool air; it is an encounter that captivates the senses.

'She liked bluebells, aye?'

Skelgill's comment is entirely spontaneous, and despite that they have been conversing naturally, when a policeman is asking questions there comes a point at which the other is likely to feel it is more than idle curiosity. Hugo Grant takes a moment to answer.

'Who wouldn't?' He casts a hand to indicate the sapphire blur. 'These remind me of the woods where we grew up. There was a spinney called Bluebell Wood. I don't seem to see them so much in Scotland. I suppose the forests are mainly coniferous.'

Skelgill wonders if he will be more forthcoming, but it seems about as far as the man is prepared to go. He ventures another question.

'What did you make of Simon Mills?'

Hugo Grant seems more comfortable with the shift of subject.

'I must admit, I barely knew him.'

'So he weren't one of your school crowd?'

'I think he was from the West Country. Daisy met him through work when she was in her mid-forties. She was PA to her employer's finance director and Eastwood-Mills was their insurance provider.'

'And he was poisoned at a party, aye?'

Hugo Grant looks sharply sideways at Skelgill.

'Well – I believe he died of heart failure. We had left, so I only heard the story second hand. But, yes, there was contamination of one of the artisan gins that he was using to mix cocktails. Several people were affected, although they suffered relatively mild symptoms.' Now he holds out a hand, palm upward, a gesture of explanation. 'But it was a widespread event – five households in the district were affected. I gather Simon Mills was just unlucky.'

Skelgill nods and shrugs rather indifferently. He does not wish to labour the point, and Hugo Grant has reined in his candour. Besides, they approach the gate where the footpath meets Church Lane and an idea has occurred to him. As they pass the small church he indicates to the public telephone booth.

'You go ahead, Mr Grant. I've got no signal and I need to call headquarters.'

They have halted, and Hugo Grant pulls his own mobile from his hip pocket.

'I have service – you're welcome to use mine.'

Skelgill for a second appears as if he might be thwarted. But he jerks a thumb over his shoulder towards the kiosk.

'Thanks all the same, sir. But I can be put through on a direct line to my department by using the 999 system.' He grins confidentially. 'That way they know I'm not an imposter.'

'Ah, of course.'

Hugo Grant however seems reluctant to make the first move. Skelgill simply strides over to the call box and heaves open the heavy door.

'Cheers for now, sir.'

Once inside, he picks up the handset and extravagantly punches in three nines while surreptitiously holding down the hook switch. He glances casually through the small pane of thick scratched glass at eye level, but Hugo Grant is already striding away purposefully. Now Skelgill begins to recite into the mouthpiece the alphabet of British fish, something he invented as a boy, Allis Shad to Zander (admittedly with a couple of international guest species included, Q and X having posed

109

particular problems). It looks like he is explaining something, should Hugo Mills suddenly turn.

But he does not. Church Lane extends only another fifty yards before its junction with the winding Keswick-to-Windermere road. Skelgill watches, his expression becoming more hawk-like by the second. Opposite the end of Church Lane is the stile and the footpath that he himself used, the shortcut to Rydal Grange. Reaching the junction, without breaking stride to check for traffic, Hugo Grant veers to his left and out of sight, taking the long route.

Skelgill shoulders open the kiosk door and gasps for a lungful of fresh air. Then he pulls out his mobile phone and calls up DS Jones. He waits while she greets him.

'I reckon that's me done. What about you?'

There is another pause before he speaks again.

'I'm just by Rydal church. My keys are in the ignition. Want to come and pick me up on the way to get your Ma's gingerbread?'

10. THE MUDDLE IN THE MIDDLE

Monday, 5.30 a.m. – M6 motorway

'Are we there yet, Dad?'
'Very funny, Leyton.'
Skelgill driving, the trio of detectives has literally just joined what is England's longest motorway, the M6, at Junction 40, Penrith and Workington; that is *Pereth* and *Wukiton* in the vernacular.

'Guess how many times I got asked that yesterday, Guv?'
'Leyton – you only went to Windermere.'
'You know my nippers – attention span's not their strongpoint.'

Now Skelgill hesitates; a note of optimism enters his voice.
'We'll be at Tebay South in about ten minutes.'
DS Jones interjects.
'Hadn't we ought to get a few miles under our belt, Guv?'
'I was thinking of more like a bacon roll. Or two.'
Skelgill grins a little sheepishly.

DS Jones, from the passenger seat, glances round at DS Leyton seated behind Skelgill. He appears to be regretting his opening remark. What Skelgill doesn't see is the imploring flash in her eyes. And subtly she tilts the electronic tablet she holds. DS Leyton gets the message.

'If it's all the same to you, Guv – since you pair are packing me off to Rutland on me Tod Sloan – I'd like to get me head round the nuts and bolts. Give me time to ask any questions.'
Skelgill pulls a frustrated face.
'I suppose we've got Killington in half an hour.'

DS Jones raises her eyebrows but immediately clicks open the tablet and pulls at her seatbelt, so that she may more easily address DS Leyton. They exchange glances of resignation as they feel the speed of the car subtly increase. While it is quite likely Skelgill has skipped breakfast, there is always the lingering threat that he will stop for food just because he can. And the three-hours-plus motorway journey to the Midlands will see them pass a good dozen service stations that specialise in the energy-sapping fry-ups on which Skelgill thrives. Determinedly, she begins.

'The overview is this. We don't have a central striking fact that tells us a crime has been committed. But we do have a death that is unexplained – that of Daisy Mills – and which is associated with certain suspicious circumstances, including references to another unusual death – that of Simon Mills. The latter was investigated – but through the prism of a poisoning outbreak. The Chief doesn't want to take any chances with the incident on her watch, so she's agreed to clear it this morning with South Mercia Constabulary, so that we can take a second look at their findings. Obviously we'll need to be diplomatic.'

DS Leyton grins broadly.

'Treading on eggshells – I'm your man!'

DS Jones turns to Skelgill, perhaps expecting some rebuttal. But he stares at the broad grey runway-like road ahead, his arms straight out, both hands on the steering wheel, apparently dedicated to his mission. His gaze flicks with regularity to his rear-view mirror, in case an enthusiastic marked patrol takes exception to the speeding shooting brake. The car stands out on the early-morning-empty motorway; for company there is just the odd HGV lumbering down from Scotland with its refrigerated haul of North Atlantic langoustines bound for Dover and beyond.

She looks back to DS Leyton.

'I'll come shortly to what we do know about Simon Mills' death – and the ensuing investigation. Obviously that's a key reason for our journey, along with visiting Daisy Mills' home. But other information has come to light – in particular messages and conversations that we've found on her phone – that justify further investigation in the context of her death.'

DS Jones is generous in her use of 'we' in relation to the midnight oil she has burned interrogating Daisy Mills' mobile. And she doubts that Skelgill has done more than skim the covering email that accompanied her report that overnight has won the Chief's consent. Skelgill remains implacable.

'If you begin with our involvement, you obviously know about the 999 call made at 07:28 bringing attention to Daisy Mills at Buckstones Jump. The call made by someone possibly trying to disguise their identity. And made from the public phone box in Church Lane, which happens to be on the route between the waterfalls and Rydal Grange.'

DS Leyton nods obligingly.

'We arrived at the scene at eight a.m. and discovered Kenneth Dalbrae, who claimed he had been there for fifteen minutes, and that he found her as we did, lying half in the shallows, on the shingle. His account is confused – but he showed no signs of having pulled the body from the water – his footwear and clothing were apparently dry. The paramedics checked him over and found no superficial injuries.' She hesitates. There is the old chestnut about the first on the scene of a crime being more likely to be the perpetrator – for instance, that by reporting it they feel it less likely that the police will suspect them, or that they may wish to conceal some evidence – and she knows her colleagues will have this thought in their minds. 'We probably shouldn't conjecture too much about that at this stage – just note it.'

Skelgill seems to grimace, which may be a reaction to the word 'conjecture'. DS Jones continues.

'There is no further forensic evidence yet, beyond that Daisy Mills definitely drowned. She had contusions on both of her wrists but Dr Herdwick thinks these were inflicted on Saturday night – although he feels it would possibly disguise further fresh bruising at the time of death, which he puts between six and eight a.m. Given the time of the phone call, it would seem more likely that this was between six a.m. and seven-thirty.'

'More like seven-fifteen – it's a quarter of an hour down to the phone box.'

DS Jones nods to acknowledge Skelgill's correction.

'We don't know when she left, other than it probably wasn't around five-thirty, when Dr Charles Rice went birdwatching.' She glances again at Skelgill. 'And we were on the lake from about six forty-five. We didn't see anyone – although we think someone may have passed through the meadow in front of the house quite early, leaving a track in the damp grass.'

Skelgill does not speak, though his features infer some cogitation. DS Jones delves into her attaché case, which is open at her feet. She extracts a single sheet of paper.

'This might help. It's everyone who was there and a short biography of each.' She hands the page over but does not wait for DS Leyton to peruse it. 'The previous night, Saturday, the group played a game with a Ouija board. There were a couple of what you might call 'celebrity' manifestations – and then suddenly the name "Simon" was spelled out – followed by the word "murder". This caused Daisy Mills to break away from the table. She had been sitting next to Hugo Grant – he showed us some fingernail marks on his hand, which he says he thinks she inflicted as she reacted. Kenneth Dalbrae went after Daisy Mills to calm her down. Then Harry Badger – who seems to be the joker in the pack – agreed with the others that he would falsely admit that he moved the pointer. He was alone with her in private for a couple of minutes. There is nothing to imply that anyone else, including Hugo Grant was alone with her around that time. It has been suggested that Harry Badger's motives were less than altruistic, to which I can add some supplementary evidence in a moment.'

She sees that DS Leyton is scrutinising the list of those who attended the gathering. Indeed he has an observation.

'Those geezers you named were all in the same year at school as Daisy Mills.'

'That's right. Along with Dr Charles Rice and Rik Hannay. That cohort is still the backbone of the group today.'

'She was popular, right?'

DS Jones is momentarily perplexed.

'How do you mean?'

'No girls from her year. Just the boys.'

DS Jones is caused to ponder for a moment. Meanwhile DS Leyton is prompted to elaborate.

'We had a couple like that – an 'It Girl' they call them, don't they? Not that I was ever –'

His reminiscence tails off rather ruefully.

DS Jones casts a sympathetic glance in his direction before she picks up her narrative.

'Possibly related to the events of the séance is an explicit selfie that was sent anonymously to Daisy Mills after everyone had gone to bed.' She looks a little apprehensively at DS Leyton. 'I can show it to you – but I think all you need to know is that it was sent by someone calling himself Darth Vader.'

DS Leyton puffs out his cheeks, emphasising his ample jowls. He inhales to remark, and then obviously thinks the better of it.

DS Jones shifts her gaze back to Skelgill.

'As I detailed in my report – there are two further aspects that I found on Daisy Mills' mobile.'

Skelgill might now nod, but it is a sufficiently noncommittal movement for him to keep open his options in terms of claiming to have read her report.

'To be honest, Guv – it could take days to go through everything in the memory – she had hundreds of contacts and she used several different apps. So I began by searching the details of the people we know about. Most striking is a text conversation between Daisy Mills and Harry Badger. In fact 'conversation' is probably a misnomer, because it's mainly one-way, from him to her. And it has all taken place since New Year – after the death of Simon Mills. I mention that, because I don't think it's a coincidence. You don't have to read between the lines to see that he's been pestering her, possibly with a view to starting a relationship. He says things like, "Fancy a walk?" and "I'll be passing later, are you in for a coffee?" And there are various toe-curling compliments. There's a message every few days. In most cases she had either not replied, or made an excuse. But there seem to be a few instances where she did agree to see him. But at no time did she invite him to her house. It appears they only met in a public place, such as a café, or with someone else present – for instance there's a reference to joining her and her sister for a walk.'

She looks pointedly at Skelgill.

'On reflection I certainly think he was economical with what he told us, Guv. I suggest that we see him after we've visited the Mills' house. We know where to find him and since he's not in employment we ought to be able to catch him at home.'

Skelgill nods meditatively. It seems to be an indication of his agreement. But DS Jones has more to reveal.

'The second item is a little controversial – on my part, that is.' She waits as though for an objection, but when none is forthcoming she continues, speaking evenly. 'I think there's a possibility that Daisy Mills was having a clandestine affair.'

This generates a raised eyebrow from Skelgill. DS Leyton squints at his list as if trying to discern which is the most likely candidate. DS Jones continues.

'There is a number in her contacts which, instead of the person's name, she has called "Do Not Ring". The number doesn't match anyone's in the party. I tried it last night. It was switched off and the voicemail is deactivated. Then I called it from Daisy Mills' phone – and her number is blocked.'

DS Leyton looks up, perplexed.

'If you don't mind me saying, Emma, how do you get from there to her having an affair?'

Curiously, Skelgill is nodding, as if her speculation achieves congruence with some sentiment of his.

DS Jones explains.

'Say there's someone who couldn't risk any trace of Daisy Mills appearing on his phone – I assume *his*. That the arrangement was that he called her. That they didn't exchange texts, because that would leave evidence that someone else might find. After he called her, they would each delete the call records. I'll keep trying the number – if it's continuously switched off, we might conclude it's someone's second phone.'

DS Leyton is not yet convinced.

'But, what's to say it ain't just someone in the past? Take 'John' – I've got half a dozen I don't even recognise – and they've probably changed their mobiles long since.'

But DS Jones has a ready answer.

'Look – I know it's largely supposition – but her phone is set to store the last hundred calls. I found one call received from that number, made last week, on Friday afternoon. She answered and the call lasted for forty-three seconds. It potentially links the mystery phone to one of them who was arriving on Saturday.'

Skelgill is now frowning again.

'What about other calls?'

'Mostly from named friends and local services. Some are just plain numbers that we can get checked out. But as for Mr Do Not Ring – that could be difficult to trace if it's a burner phone. They can be bought for cash and come pre-loaded with credit.'

Skelgill makes a noise that might be a sigh.

'Okay.'

It is "move on" okay.

And now DS Leyton requests a reprise.

'Let me see if I'm getting this right. I'll go by what they taught me at detective school. The central strand – the facts we know. There's an anonymous claim that Simon Mills was murdered and within a short time Daisy Mills dies. Therefore, she moved the Ouija board – showed her hand – and the killer silenced her before she could blow the gaff?'

DS Jones lets go of her tablet and holds up her hands. It is an involuntary reaction – but probably is somewhat to Skelgill's relief. Solving the conundrum before breakfast seems to be acting with uncivilised haste. DS Jones now qualifies her own impressions.

'It's a Catch 22. There's no actual evidence that either of them was murdered. We're tempted to think Simon Mills was murdered because Daisy Mills died immediately after it was suggested that he was. And therefore perhaps so was she. It's a circular argument without a proper starting point. It's like a merry-go-round – and, worse, the more we discover the more it seems to gain momentum.'

They listen to the rumble of the tyres over the tarmac and the headwind across the screen. They are motoring due south, and the rising sun to their left troubles them all as Skelgill brings the car up out of the sheltered Lune Valley and over the rugged sheep-flecked shoulder of Lambrigg.

DS Leyton is first to break the silence.

'I mean – call me – what is it you call me, Guv? A doughnut – that's it.'

'A *donnat*, Leyton! Not doughnut. It means good-for-nowt. Donnat!'

DS Leyton grins amiably, as though he has received some minor promotion.

'Whatever, Guv – but, what I'm saying is – call me stupid, then – but if they were both murdered – taking out a husband and wife, a few months apart – assuming it's the same person. Who gains – ain't that the question? Your Dalbrae geezer was on the scene – and we know the stats about that – but he doesn't gain, from what you've told me about him.'

Skelgill and DS Jones exchange brief glances. This was a subject they inconclusively considered after leaving Rydal Grange. But it was also a key aspect in determining their direction of travel today.

DS Jones answers.

'Simon Mills had no living relatives. We're assuming Daisy Mills inherited his estate. In her case there are just an elderly father in a care home, Rex Lux – and her sister, Poppy Lux. As far as wills are concerned – it's one of the things we're hoping to find out today.'

'Where there's a will, there's a way, Emma.'

DS Jones smiles appreciatively.

'So, purely in terms of money, Poppy Lux is a possibility. The other potential financial beneficiary is Karl Eastwood, Simon Mills' business partner. Additionally, it may be that Daisy Mills inherited some share or control in the firm that was problematic to him.'

Despite the sunlight slanting into the car, DS Leyton's eyes appear to widen.

'In which case it could be just as simple as Daisy Mills being onto the Eastwood geezer's shenanigans – and making the mistaking of hinting at it.'

He slumps back into his seat and turns his head to stare at the flickering blur of the passing central reservation. Is the car moving or is the earth moving? He runs the fingers of one hand through his thick dark hair.

'Cor blimey – ain't this a rum do? Guvnor – it's a right old kiss and cuddle.'

His words reflect Skelgill's own inner discord. Take a dozen people with varying degrees of connections between them, and begin to scratch beneath the surface of their lives, you will find irregularities, ranging from the innocent to the sinister. It is the risk that comes with the 'follow the evidence' method of policing. Throw in your own prejudice and you can contrive exactly the outcome you're looking for, and miss the real story altogether.

The analogy that has taken shape in his mind's eye is Wainwright's advice about being lost in low cloud upon the summit of Haystacks, where every direction looks the same. *("Kneel down and pray for safe deliverance.")* He is only glad that he has DS Jones, in particular, whose capacity to organise and communicate the facts and assumptions does not seem to faze her, leaving him in his own good time to float above the fog and see the dawning.

And now further relief arrives in the form of a blue motorway sign. Killington Lake Services. He senses a hint of resigned deflation in the demeanour of his colleagues, but does not let it deter him from taking the slip road.

*

'They were decent bacon sarnies, Guv. Very generous on the rasher count.'

'Aye, well – it helps to have local contacts.'

Skelgill just about manages not to gloat in being vindicated; breakfast went down unanimously well. Instead he refers to the phenomenon that sees distant cousins seemingly planted for his convenience in eateries across the county.

DS Jones, meanwhile, is interrogating the maps app on her mobile phone.

'We're still looking good for a ten o'clock ETA.'

Skelgill makes a confident clicking noise with his tongue.

'If it's saying ten we'll hammer that. Those timings are set up for Sunday drivers.'

DS Jones does not argue; they are set up for drivers who obey the speed limit; that is for sure. And Skelgill has a further timesaving tactic.

'Happen we'll run into the tail end of the Birmingham rush hour. I reckon if we take the M6 toll it brings us out just above our junction.'

But he puts his foot down just in case.

DS Jones makes a sound of satisfaction – but she is now checking her messages. She turns to address DS Leyton.

'That's confirmation of your schedule. It's a DC Garth – who oversaw the poisoning inquiry – that will meet you at ten with a pool car at the Middlemarch junction café to run through the files and take you to see the off licence. Then you're to drop off the constable and continue on to the distillery. They're estimating you'll be in Rutland by one p.m. at the latest – so you could be back with us comfortably for six.'

'Or not, if you start sampling the gin, Leyton.'

'No danger there, Guv – evil stuff – tastes like perfume.' He waves a hand. 'I mean – not that I've drunk it – but you know when you get a splash of aftershave in the old north and south?'

DS Jones is smiling.

'There are so many unusually flavoured gins now – there are probably some that would pass as fragrances. I saw orange blossom and jasmine the other day.'

'Did you try it? You're partial to the occasional G&T, ain't you, Emma?'

DS Jones glances briefly at Skelgill.

'I prefer the traditional taste – of juniper. Although I suppose sloe gin is a traditional recipe?'

Her intonation invites a response. Skelgill, whose attitude is that anyone who doesn't want to drink real ale must have something wrong with them seems momentarily distracted – but he does have an angle now.

'Have you ever tasted sloes?'

DS Jones shakes her head.

'Aren't they wild damsons?'

'Until you bite into one. Wersh isn't the word. It's like your mouth's collapsed in on itself.'

Now DS Leyton chuckles.

'I'll remember that if they offer me one. It was sloe gin that was poisoned, right?'

DS Jones takes the opportunity to move the conversation back to the subject of DS Leyton's mission. She swipes at her electronic tablet.

'I was only able to access the digest last night. No doubt they'll give you more details when you arrive. But the top line thinking is that berries of deadly nightshade that were mistaken for sloes contaminated a batch of commercially produced sloe gin. The poisonous component is normally bitter but the manufacturing process disguised the taste – just as it must for the sloes – so nobody who drank it was any the wiser. One of the effects of the toxin can be to depress the heart rate and Simon Mills was vulnerable. The vast majority of those affected in the outbreak were young people with no underlying health conditions – perhaps a small mercy that it's a fashionable drink – and it being Christmas there were sizeable gatherings, so the bottles were consumed by a large number of individuals who each drank a relatively small amount. Five separate households in the Middlemarch area were affected – and they'd all purchased the sloe gin from the same retailer.'

DS Leyton is listening with interest. But gradually his features become perplexed. He ruffles his hair, which is normally a reliable sign of consternation.

'I don't want to be a party pooper – but ain't it a bit of a leap to get to Simon Mills being murdered out of this?'

Skelgill is quick to interject.

'Leyton – we're not trying to get him murdered out of it. If anything we're trying to get him *not* murdered. Our lives start to get complicated if he were.'

DS Leyton takes a moment to absorb his superior's inelegant prognostication.

'Mind you, Guv – what if, say, he fell ill – and then someone took advantage of that?'

'Like what?'

'Well – maybe interfered so he didn't get treated when he should have.'

'That comes back to them knowing about the poison.'

'Not necessarily, Guv. Not if someone recognised the symptoms of a heart attack and played them down as indigestion. Pack 'em off to bed with a couple of Rennies and glass of Alka-Seltzer. It's been done before. Someone biding their time.'

DS Jones is staring with considerable interest at her colleague. While Skelgill seems unmoved by this new bout of guesswork, she decides to test it out.

'That would surely require someone who was close to him. As I understand it, he was generally believed to be in good health. It would really bring us back to Daisy Mills.'

DS Leyton is happy to surmise.

'There you go, then. If she were responsible and then realised someone knew – maybe she did commit suicide – rather than face the music.'

'Nay.' Skelgill's intervention is abrupt and decisive. 'Forget suicide. Leave that for them to think it's what we think.'

While it is not unusual for Skelgill to kybosh speculation that he feels is gaining a life of its own, it is rare that he would denounce as completely off-limits an apparent blind alley, for he is not averse to poking into them himself. Perhaps it is more the intent – blind alleys are fine if one doesn't try too hard to draw conclusions from them. Feelings are fine but don't try to weave them into some pattern before they are even spun as tangible threads. Less fine – from the unenviable perspective of his colleagues – is that such subconscious analysis (moreover, an oxymoron) cannot be communicated. Skelgill does not remember much from school, but he does recall an English teacher who seemed to understand something of his nature. *"We must keep the germinating grain away from the light, eh, Skelgill?"*

A silence ensues. DS Jones meanwhile gathers her thoughts. She has plenty to cover and is undaunted by Skelgill's predictable retreat into his shell. To deal in facts is usually the best way to draw him back out into the conversation.

'I was thinking, Guv – reflecting on the interviews yesterday. While the majority of the group kept to themselves, those that didn't were most of the males in the same school year as Daisy Mills.'

Skelgill glances at her in a way that she takes as permission to elaborate.

'Kenneth Dalbrae – he could have made the anonymous distress call and returned to the scene, in which case he certainly put himself in our path. When we visited Rydal Grange for the first time Rik Hannay interrupted – and was eager to speak with us. The second time, Harry Badger intercepted us in the garden. Shortly afterwards, Hugo Grant came out, also unprompted. The only one of the five who didn't immediately present himself – when he finally returned – was Dr Charles Rice.'

Skelgill does not appear particularly moved by this assessment. This is not to say that each of the men she has named left no impression upon him, or that in their behaviour he sensed no underlying motive. Hugo Grant, for instance – not only was there the willing interview that DS Jones has highlighted, but there was also the solo visit to Buckstones Jump. Surely his was a reaction that went somewhat beyond the fraternal compassion that might reasonably be expected by members of Daisy Mills' old school circle. As Harry Badger had let slip, there was once a relationship there, albeit forty-plus years ago. But perhaps more salient in Skelgill's mind is the reaction of Dr Charles Rice, who seemed outwardly no more concerned than if he had pranged his car. Indeed, perhaps less so – and

Skelgill is reminded of the image of the pristine, identical sets of clothing on the rail in his wardrobe.

DS Leyton, perhaps becoming impatient with Skelgill's apparent lack of engagement, offers a word of encouragement.

'So what's your theory, Emma? About these geezers? Are you saying they were working a relay – trying to pump you for what you knew?'

DS Jones glances rather apprehensively at Skelgill. She opts to stick to the impartial line that she has begun to develop.

'It's more just an observation at this stage. There are certain parameters that might help us frame the investigation. For instance, it's worth reminding ourselves that it was the same group of people who were present at both events – the Mills' Christmas party and this gathering at Rydal Grange. Then there's the issue of who moved the pointer on the Ouija board – surely a significant event, if anything is. It could only have been one of the eight people at the table – four of whom were males in this 'Class of '79' – that's Kenneth Dalbrae, Dr Charles Rice, Harry Badger and Hugo Grant. The other participants were Karl Eastwood, Gail Melia and Poppy Lux. Plus, obviously, Daisy Mills.

'There's also the question of who was awake and up at the time of her death the next morning. That's more difficult to ascertain – it not being a communal activity – but as far as we can establish, most of them were in bed with hangovers. Dr Charles Rice says he set off early, probably before Daisy Mills, and in the opposite direction. Kenneth Dalbrae says he woke after she had left, and correctly guessed that she had gone to see the waterfalls. They were the only two who have admitted to being abroad during the interval in which she died. I learned from interviewing Karl Eastwood that he drove to Grasmere to buy a newspaper at around seven-thirty. He was away only ten minutes, and says he saw nobody and went back upstairs to read it with a coffee.'

She grins contritely.

'Sorry – that was a bit of a monologue.'

DS Leyton waves his hands in deference, although his expression is certainly erring towards the bewildered.

'Nah – you're alright, girl – you're doing a cracking job. It's just there's a lot to take in. Not so easy coming to this fresh – especially if you've got a doughnut for a brain.'

Skelgill shakes his head resignedly.

DS Jones seems unsure of whether she should call it a day – but she makes one final entreaty. She turns again to DS Leyton.

'I could just run over the top-line details of what the others told me? There's nothing particularly demanding. Then we're done and you can refer back to the report as and when you need – at least if something crops up when you're on your own it might just ring a bell, rather than pass you by.'

'Sold.'

DS Leyton settles back and folds his arms, as if he is readying himself for one last act of concentration.

'Okay. Well, we've covered the 'Class of '79', so to speak. Three years behind at the same school were Daisy Mills' sister Poppy Lux and Dr Charles Rice's sister Sarah Rice. Gail Melia is a relatively recent friend – she's a bit younger still. And the other two males, Ben Lomond and Karl Eastwood are, in a sense, acquaintances – Ben Lomond as Kenneth Dalbrae's partner, Karl Eastwood as Simon Mills' business associate. And finally there's Jane Grant, Hugo Grant's wife. She's probably more of an outsider than any of them, and has had limited contact with the group.

'In the order that I saw them – starting with Ben Lomond. He was – what would you call it – quite charming, but suitably diplomatic given the circumstances. He said he didn't really appreciate anything of what was going on during the séance. He was chatting with Jane Grant in a separate part of the drawing room – there's a kind of terrace room – they'd moved away because the music was quite loud. Then in the morning he said the first thing he knew was Kenneth Dalbrae waking him when I took him back. He says he saw Daisy Mills reasonably often – every couple of months she would stay with them in London or they'd meet in the Cotswolds for lunch – or they'd stay at her house. He said the only people he knew remotely well were Daisy and Simon Mills. He's over ten years younger than most of the others and is originally from Croydon. One thing he did mention was that Simon Mills wasn't keen on Kenneth Dalbrae – when I pressed him, all he would say was "chalk and cheese". I didn't like to offend him.

'Karl Eastwood. I mentioned what he said about going out for a newspaper. He would have passed Church Lane in Rydal – with the phone box – but maybe five minutes or so after the emergency call was made. He said he was unaware of any movement in the house, and he didn't see anyone as he drove round. Again, he's an outsider – he said he'd occasionally met some of the others over the years, at the Mills' place for a meal, or when he was there for a meeting with Simon. But he said none of them are really what he would call his friends. Read into that what you wish.'

DS Jones pauses, as if she expects a response on this point. After a moment, Skelgill obliges.

'What did you make of him?'

'Confident. A smooth-talker. He's an insurance salesman.' She hesitates. 'He seems to have quite a high opinion of himself.'

Skelgill is scowling.

'Makes you wonder why he was there. The first party – with his oppo – I get that. But why the one up in our neck of the woods – if he's not one of their crowd?'

DS Jones is wishing she had probed on this point. She makes a note before she moves on.

'The others were the four females present. I didn't do a further interview with Poppy Lux. I felt she was probably too upset – but I'm planning to call her nearer our time of arrival to meet us and let us into the Mills' house this morning. She is a medical receptionist at a local surgery – I'm assuming for obvious reasons that they will have granted her compassionate leave this week – although we do have the contingency of Daisy Mills' keys.

'Gail Melia – you chatted to her a couple of times, Guv –' She breaks off to see if Skelgill will comment, but he merely makes some kind of indeterminate face. 'She's Dr Charles Rice's partner of the last three years. She is, I think, a lady of leisure, but she has some conservation interests and keeps bees. You probably noticed, they live in a village called Stoke Dry, in Rutland.' This is presumably aimed at DS Leyton – Skelgill previously having raised it – but she does not look up from her electronic pad, and no remark is forthcoming from the back seat. She continues. 'I would say she has become quite a close friend of Daisy Mills – I think they both had plenty of spare time on their hands. I asked her if Daisy Mills had confided anything in her that could be considered significant – I kind of felt she was being a little tight-lipped – but the answer was no. What she did tell me is that Dr Charles Rice has been diagnosed on the autism spectrum, mild Asperger's. She said don't be surprised if he seems rude.'

She sees that is Skelgill frowning. She waits and in time he responds.

'I thought he was alright. A bit anoraky about his birds. But there's nowt wrong with having an interest.' However he glances sternly at her, before returning his glare to the cluster of slow traffic that presently impedes their progress. 'That said, the distance he reckons he covered – you could do it in less than half the time.'

DS Jones looks a little alarmed, as though this is an observation he ought to have shared with her earlier. But when Skelgill says no more, doubling down on his concentration upon the road ahead, she returns to her account.

'Sarah Rice, as I said, was in the same cohort as Poppy Lux. She lives at Cowes on the Isle of Wight and works for a yacht-hire business. She said she's been a regular friend of Daisy Mills, and that they would often meet up in London with Kenneth Dalbrae and stay at his flat. But she said she's seen less of her in the last few years – apparently Daisy Mills developed an interest in birdwatching and started to spend more time visiting Sarah Rice's brother and Gail Melia at their house in Rutland.

'And finally there's Jane Grant. She's a lecturer in Physics at the University of Glasgow. They live in a suburb called Milngavie – if I'm pronouncing it correctly.'

She has said something that sounds more like "Mill-guy" – which neither Skelgill nor DS Leyton shows any inclination to gainsay. It seems they are suffering the post-fried-food slump. Head bowed, she soldiers on.

'Jane Grant said she only met Daisy Mills on two occasions, as it happens the Christmas party and this weekend past. She said she didn't know any of the people well – just through references her husband has made over the years. She said that Rik Hannay and Harry Badger have stayed with them in Glasgow – just for a night when they've been passing through – but that Hugo Grant took them out for beer and curry, and that she was away to work early in the mornings. Both visits she thinks were over ten years ago. She made one interesting observation about the séance. She said she had declined to play, but she noticed that Daisy Mills was keen and literally dragged Hugo Grant to join in. So she was surprised when the histrionics took place and said it seemed rather like attention-seeking behaviour. She's quite a serious sort, and I think she considered Daisy Mills as childlike.'

Again there is no reaction from her colleagues. DS Jones looks round. DS Leyton has nodded off. She gives a small involuntary gasp. Skelgill cranes into his rear view mirror.

'He was probably changing nappies at three in the morning. Leave him be, he's got a long day. We'll wake him when we stop for a mash. I reckon it's just above an hour to Knutsford. They do cracking Eccles cakes.'

11. SHENTON MAGNA

Monday, 9.30 a.m. – 'Mills' Manor'

'It's some size of place, Guv.'

Squinting, Skelgill holds the car on the clutch for a moment before decisively aiming the vehicle between imposing gate pillars.

A broad gravel driveway curves between manicured lawns, on one side a mature cedar sprawls its shadow while across on the other is a small birch copse where the blur of bluebells catches Skelgill's eye. They pass a stone-built barbecue area beneath a vine-covered wooden pergola. Then the manor house comes into full view. It is clearly of considerable antiquity, a framework of warped black timbers with whitewashed stucco between, two storeys, triple gable-fronted, the porch recessed in the centre one, and a steeply pitched rust-red tiled roof with matching brick chimney stacks at either end where there protrude smaller hip-on gables. It is majestic, fantastical, and yet the dominant feature is not the house itself but a blooming wisteria that has been trained across much of the frontage, a cascade of flowers, pendulous violet racemes, as if the bluebells have been piped by circuitous trickery to pour like a waterfall from the cast-iron gutters.

'They obviously weren't short of a bob or two.'

Skelgill's tone is objective, free of envy – perhaps he is calculating the upkeep, and is reminded of the silver lining of a frugal existence.

DS Jones checks the time on Skelgill's console clock.

'It looks like she's not here yet. I could have said a bit earlier.'

'I told you that app's for Sunday drivers.' Skelgill grins triumphantly. 'But she might be parked round the back.'

The driveway continues around the left-hand side of the house and Skelgill keeps going into a paved yard where stables have been converted into garages and stores. But there is no other vehicle. He draws to a halt and they get out and stretch.

'It's a lovely day. Should we sit in the garden? We'll see her coming.'

Skelgill is flexing his spine and at the same time peering through the window of a garage. A row of small Perspex panels admits some light within.

'There's a car in here covered with a tarp. And another one – looks like one of those daft Fiats.'

He turns to his colleague.

'What's on those keys? Is there a zapper?'

DS Jones regards him with a look of disquiet.

'Shouldn't we wait for Poppy Lux?'

'Why would she worry? We'll save her the trouble if we look now. It's hardly breaking and entering. You press a button – a door goes up. You close it afterwards.'

DS Jones is not sure what 'trouble' he is talking about, but she swings her attaché case round on its shoulder strap and delves into an inner pocket. She produces and examines a bunch of keys on a stitched blue leather heart-shaped fob.

'There is a remote. No car keys on this, though.'

'Aye – she probably left them locked in the house.'

DS Jones is still plainly reticent, but she passes them over.

Skelgill without further ado presses experimentally at the remote and with a clank the whole door of the double garage begins to tilt and slide back inside the ceiling. Automatically a light comes on.

Skelgill ducks beneath the door even before it is fully retracted.

Then he stops abruptly and hands back the keys.

'You better stand there – just in case it decides to close of its own accord. Don't want us both to have to be rescued.'

DS Jones seems content with this arrangement.

Skelgill first approaches the car covered by a red tailored dustsheet. He stoops and lifts it at the front and emits a hiss.

'Look at this.'

He reveals a registration plate with the number M1 LLS and above it a yellow badge with a black prancing horse.

'A Porsche?'

'Close, but no cigar. It's a Ferrari.'

'How much would that cost?'

Skelgill drops the hem of the sheet and straightens with an affected groan.

'Leyton would know. Probably more than most folks' houses. We're in the wrong game, lass.'

DS Jones grins.

'You'd never let yourself be seen in one of those, Guv. Besides, where would you put your fishing rods?'

Skelgill wheels away. There is a small compliment that pleases him and he hides his reaction. He approaches the other car. It is a new-looking Fiat, in classic white, shiny and clean. The registration is D7 1SY. Not quite as literal as her husband's but not difficult to guess the attempt at 'DAISY'. Then Skelgill notices a scrape and dent in the front nearside wing. He drops to one knee to examine the damage.

'I know just the man for the job. Cash in hand, no questions asked.'

He does not elaborate, although DS Jones can guess whom he means.

'Given Simon Mills' occupation she probably had fully comprehensive insurance, Guv.'

But Skelgill does not answer.

He is feeling beneath the wheel arch, as a panel-beater might before getting to work. He has done plenty of rudimentary jobs like this in his time, with equally rudimentary results.

'I could soon knock this out.'

But DS Jones now sees him stiffen. His arm crooked inside the wheel housing, it appears he detects an irregularity. Indeed, with a sudden tug, he pulls something away and springs backwards to his feet.

'What is it, Guv?'

He extends his arm. In the palm of his hand is a small black rectangular object, salt-and-grime-encrusted. He rubs at the gritty patina with his thumb. It reveals the printed legend "GPS Tracker".

'Happen it does what it says on the tin.'

'It's magnetic?'

'Aye.' Now Skelgill uses his thumbnail to prise open a flap at one end. 'Look – there's a SIM card. You activate it by sending it a text. Saves the battery life. Woody's just hidden one on his boat – he showed me the app on his phone when I met him for a pint in The Partridge last week.'

'Who do you think –'

But DS Jones cuts off her question.

Muffled, but distinctive, there comes the crunch of approaching tyres on gravel.

Skelgill pockets the device.

'She'll probably park at the front.'

But they both know what to do – and DS Jones is quick to press buttons on the remote switch.

The descent of the door seems painfully slow.

They hear the vehicle stop just as the rollers hit the end of their tracks to produce a resounding boom from the steel door. They flinch in tandem but continue walking, skirting the main house.

But the surprise now befalls others.

Standing beside a large black-metallic BMW that is instantly recognisable to Skelgill are its owner Karl Eastwood and Poppy Lux. They are clearly not expecting the police to be here, still twenty minutes ahead of their agreed time of rendezvous. They noticeably step apart – and indeed Karl Eastwood, wearing a smart business suit, climbs into the open driver's door, which he pulls shut and simultaneously lowers the powered window.

'I'll leave you to it – the in-tray beckons.'

He smirks, rather superciliously. The engine is running, and he pulls away, leaving a clearly flustered Poppy Lux to face the detectives. She looks at them apprehensively.

'My car's off the road. Karl only lives in Nuneaton. And he drove us to the Lake District.'

She has provided an explanation when really they have neither entitlement to, nor expectation of one.

DS Jones picks up the thread, however. They know that Poppy Lux lives in the next village.

'How were you planning to get home?'

'Well – I could walk. It's not much more than a mile if you use the footpath.' She is fumbling in her handbag. Then it seems she comes clean, albeit she is self-conscious. 'I thought I might be able to use Daisy's car.'

She is edging towards the house. Skelgill inquires casually.

'What kind is it?'

Poppy Lux glances up sharply, but Skelgill's expression is merely one of interest.

'Oh – I expect you've heard about Simon's Ferrari? Daisy's is just a small Fiat. She's not – she wasn't – ostentatious about cars.'

The present-to-past-tense correction reminds them of the sombre circumstances and they follow Poppy Lux in silence but for the crunch of stones beneath their feet. At the front door they notice her hand shakes as she inserts the key – but then she bustles ahead – for there is the warning tone of a burglar alarm. The detectives exchange knowing looks – it would have embarrassed them had they intruded unaccompanied.

The entrance hall is as impressive as the exterior, with its minstrels' gallery and grand staircase; Skelgill considers it a much superior house to Rydal Hall, albeit in its pastoral Midlands setting it lacks the star quality of Rydal Water.

Now he takes the initiative.

'Madam – first things first. Like you say, you've recently done the journey down from Cumbria – it's a decent trek and I'm fair clemmed, as we say. I wonder if you'd do the honours of a cuppa? And – er – perhaps I could use the bathroom while you're at it?'

He glances up to the gallery. It is an action that causes Poppy Lux to follow his gaze and instinctively she raises a hand –

Skelgill can see the upper of part of a series of doors and one is adorned with a Romanesque plaque that might be a female nude in a bathtub. Then Poppy Lux changes the direction of her indication.

'There's a loo on this level – through the kitchen, in the extension.'

But Skelgill is already accelerating towards the foot of the staircase.

'Needs must.'

He grimaces for effect and does not wait to debate the matter further. As he climbs he glances back to catch DS Jones's eye – she is already chaperoning away a slightly bewildered Poppy Lux.

They disappear from his sight, but now his progress is halted. At the head of the stairs is a portrait – and it is his first lifelike encounter with Daisy Mills. The features he recognises – but it is the eyes that captivate him – for these were closed when he saw her in the flesh; now he thinks the artist must surely have embellished the iridescent blue-violet irises.

But time is short and he proceeds to the bathroom where he opens and then loudly closes the door without entering. Instead he stalks around the landing and intuitively locates the master bedroom. It is heavily beamed, with a dark oak four-poster bed – just as would be expected in a property like this. The wallpaper is white with a delicate blue motif in different shades – he realises it is a subtly repeating bluebell pattern.

Along one wall there are recessed wardrobes with curtains instead of doors. He sweeps them aside in a couple of places. He sees no men's clothing, just rails of dresses and blouses, the blue floral theme dominant here, too – although beneath are racks of shoes, long and slender, and some with the red soles that he has noticed DS Jones admire wistfully on occasion.

He opens the drawer of a nightstand on the side of the bed nearest to the latticed window. Among the objects there is a packet of tablets with a prescription sticker affixed. He reads off the address of the medical centre and scowls at the brand name, pausing for a moment before returning the box to the drawer.

The bedroom has one door that reveals an ensuite bathroom and another a kind of study with a view over the grounds from a desk set beneath the gable. Skelgill can see immediately that this was Simon Mills' den. The walls are carefully ornamented with various framed pieces: certificates, awards, and mainly enlarged photographs – what Skelgill would call 'macho' shots, showing off, Simon Mills (presumably) undertaking various exploits, such as canoeing, water skiing, one astride a Harley-Davidson. The man is balding, sturdy, pugnacious. In other photographs he is with Daisy Mills – at formal dinners and less formal parties, by the look of it, though they are extravagantly dressed. Skelgill stares pensively, and two things strike him. The first is that Daisy Mills looks like an accessory to her less attractive husband; there is a sense that he displays her like an expensive wristwatch. The second is that the portraitist did not after all exaggerate the radiant ultraviolet lustre of her eyes.

But once more Skelgill does not dwell. He approaches the desk. It is clear but for a pile of unopened mail. On one side there are drawers that contain stationery and files. There is no sign of a laptop or a mobile phone, although Skelgill notes there is a bank of plugs to one side and a printer cable and a charger among those attached.

He flicks through the mail. It comprises mostly trade magazines and circulars for Simon Mills. But there is one item – recently postmarked, addressed to Daisy Mills – a distinctive long narrow manila envelope. A legal envelope. Skelgill turns it over, and now for the second time he commits to memory a name and location.

He retraces his route with careful steps; there are creaks beneath his soles but none he thinks that would penetrate to the floor below. When he enters the kitchen he is shaking his hands as if to dispel the last vestiges of water.

'Sorry about that, ladies.'

He offers no elaboration – which the ladies might think is just as well. He joins them at an island breakfast bar, where in front of one of six oak stools there is a mug from which rises a wisp of steam. The kitchen is sumptuously equipped, like that from a television cookery show.

DS Jones interrogates him with a subtle glance; he manages to communicate that she should continue.

'Miss Lux was just telling me she has been in touch with a local funeral director. I've got their details and can notify them when Mrs Mills' body can be released. I've explained about the process for obtaining a death certificate – and that under the present circumstances we're still waiting for the Coroner; that it might be a few days.'

Skelgill, his nose already in his mug, contrives to nod.

It would seem a morbid conversation for a Monday morning tea break; but for the police it is not an entirely rare event; and now Poppy Lux appears considerably more composed, albeit she looks drawn, and her manner is reserved.

DS Jones continues.

'Miss Lux, have you informed your father?'

The woman frowns.

'I don't think I'll tell him.'

'Oh.'

'You see – he doesn't know who we are any more.' She allows a considerable pause. 'I don't even think he knows who he is.'

After a few moments she looks at the detectives expectantly. From their perspective, they are acutely aware of an elephant in the room. She must be wondering why have these police officers travelled half the length of England to see her – or, at least, to see Daisy Mills' house? And this talk of the Coroner; it surely cannot be that all is well.

Also familiar for them is the eternal conundrum. When there is only a *potential* crime, concomitant is the challenge of discriminating between suspects and witnesses. How to avoid alerting the one while at the same time gaining essential information from the other – tricky when it is the same person in the spotlight.

Poppy Lux has not helped her perceived status on this spectrum, thanks to her somewhat inexplicable and certainly uncomfortable arrival with Karl Eastwood. Now it seems to Skelgill there are things she would like to say – or know – but she senses that to speak would not be in her best interest. He regards her critically –,but the notion that grabs him is peculiar – with her dull brown eyes and not-quite-symmetrical features she is like an early, failed, discarded attempt at the Mona Lisa – the final masterpiece hangs out in the hall, at the head of the stairs.

DS Jones detects that some catalyst is needed. They have agreed that suicide – much as it is anathema to Skelgill – is the line that they will openly pursue when the requirement arises. It enables them to ask questions about Daisy Mills and, indirectly, those in her close circle.

'Miss Lux, is it possible that your sister was involved in a new relationship? And this was the thing that drastically upset her?'

Poppy Lux shoots a wary glance at DS Jones, who presses on unperturbed.

'Among the men in your friendship group – the one who lives locally is Harry Badger – we understand that Daisy met him from time to time, and quite recently.'

Again there comes the frown; it is a rather childlike expression of denial.

'Daisy would never have got involved with Harry.'

DS Jones waits but Poppy Lux does not freely particularise.

'What makes you so sure?'

'There are just some men you wouldn't go out with.'

'Do you mean – in a sinister way?'

'No.' She inhales, but it is a moment before she elaborates. 'Well – I don't like to use a bad word – but if you insist – round here they would call Harry a –'

At this Skelgill shrugs and shifts in his seat. He has been called it often enough by his pals in the pub. But language is fickle. A word that can end a lifelong relationship in the USA is bandied around in England meaning little more than that the subject is a congenital twit. But he gets the gist – banter among mates is one thing, but for a woman to use of it a man is a fairly categorical denunciation; D-minus as far as suitability for company goes.

Now Skelgill interjects.

'So, you're saying she wouldn't have lost any sleep over him.'

Whether she thinks he is speaking euphemistically, or simply metaphorically, she mirrors Skelgill's shrug of a moment earlier.

'No.'

Skelgill continues, as self-deprecatingly as his limited proficiency permits.

'It's easy for a bloke to get the wrong end of the stick. Could he have imagined she'd encouraged him?'

Poppy Lux is beginning to look positively alarmed. Not unreasonably, she might deduce from the detectives' casual persistence that they have some evidence to support this line of inquiry. She appears to give a slight shake of her long dark hair, but does not answer.

Skelgill does not press his point; DS Jones picks up the baton and proceeds patiently.

'Miss Lux, surely she would have confided in you if there were another person? Or, even, you would have known or suspected – since presumably you saw each other most often?'

'I didn't – I don't. I –'

She stumbles – but clearly a thought has come to her.

'I suppose – when Daisy and Simon were getting together. Both were still married. Daisy was in middle of a divorce but she still lived with her ex. Simon had separated but wasn't divorced. So they didn't tell anyone they were an item – until after the divorces.'

The detectives' eyes meet briefly – they can read between the lines. Daisy Mills could keep a secret.

DS Jones decides to move briskly on.

'Miss Lux, could I just ask you about Simon Mills.' Her inflexion does not allow for a question mark and she continues without waiting for a sign of assent. 'How would you describe his attitude towards your sister?'

Her use of words – attitude, towards – makes this unashamedly a leading question, although Poppy Lux surely cannot know about the tracking device they have just found; indeed she seems to read the inquiry in a positive light.

'He worshipped the ground she stood on.'

DS Jones waits in silence. Poppy Lux – as if this extravagant response has not been enough – indicates to their surroundings.

'He gave her everything she wanted.'

DS Jones makes a one-handed gesture of acquiescence.

'Did they usually do things together?'

'He was – inseparable.' Poppy Lux seems to realise she has spoken ungrammatically – but she continues after a moment's hesitation. 'He would always have his arm round her at parties. Simon's job was very time-consuming. He had to travel away a lot. And Daisy – remember, they only got together in their forties – most of Daisy's friends are from before that.'

The answer is somewhat disjointed, as if she has been assailed by a flurry of contentions and has made an untidy job of plucking them down.

DS Jones picks up on the latter point.

'She spent a lot of time with former schoolmates.'

But Poppy Lux appears to disagree.

'Well – maybe Kenneth and Sarah, with Daisy – they were like a little clique at school – and they've always met up – in London mostly. It was halfway for Sarah and Daisy, and I suppose good fun to stay at Kenneth's flat in the West End. But not so much in the last few years. And never really the rest of them. Everyone's getting a bit too old to go gallivanting around the country. These long journeys are tiring – what with the traffic and roadworks everywhere.'

'And your sister – how had she coped with the loss of her husband in that regard?'

'What I said about Simon – he was protective – he would drive if they went somewhere. But like I say – she wasn't dependent on him for what to do – she had plenty to fill her time – afterwards.'

'Do you mean she perhaps kept herself busy to avoid thinking about it, processing it – that Simon had died?'

'Could be.'

DS Jones probes gently.

'Might the Rydal Grange house party have had the opposite effect? That it brought to the surface feelings your sister had suppressed?'

Poppy Lux appears to be moved by this line of argument.

'Well – there was the séance – I mentioned that, didn't I?'

DS Jones nods encouragingly. But then Poppy Lux frowns, more deeply than hitherto. 'But she seemed alright a little while afterwards. She knew it was just a game – that someone messed about.'

They wait, but she has no more to say.

Skelgill clears his throat.

'What will you do now?'

The question is something of a blindsider – a sudden leap from the specific to the general, from her sister to herself. She blinks vacantly, like someone who has awoken to find herself marooned at a crossroads on vast open plain, where the surroundings appear no different in any direction.

It seems she is genuinely unable to answer.

But the rattle of a key in the front door reaches their ears.

And now she puts a hand to her mouth.

'*Magda.*'

'I'm sorry, madam?'

'It's Magda – Daisy's cleaner. She doesn't know. She's been coming for years.'

She begins to rise and then seems to wonder if she has permission. From the hallway come sounds of the front door opening and closing, and shoes being kicked off, and a cupboard opened. Then there is a silence. Perhaps the cleaning lady has realised the alarm should have been activated.

Skelgill catches DS Jones's eye and gives a little sideways jerk of the head.

'Miss Lux, our car's at the back. We'll nip out there and leave you to it. DS Jones will be in touch about the death certificate.'

Poppy Lux remains torn between the demands upon her to make a decision – in the event she simply watches in silence as the detectives depart. But, the moment the back door clicks shut, she reaches for her mobile phone that lies on the island counter.

12. SOUTH MERCIA POLICE

Monday, 10 a.m. – off-motorway café

'Alright, me duck?'

DS Leyton glances up from his newspaper and quickly closes the page, for it showcases not the best of the British tabloid press's output.

'DC Garth?'

'Call me Mary – and don't sound so surprised.' Her tone is jovial; she has a strong local accent.

'Sorry – I was – distracted.'

He utters a nervous laugh and struggles to his feet, making a loud scraping with his chair that attracts glances from around the cafeteria. He offers a hand, which the woman accepts and shakes firmly. She is in her mid forties, short and stout, clad in a slightly loose-fitting navy business suit; she has shoulder-length curly brown ringlets that frame a round friendly face, rosy-cheeked, button-nosed and bright-eyed.

DS Leyton moves gallantly to pull out a chair.

'There you go then, Mary – I'll fetch you a coffee – or would you prefer a nice cup o' Rosie?'

He is getting back into his stride.

She removes from under one arm a red plastic wallet file and slides it onto the table, and takes the offered chair.

'I'm alright – thanks all the same – I had a brew before I left the station.'

DS Leyton resumes his seat. He casts a hand about the busy eatery.

'How did you know it was me?'

'I looked up your profile –'

Now she hesitates, but plies him with a look of intrigue. DS Leyton begins to colour – he knows what might follow and it is always a source of embarrassment. Skelgill would revel in such moments. But she detects his discomfort.

'You're a Cockney – I was expecting an Ecky Thump type – you coming from Up North.'

DS Leyton grins, clearly relieved. And he wonders with some amusement how Skelgill might react, being so described. He expands upon his own provenance.

'I served my time in the Met – they gave me parole.'

She smiles at his joke, that he has made his career sound like one long jail sentence.

'What made you go to Cumbria? That's nigh on Scotland.'

DC Mary Garth is candid and apparently unfazed that he ranks above her; but the no-airs-and-graces Midlands informality is refreshing to him.

'Me and the missus – went to Windermere for our honeymoon. We thought the Lakes would be a better place to bring up kids. Never looked back, once we bought an umbrella.'

She laughs.

'Good on you.'

DS Leyton sees that she wears a wedding ring, and feels that he ought to return the bonhomie and inquire after her circumstances and family – but again she is on the ball and pre-empts the need. She taps the wallet file in a businesslike manner.

'I've read your colleague's report – DS Jones?' (DS Leyton nods in confirmation.) 'It's a bit of a thorny one for you. I hope you find something at our end – but I'm not optimistic, I'm afraid.' She regards him with an expression of wistful frustration – perhaps as if she is debating whether to say something – and then she does. 'I looked for foul play – but the powers that be knocked it on the head. I reckon that shopkeeper's in the same lodge as our Chief.'

She grins, because she renders DS Leyton a little open mouthed.

He strives to make a suitably neutral exclamation of interest.

She leans forward conspiratorially.

'I read a lot of crime – I mean, not fiction, obviously – *hah*. True crime. Have you heard of the Agutter case?'

DS Leyton shakes his head but indicates that he is all ears.

'Edinburgh it were. 1995 the trial. You can look it up online. He was a lecturer in biochemistry. He was having an affair. He laced his wife's gin and tonic with atropine and to cover it up he'd contaminated a batch of bottles of tonic and secretly returned all but one of them to their regular supermarket. The concentration in these wasn't fatal – but quite a few local people fell ill. The police thought it was a blackmail plot – but nothing came of that. Although it didn't help in the first place that some attention-seeker made a false confession.'

'What happened to his missus?'

'She was lucky. It's a bit of a long story – but she basically got fortuitous medical attention. Agutter only left a message on the doctor's answering machine at night – that she was a bit poorly. The prosecution claimed his plan was to leave her to die. But there was a duty locum who was keen and was checking the messages out of hours. He sent an ambulance and by good procedure they impounded the drinks. Agutter's idea was that the bottle of tonic would only contain the same weak dose as the other bottles he planted – so it would look like they were accidental victims of the blackmailer, just like all the rest. But the wife's glass had dregs in it and when they analysed it they found it was a potentially fatal concentration.'

'Cor blimey.'

'There's more to it than that. You should read up on it. For instance it turned out that he was recognised tampering with bottles by one of his students who was a part-time shelf-stacker. But when I heard about this case I couldn't believe the similarities – same poison, same thing with a batch of contaminated bottles in a local shop. And only one person dies – well, if you see what I mean?'

DS Leyton nods – although now that it comes round to his investigation, some questions arise in his mind.

'But no toxicologist – no obvious suspect – or obvious victim, really?'

DC Garth is in agreement.

'That's the thing. You can always make up a reason why a person might wish someone dead – if I'd had atropine there's plenty of nights I'd have gladly poisoned my other half!'

DS Leyton looks like he is thinking he might have been similarly reprieved.

DC Garth continues, playing her own devil's advocate.

'And the circumstances were that Simon Mills was serving the drinks – he was hosting the cocktail party.'

Now DS Leyton feels he should offer a counter argument.

'But he was drinking, right?' (She nods.) 'And people are coming up to him all night for refills? Easy enough to slip him a Mickey Finn.'

Again she nods in agreement; but she continues fair-mindedly.

'There was another fly in the ointment there. It's not easy to obtain the poison unless you've got scientific or medical contacts – or the botanical knowledge to find it in the wild. And the berries disappear after October – the party was late December.'

DS Leyton ponders her words – she has certainly been thorough in her thinking – albeit guided by the Edinburgh case history.

'What about the off licence?'

She shrugs a little resignedly.

'You'll see, shortly. But it's an independent shop in the old part of town – it's a maze of high shelves and they've only got basic CCTV at the till. It's grainy footage – you'd struggle to identify someone even if you knew who you were looking for. They don't have EPOS so we couldn't match purchases to credit card numbers.'

DS Leyton regards her pensively. He is wondering if the shop is worth a visit at all.

'Sounds like a good place to pull a stunt like that. The surveillance in supermarkets these days – never mind what you're doing – they even know what you're thinking!'

She seems to share his complaint. But her tone remains a little downbeat.

'Thing is, at the end of the day we couldn't identify any criminal connection – Simon Mills' death can be explained by the amount he'd drunk and his underlying medical condition. Plus there's what you might call a natural explanation for how the poison got into the gin at source – although the distillers are not too chuffed about that.'

DS Leyton frowns.

'What about the bottle at the Mills' place – the concentration of poison, I mean?'

DC Mary Garth nods – she gets his point.

'It'd been chucked out. Remember, they thought he'd had a heart attack due to health reasons – and he was dead before the ambulance even arrived. Although there were other members of the party that were mildly ill, no one else complained of it at the time. They'd drunk a lot and put it down to that and the shock. Everyone went home. His body was taken for tests and his wife stayed at her sister's that night. It had been arranged for the cleaner to come in the next morning – she didn't know anything about what had happened. They don't have a glass waste collection in the village – she took all the empty bottles to a central recycling point. All the used glasses – everything – went in the dishwasher.'

DS Leyton moulds his malleable features into an expression of commiseration.

'So, how about the wider incident – how did that unfold?'

She lays her hands palm up on the table surface.

'Slowly, is the answer – though if you saw the local paper you'd think we'd had another Salisbury on our hands. A few people were admitted to hospital – in dribs and drabs, so it didn't look like a sudden emergency. And most who were poisoned just felt a bit ill. Stomach cramps, headaches, giddiness. Apparently, the body metabolises atropine quite quickly, so it's hard to pick up in blood tests. It was only when Simon Mills died that the compound was identified and a consultant at the hospital put two and two together. They called in the local environmental health officer, and together with Public Health England they traced it back to the batch of Rutland gin.'

DS Leyton is listening intently.

'Can you even be certain that they had the Rutland gin at the Mills party?'

She is nodding vigorously – she acknowledges it is a good question – but also to show she has dealt with it.

'By a process of elimination across the various households they narrowed it down to that make. Then they contacted people who'd been at the Mills' party and some of them could remember the distinctive bottle design – it's like a picture of a gin-trap that's crushing the juice from the berries of the blackthorn.'

'Did they find out who bought the bottle?'

DC Garth shakes her head ruefully.

'The conclusion they came to was that it was Simon Mills. After all, he was the organiser of the drinks – the host of the party. Gin cocktails were his idea.'

DS Leyton purses his lips.

'You'd usually take a bottle as a gift.'

'True. And the theme was advertised. But no one admitted to taking Rutland gin.' She makes a face of reluctant acceptance. 'I don't suppose anyone would – once the word got out. And they had to publicise it straightaway for public safety. As it is, we've only identified five out of six bottles – unless they had two at the Mills' do.'

DS Leyton is thinking of his day ahead.

'Did you investigate the distillery?'

Perhaps a little to his surprise she shakes her head.

'At the time it was treated as a public health matter. They've got more powers than we have – they can close a factory down, for example. We have a weekly liaison committee with the local authority and it came up on that. I only found out about the Edinburgh case a month or so later – I was searching online for information about Deadly Nightshade. By then the incident had been more or less put to bed. Rutland Gin-Trap Gin is just a man-and-wife concern – it's not like it's a big company or some sweatshop with a slew of disgruntled employees. And they have no control of where their product ends up once they've

147

despatched it to the wholesaler. So, like I say, there was no actual indication of a criminal involvement at any stage in the process – until –'

DS Leyton supplies DC Garth with her unspoken line.

'Until we stuck our flippin' great oar in.'

She grins amiably.

'No – you can't help it.'

He notices the vehemence in her tone that causes her accent to become more acute. She says *nar* for no and *kernt* for can't and drops the *h* on help. He might only be ninety miles from his home town of London, but it is a reminder that he is very much in alien territory. She seems to be thinking along similar lines.

'Besides – you've got yourself a nice jaunt down to the Midlands. Have you been to Rutland?'

DS Leyton shakes his head.

'It's like East Leicestershire – rolling countryside, wooded, a lot of water – but you'll be used to that. Mind you – blink and you'll miss it – smallest county in England, so they say.'

'Sounds perfect for my detecting abilities.'

The woman appreciates his self-deprecation and reaches to pat his forearm in a gesture of a friendly reprimand.

'With your record – you're sure to find something we missed. Now you know what you're looking for.'

DS Leyton regards her gratefully but still with some doubt.

'Trouble is, Mary, I'm not sure we do. It may be that Simon Mills was the kind who'd get himself killed over money. But then the missus, too – why would that be?'

She regards him shrewdly.

'Where does the Mills' money end up?'

DS Leyton nods.

'That's exactly what my colleagues are trying to find out. There's a business partner of the husband – a geezer called Eastwood – and a sister of the wife.'

She nods as though she is loosely familiar with the characters involved.

'They could be in it together.'

She says it casually – but DS Leyton glances sharply at her. Of the various theories that could be developed, he is not sure if this was one they considered on their journey. But it has a simple appeal. Moreover, it strikes him that, without Skelgill there to belittle his efforts or shut him down altogether, he is presently free to speculate. He flies an alternative kite.

'There's a suggestion that Daisy Mills was having an affair.' (DC Garth's gaze fixes upon him.) 'Nothing concrete, mind – and it might have been since her husband's death – in which case, maybe it's no big deal. In fact, that's where it don't really pan out. And by all accounts she was popular – the queen bee at the centre of her little swarm. Most of them have been friends since they were at school together.'

The woman ponders for a moment, as though his suggestion has prompted a new way of looking at things.

'It sounds like a spiteful thing to do to her – that business with the Ouija board. Maybe she was too popular?'

'You mean, like someone was jealous of her?'

The woman turns out her lower lip and tilts her head to one side – a gesture of "why not?"

'Some people carry bad thoughts all their lives. What is it my Nanna Garth used to say? *A grudge is a worse enemy than pain.*'

DS Leyton finds himself in accord with Nanna Garth. Though he realises he ought in the absence of Skelgill to find a counterpoint.

'I get all that – and if you take Daisy Mills' death in isolation – if she were murdered, then it does open up a range of motives. But, if it were something against her personally – then how do we match that up with Simon Mills being murdered? It breaks the connection. It's hard to see how someone would hold a grudge against them both.'

The woman folds her arms and glowers, as though this line of conjecture has run up against the buffers and she is irked by the condition. She sighs.

'Well – maybe his death *were* an accident.'

She sounds substantially dissatisfied – despite that the corollary would be that South Mercia Constabulary have reached

149

the correct conclusion. DS Leyton, however, appreciates her candid encouragement. He has not had to tread on the eggshells about which DS Jones had cautioned him. He finishes his tea. DC Garth is watching him. Now she hands over the red file.

'Well, me duck – you'd better get on with finding that out.'

13. HARRY BADGER

Monday, 10.20 a.m. – Jericho Park

'It's a trailer park.'
'Jones – you've been watching too much American TV.'
'Guv – when do I get time to watch TV?'
Skelgill does not answer. He is busy scowling at the entrance sign. Jericho Park, Burton Magna, they had assumed was a street address, but in fact it is the residential site before them. The signboard, beneath the name, offers "Luxury Park Homes For Sale" but the first impression is of poorly repaired tarmac and unkempt verges, and the handful of low-grade properties that are in partial view make an unappealing sight, with budget motor cars squeezed into inadequate plots and no pattern to the arrangement or style of panel fencing and shrubs, which seem to have been entrusted to the questionable whims of each resident.

There is a one-way system and DS Jones is a little surprised that Skelgill now complies with it, for she is sure he will have calculated that, at number 77, Harry Badger's property is likely to be closer to what will become the exit on their way out. It must be a refuse collection day (and the pick-up recently made), for brown wheelie bins have been untidily abandoned at intervals, requiring Skelgill to snake between them; there is no actual pavement, perhaps a space-saving omission to pack in more homes. And it could be the expectation that anyone who lives here will drive; Burton Magna is little more than a hamlet, with few amenities. DS Jones gazes pensively as Skelgill navigates the obstacles. She wonders what is the demographic profile of residents. There is no indication of children – no play area or carelessly discarded cycles or punctured footballs – or even pre-school children playing out, come to that. Is it elderly people who have made a conscious decision to downsize, or those driven by economic hardship? It is an unfamiliar environment. Britain might be a land of holiday homes and static caravans – Cumbria being no exception – but residential parks like this are comparatively few and far between. Despite the bright conditions, and horticultural efforts some have made with their displays of bedding plants, she has a feeling of foreboding – although she is cheered when they pass an extensive gnomery where multi-coloured plastic windmills spin in the breeze.

They make successive left turns around the compressed rectangular track, their progress further slowed by a superfluity of sleeping policemen that Skelgill curses. And they are indeed on the back straight to their point of entry when he pulls up outside number 77, which he identifies by the carelessly daubed white numerals on its wheelie bin. While the properties vary in their size and permanence – some are cabins set on brick-course bases – this is a static caravan on a steel box-section chassis, not particularly new-looking. There is no car in the parking space; only a bicycle – an old-style Claud Butler road racer with drop handlebars and full mudguards – chained to the tow bar alongside a tall red propane cylinder. DS Jones realises that Skelgill is staring vacantly.

'What is it, Guv?'

'Eh?' He seems only half roused from his reverie. 'I'd always fancied living in a caravan.'

'Really?'

DS Jones notes the past tense in his admission. Was there an 'until'?

'Aye – well – a canal boat, actually.' His tone is distinctly wistful. 'At junior school – the teacher used to read us these stories – it were a badger character that lived on a narrowboat – had its own woodstove, oil lamps, cosy at night, self-contained – he could go wherever he wanted – fish whenever he liked.'

He seems to realise he has digressed from their purpose and that his colleague is smiling in the way of: surely he does not seriously expect her to have a conversation about a fishing badger? He emits a contradictory growl of disgust. It must be the 'until'.

'Hired one with some mates one year – it were a nightmare. We kept crashing into bridges – it's like steering a bathtub. Inside you couldn't swing a cat. It rained most of the week – we couldn't get owt dry. None of us fitted in the bunks – and you don't want to know about the chemical toilet.'

Now DS Jones makes a suitable face.

'I think you're probably right there. Should we see if our other badger is home?'

Skelgill utters a strange little laugh – he realises the connection had not struck him.

They climb out, closing the car doors judiciously in what seems to be a required yet unnecessary precaution. The caravan is sited perpendicular to the roadway, and what looks like the main living area protrudes towards them in the shape of the blunt prow of a riverboat, although the curtains are closed. However, they can hear what sounds like a television set, and they exchange brief nods.

The door is on the side with the parking space, set back about six feet from the front. There is a metal step, not deep enough actually to stand upon, but merely for passage when in motion. Skelgill reaches up and knocks on the frosted glass.

There is no response.

Indeed there is no change – the TV continues to blare. The background score seems vaguely familiar, but he is unable to put a name to it. A recording, though – since he has noted that, while satellite dishes and terrestrial aerials abound, this van lacks either form of receiver.

There is a letterbox. He raps at it, and then bends forward and calls through the raised flap.

'Mr Badger? Mr Badger – it's Cumbria CID.'

It takes Skelgill three more attempts before the television is muted.

Then come hollow footfalls – and the click of a cupboard opening and closing and a tap briefly spluttering and the clunk of a metal sink.

Now a figure looms up at the door.

It opens outwards to reveal a dishevelled-looking Harry Badger. His thick black hair is tousled, the whites of his dark eyes are reddened, the flesh around them puffy. Ironically there is something of a badger rudely evicted from his sett by unwelcome terriers.

He wears a grey tracksuit with food stains on the top; Skelgill skips the midriff. But he notices the man is barefooted, and there are unappealing toenails.

'Can we come in, sir – just a quick word? We were in the area – and a couple of points have cropped up that we thought you might be able to help us with.'

'What? Er – yes, er – yes, be my guest, Inspector.'

Despite his words his body language is not so welcoming.

Rather than gracefully usher them in he merely turns away and reaches for a remote control and switches off completely the television. After the bright sunshine the interior seems positively troglodytic – but at least Harry Badger seems to appreciate this and works around the three sides on which there are windows, pulling back the curtains. Skelgill glances at DS Jones to see that she is striving to repress a look of distaste. The unventilated caravan is uncomfortably hot and the air foetid. He notices that she leaves open the door.

From the arrangement of squashed cushions on the settee at one side it is apparent where Harry Badger has been lying, and now he sits back down. The van is quite spacious, maybe eight feet wide, and they settle opposite. Again Skelgill notes that his colleague suffers some discomfort – the interior is not exactly untidy, indeed its contents are sparse, much like a holiday caravan would be found on arrival. But, while not ranking high on Skelgill's radar, even he can see that duster, vacuum and cleaning spray are long overdue some action.

'You're probably wondering, officers, what I'm doing in a place like this.'

It seems Harry Badger feels he should take the initiative – and his rather pompous tone suggests that the circumstances in which they find him are infra dig, and far from the normal state of affairs. But Skelgill is quick with a counterpoint.

'Not at all, sir. I was only saying to my colleague how I've always fancied living in a caravan.'

But Harry Badger looks like he thinks he is being humoured – and, in any event, there is a certain admission in this – it reveals that they have discussed his status. He looks away, knowingly.

He makes no offer of refreshments. But for once Skelgill is not unduly bothered. Perhaps it is the uncleanliness, the stale air that dulls his thirst. Only the occasional waft of scented stocks from a neighbouring plot through the open door provides a respite. He glances at DS Jones. They have agreed, they have little to go on – a modicum of hearsay and the mobile phone communications. And they do not particularly want to show their hand. But they know it does not take a rocket scientist to deduce they have Daisy Mills' phone – or indeed to form a theory about why they might be here asking questions. DS Jones starts up accordingly.

'Mr Badger, we are trying to build a more complete picture of Mrs Mills' state of mind over the past few weeks. Apart from her sister, you're her closest neighbour – and you mentioned that you have run into her once or twice. Can you remember the last time you saw her – prior to the weekend, at Rydal Grange?'

Harry Badger has watched DS Jones with the same sly sideways look that Skelgill now recalls from their previous conversation beneath the oak trees. He is glad his colleague is not alone – he could have opted to accompany DS Leyton – there was the temptation of a sight of the great Rutland Water, six times the size of Bass Lake, with its legendary leaping trout and swooping ospreys. But in response to DS Jones's question the man shifts a little uneasily in his seat, and his eyes close for a moment; he is slumped as though he could easily fall back to sleep. Skelgill did not approach sufficiently closely to smell his breath – nor did he want to – but he has the distinct impression that the man has been drinking. Was that among the sounds they heard – of a bottle being secreted in a cupboard and a tumbler rinsed and inverted on the drainer (where there stands one now)? And of course he was drinking at Rydal Grange – quite openly there – though he was more alert and seemed to have his wits about him. Slowly, the man returns his gaze to DS Jones.

'I don't remember, actually. When you're unemployed one day merges into the next – groundhog day – *hah!*'

As if he refers to the eponymous movie he waves a hand grudgingly towards the television set, angled on a corner unit at Skelgill's right. Beneath it there is a DVD player and a tightly packed shelf containing a collection of discs; these must be his limited fare in lieu of subscription services and BBC licence. Skelgill looks up to see Harry Badger regarding him furtively.

'I might have cycled past, one day last week – or the week before, maybe.' Again he makes a loose hand gesture, this time towards the back of the caravan, the kitchen-dining area, and beyond two doors – presumably a bedroom and toilet. 'Naturally I have to buy provisions. There's a supermarket at the edge of town. On the bike I can only carry so much – so I need to go most days. It's nice to have fresh bread and fruit and vegetables.'

Skelgill suspects that it is not these items that he needs to buy fresh every day, but a less wholesome form of consumption. But he is not hopeful that DS Jones will extract a useful admission out of the man concerning an encounter with Daisy Mills. Already he has effectively sidestepped the question. And, while they know he had texted her during both of the last two weeks, there were no replies – so any outcome is in his power to render inconclusive. Now that Skelgill has the lie of the land, the juxtaposition of these rural Midland villages, he can see that if Harry Badger – for want of something to do, for want of company, for want of much more, for want of a wealthy woman, even – were in the habit of turning up at the Mills' property, there was probably not a lot Daisy Mills could do about it. But there is not a lot of evidence to prove it.

Moreover, probe as they might, there is one other indisputable fact that points to the futility of questioning Harry Badger on this subject. Until some time between six and seven a.m. on Sunday morning, Daisy Mills was seemingly fine. What went before may have little or no bearing on her condition.

It seems that DS Jones has reached the same conclusion. For now she does not directly challenge him on these points as she might. Instead, she lets him have the one decent shot in their locker.

'Mr Badger, do you know anything about a mobile message – a photograph, in fact – received by Mrs Mills at approximately one a.m. on Sunday morning?'

Sluggish he may be, his senses dulled by post-sleep stupor and quite likely alcohol, Harry Badger cannot fail to detect this entirely blatant switch of subject from Daisy Mills to him.

Skelgill is watching the man's reaction closely. But other than the underlying shiftiness to which they are becoming accustomed, he detects no trace of alarm. Harry Badger holds DS Jones's gaze. His brow slowly furrows and he purses his full lips.

'I've no idea what you are talking about, Sergeant.'

DS Jones nods, and tries to make it appear as though this were just some incidental, of no great importance. But while she is gathering her thoughts, the silence seems to prompt Harry Badger to elaborate.

'I was out like a light the second my head hit the pillow. And, as I explained previously, the first thing I knew was in the morning, when Kenneth came banging on my door at ten.'

DS Jones is quick to catch on. She has witnessed Skelgill often enough – though he seems to be able to brazen out a pregnant pause without the embarrassment most people would naturally feel. She has a notebook, and now she turns over several pages, apparently perusing them. At her side, Skelgill is amused – he knows full well that she has everything she needs to know in her head. He glances amenably at Harry Badger – he is all the more certain he is drunk – but inebriated in the way of one who is used to concealing it. And now the tension succeeds in winkling out an admission.

'Sergeant – you're making me wish I had a cast-iron alibi – like good old Rik – the dirty old man.'

157

Harry Badger laughs – sneers rather – at his own words. DS Jones regards him innocently.

'I'm sorry, sir?'

But he looks at her as though he thinks she is being disingenuous.

'I'm sure you've had it from the others, Sergeant?' But he does not wait for an answer. 'Oh, it's no secret – Rik and Sarah are at it like rabbits every time they meet – t'was ever thus.'

Now he leans towards Skelgill with a locker-room leer. Skelgill offers no response, but Harry Badger is undeterred. He cackles salaciously.

'You'd think we were getting a bit old for that kind of thing.'

He returns his gaze pointedly to DS Jones. His eyes are appraising, wolfish, as though the subject has stimulated him and he cannot control his inhibitions.

Skelgill thinks back to what Poppy Lux called him, and he decides he agrees.

He rises to his feet. The first impression is perhaps that he needs to flex his spine, but he walks instead to the door.

'We have to be getting on, sir. We know where to find you.'

He glances sharply at DS Jones. Then he briefly points a warning finger at Harry Badger, and turns and descends the steps.

DS Jones has no alternative but to wrap up. She makes a somewhat more diplomatic if brief exit speech, and joins Skelgill, already in his car.

He drives away immediately, taking less care than before over the speed bumps. But at the entrance he parks on the hard standing beside the site office, checking that they are out of sight of Harry Badger's caravan.

DS Jones regards him inquiringly.

'I had to get out of there – couldn't breathe – it was like that narrowboat I was telling you about – the morning after the night before.'

DS Jones grins – but she humours him and drops any further such interrogation.

'What did you think about what he said, Guv?'

'About the Hannay bloke?' He shrugs. 'He's probably right. They were knocking about together, weren't they?'

DS Jones nods.

'It does correspond to accounts of the evening. I don't suppose we should read too much into it – they're both singletons.'

'T'was ever thus.'

Skelgill's somewhat nettled-sounding repetition of Harry Badger's words causes DS Jones to look twice. He responds.

'He filmed his detective series in the Isle of Wight. That's where she lives, aye?'

'That's right.' This point has not in fact eluded her photographic recall. 'But the filming was a long time ago – and, besides, they probably go right back to schooldays.'

He understands she means a relationship, and whatever variety of casual hooking-up has suited them since. But he remains thoughtful, and does not speak for a while. Then he leans abruptly behind DS Jones and pulls his road atlas from the seat pocket. Efficiently he finds the spread that covers their location.

'What is it, Guv?'

Skelgill indicates with a long rough index finger.

'Here's us – Burton Magna – here's Middlemarch.' He pauses, but when she says no more he taps the map. 'Then – here – the Mills' house is in completely the opposite direction from Badger's daily booze cruise. He'd have to go there deliberately.'

Now DS Jones is silent for a few moments.

'Last time – *you* asked me, Guv. What do you think of him?'

Skelgill does not hesitate.

'Happen Poppy Lux was right. But I reckon he's a harmless –' He repeats the word the woman had used.

'Really?'

'I reckon Daisy Mills could handle him. Couldn't you?'

DS Jones grins broadly.

'I might have to punch him.'

'You'd be in the queue after me.'

159

But DS Jones is a little surprised – it is not like her superior to rule out someone who is ostensibly a promising suspect. She is not quite ready to concede this detail.

'But – like he pointed out, Guv – he doesn't have an alibi for Sunday morning.'

Skelgill is squinting, the cause a blend of sunshine and dissent.

'Nor do most of them.'

'Guv – there were three couples – and now it sounds like four. That only leaves three of the party who slept alone. Karl Eastwood, Poppy Lux and Harry Badger.'

'Aye – but the rest – you've still only got their partner's word. Most folk were out cold, by the sound of it. The shower lady reckons the Doc never woke her.'

DS Jones remains pensive; she resists the temptation to comment upon his casual terminology.

'What did you make of his reaction when I asked him about sending the photograph?'

'Could have been him.'

Now she is shocked – this seems to be a sudden volte-face.

'Why do you say that?'

'Didn't you notice his DVDs?'

'I couldn't really see, from where I was sitting.'

'Seventies stuff – if I've got my dates right. Monty Python. Jaws. The Exorcist. Grease. Dirty Harry. And I reckon the whole set of Star Wars.'

Skelgill seems like he is not entirely paying attention to his own words. He has turned the page of his road atlas and is apparently searing a route onto his mental map with a laser-like stare. He closes the book and hands it to DS Jones and slots the car into first gear.

'Royal Leamington Spa.'

14. GIN-TRAP GIN

Monday, 12.45 p.m. – Rutland

Starting in the vicinity of Middlemarch, DS Leyton has charged his navigation app to convey him to the Rutland town of Uppingham. As in much of England, while there are motorways and dual carriageways that hasten the motorist's progress the length of the land (some legacy of the Romans having been in a hurry to subdue the troublesome Picts), travelling cross-country can be another matter. Thus consigned to mainly B-class roads, DS Leyton finds himself jinking through a string of small villages, for he must traverse the entire county of Leicestershire.

From Burbage on the western boundary, through Sapcote, Cosby, Countesthorpe, Kilby, Kibworth Harcourt, Tur Langton, Cranoe, Hallaton, Horninghold and finally Stockerston on the eastern. And, while he has only just begun to get his head around the curious Old Norse nomenclature of Cumbria, this abrupt descent into what must be largely Anglo-Norman has him blinking with bewilderment as he approaches each new habitation; this is the land of the Domesday Book.

In due course he enters Rutland. The ground rising from the crossing of a stream, a discreet sign in the verge, slightly askew, announces the county name, and its impenetrable motto, *Multum in Parvo*. (Back to the Romans?) He is thinking he must ask DS Jones about it, if only he can remember the words. But another sign galvanises him: Uppingham, two-and-a-half miles.

The settlement is decidedly pleasant, a quintessentially English market town of Georgian and Victorian sandstone and red brick and white-painted stucco, the shops mainly independent traders, by the look of it – he spots a butcher's ("Established 1898") and an ironmonger's ("On this site since

161

1761") and a Melton Mowbray pork pie shop, and he delights in the pleasure of Skelgill's absence, and therefore the ability to drive past without stopping.

But since it is almost lunchtime, and he has fifteen minutes to spare, he does stop, and avails himself of one of Melton Mowbray's finest. Small, but dense like a World War II handgrenade, it is extraordinarily filling; however he contrives to wash it down with a can of Diet Coke and the dual satisfaction that the beverage will cancel the excess calories in the pie.

He has his window lowered and hears a bell sound from the impressive edifice across from which he is parked. The institution extends a good distance along the main street in either direction, and beneath a central tower has a grand entrance like that of a castle. There is a sign, "Uppingham School". Boys in smart blazers and girls in kilts begin to stream out, laughing and joking – lively, but a contrast reflecting upon his own experience, where the boys would be shadow boxing and catcalling and the girls chewing gum and hoisting their skirts to indecent heights. Of course, it is a public school – that is, public to the extent that a parent can afford annual fees equivalent to the average household income. He watches pensively, perhaps wrestling with some mental arithmetic. He sighs and gazes admiringly at the architecture – the sign informs him that the venerable college dates back to the sixteenth century, and is the beating heart of the town.

In this context The Rutland Gin-Trap Gin Co. for all its reported artisan credentials proves to be a disappointment at first sight. DS Leyton's satnav takes him off the old high street and along a road lined by more recently built properties, where he arrives at a modern low-rise industrial unit sandwiched between the local fire station and a Harley-Davidson dealership. He pulls in and stares, frowning. He realises he does not know what he thought a gin distillery would look like – in his mind's eye is an image of a whisky distillery, an ancient building with pagoda-like vented cupolas and, inside, towering copper pot stills. At most, here, there are some box-shaped extractor units towards the rear on one side. This place looks more like it would house a small IT company or an electrical repair shop.

At the front there is a loading bay with its roller door closed. A sign marked "Office" indicates around one side. He follows, conscious there is CCTV monitoring his progress – fair enough, given the desirability on the black market of the contents therein. He presses a buzzer and is immediately admitted into a small brightly lit corridor with several doors off it, "Staff Only", "Ladies", "Gents", "Danger – Do Not Enter" and "Reception". Weighing up his options he selects the latter. His immediate impression is of clean modern efficiency. There is a pleasant floral scent, perhaps piney.

This impression continues into the reception area. Although windowless it is a bright room equipped with modern office furniture. There is a casual seating area and opposite a workstation with a desktop computer. Poking just his head around the door he sees a woman is evidently winding up a phone call – she greets him with a welcoming smile and beckons him urgently to sit. She completes her transaction – something about "approving visuals and getting the artwork to the label printer by Friday". Then he notices, from beneath the woman's desk, two Labrador retrievers are eyeing him – distrustfully, he thinks.

'Sergeant Leyton, in't it? From up the Lakes?'

He recognises her accent as akin to that of DC Mary Garth. Now she rises and crosses to meet him halfway.

'I'm Gillian – call me Jill.' She extends a hand and with the other indicates towards her desk. 'That's Bill and Fudge – take no notice of them – they're getting on a bit now.'

She had evidently detected his look of trepidation when he spotted the dogs, an affinity with canines not being a strong suit.

The woman is in her early fifties he would guess, active looking, with strong regular features and a smooth complexion and a broad smile, wavy shoulder-length brown hair and hazel eyes, and buxom might be a word that springs to mind. She is dressed in smartly pressed white workwear with The Rutland

Gin-Trap Gin Co. logo emblazoned on the blouse breast – the graphic a toothed spring-trap grasping a bottle.

'Sit yourself back down and I'll get you some dinner.'

DS Leyton is trying to conjure a diplomatic answer, but he has already noticed she does not allow much more than a second's hesitation before making a presumption of agreement.

'Jack's just finishing off a spirit run – he'll be a few minutes if that's okay – then he can take you through. He says he doesn't want to blow up a policeman – or get you drunk on the vapour – that wouldn't do, would it?'

DS Leyton grins rather sheepishly – he wonders if the woman – Mrs Gillian Battlingbrook by her full name – is referring to the subject that underlies his visit; that another mishap would not be expedient; however she does not appear harried by the former experience, merely innately cheerful.

Now he manages to introduce his protest – that he cannot put her to the trouble of preparing food. He counters with the suggestion that a "nice cuppa" will suffice; though she looks rather hurt, and they settle the negotiation with tea and that she will see if there is "a little bite of something" in the fridge.

While he is waiting he begins to peruse the wall behind the seating area. There is a display shelf on which stand various pristine specimen bottles of gin, and several gleaming silver trophies, and above this a neat array of award certificates, and framed press cuttings. Among them is a certificate of insurance, which makes him ponder, given what fate has befallen this company – and something about this seems to be nagging him – but now the door re-opens, and he is obliged to drop the notion.

Mrs Battlingbrook has evidently been unable to cope with the idea of not feeding a guest. She bears a small round tray.

'There you go, me duck – I've put you up a nice cheese cob. Best Red Leicester it is, from the local dairy. And homemade ploughman's pickle. Just a little snack to keep you going.'

DS Leyton groans inwardly, but he sits and gallantly receives the well-meant offering. It is a large round bread roll in which is sandwiched a quarter-inch-thick slice of orange-coloured cheese and an equivalent layer of shiny brown pickle. He doubts even a hungry Skelgill would finish this. Then again – of course he would.

The woman takes the seat beside him; it seems she is determined to see her handiwork devoured. Across the room, DS Leyton observes that the snouts of the two dogs are raised; although the creatures seem to know that any greater interest is forbidden; they have a kind of hangdog expression, which seems to heighten as he takes a tentative nibble at his sandwich.

'We love it, up the Lakes. Jack and me normally stay at a caravan site at Braithwaite. They don't mind the dogs there. We've not been for a few years, though – since we set up the business we've not had a proper holiday.'

DS Leyton makes a sympathetic murmuring sound, and a face to accompany it. He thinks of saying that he lives quite close by, but she continues quickly, making pleasant if rather one-sided conversation. He learns they are literally a man-and-wife team (as DC Mary Garth had intimated); that this was their pipe dream to run their own business; that husband Jack was a mechanical engineer in the brewing and distilling trade; and she a pub manageress. He knows how to make it – the production department. She knows what folks like – the marketing department. Then came the gin boom and they decided to chance their arm while they were still young enough.

DS Leyton, having made only minor inroads into his cheese roll, decides to play for time. Perhaps if he can keep her distracted, the husband will appear and he can ask for a doggy bag.

'Jill – what made you call it Gin-Trap Gin?'

She seems pleased that he uses her name in its contracted form. However, she waves a hand airily, as though to indicate that he has touched on a source of contention.

'I know, it sounds a bit daft, don't it?'

DS Leyton does his best to sit on the fence; he chews stoically.

'The in-laws used to have a van up Norfolk – it were Jack's granddad's, originally. There was a pub not far, called the Gin Trap. You see, a gin trap's a bird trap, like a miniature mantrap.

A gamekeeper sets it on a post where a bird might perch. The pub had them dangling from all the beams for decoration.'

She points to the logo on her blouse. She seems uninhibited about drawing his eye to the curve. He blinks and nods innocently.

'Jack can tell you – he's the expert. Gin's just short for 'engine' – it were an old word for any mechanical device. So it's nothing to do with the drink gin – but we always used to joke about going for a Gin-Trap Gin when we courting over there. Then, when the time came, we thought it would be a good name for our own product. It meant something to us – and a gin-trap's a country thing – and it's got the word gin in it.'

She looks at him artlessly, as though to say what could be more reasonable. DS Leyton is presently having trouble swallowing, but he emits another suitably soothing noise and reaches for his mug of tea.

Gillian Battlingbrook suddenly seems to remember why he is here – that he is on important business of his own – and turns to look at the wall clock above her desk. The time reads twenty minutes past one.

'I tell you what – I'll just go and check on Jack – make sure he's not gassed himself!' She emits something of an involuntary laugh. 'You can be drunk in seconds on alcohol fumes.' She rises, but hesitates and looks with some concern at DS Leyton's plate. 'All this nattering – you've hardly made a start – you finish your snap, me duck.'

The instant she has left the room – heading presumably for the door marked "Danger" (indeed, he hears the chime of an alarm) – the dogs make their move, what looks like a well-practised pincer movement. When DS Leyton would normally feel trepidation – long in the tooth or not, to be trapped with two overweight slavering Labradors is his idea of Room 101 – now, paradoxically, he recognises salvation. He has a good three-quarters left of his 'cob'. He breaks it into two roughly even pieces and, with frictionless glee posts them into accommodating jaws.

He is basking in the glory of such serendipity when the alarm sounds again. Someone is coming back. He begins to panic. The dogs are licking their lips and looking for more. But, then, with an alacrity that belies their years they turn tail and slink back to their den. Before the door is even opened, they are curled up with merely half an eye open. DS Leyton could swear that the slightly smaller chocolate Lab (presumably 'Fudge') winks at him.

Wresting his bewildered gaze from his co-conspirators he rises as Gillian Battlingbrook re-enters the office. For a moment he thinks she is alone, but then realises that behind her follows a man of smaller stature, if of similar age. This must be the happily un-gassed Jack Battlingbrook.

Size aside, his outstanding feature is a bristling moustache, like a yard brush. He is of wiry build, clad in the same uniform as his wife. He has straight mousy hair, a large, long nose and beady brown eyes; features which, together with the moustache, confer upon him the look of a small wild animal, though DS Leyton is not entirely sure what species.

Gillian Battlingbrook makes a convergent ushering motion with her arms.

'This is me husband, Jack. Detective Sergeant Leyton.'

The man shoots out a hand.

'Alright.'

The greeting is terse; the intonation does not invite the usual reciprocation. DS Leyton feels he ought to say something.

'Nice little place you've got here.'

The man seems to take offence. His features contract fiercely. Perhaps ferret is the creature DS Leyton is looking for.

'Multum in Parvo! Multum in Parvo, mate.'

He appears unconcerned that DS Leyton is a ranking police officer, and that it is customary to exhibit some qualitative recognition of the fact; not that DS Leyton is the type to hold it against him. The man continues to glare at him.

'Rutland's small – in't it? But it's only got the biggest manmade lake in England. If Rutland were North America – Rutland Water would be eight times the size of Lake Superior. Put that in your pipe and smoke it.'

He glances at his wife, who nods admiringly. DS Leyton is somewhat baffled by the logic – it is the sort of obtuse analogy Skelgill might employ to win an argument. Besides, there is no argument. But it dawns upon him that there is something of an inferiority complex at play here – for a start, it is not often he is the tallest person in the room. Now his unaffected Cockney nature provides him with a spark of inspiration.

'I travelled down with two colleagues. We drew straws on who'd get Rutland and who'd get Middlemarch.' (There is a small white lie here). 'My Guvnor – he's fishing mad, kicking himself he is – that he never got a butcher's at your Rutland Water. And my fellow sergeant – gin-and-tonic's her middle name.' Beaming, DS Leyton now gestures down to his empty plate, on the coffee table beside the settee. 'And yours truly here got the long straw on all fronts!'

Gillian Battlingbrook flushes with pleasure (DS Leyton's only concern is that she will make him another one), and her husband seems adequately placated. He gets down to business.

'Right, come on then, if you want to see the engine room. There's a ten-minute window before I start the next boil.'

The man does not stand on ceremony and leaves without further ado. DS Leyton hustles after him, hearing behind him the woman's voice inquiring of the dogs if they are ready for their dinner. He has no doubt they are.

Behind the door marked "Danger" is a laboratory-like chamber, impeccably clean, where various shiny copper and stainless steel contraptions and pipes interweave in a baffling array. The centrepiece, however, DS Leyton does recognise – a copper pot still, like a scale model of those he saw on his one and only leisure trip to Scotland (another distant memory of his honeymoon, when they took a coach tour into the Borders). His host informs him that this "mighty midget" can produce a batch of 250 litres, or 55 gallons in "proper money". It is a descriptor of which Skelgill would approve, and complemented with another rendition of the battle cry, "Multum in Parvo, mate!"

But DS Leyton is conscious that time is short. He must focus on the crux of the matter – if the contamination was here, how did it happen? The public health authority's report in DC Mary Garth's file could not entirely exonerate the artisan distillery. He becomes rather acutely aware that, if there were indeed a moment in his mission for treading upon eggshells, this is it. But he senses that the man, too, would rather come to the point than go through the motions of a guided visit.

'Sir – has anything struck you, since the original investigation, that could explain what happened? I mean – I imagine you want it cleared up as much as the next man.' He casts about admiringly. 'You and your missus – you don't deserve to be under the cloud of suspicion.'

Despite a fierce scowl being elicited by the phrase "cloud of suspicion" he seems to strike the right note. Perhaps, in private, away from his spouse where no bravado is needed, the man is willing to soften. He shakes his head, ruefully.

'I've racked me brains, mate. It couldn't have been here, though. I mean – for a start – why would we queer our own pitch? Six years work we've put into this, round the clock, fingers to the bone.'

DS Leyton is nodding. Of course they would not want to queer their own pitch, but could it have been an innocent accident?

However, this is the sixty-four-thousand-dollar question, and the man does not shirk it.

'Even if we did pick Deadly Nightshade by mistake – which I'm telling you, we wouldn't, the berries are completely different and it was too late in the season – but even if we did, why was *only one case* contaminated?'

He puts his hands on his hips and literally bristles, challenging DS Leyton to gainsay him.

DS Leyton responds in the way he thinks best.

'Run that by me, then, sir.'

Jack Battlingbrook points to a large stainless steel cylinder.

'*Nice 'n' Sloe* was a liqueur. You leave the sloes to macerate in the gin for six weeks. It were a one-off – a new line we thought we'd try for Christmas.' He slaps the side of the vessel, producing a hollow ding with his wedding ring. 'That made

169

twenty cases – all from the same batch. A hundred-and-twenty standard bottles.'

DS Leyton suddenly sees why there has legitimately been an air of defiance tinged with affront about the man's demeanour. He responds soberly.

'There were no other reports of contamination.'

The predatory ferret, coiled for action, pounces upon his words.

'Not a dicky bird.'

DS Leyton compresses his lips. The man points to one part of the room and then another.

'The bottles were capped and sealed into cartons. They stayed untouched in our bond until the courier picked up the order for the wholesaler. After that – it's a free for all.'

He swivels and reaches for a squirt of sanitiser from a wall-mounted dispenser, and rubs vigorously, as though acting out the metaphor of washing his hands of the problem. He continues, becoming more animated, the moustache seeming to fan out with a life of its own and his arms shooting hither and thither.

'Think of all the folk that could have handled it. You've got your delivery driver, your goods inward, your forklift driver. Then it's on the rack at Merry's Cash & Carry in Leicester for a good month – on public display – to the trade at least. Then that off licence bought the single case in question. Another driver, shelf-stacker – then the bottles are on open sale – any old Tom, Dick or Harry could have messed with them.'

DS Leyton nods pensively. His assumption, led by the initial investigation, had been that, if not at source in Rutland, then the Middlemarch retailer was the most likely location of contamination, but he sees now there would be other opportunities. That said, only a local retailer could provide the cover of an apparently rogue incident within a tight neighbourhood – much in the way of DC Mary Garth's Edinburgh case study, with the perpetrator holding back one or two of the batch for their own devices.

Jack Battlingbrook still has more to add.

'We got most of them recalled. All independently tested. There were no other problems.' He exclaims in frustration and curses. 'What a waste. Thick end of two grand at retail.'

'Did they all go to the same wholesaler?'

The man hesitates a moment, and folds his arms.

'The local wine shop took a case. They stock all our lines – local product – local shop for local people. They sold out straightaway – over a month before the rest. None were returned. No one was poorly round here.'

However, there seems something odd about his manner, but before DS Leyton can render a follow-up question the man checks his wristwatch.

'I have to get a shift on. Is that your lot?'

DS Leyton would like to think of some clever parting question – Skelgill has a bit of a knack for them, when apparently he has not been paying attention – but it is a difficult skill to be questioner and analyst at the same time. He supposes he can always phone from the car. He proffers his thanks in a manner that he hopes will be reassuring, that he is not leaving them with doubt in his mind. He reiterates his compliment of it being a nice little operation.

Having thus been let out of the locking door system with a parting shot of "Multum in Parvo" ringing in his ears, DS Leyton returns alone to bid farewell at reception.

'Ooh – just you wait a minute, me duck – I've got something for you.'

Gillian Battlingbrook bustles past him and out of the office; he curses his good manners – what if this time she stands over him until he finishes the next sandwich? Clearly, one had not been enough. While he waits he tries to distract himself with the wall display. Now he is reminded of his earlier unease – and by chance his eyes light upon what must surely have been the source of his disquiet. In something of a panic he pulls his mobile phone from his jacket pocket and fumbling with the commands he takes a photograph – only just in time before the door opens and he can pretend he is checking a message.

'Here you are, me duck.'

171

To his relief the woman holds out a plain white polythene carrier bag – something to take away?

Politely he accepts the offering – it is quite weighty. As he delves inside she provides a commentary.

'It were for our tea tonight, but I'll pop out and get another. That ought to keep you going on your journey home.'

A pork pie, more than twice the size of that he ate for his lunch, accounts for about half of the burden. It would feed his family, if only he could get them to eat it. The other item is a slim rectangular box printed with The Rutland Gin-Trap Gin Co. livery. He lifts it partially out.

'And that's our souvenir pack of three miniatures – our most popular lines – London Dry, Navy Strength and Rutland Rhubarb. *They're* not for your journey, obviously – but don't worry, when you do drink them, they won't poison you!'

15. JARNDYCE & JARNDYCE

Monday, 1:45pm – Royal Leamington Spa

'Leyton – I've got you on hands-free so Jones can hear when she comes back.'
'Righto, Guv – where are you up to?'
'Outside the Eastwood bloke's office. You only just caught us. Jones is sorting the parking ticket. The vultures are circling.'

DS Leyton understands that Skelgill would expect him to convey directly any startling finding (which he does not have); equally, there is their mutual appreciation that Skelgill does not do small talk. So DS Leyton has to chart a course somewhere down the middle.

'Top line – the South Mercia report seems largely corroborated, Guv.' Now he hesitates, for a small commotion disturbs him – but it is merely DS Jones re-entering the car. 'Actually – I've just sent you both a photograph. It's easier to explain if you can see it.'

DS Jones has paid for parking using her mobile and hearing her colleague's words she opens the message. Skelgill leans over.

'What is it?'

DS Leyton assumes the question is intended for him.

'At Rutland Gin, Guv – they've got a display in reception – awards and whatnot. This was one of the framed press cuttings. The Uppingham Times – from September last year.'

'That's Dr Charles Rice.'

It is DS Jones that makes the identification. Now she manipulates the message. They read the headline:

"Local Gin Sponsors TV Naturalist's Anti-Trapping Campaign."

Skelgill settles back in his seat and folds his arms. DS Jones, taking over, paraphrases the content of the article.

'It says – Uppingham-based gin manufacturer – The Rutland Gin-Trap Gin Co. – has teamed up with celebrity birdwatcher and local resident Dr Charles Rice. Host of popular TV show Wild Side – he is petitioning for a controversial change in the law – to make landowners liable if any kind of bird trap is found on their property, whether set for use or not. And, er – promotional packs of gin will feature the campaign message – invite donations to Dr Rice's crowd-funded charity – plus the chance to win a distillery tour and birdwatching at Rutland Water with Dr Rice.'

'That'd be a fun.'

Skelgill utters this without emotion, which DS Jones equates in his case to maximum sarcasm. For a moment she thinks about comparing it favourably to a day with some fishing icon (they must exist) – but she realises that Skelgill would hate every minute of it.

Skelgill points rather indifferently at her screen.

'What does it say under the picture?'

DS Jones enlarges the caption.

'Just that it's Dr Rice with company directors Jack and Jill Battlingbrook.'

'That's right, Guv – that's the pair I met.' It is DS Leyton that now chips in. 'Dunno about directors – it's a one-man-and-his-dog operation. Well – one man, one woman – and two dogs.'

The jocular aside does not elicit any further reaction from Skelgill.

DS Jones is flicking through her notes. After a short silence she ventures an opinion.

'It's quite a coincidence. Although I see that he does live nearby. I guess he's well known in those parts.'

Skelgill looks like he is struggling to process this item of news – as though he has been methodically solving a jigsaw and has suddenly been presented with a piece that seems to be from another puzzle altogether. He looks again at DS Jones.

'Any mention of this in the reports?'

She shakes her head – while over the airwaves DS Leyton simultaneously answers in the negative.

'That's why I'm calling, Guv. Since I'm in his neck of the woods – I could drop by.'

Skelgill does not reply.

'Guv!'

It is DS Jones who exclaims. And she causes Skelgill to start, not least by giving him a sharp jab on the thigh with the end of her pen. A fly on the wall might think she is annoyed at him for ignoring her colleague – but he sees she is staring through the windscreen, willing him to look. He follows her gaze. Amidst the pedestrians milling about the pavement the tallish figure of a man, with swept-back dark hair and perhaps a tanned complexion, is moving purposefully away.

'That's Karl Eastwood.'

Skelgill watches for a moment.

'Happen he's hungry.'

But DS Jones is shaking her head.

'He came out of that door. He looked at us. He's got a briefcase with him.'

Skelgill, seated on the kerb side, rolls down his window and cranes up at the buildings. In typical fashion the high street has shops on the ground floor and offices on the first. From his acute angle he can just make out half-lowered blinds that read, "Eastwood-Mills Assurance." And thus someone looking out could surely see enough of the distinctive brown shooting brake parked beneath.

'Would you take a briefcase to buy a sandwich, Guv?'

Skelgill treats the question as rhetorical. But if DS Jones's observation was accurate, then it is the second time today that the man has made himself scarce. He knows well enough that they are in the area. Finding them outside his office could only mean they were here to speak with him. And, if he did recognise them, surely it would be normal to make at least an acknowledgement, and offer a few words of explanation for his departure.

Skelgill looks at his wristwatch.

175

'How long did you put on the meter?'

'An hour – but I can just extend it with a text. Three is the limit along here.'

Skelgill now ponders for a moment.

'May as well try the solicitor.'

'Sure.'

DS Leyton, still on air, has held his peace – deducing from the exchange that what is afoot does not require complication. Now he comes back in.

'What do you reckon, Guv – should I see the twitcher geezer?'

Skelgill again seems distracted. It appears he is finding Karl Eastwood's behaviour more unfathomable than he wishes it to be.

'Aye – as you like.'

It is not a particularly encouraging or helpful response – but Skelgill now opens the car door, and in yanking his phone from its hands-free cradle he inadvertently disconnects the call. Slamming the door, he looks blankly at his handset. Then he pockets it, and beckons with a jerk of the head to DS Jones.

'This way, I reckon.'

There is something dubious about the manner in which Skelgill sets off; DS Jones recognises the body language – when a 'speculative' diversion will conveniently take them past a café or cake shop. But they have already stopped for lunch – Skelgill playing the petrol card to pull in at a Little Chef on the Warwick Bypass. Dutifully following, she wonders at what point he worked out where to go. He claims never to have visited Leamington (Royal Leamington Spa, to give it its full title), yet he drove them more or less directly without assistance to the Parade – their present location – an almost grand Regency thoroughfare where the buildings exhibit a unanimity among owners (or maybe a diktat of the town council) in their creamy white facades, bright on the eye. Skelgill has them striding south, squinting into the early afternoon sun. DS Jones concludes that he must have consulted the maps app on his phone when she was powdering her nose.

But her suspicions are compounded when they reach a bridge and he abruptly slows his pace. A river, fairly modest in width, flows slowly beneath.

Skelgill veers to lean over the classical-style balustrade.

'River Leam.'

He pronounces it as per the spoken 'lemm' of Leamington.

'Ah, I see.'

DS Jones makes the connection. The town on the Leam. Of course, like most place names, this one has rudimentary origins – although, unlike most, it acquired rather grand embellishments. Indeed, she turns away to scrutinise an impressive building diagonally opposite: "Royal Pump Rooms & Baths – 1814".

'Guv – do you think that place is still in use?'

But a question asked of Skelgill under circumstances such as these is liable to be screened out. DS Jones is unperturbed. She joins him at the rail; he is staring, unblinking. After a few moments, she raises a more apposite query.

'It seems a bit stagnant for spa water. What do you think, Guv?'

'There's a shoal of decent-sized bream feeding under those willows.'

When she laughs he seems to realise he has perhaps been on his own private wavelength. Now he makes an effort.

'There'll be a weir downstream. It was common practice in town centres – to create a body of water. This would have been a sewer, mind. The spa water was drawn from underground springs, not the river.'

DS Jones makes an encouraging murmur.

'Ought we to go?'

Skelgill seems to understand that she is rescuing him from a rising tide of frustration – another day not fishing.

'Howay, lass.'

He moves on hurriedly, as though it were at his insistence. And, now, clearly knowing where he is taking them, he crosses the bridge at a tangent, towards Victoria Terrace, a three-storey Georgian block in obligatory cream, its northern elevation overlooking the river. He stops at a freshly painted black door between two shops, one that retails expensive paint and wallpaper and the other extravagant home accessories.

A brass plate announces, "Jarndyce & Jarndyce". In this regard, DS Jones is not entirely in the dark. They had kept an open mind about whom exactly they would try to see in the Midlands – Harry Badger a probability, Karl Eastwood a possibility – but the rendezvous with Poppy Lux at her late sister's home was the only definitive advance arrangement. Thereat, events indicated an interest in Karl Eastwood might be of merit. This sentiment was fortified – albeit indirectly – when Skelgill came across the envelope that revealed the Mills' private solicitors were domiciled in Royal Leamington Spa, where Eastwood-Mills have their office. Thus two birds could be targeted with one stone – the comparatively short journey south into provincial Warwickshire, with its cluster of historic towns, Warwick itself, Kenilworth, Leamington of course, Rugby and Stratford-upon-Avon, variously famous for their imposing Norman castles, eminent public schools and a none-too-shabby playwright.

While they had decided to call upon Karl Eastwood unannounced (taking him at his word that his in-tray beckoned), such a tactic did not seem appropriate for a member of the legal profession, so DS Jones had telephoned ahead. It was however a flexible arrangement; they would drop by some time after lunch. The receptionist had confirmed that would be satisfactory.

Now DS Jones states their identity via an intercom and they are buzzed into a well-maintained communal atrium where they mount a stone stairway with black-painted cast-iron balusters and a polished oak handrail to a further door on the first floor. A sign invites entry.

Skelgill steps aside to allow DS Jones to go first. The door gives on to a small windowless though brightly lit anteroom and over his colleague's shoulder he sees standing facing them a woman of slender build, in her early thirties, he would guess, rather formally dressed in a dark suit, dark stockings and black flat shoes. She has red hair drawn tightly back; her complexion is pale and her features are fine and regular; she makes him think of

Elizabeth I, although when she fixes him with her penetrating blue eyes the image is superseded by that of the portrait of Daisy Mills.

'Please, come this way.'

She leads them into a short, carpeted passage with doors off and mounted on the walls paintings of men – lawyers – wigged and gowned, towards a long sash window with internal shutters before which she turns off into a room on the right. A pair of carved Chippendale chairs are set before an expansive mahogany desk, behind which the wall is shelved and lined with sets of leather-bound books in an immaculate display. Skelgill experiences the curious feeling of entering a period drama, and finds himself drifting towards the window as if to ground himself in the present day. Then again, there is the river to see – except that a stand of white poplars thwarts his ambitions and he is obliged to take up the offer of a seat.

'May I order you some refreshments – tea, coffee – or mineral water, perhaps?'

The woman is well spoken, her accent neutral and her intonation precise, as befits one accustomed to the importance of clarity in communication.

To DS Jones's surprise Skelgill declines. He raises a palm as he approaches the desk.

'We've not long ago stopped, thanks, er – madam.'

The woman seems faintly intrigued by his apparent awkwardness in addressing her, but she takes her seat and hands across the desk a business card, first to DS Jones and then a second to Skelgill, in the latter case holding onto the card such that he makes eye contact with her.

'Esther Jarndyce.'

She releases her grip and Skelgill leans back, squinting at the legend. He has noticed that she wears no rings.

'Are you a husband and wife –'

'Partnership?' She completes the legal definition, and now she smiles for the first time, transforming what has been a rather stern if good-looking countenance into something considerably more of the latter. 'Father and daughter. We have a long family

179

tradition in the law. I am the sixth generation. Our first case was in 1852.'

She indicates with the ringless left hand to the antiquarian tomes at her back.

Skelgill grins rather sheepishly.

'We're only talking six months.'

'In which case you have the right person.'

It seems that Skelgill finds Esther Jarndyce's inscrutability discomfiting; now he turns to DS Jones to see she is regarding him with a look of bafflement. But she realises she should take the initiative.

Succinctly she elaborates on the information she had conveyed in arranging their appointment. The drowning at the weekend of Daisy Mills. The Rydal gathering and the group of people present. The earlier death of Simon Mills. Their visit to the Mills' house with Poppy Lux, and subsequently to Leamington; and their intention to interview Karl Eastwood. She restricts herself purely to the facts, and makes no suggestion of causation, or even of correlation.

The solicitor reacts calmly. She appears to appreciate DS Jones's forensic approach.

But she is not immediately forthcoming, and Skelgill wonders if she is formulating a defence on behalf of her erstwhile clients. Perhaps rather uncharacteristically, he butts in.

'Obviously we're not asking you to break any confidences – and we appreciate that Eastwood-Mills is still operating.'

'We do not act for Eastwood-Mills. We are family lawyers, not commercial.'

Skelgill seems a little chastised. However, he has a rejoinder.

'How about Mr Eastwood, do you act for him personally?'

'No. Nor have we in the past.'

The lawyer's tone is perhaps just a little terse – that despite his suggestion to the contrary she suspects he will quite glibly transgress the rule of confidentiality. But, if she is inwardly irked, her expression is more that of the schoolmarm reproaching an incorrigible pupil of whom she is secretly fond.

For her part, DS Jones now moves to regain control of the interview. She reads that there is no requirement for a game of cat and mouse.

'Miss Jarndyce, plainly we wouldn't be here if there were not some doubt over these deaths. And we have to report to the Coroner in that regard.' (The lawyer nods; the legal obligation strikes a chord.) 'One clear line of investigation is to look at who might benefit from the passing of either or both of the Mills couple.'

The solicitor does not need further prompting. And now it seems she has prepared for their visit. She places a delicate hand on a manila file at the top of a pile on one side of her desk.

'Since a grant of probate was required in order for us to fulfil our role as executors of the estate, the will of Simon Mills is a public document. I think what you want to know is that Simon Mills left his estate in its entirety to his wife – his *late* wife. There was a substantial liability for inheritance tax, which is yet to be determined and settled. Simon Mills' shares in the business transferred to his co-director in return for a keyman insurance payment – a valuation is necessary. As executors we are awaiting information in that regard from various professional sources.'

There is potential for deviation here – and it might be that DS Jones is trying to process the possible implications before she chooses her route. But Skelgill reads her wavering as a polite reluctance to tread on forbidden territory. Suffering no such inhibitions, and despite the subtle warning he has received, he takes the view that there is no point driving from Cumbria and not asking.

'What about Mrs Mills' will?'

Esther Jarndyce turns what is now categorically a reprimanding glare upon him.

'Naturally, at such a juncture as this, I could not divulge the contents.' But now she leans towards him and rests her chin upon the backs of her hands. There is a flutter of lashes over the fluorescent blue eyes. 'But what I can tell you is that unless she used a different law firm, *she did not make a will.*'

She raises her eyebrows interrogatively.

Skelgill makes a gesture of guilty apology, raising both hands, palms outward. Then he looks to DS Jones, and mimes out what looks like a rugby offload – that she should run with the ball.

She turns to address the lawyer, and it seems for a moment that there is a flash of mutual empathy that transmits between them. She brings her notebook up to her chest.

'Miss Jarndyce, which do you think is most likely?'

The woman seems perfectly happy to deal with such conjecture, but a small frown creases her hitherto smooth brow.

'Firstly, I should stress that I never met Daisy Mills. And Simon Mills only briefly over the signing of documents on a handful of occasions. We undertook the conveyancing of their properties when they last moved house – it was almost a decade ago. There have been a few minor matters since – for instance planning permission for an extension and barn conversion that required a change to title deeds – but nothing I think that would give you cause for concern. So, as to your question, I do not know if Daisy Mills consulted other solicitors, or indeed wrote a will privately. It does not require a solicitor for a will to be legally valid – although there is the risk that invalidating flaws could creep in. A common mistake is that people enlist beneficiaries as witnesses.'

DS Jones is listening carefully.

'A sister survives her, and an elderly father who is in care. There are no other relatives. Assuming she left no will, who would inherit her estate?'

The lawyer responds efficiently.

'Then the rules of intestacy apply. The two surviving relatives you mention would inherit equally. Do you know if the sister has power of attorney for her father?'

DS Jones shakes her head.

'I don't know. Is that significant?'

'To be frank, it would be normal. And it does not give carte blanche to raid a person's assets. There are strict rules governing reasonable expenditure. It is a trustee-like role.'

'Do you know if Daisy Mills *intended* to make a will?'

DS Jones senses that Skelgill glances at her – as if in surprise that she poses an off-limits question that ought to be reserved for him.

Esther Jarndyce bites her lower lip. But she might be trying to suppress a smile. And perhaps she concludes that she ought to cooperate as far as possible; after all, when it comes to the scales of justice, they share the same plate.

'We have been corresponding with Mrs Mills over matters of probate. If you asked me, would it be our professional duty under such circumstances to recommend a client made a will, then the answer is yes.'

She reaches out briefly towards the two detectives, as if to include them in her advice, that it is a universal truth. Reading between the lines, they nod obediently.

Skelgill is thinking back to the letter in Simon Mills' study from which he memorised the sender's address, Jarndyce & Jarndyce, Victoria Terrace, Royal Leamington Spa. He is pretty sure it had not been opened or tampered with. He gestures with a hand to show he has a question.

'When were those letters about probate sent?'

Esther Jarndyce regards him evenly.

'I believe there have been five items of correspondence since the turn of the year.'

A short silence ensues, and it is DS Jones who is next to speak.

'Miss Jarndyce – if Daisy Mills made no will – who would be the executor of her estate? Would that automatically fall to your firm?'

The woman sits back in her chair. She compresses her lips into a narrow rosy line.

'No. We have no connection in law in that context, since we were not formally appointed.' And now she pre-empts the logical follow-up question. 'In the absence of any such request, a beneficiary of sound mind is tasked to step in as administrator.'

DS Jones ponders for a moment. The algorithm they have covered tells her there is only one person that fits the description.

183

'Poppy Lux.'

16. RICE RESIDENCE

Monday, 2.15 p.m. – Stoke Dry, Rutland

It strikes DS Leyton that Stoke is another one of those place names more prevalent in the Midlands, like Magna and Parva. In typing it into his satnav he is provided with a plethora of options, such as Stoke Golding, a village near Hinckley, not far from his rendezvous with DC Garth; plain Stoke near Coventry (also a village, and in roughly the same vicinity); and Stoke-on-Trent, a city famed for its pottery, and named he has always subliminally assumed from the verb to stoke the kilns.

But the Stoke he needs is Stoke Dry, on the map a dot of a place just inside the Rutland-Leicestershire border.

From the Uppingham-Corby road he takes a single-track lane with broad grassy verges white with cow parsley and a view across arable farmland dappled with copses and spinneys. The general vista is a tricolour of spring green, and blue and white above. Snatches of indeterminate birdsong reach his ears. A buzzard lifts off from the tarmac as he rounds a bend – and there must be plenty to eat, for there is no shortage of roadkill. Pressed by passing tyres into two dimensions he believes he identifies the remnants of a hedgehog, a hare – and could that little caramel-coloured one have been a hamster? The Guvnor would know.

The lane begins to descend into a shallow valley. He thinks he gets a glimpse of a lake – though surely it cannot be the much-vaunted Rutland Water, for in Uppingham he saw signs indicating in entirely the opposite direction. But trees rise up and begin to thicken and thwart his view. There are occasional cottages built in what he would think of as Cotswold stone, though he is nowhere near the Cotswolds. However, it is evidently one such property that he seeks, for the omniscient satnav lady announces: "Your destination is ahead on the right". A large circular driveway exit mirror marks the spot.

He pulls off into a recessed gateway. Ahead between the spars of ornate wrought-iron gates he can see a splendid country home in the same creamy limestone, perhaps once a farmhouse with steadings, now interconnected through cleverly blended extensions, and loft rooms with jutting dormer windows. He lets out a soft whistle; it is something of a dream home.

Switching off the ignition he gets out. On tiptoes he can just see over the top of the wall that flanks the pull-in. Two cars are parked in front of stables converted into a triple garage with white-painted doors. A classic soft-top MGB Roadster in British racing green – in mint condition, he wonders if it is a modern clone – and a more regular VW hatchback, though not unstylish in sporty livery. He cross-references the vehicles against the list provided by DS Jones. There is no sign of the diesel-electric hybrid that belongs to Dr Charles Rice.

He finds an entry system set into one of the gate pillars. There is a camera and he realises that someone could be looking at him on a mobile phone doorbell app. Belatedly he smoothes his hair and straightens his jacket. And suddenly he becomes aware of the afternoon heat. The air is still and there is an intensity of humidity that reminds him of London and the Thames; he has grown accustomed to the cooler breezy mountain climate of Cumbria.

'Yes?'

It seems he was right. Before he has pushed the call button a woman's voice challenges him, it is husky and seems amused in tone, and perhaps there is also a second higher-pitched voice that laughs in the background.

'Hello? It's, er – DS Leyton from Cumbria Police. I believe you may have met my colleagues – DI Skelgill and DS Jones. I'm doing some follow-up work for them and wondered if I might have a word – it was Dr Rice I was hoping to see.'

'Stand back a little.'

He obeys the woman's entreaty – he assumes it has something to do with opening the gates.

'You look like just the man we need.' (Was that more suppressed sniggers?) 'Come around the right-hand side. Follow the path.'

Somewhat bewildered he hears an electronic buzz to his left and realises there is a small access gate in the stone wall that is being remotely unlocked. He makes a dart and pushes it open while the vibration lasts. Once inside the fortifications, he pauses to get his bearings. The driveway has been paved at no little expense in complementary amber brick, and despite the age of the property in general, there is also the impression of it being a new development. Around the building are flower borders with what looks like fresh planting. He stands for a moment – there are white butterflies that bounce erratically and the hum of bees, busy in the colourful beds.

He follows an offshoot of the brick paving around the nearest corner and skirts the building, momentarily passing into welcome shade. There is a long, low extension, perhaps another stable conversion and when he rounds this and its next corner, all is revealed before him.

The property stands on sloping ground and from here, without the trees that border the lane a magnificent view opens out over the low valley, in which a narrow lake glints. In the foreground an expansive lawn, of maybe a couple of acres stretches to a boundary of mature hawthorn fringed by meadow-like grass. More immediately still is a stone-flagged patio area – and, here, two largely naked women recline on slatted wooden loungers, turned away from him into the sun. One, a honey blonde, sips a long pink drink through a straw. The other, auburn beneath a cowboy hat, reads a Kindle.

DS Leyton stands motionless. They do not appear to be anticipating his arrival with the enthusiasm suggested in their exchange over the intercom. He casts about. The back of the main house and the extension form an L-shape around the patio. A stable-type kitchen door has its top section open, and a floor-to-ceiling sliding glass pane in the annexe is also open, where an imposing telescope on a tripod stands sentry. The sandy-hued environs create a substantial suntrap and the besuited DS Leyton feels a bead of sweat trickle down his spine.

He is reticent about stepping too close, because from his present angle he cannot tell just how much – if anything – the two women are wearing. He clears his throat, rather in the manner of a butler who has been summoned but is now ignored by his aristocratic employers.

But now the nearer with the cocktail sits up and swings her legs elegantly around, keeping her knees and ankles pressed together. To his further relief he sees that she is wearing a glossy gold bikini – albeit that in some respects it only serves to emphasise a bronzed figure that would be a credit to a woman half her age. That is to say, if she is who he thinks she is from DS Jones's briefing notes – Gail Melia, partner of Dr Charles Rice, and aged fifty-five. And presumably the other woman – who puts down her device and turns to regard him over a bare shoulder with a languid smile – is the man's sister. He sees that she, too, wears a bikini, alarmingly flesh-coloured. He averts his gaze – but he finds it difficult to strike up a conversation without looking at either of them.

Not that they appear threatened in any way, or even remotely inhibited. And they seem quite lackadaisical about letting him in – a stranger they have never met. Indeed, the whole scene is incongruous – is this what he should expect of two women who only the previous day lost a friend in tragic circumstances? They are acting like they are still on their holiday, as though nothing has happened. But – he reflects – what is the right manner? Perhaps they are suffering from shock – he knows it himself – that period when some inner switch is thrown and the body is put into autopilot until it is ready one day for reality to be restored.

'Ah – you are heaven-sent. Sarah and I were just saying how we needed a strong young man.'

The woman rises gracefully and moves rather ominously towards him.

'Please, come this way.'

It seems she intends to chaperone him into the house, for she reaches as though to take his hand – but when he does not reciprocate she pinches the sleeve of his jacket. But she draws him instead in the opposite direction, across the patio and onto the spongy turf of the lawn.

'I have had a minor mishap with one of my hives.' She indicates towards the garden border with her free hand. 'There – you see?'

Now he does see. A row of pale wooden beehives is set amongst the wild grasses beneath the hedgerow. They seem to DS Leyton like a London housing estate viewed from afar, blocks of flats with tiered storeys and pitched roofs. One appears to have suffered from a failed attempt at demolition, and is leaning alarmingly. The same ambient drone that he heard at the front becomes audible, growing in intensity as they approach. And he begins to see that there are bees moving everywhere, entering and leaving the hives, and generally milling around and buzzing about, and feeding upon the abundant white blossoms of the hedge – the sickly scent reminds him of something slightly unpleasant, though he cannot quite place it.

Now he recalls a childhood experience with bees (or was it wasps?) – when his pal Dev's wire-haired ratter had belligerently dug into a nest on a patch of waste ground. The insects had attacked with a vengeance, like a kamikaze squadron – they were forced to flee for their lives and were gingerly picking them out of the poor terrier's fur for the next half hour. He contrives to voice his concern from the perspective of chivalry. He gestures to the woman's lack of attire.

'Is this safe?'

'Oh – they know me.' She gives her throaty laugh. 'It's you they'll go for. Just don't show any fear – they smell it.'

She must sense his alarm.

'Don't worry – there is protective equipment.'

Indeed she diverts to what looks like an incomplete hive standing apart from the rest and lifts a hinged lid. She pulls out a beekeeper's veiled hat and a pair of thick cotton gloves that extend past the elbows to elasticated cuffs.

He finds himself powerless as she helps him off with his jacket, and then steps close to face him, gazing with just the hint of a smile as she raises and fits the hat and adjusts the veil. Now there is another scent – a mixture of perfume and perspiration that is just a little intoxicating. She murmurs and assists him with the gloves, and lingers within range of an embrace – before she exhales and steps back to admire her handiwork.

'There – perfect.' She gestures to the task at hand. 'And – *there*. One of the legs has given way. The hive is too heavy for me to lift. All it requires is to raise it and slide a brick into place – I brought one earlier.'

They are about fifteen feet from the tilting hive. DS Leyton frowns behind his veil. The more one thinks about certain situations the worse they can seem.

'Geronimo!'

Without further ado he strides into action. As he approaches he sees exactly what needs to be done. One of the front legs – a section of baton about three inches long – has folded beneath the brood box. A brick sits beside it. It is ostensibly a simple job.

Except the hive weighs a ton.

His first attempt – expecting to be able to raise it one-handed like an empty tea chest, while slipping the brick into place with the other – finds the hive not prepared to budge. Kneeling, he tries with two hands. Now he begins to hear buzzing at close quarters. And some bees are crawling over the gloves. There is a hint of movement – but the strength of his arms is insufficient. And anyway how is he going to slide the brick when both hands are hoisting the hive? This is a two-person job. But he can't ask the near-naked woman, despite her claims of immunity. The buzzing is becoming louder and its frequency increasing.

He senses time is running short. There must be a million bees in these hives – if they mobilise their forces he could be overwhelmed in seconds, gloves and veil or not – his shirt will only give him so much protection – he's been bitten through his clothing often enough by the winged fiends that Skelgill refers to as 'clegs'.

He will have to put his back into it. He struggles to his feet and with a grunt bends double and grips the base of the hive, just above the ground. Still it feels like it will not shift – but in contorting he has pulled the tail of his shirt out from his trousers and at this second a bee finds its way in. To his horror it begins crawling northwards.

Emitting a kind of war cry and almost bursting blood vessels he gives a desperate heave and the corner of the hive comes up. With a deceptively sure-footed shuffle he kicks the brick into place and lets go of the box and staggers away flapping his arms.

'There's one up me flippin' shirt!'

Gail Melia moves in swiftly.

'Stand still – they react to violent movement.'

He manages to steel himself.

The woman pulls out his shirt completely and lifts it.

'I don't see anything.'

'Aargh – it's in the hood!'

DS Leyton tugs at the hat but the drawstring of the veil holds it on. The woman's deft fingers set to work and she loosens the cord and yanks off the whole ensemble. But not before the bee has stung him on the nose.

Gripping the injured appendage he seems more self-conscious about his flabby and decidedly pale torso. With his free hand he fumbles to restore his shirt, but she brushes away his efforts and methodically works her way around the waistband, tucking in rather well at the front.

'Oh dear – don't worry – I have some special antihistamine cream – it is very effective.' Her voice is honeyed and soothing. 'They sting Spike all the time – they seem to know he is a conservationist.'

She picks up and hands him his jacket, and grips him by the arm. Feeling somewhat disoriented he complies, still holding his nose and not really taking in what she is saying – but it is something complimentary about muscles, and deserving a drink.

'The hero returns!'

191

Gail Melia announces their success to Sarah Rice, who has remained on her recliner, having witnessed the minor drama from a safe distance.

'I know – I saw.'

From the shadows of her hat she regards DS Leyton appraisingly.

Gail Melia notices her interest.

'Darling – would you fetch the antihistamine cream for Sergeant Leyton? It's in the cupboard above the microwave. And perhaps a fresh round of Pimm's from the jug in the refrigerator. And a glass for our guest.'

DS Leyton protests – and meets some resistance – but on this subject he holds firm and it is agreed that iced water will suffice, and double up to salve the swelling on his nose.

Gail Melia drags over a wooden chair and positions it beside her recliner, onto which she sinks. There is a silky gown draped over the raised back, but she makes no attempt to don it, and seems entirely uninhibited in her scanty outfit.

DS Leyton decides he ought to get down to business. He lowers himself gingerly onto the seat.

'Madam, I take it Dr Rice is not home at the moment.'

She looks a little surprised, that he apparently has some other reason to be present.

'Oh, well – he left early this morning – it is normal for Spike – for a famous communicator he does not excel in communication. He has probably gone birdwatching to Norfolk. I expect he will return tonight. *After dark.*'

She adds the rider with emphasis, as though this fact is intended to be both reassuring and significant, and now she reaches for her glass from the side table, discards the pink-and-white striped straw, and tips back her head to swallow the remaining contents. DS Leyton, hand to nose, watches with some disquiet. He wonders – doubts – if there is any merit in pursuing his rather tenuous line of enquiry. And what would he say? "Madam, I'm looking for a connection between your partner and the sloe gin that poisoned Simon Mills." Hardly. For that matter, how exactly was he going to broach the subject with the man himself? It had seemed a good idea at the time – when he phoned Skelgill – a possible brand new lead when his role in the mission so far has revealed little other than that the local police and public health authorities did their job. Frustrated, he blurts out a spontaneous question.

'Why do you call him Spike?'

Gail Melia laughs – and at this moment Sarah Rice appears from the kitchen door bearing a tray. Perhaps for the purpose of modesty she has put on a short scarlet sarong, but split to the waist it has an alluring effect all of its own.

'Sergeant Leyton is asking why your brother is called Spike.'

Perhaps the hint of a smile teases the corners of Sarah Rice's mouth; it seems to DS Leyton that her lips are freshly applied with lipstick that matches the new garment. She offers the tray so that he may take his water, and then she does the same for Gail Melia. She lifts off her own glass and takes a sip, looking unblinkingly over the rim at DS Leyton.

'He liked to get girls drunk.'

'All before my time.' Gail Melia makes a soft growl in her throat. 'I don't require any such encouragement.'

Sarah Rice's full lips now curve up into a definite smile. She pulls from the hem of her sarong a small white tube.

'Let me do it, Sarah.'

Gail Melia gives no explanation – perhaps there is some unspoken exchange – but the other woman yields the medication to her. Still seated, DS Leyton holds the cold glass of iced water to one side of his nose.

'Turn to me please.'

Gail Melia raises a hand, a blob of cream on her middle finger, her long nails silhouetted against the sun like the claws of a cat. In reaching across, the thin glossy material of the bikini top stretches across the fine details of her contours. Once again the tentacles of the perfume-perspiration concoction assail DS Leyton. He holds his breath and averts his eyes, like a patient awaiting the dentist's drill. But the sensation that follows is the lightest of circling touches. Quite unnerving.

'There – that ought to reduce the pain – if not take away your swelling.'

Multiple thoughts are competing for precedence with DS Leyton's baser emotions. And there is the bizarre admission that Sarah Rice has just made. Moreover, in the back of his mind there rattles some distant memory about the difference between wasps and bees – that a bee leaves its barbed sting in the wound. But the last thing he wants to do is invite closer inspection. Perhaps he could make an excuse to visit the toilet – but there seems to be the real risk that he will be followed and corralled into the house. Then he has the idea of the reflective glass of the extension. He rises to his feet and stretches, as though to shrug off the effects of his exertions.

'Thanks – it's just a scratch. I'll be right as rain in no time.'

'I am sure a little Pimm's would help with that, Sergeant. I really must repay you for your bravery.' Gail Melia regards him invitingly, her large brown eyes so dark with the sun at her back that the pupils and irises seem to merge. She puts a hand briefly against his thigh, and then gestures sinuously to indicate Sarah Rice and herself.

'We *have* had too much to drink of course.'

In her tone there is the clear suggestion of a corollary.

DS Leyton takes an involuntary step back and almost stumbles over his chair. But he keeps his wits and contrives to turn her words in a more suitable direction.

'It's only natural. It'll take a few days to get used to what's happened to you – the loss of your close friend.'

Gail Melia regards him intently for a moment. Then she lies back and sighs gently.

'Sarah's close friend, really. I have only known Daisy these past few years. I met her through Sarah. Sarah has been in cahoots with her since their schooldays.'

'But I think she preferred you.'

Sarah Rice is quick to speak up from the sunbed, a voice from the shadows beneath her wide-brimmed hat. To DS Leyton's ear her tone is entirely artless – if somewhat tipsy and reinforcing of her loose-tongued condition.

Gail Melia waves a dismissive hand.

'Oh, no, darling – not at all. How can you possibly say that?'

'Well – for instance – we always meet Kenneth on his birthday – religiously – we go to The Ivy for lunch. Kenneth had it booked this year – but Daisy phoned me to say she couldn't make it after all – that she was going to a beekeeping fair with you at Oakham. I've never known her put off anything for Kenneth's birthday – she just loved having him wrapped round her little finger.'

A slightly hysterical titter escapes the scarlet lips.

DS Leyton is wondering what he should do. They have struck up this conversation as if he weren't in their presence. He is just thinking it might be a good time to make an expedient exit, when Gail Melia drops her little bombshell.

'Sarah, darling – you must be mistaken. Daisy told me she couldn't come to Oakham – precisely because she was lunching with you and Kenneth in Covent Garden.'

DS Leyton feels the hairs on the back of his neck bristling. As if to remain under the radar he turns and affects an interest in the annexe, and drifts towards where the impressive-looking telescope stands.

Behind him, Sarah Rice is now gazing inquisitively at her brother's companion.

'Gail – she didn't come to The Ivy. In fact she messaged me afterwards to say she got sunburned at the fair because it was an unexpectedly hot day for April.'

DS Leyton hears Gail Melia inhale to speak – but then something must strike her, for the retort never comes. At least, not for an unnaturally long moment.

'Oh – well, I must be thinking of something else.'

Sensing that he might be suspected of eavesdropping – not that he could help it – but of showing an interest, then – DS Leyton steps into the open annexe. It is a magnificent viewing room and study, entirely glass-fronted and minimalistic in its design and contents; he notices a shelf with bird books arranged in ascending size order; and three identical looking outdoor jackets hang neatly on a row of hooks, each with an identical hat.

195

He rounds to the back of the telescope and has to raise himself on tiptoes to look into the eyepiece. Now Gail Melia calls out; her voice has regained its customary purr.

'I am afraid Sarah and I might be in your line of sight.'

He senses he really ought to respond in kind – something jokey, like, isn't that what it's for – for spying on 'birds' – when he realises that the telescope is indeed focused upon a distant cottage, with a patio where, if he is not mistaken, a young female lies prone upon a lounger.

'I just thought I'd see if there's any rare ducks on that lake. Now it's not Rutland Water reaching all this way, is it? I know it's supposed to be big, but –'

Gail Melia enlightens him.

'It is called Eye Brook reservoir. Apart from its ornithological interest, apparently it is where the Dambusters performed their final practice runs before they set off to Germany.'

'Whoa – what a sight that would've been!'

DS Leyton sounds genuinely enthralled by the prospect. He has a vague idea of how to use the twist-grip and now makes a show of adjusting the trajectory. What is not apparent is that he does indeed home in on the two women before him – they are much too close to focus upon, indeed, blurred they more than fill the picture – but what he can discern is that they are both now facing away, back into the sun. Deftly he slips his mobile phone from his pocket and undertakes a brief transaction. Then he returns his attention to the reservoir, and performs a sweep just above the water, imagining the reverberating throb of the Lancaster bombers as they ran the gauntlet of the Nazi guns. Never mind taking on a swarm of bees; that was heroism.

Then his phone rings.

Rather than answer it immediately he leaves it in his pocket – and makes a few adjustments of the telescope, to return it to its original position. He notes that the girl has gone.

Since the phone continues to ring Gail Melia raises herself on an elbow and turns her head – just as DS Leyton is stepping out of the viewing gallery and tapping at his handset.

'DS Leyton.'

Evidently it is a police call. She watches as he listens. A frown creases his brow and he looks at her and contorts his features resignedly. He consults his wristwatch.

'Righto, Guvnor – I reckon I can be there within the hour. Leave it with me. I'll call you for the address once I'm on the road. I'll just say my goodbyes and get back to you in two ticks.'

17. MEANDERS

Monday, 5.30 p.m. – Middlemarch

'Here he comes, Guv – perfect timing.'

DS Jones is watching the nearside mirror from the passenger seat of Skelgill's car. They are parked outside a busy fish and chip shop. Skelgill glances at his wing mirror. A familiar stocky form has rounded the corner of the suburban street and is marching with a rolling gait along the pavement in their direction. He has his briefcase in one hand and a white carrier bag in the other. Skelgill lowers his window and calls out as their colleague comes within earshot.

'Step on it, Leyton – your chips are going cold.'

DS Leyton slides into the bench seat behind Skelgill. A packet wrapped in newspaper rests in the centre.

'Nice one, Guvnor – you don't mind eating in the car?'

This is a moot point: Skelgill and DS Jones have their part-consumed meals spread on their laps.

'What – like it might make it smell of fish?'

DS Jones glances over her shoulder with a grin – it is always a good sign when Skelgill takes the mickey out of himself. DS Leyton winks at her.

'Nothing like eating it piping hot from the good old Currant Bun, Guv.'

They know enough of their colleague's East End vernacular to understand he means the infamous tabloid. Skelgill has another take on it.

'Saves on the washing up, Leyton.'

DS Leyton wastes no time in unfolding the reassuringly warm parcel. As he does so, DS Jones comments.

'We got you a large cod and chips – in case you haven't had lunch.'

DS Leyton is reminded that he ought hardly need to eat at all – but the pungent aroma of salt and vinegar strikes straight at the hunger cortex of his brain. He tucks in. He can see DS Jones, too, has a battered fish.

'What have you got, Guv – cod and chips an' all?'

'Aye.' Skelgill glances rather sheepishly at DS Jones. 'And a steak and kidney pie.'

DS Leyton chuckles.

'They like their pies round here.'

Skelgill stretches his neck to look into the rear-view mirror – as if to check whether DS Leyton is ribbing him – when he spies the swelling on his sergeant's nose.

'Hey up – it's Conky the Clown! What happened to you?'

DS Jones turns urgently – her colleague's nasal distension is on the side away from her and she had not noticed it. DS Leyton seems to be making light of Skelgill's jibe, though he would be entitled to think that Skelgill is the last person to be teasing anyone about big noses.

'You might say I got a bee in my bonnet, Guv. Although that's only half the story.'

He breaks off and bites into a crunchy chunk of battered cod. It is indeed piping hot, and he has to pant rapidly to cool it.

DS Jones fills the little hiatus.

'Is that why you sent your SOS?'

She refers to his text message urgently imploring her to phone him – his excuse to escape the overbearing company of Gail Melia and Sarah Rice. Now, with his mouth still full, DS Leyton can only move his head in an unstipulated manner that might mean either yes or no, or indeed both. He gulps rather prematurely, trusting the filleter did their job well.

'You ever seen that film, The Witches of Eastwick?'

DS Jones regards him wide-eyed. She glances at Skelgill – no doubt he has heard of it – but he is less likely to have watched it, and he carries on eating, unconcerned. DS Leyton pulls a face that seems to convey that he experienced a narrow escape.

'That Gail Melia – she's a – friendly sort, you might say.'

The euphemism prompts Skelgill's eyes to flash at him in the mirror as though it strikes a chord. But DS Leyton steers away from the potentially more prurient aspects of his encounter.

'She roped me in with her flamin' beekeeping – one of the hives was standing all to cock. I had to right it. The bees didn't take kindly. That's how I got stung. The doctor geezer wasn't there – he'd done a bunk, birdwatching over in Norfolk. But I had a butcher's through his telescope. Tallish cove, is he, Guv?'

'About my height, aye.' Skelgill's tone is that of, "So what?"

'Where they live – it overlooks Eye Brook reservoir. Fair enough – he's one of those twitcher types – but the telescope was focused on a cottage where a young female was sunbathing on the patio. It couldn't have been either of the women set it up, they weren't tall enough – I had to stretch to see, myself.'

He signifies that he has concluded this little piece by eating a cluster of chips. Skelgill looks like he could be thinking, "telescope – attractive girl – is there any surprise?" Lock a man in a room with a tea cosy and a mirror and wait to see just how long it takes for him to try it on. His mantra in this short investigation has been to warn of the inevitability of erroneous revelations rearing their heads.

But DS Leyton has a follow-up.

'Did you happen know how he got his nickname – Spike?' (Both eating, his colleagues shake their heads.) 'Seems he had a teenage thing for getting a girl drunk. And I looked up his Wikipedia profile. It says he studied for a PhD in bird migration – but before that he took biochemistry at the University of East Anglia.'

It is a contribution that is harder to dismiss. There is an unarguable correlation when it comes to biochemistry, spiking drinks and the death by poisoning of Simon Mills. Skelgill responds accordingly.

'What about his connection to Rutland Gin?'

Now DS Leyton emits a low groan.

'Him not being there – I couldn't find a way of introducing the subject.'

Having reviewed this failure driving away, he suspects that had he so much as mentioned an interest in alcohol the two women would have pounced, and he would still be there now, sipping cocktails whilst bathing in a Jacuzzi filled with melted honey.

'To be honest, Guv – on reflection I don't reckon the sponsorship deal is much of a lead – I'll explain why in a mo. But I am fairly certain that the sloe gin was tampered with.'

In the mirror he sees his superior's brow furrow with dissatisfaction.

'I thought you said it was all above board?'

'What I meant, Guv – the reports were accurate as far as it went. But listen to this. There was an incident in Scotland, back in the nineties, when a similar thing occurred. This geezer worked at a university and had access to the poison – same stuff, atropine – apparently tried unsuccessfully to bump off his missus by contaminating a batch of tonic water in a local supermarket – kept one of the bottles for himself, and gave her a stronger dose. Since there were other poisoned bottles circulating in the community, it made it look like random chance – and that some blackmailer was at large.'

To his surprise he sees that Skelgill is nodding. Indeed Skelgill speaks.

'The Grisholm case – this came up.' He glances at DS Jones, his tone inviting her to agree. 'The prof – Hans Sinisalu told me about it. That wasn't so much the MO we were looking at – but more about detecting the poison – atropine, it's metabolised quickly and leaves few traces.'

There is a pause before DS Leyton responds.

'Well, this Edinburgh case, Guv – it *is* a blueprint for the MO. They say there's nothing new under the sun. And the geezer who runs the distillery, he's adamant it couldn't have happened there. A single batch of sloe gin was made, and yet only one case of six bottles, a fraction of it, was contaminated. So that case must have been doctored somewhere further down the supply chain.'

'Up to and including the off licence?' It is DS Jones that chips in. 'Surely that would be the only stage in the process when it would be possible to take a bottle, apparently innocently, and target someone?'

DS Leyton is nodding.

'That's right – that could only have been done at the store.' Now however he rows back a little. 'But it doesn't stop it having been someone with a grudge, a nutcase – or an extortionist who lost their nerve – someone who had nothing to do with the Mills crowd. And I suppose there's also the possibility that it could have been a rival shopkeeper, trying to kybosh his competitor's business at Christmas.'

Again they sink into silent rumination, although in Skelgill's case he does not let it interfere with his supper. After a while DS Leyton feels mounting pressure to elaborate upon his conclusion.

'I reckon, even if Dr Charles Rice had got himself a bottle of that particular gin – he might have bought it in Uppingham – there's no way he could have known there'd be another case of the stuff waiting in a shop in Middlemarch. They only produced twenty cases for the whole country.'

With a sudden vigour Skelgill screws up his newsprint chip wrappings and casts about outside the car for a waste bin. He notices the shop has no queue.

'Reet – I'll fetch tea while yon chippy's quiet. You want a mash, Leyton?'

'I'll get 'em, Guv.'

DS Leyton opens his door but he is impeded by his luggage in the footwell. He pulls free the carrier bag.

'While you're waiting – I've come bearing gifts from Rutland.'

He produces first the carton of miniatures.

'There you go, Emma – for the gin connoisseur. I'm assured they're quality tested and poison-free.'

She seems suitably amused and delighted and examines the pack.

'Multum in Parvo?'

'Yeah – now what the heck does that mean, girl? You're the educated one around here – no offence, Guv – but I'm guessing you never took Latin.'

Skelgill growls but lets it pass. DS Jones holds up the item.

'Quite appropriate for miniatures. I suppose a modern iteration would be along the lines of "punches above its weight" – literally *much in little.*'

'Hah – there you go, I knew it was something like that.' DS Leyton delves again into the bag. 'And for you, Guv – no need to punch above its weight – it's already a flippin' doorstopper.'

He hands over the hefty pork pie in its artisan paper wrapper. Skelgill, never one to find it easy to accept a gift – something about the social convention of having to act pleased when one might not be – looks relieved that the offering is not of a personal nature. He raises an inquisitive eyebrow.

'Cheers, Leyton.'

'Thought it might do for your tea, for the next couple of nights, Guv.'

Skelgill weighs the item in his palm, as though he is assessing its poundage by reference to his long experience with fish. However, he cannot seem to think of anything to add, so DS Leyton resumes his mission.

'Right – three cups of cha coming up.'

'Plenty of sugar, Leyton.'

DS Leyton closes the door but raises a hand in acknowledgement as he moves away – in fact showing four fingers with his thumb tucked in which might indicate his understanding of what will be suitable. When he returns a couple of minutes later with three takeaway drinks in a cup carrier he thinks of passing it into Skelgill's open window – when he realises that his boss has both hands full and his nose buried in the pork pie wrapper. He rounds to DS Jones's side – she grins at him helplessly and relieves him of the card tray. He resumes his seat and DS Jones passes back his tea.

'Would this be a good moment for me to say I've saved the best bit until last?'

There comes something of a splutter from Skelgill.

'What's that supposed to mean, Leyton?'

'Well – thing is – forget Dr Charles Rice for a minute, and the poisoning malarkey – this is something about Daisy Mills – that her female friends let slip and then tried to gloss over.'

He has their attention, and now relates the account of how Daisy Mills had committed to be in two places at once, and in fact was at neither. DS Jones shifts directly into action mode. She places her drink in the central console and extracts her notes and phone from the door pocket. First she scrutinises the printout.

'Kenneth Dalbrae's date of birth is the 6th of April.'

Now she performs a search on her mobile. She looks up questioningly at Skelgill and then turns to DS Leyton.

'Exactly the same day as the Oakham Beekeepers' Fair. About a month ago.'

Another silence ensues, broken only by Skelgill's crunching of pie crust and DS Leyton attempting a slurp of tea that is still too hot for him.

Skelgill now shows some interest.

'What day of the week was it?'

'Wednesday.'

Skelgill is not wishing to read too much into this development, but there are straws in the wind – which tally with DS Jones's earlier supposition that Daisy Mills might have been seeing someone – someone whose identity needed to remain unknown – indeed even that the act of meeting must remain secret – and a weekday would suggest someone who works, or at least for whom being absent on a Saturday or Sunday might be more difficult to explain. But he checks himself. It is so easy to take conjecture a step too far. Suddenly, branches open up in the path ahead, and only one of them can be right. However, he knows his colleagues will be thinking along similar lines, and he offers a little encouragement to DS Leyton.

'We found a tracker on her car. It were clarty – like it had been there a good time.'

Skelgill looks interrogatively at DS Jones. Obligingly she flips open the glove box and draws out the item in a clear evidence bag. She holds it up for DS Leyton to see. He appears fascinated.

'You reckon her old man was on her case? Like he suspected her – before he died.'

'He could hardly suspect her afterwards, Leyton.'

But the suggestion from Skelgill's manner is that it is considered most likely.

'You know what I mean, Guv.'

DS Jones inhales to speak but hesitates, as though the thought is not fully formed. Her colleagues regard her with anticipation.

'Then why not come out, once he did die? She was a free agent, you might say.'

Her tone, her adjustment, suggests she already has an answer.

DS Leyton obliges her. In company with Skelgill, he is reminded of her hypothesis.

'Like you said before, Emma – when you were talking about that "Do Not Ring" phone number – what if it's someone whose identity can't be revealed? A married man.'

DS Jones regards him with a twinkle in her eye, as though she thinks he is demonstrating predictable naivety.

'Or just someone who is going out with one of her best friends?'

DS Leyton regards her intently. He gives a small nod.

'Fair point, girl. So who does that cover?'

DS Jones looks down at the sheet of notes.

'Well – best friends – we have Sarah Rice possibly involved with Rik Hannay, Gail Melia certainly in a relationship with Dr Charles Rice – and –' (she glances apprehensively at Skelgill) ' – if we include her sister, I wouldn't rule out that Poppy Lux is involved with Karl Eastwood. He is also married, of course, as is Hugo Grant. For completeness I should add that so are Kenneth Dalbrae and Ben Lomond.'

'Wait a minute – who's left?' DS Leyton starts counting on his fingers. 'Among the geezers that only leaves Harry Badger!'

'No danger there.' The cynical quip comes from Skelgill. 'But you're right about the other half dozen.'

DS Leyton shrugs resignedly.

'At least we've got the 6th of April, Guv. Maybe we can find out where each of them were?'

Skelgill laughs.

'I think I can tell you where Kenneth Dalbrae was.'

DS Leyton looks suitably chastised. He touches his nose with his index finger and points at Skelgill.

'Good point, Guv – I guess that gets him off the hook – and presumably his partner.'

Skelgill shrugs at this. And he raises his eyes to the watery evening sky, its flotilla of clouds becalmed and attenuated.

'That tracker – happen that could do us a favour. If only.'

DS Jones knows he means that it most likely has not been active of late. But she puts it with extra care back into the glove compartment. With similar attention to detail Skelgill folds the wrapper around the remnants of his pork pie and sets it on the dashboard. He pushes open his door.

'Come on – let's stretch the old shanks. We can talk and walk.'

DS Jones notes that, as in Leamington, Skelgill seems to know the way. Twenty minutes earlier they left the M69 motorway and entered a sprawling dormitory village that borders on Middlemarch, using satellite technology to locate the nearest fish and chip shop, near to where it was also convenient for DS Leyton to be dropped off by the PC collecting his pool car. Now Skelgill wheels left-handed around the block of shops and takeaways above which modest flats are built, onto a generously wide road that forms the central avenue of a 1950s housing estate. The properties are constructed of low-grade red brick, unprepossessing, their architecture the basic lines that a child would draw, former social housing snapped up for a song by their tenants, a not-inconsequential skirmish in Mrs Thatcher's war on society. Most have their front boundaries dismantled and their small gardens paved, and an excess of mid-range cars crammed onto these makeshift driveways. For a few minutes the three colleagues walk in silence, alone with their thoughts – perhaps it is just the introduction to this community, of which there are thousands like it across Britain; perhaps wondering what the people are like who live here – right now it seems they are all indoors having their tea.

Also as in Leamington, DS Jones suspects an ulterior motive for Skelgill's choice of route. Having gently perambulated downhill, they turn into a long straight level road called Brookside. It won't be called "brook side" for nothing! But, if there once were a brook by which locals navigated, Skelgill is disappointed – for when he departs at a right angle onto a footpath between allotments and waste ground, where a stream might reasonably be expected to flow, they reach only a bridge over a railway line, and indeed a small railway station. Skelgill mutters something unintelligible about a culvert – but they pause on the bridge, since a train approaches from the east. It is of the short-hop variety, its destination plate, "Birmingham New Street". It stops and a few people get out and quickly disappear; they look like commuters arriving home. Skelgill ventures that the train has come from Leicester, and ushers them on. They cross the bridge and leave through the station, which appears to be unmanned. They head away, now moving up a mild gradient, the road lined by more substantial Victorian villas in the same red brick as the station, some quite grand, four storeys with large bay windows on the ground floor and gable rooms in the attic, a mixture of residential and businesses – dentists, doctors and lawyers. Skelgill glimpses a nameplate that seems to read "Pray & Pray, Solicitors".

Perhaps it is the latter, or perhaps they have had sufficient of a break to clear their heads and assimilate DS Leyton's news – but now Skelgill offers a prompt to DS Jones.

'Want to tell Leyton about the wills – or not?'

His words might seem confusing, but DS Jones understands his meaning. She and DS Leyton are walking on either side of Skelgill, but now she and Skelgill swap places so she may more easily be heard without raising her voice.

'We got the address of the Mills' firm of solicitors from an envelope at their house.' Her explanation is diplomatic, given that Skelgill employed a somewhat sneaky tactic to achieve this

207

without alerting Poppy Lux to their interest. 'They're based in Leamington, where Eastwood-Mills Assurance also has its office. An insurance policy paid out such that Simon Mills' shares went to Karl Eastwood in return for a cash sum to the estate – which was left in its entirety to Daisy Mills. She, it appears, despite written prompting from her solicitor, did not make a will. She was in the process of inheriting a substantial fortune. To all intents and purposes, that now goes to her sister, Poppy Lux.' DS Jones glances at Skelgill. 'Here I should add that we got to the Mills' house early. Poppy Lux arrived with Karl Eastwood – which you may think was curious. He made himself scarce – and did the same thing when we turned up outside his office later.'

She checks briefly that Skelgill seems satisfied with this aspect of the account – he nods cursorily. She turns to DS Leyton, inviting his reaction; it is typically forthright.

'So that's why you're saying they might be canoodling? In cahoots, even. She gets the dough, he gets the business?'

There is a silence before Skelgill pronounces.

'That's what's happened, Leyton, canoodling or not.'

But DS Leyton sees that his female colleague is unsettled.

'You not happy with that, Emma?'

DS Jones makes a conciliatory gesture, raising her hand to touch her associate's sleeve.

'Look – I certainly see that Poppy Lux is what you might call the poor relation. Daisy got the good looks and a string of rich husbands. Poppy has probably walked in her shadow for much of her life. But conspiracy to murder – that feels impossible to me.'

She notes that Skelgill begins to nod reflectively, as though he gives credence to her intuition above any rationale. However, DS Leyton is happy to extend the speculation.

'But she'd have the Eastwood geezer to do all the dirty work. First he poisons his business partner, then he waits for an opportunity to bump off the widow. He was present and correct on both occasions – and we've only got his word that he went for a newspaper on Sunday morning. What if he followed Daisy

Mills up to that waterfall? And it could have been him that dialled 999.'

Skelgill makes an exasperated growl.

'Leyton – I thought you'd got Dr Charles Rice down as prime suspect?'

DS Leyton holds out a palm in an accommodating gesture.

'Look – I'm just trying to keep an open mind. Right enough, he seems like a queer old cove. I've seen him on the telly – he never looks straight at you.'

DS Jones chuckles, although she does not offer an explanation, and DS Leyton continues.

'He goes back a long way with Daisy Mills – him and his sister, who seems to have had her nose put out of joint. Driving back, I've been racking me brains, obviously.'

'We could hear you in Warwickshire, Leyton.'

'Very funny, Guv – but what I'm trying to say is – when Gail Melia clammed up – I thought, who was she trying to protect? What if it weren't Daisy Mills but Dr Charles Rice? What if she realised he was away that day, an' all? Maybe he's the secret bloke – maybe he's our Darth Vader?'

Now Skelgill laughs, too – although it is a laugh that as much as anything speaks of vindication – that their latest discussion only serves to confirm his theory – in just a few minutes they have constructed two entirely opposing outcomes.

'Leyton – if it's any consolation we've put Harry Badger down as Darth Vader. He's got the full Star Wars collection in his caravan.'

'Caravan?'

Skelgill looks at DS Jones.

'Do you want to tell him?'

She grins – but cautiously – for she is not entirely sure where Skelgill has come out on Harry Badger. She relates their encounter at the residential site; that there was little to learn other than it reiterated their view of him as sleazy, bitter, hard up and boozed up. To add to which there was Poppy Lux's vehemence that her sister would have had nothing to do with him. He had admitted he was unemployed rather than retired, and that he cycled about the vicinity – within easy reach there being a supermarket on the outskirts of Middlemarch (where he was probably no stranger to the drinks aisle) and in the other direction the Mills' property. At the end of her account, DS Leyton requests clarification.

'But you're writing him off?'

'Nay.'

It is Skelgill's interjection. DS Jones nods to herself. Skelgill notices her reaction – he points an accusing finger at her and then at DS Leyton.

'Look – you pair have come up with your pet ideas. Let's make the case for Harry Badger, why don't we?' Skelgill's tone is thickly laced with sarcasm. 'It's obvious he's been pestering Daisy Mills – maybe Simon Mills warned him off and made an enemy of himself. What did Harry Badger do for a living? He was a pharmaceutical rep. There's your poison. As for Daisy Mills – there was the whole fracas surrounding the séance. Badger could have moved the pointer – and then we know he was alone with her. He could have tried it on – hence the bruises on her wrists. He could have sent the photo – with the enticing message about Simon Mills. She might have agreed to see him at the falls. He turns up drunk or deluded or both. He tells her he poisoned her husband so she can be with him. She resists his advances – or maybe threatens to report him – there's a struggle – and he drowns her. On his way back he sees Dalbrae heading up through the trees – he hides – and makes the phone call to put him in the frame. He creeps back in and pretends he's sleeping off a hangover like half of the others.

'Or – while we're on the subject of Kenneth Dalbrae – let's not forget we found him alone with Daisy Mills' body. Aye, he was a convincing witness – but now we know there were tensions between him and Simon Mills. Meanwhile Daisy Mills stood him up on his birthday. What if it were his partner she was seeing? Hardly grounds for murder – true – but who arranged the trip to Rydal Grange? Who organised the séance? He did. He could have moved the pointer. He was alone with her before the others could react. And next morning he followed her to Buckstones Jump. And he also had time to make the phone call.'

This little diatribe stuns Skelgill's colleagues into silence. Not just that he has confounded them by breaking his own rules of analysis, but also that he has reeled off a couple of perfectly plausible alternative explanations for what took place. In the absence of any feedback, Skelgill veers away and peers into the window of a public house they are just passing. He emits a scornful snort and stalks back.

'Keg palace.'

But the suggestion that they could all do with a drink does not meet any dissent. They are approaching the town centre. DS Leyton perks up.

'Wait a minute – this is where I was this morning – that's Castle Street on the right. It's where the off licence is. Up at the top, pedestrianised. We had to park in the market place just past the junction – if I recall, there's a couple of decent-looking boozers, Guv.'

Presently, Skelgill is drawn to a sign, "Finest Cask Ales". The pub is The Knitter's Arms, in his eyes suitably lacking in ostentation. This is of course a town whose captains of the industrial revolution made their money in hosiery and textiles, and whose ragtag army of dexters and quillers and reelers *spent* their money in hostelries such as this. From a corridor they select the "Tap Room", Skelgill following his nose to the real ale. Still early, only a couple of old fellows play dominoes and a young Goth girl aimlessly throws darts at a board. She proves to be the barista, taking up her station and eyeing them suspiciously. Skelgill, too, scowls, but in his case at the unfamiliar badges on the polished oak hand-pumps.

'I'll get 'em, Guvnor.' DS Leyton moves forward. 'You got the chips.'

In fact it was DS Jones who paid for their supper, but Skelgill is preoccupied.

'Whichever's the ordinary bitter.'

The girl, despite her apparent disinterest, reaches below the bar for a glass and takes firm hold of a pump marked "Burton

Ale"'. She is stronger than she looks, or she has mastered the technique, for a jet of pale amber liquid spurts reassuringly into the vessel. Skelgill turns away; he spies vacant seats in an alcove. He calls over his shoulder. 'Get us a couple of bags of cheese and onion, Leyton.'

DS Leyton grins at DS Jones.

'G&T, Emma?'

'So long as you watch carefully.' She returns the smile. 'I'll skip the crisps.'

DS Leyton brings the drinks to their table, three glasses clamped together and the crisps tucked under his chin. He drops the crisps like a faithful hound returning a trophy to its master; he beams.

'Cheap round, Guv. I got change of a tenner.'

Skelgill seems to have been expecting this.

'It's a proper town, Leyton. Don't forget, in the Lakes we're brainwashed – we get stung for tourist rates.'

DS Leyton takes his seat; they have all three sides of the bench that lines the niche, a cosy arrangement.

'I don't suppose I drink enough for it to make much difference. Just the odd pint of Forsythe Saga.'

He lifts his glass by way of illustration; he watches Skelgill, who sips tentatively, and then sups more substantially.

'How's your real ale, Guv?'

Skelgill smacks his lips.

'Surprisingly good. Cheers, Leyton.'

Skelgill puts down his bitter and pops open bag of crisps; then he seems to realise he ought to share and he tears apart the wrapper and lays it on the table so they may all partake.

It is DS Leyton, however, that gets them back on track with their business.

'So where are we – looking for the geezer that Daisy Mills might have been having a secret affair with? Is that the key to all this? Find out who he is and we unlock the rest of the story?'

Skelgill's reaction appears ambivalent – indeed he seems more interested in his newly discovered brand of beer. He has heard of 'burtonisation' to improve the quality of water for brewing –

but around here it comes out of the ground naturally smelling of sulphur. Some folk would prefer to bathe in the mineral springs – but he reckons the brewers got it about right.

DS Jones gently swills the ice about her glass and regards it pensively. From her perspective – their emphasis today upon matters financial, Poppy Lux and the elusive Karl Eastwood, makes DS Leyton's diagnosis seem too constraining; and she would not expect Skelgill to pin his colours to a single mast just yet. She puts forward her own suggestion.

'I know it's a Catch 22 – like we've said – if one's a murder it makes the other more likely to be a murder – and that the complete opposite applies. But are we trying too hard to connect the two deaths?'

What DS Jones says has logical appeal, for in looking at one death they are hamstrung by the idiosyncrasies of the other; this is no 'serial killer' situation, where the evidence of successive slayings is helpfully cumulative. They probably *are* trying too hard. But for the first time, and yet with no immediate rational counterpoint coming to mind, Skelgill finds himself harbouring a powerful sentiment. Somewhere in the mists between his subconscious and his conscious drifts a certainty, vague though its present form may be, a ghost ship bereft of crew; he can hear the black waters lapping against the decaying hull.

That moment at the Ouija board when "murder" was spelled out, for him indisputably links the two deaths. As to who would do that, and why, maybe they are no clearer. But to cast off and float separately the two events does not sit comfortably with his instincts. And, while his colleagues have stressed 'money' or 'love' as pre-eminent motives, he senses more sinister forces at play, their darker counterparts, greed and envy, harbingers of wrath.

However, as is often the case when such abstractions threaten to confound him, Skelgill has a practical solution. He rises abruptly and waggles his empty glass.

'I don't know about you pair, but I could murder another pint.'

213

18. POLICE HQ - 1

Tuesday afternoon – DI Skelgill's office

'See if I can get this thing to work, Guv. She said she'd cued it up after the preamble. She said not to wait – the Dalbrae geezer's just returned her call and she didn't want to miss him again.'

DS Leyton has DS Jones's electronic tablet. He settles across from Skelgill in the latter's office and reaches with a groan to place the device on his desk. He taps where instructed and a recording begins to play. There is background sibilance that suggests one of the parties is speaking hands-free in a moving vehicle. Then comes DS Jones's voice.

"Mr Eastwood, we were hoping to meet with you yesterday when we came down to the Midlands."

"Ah? I didn't realise. I imagined you wouldn't want me cramping Poppy's style – me not being one of the family. I thought I should get out of your hair."

Skelgill now appreciates that the man's accent has a distinct West Midlands nasal twang, although his enunciation is clear and precise. He sounds older than Skelgill would have guessed from his rather slick appearance.

'Actually, sir, I meant in Leamington."

"Oh?"

DS Jones inserts a deliberate pause, but the man does not rise to the bait.

"We were parked outside your office at about a quarter to two. You were just leaving. You seemed to see us."

"I had no idea you were coming."

The answer is potentially evasive, but DS Jones evidently decides not to put him any more on the defensive. When they had telephoned after their meeting with Esther Jarndyce, Karl

Eastwood's secretary had informed them he would not be back that afternoon; meanwhile his mobile was diverting to voicemail. DS Jones had not left a message in either case, nor revealed her identity to the receptionist. If they really needed to check his whereabouts, it was well within their powers.

"Mr Eastwood, in trying to understand what happened to Mrs Mills, we intend to carry out a form of reconstruction next Sunday morning. People have regular habits, and it may jog the memory of someone who was passing, who might have seen her."

"Are you saying I will be required?"

Thus far confident, a distinct note of unease has entered the man's voice.

"Not in person. If we replicate known events we use stand-ins. It is from unrelated members of the public that we would hope to gain information. I just wanted to re-confirm the timings that you gave us."

There is another pause, and the man seems to realise the onus is upon him to speak.

"When I woke I had a feeling nobody would be up and about for a good while. I'd noticed the local shop as we were arriving. I figured it might open at seven-thirty, and the time was shortly before – I couldn't say to the minute, I'm afraid. All I did was to drive there, buy the Sunday Telegraph, and drive back. I was gone at most fifteen minutes."

"You said that you travelled directly to Grasmere via the lane from Rydal Grange and the A591 and returned by the same route. You didn't stop or deviate. You didn't see any member of your party, either from the car or at Rydal Grange."

He hesitates to answer – though he seems to understand these statements are questions.

"Look – if you're doing a reconstruction – I must have passed another vehicle or two coming in the opposite direction. But I couldn't swear to it. When I got back no one was stirring. I took a coffee up to my room. I read some of the paper and I must have nodded off. The next thing I was aware of was voices and movement around nine."

"Sir, could you have been mistaken? Could it have in fact been an hour earlier that you went out?"

"What? I don't see how, officer." He is plainly disconcerted by this rapier-like thrust that verges on an accusation. "I mean – well, they must remember me in the shop – surely they have CCTV?"

Skelgill and DS Leyton exchange significant glances. They know DS Jones was not thinking of the shop, but of the possibility that Karl Eastwood left at the same time as Daisy Mills, and later went to purchase a newspaper. But he would hardly admit it. Her question can only be to "rattle his cage" as Skelgill sees it. And he does sound a little rattled. It interests Skelgill that the man has cottoned on to the idea of having an alibi of sorts. Also of note is that DS Jones simply moves on.

"Mr Eastwood, Mrs Mills – together with her sister – travelled up to the Lakes in your car. Was there anything she said or that was discussed which on reflection might be connected in any way to what happened to her?"

Karl Eastwood seems to have gathered his wits, and counters with a question of his own.

"Sergeant Jones – may I ask, what are you driving at?"

"It's just a simple question, sir – you were one of a few people that spent an uninterrupted period in Mrs Mills' company."

"Actually, officer, Daisy slept most of the way. She and Poppy started out by sharing a half bottle of rosé. What conversation took place consisted mainly of them talking about their old school friends – whom I barely know and so I was largely zoned out."

DS Jones is quick to make an inference.

"What you just said there, sir. How did it come about that you were included in the party?"

There is a delay before Karl Eastwood speaks.

"Sorry – you broke up for a moment. I didn't quite catch – "

He could be playing for time. DS Jones repeats the question. But when he answers there is a distinct change of tone in the man's voice – what sounds like self-deprecation.

"I think it was probably an error in the first instance."

"Could you explain that, sir?"

"The Christmas party – the cocktail evening that Simon hosted for Daisy – the idea was a 'friends reunited' thing – something to do with them all beginning to hit the sixty mark. I don't know why Simon got me along – keep him company, maybe. Although as it turned out there were a handful of partners, outsiders – five of us if you include Simon. Anyway, when they started to arrange the second reunion in the Lakes, they cc'd the same group email list. I rather suspect they thought they couldn't very well exclude me once the invitation went out."

"Just to clarify, sir, "they" being Kenneth Dalbrae and Daisy Mills?"

"Well, Kenneth Dalbrae started the ball rolling, but several people chipped in with suggestions before the date and location were finalised. Certainly Kenneth Dalbrae was the principal organiser."

DS Jones again demonstrates her aptitude for listening and questioning simultaneously.

"Mr Eastwood – you said in the *first* instance?"

Now the man gives a rueful laugh.

"Well – I don't think it escaped Daisy that a chauffeur might come in handy." He clears his throat. "But of course I was happy to support her – she'd lost Simon, after all."

To Skelgill's ear he sounds like he considered that he had been going through the motions, doing what would be expected rather than what was necessary. Of course, he could have declined to take part in the trip. DS Jones is thinking along similar lines.

"Sir. You mentioned that several of the group took their partners. What was the situation regarding your wife? Was she not invited?"

"Ah, well – she opted out of the original cocktail party – she doesn't drink alcohol – and she really wouldn't have known anyone. As for the Lakes, in any event she was unable to come. This week she is a delegate at an annual conference in Brighton."

"What would that be, sir?"

He seems to consider whether he ought to answer.

"I think you would know it as NPCC."

They hear DS Jones draw breath – Skelgill and DS Leyton look at one another in alarm. They indeed know NPCC – as the National Police Chiefs' Council. Only very senior ranks and executives are members. However, DS Jones quickly regroups.

"Your wife is a police officer?"

"She is on the staff side. Director of Finance for South Mercia Constabulary."

DS Jones pauses. Her colleagues can almost hear her mental machinations, determining not to become sidetracked. But it creates a respectful gap before her next question.

"Sir, how well did you know Daisy Mills?"

Perhaps subconsciously she avoids the use of the title, Mrs.

"Not that well, actually. We didn't socialise – as couples, I mean. I've had dinner – well, takeaways – at Simon's place a few times, when we've travelled in one car and have arrived back late. But we set up the business as colleagues rather than friends – we had different interests and our own established social groups."

"Did you form an opinion of the relationship between Mr and Mrs Mills?"

"Frankly?"

"That would be most helpful, sir."

"To be honest, sergeant – and I would never have said this to anyone – but, now – well, they are both gone and there's no one to harm – in my view Daisy was badly spoiled, and Simon pandered to that."

DS Jones pulls him up on a technicality.

"There is Poppy Lux – to be offended."

"I think you'll find she holds the same view – though she may not admit it publically."

Their own findings are consistent with the man's assessment. And perhaps the revelation of his wife's job now casts him in a somewhat different light. DS Jones evidently decides to confide on this issue.

"In fact she suggested to us that Simon Mills was doting to the point of being possessive. Would you agree with that?"

"I would say he was potentially that sort of guy – but that it was Daisy who would bring it out of a man. She was a good-looking woman – and she made you think there were possibilities, when she engaged with you."

"Possibilities?"

"I can't say more than that. She liked to be popular amongst the men, put it that way – but her chief confidante was Kenneth Dalbrae, as far as I could gather."

DS Jones is evidently supposed to draw her own conclusions. But she has a point here.

"There was some suggestion that he wasn't in favour with Simon Mills?"

"Maybe he liked to monopolise her time."

DS Jones considers the suggestion.

"Was that an issue for Mr Mills?"

Now Karl Eastwood takes a moment to reflect.

"Simon and I had separate offices. I occasionally overheard him on the phone to her. I would say there was something of a father to a slightly wayward teenage daughter. My impression is that Daisy's personality was a conflation of the free spirit with the unworldly. And sometimes I would suspect the latter was more for convenience than it was genuine. Perhaps Kenneth Dalbrae was a harmless scapegoat when she suddenly found herself drunk in Soho and unable to drive home for dinner. And she would annoy Simon by letting her phone run out of charge."

Skelgill is reflecting that, despite his protestations to be an outsider, Karl Eastwood is in fact probably giving them the most objective appraisal of Daisy Mills to date, to complement the more abstract insight provided by Hugo Grant. And – he suppresses a grin – the flat batteries scenario strikes a chord; a person needs a tactic for preserving their sanity.

It seems DS Jones is now prompted by the description of Daisy Mills – that quite probably she had ignored correspondence from Esther Jarndyce.

"One related aspect you might be able to shed light upon. Were you aware of any financial issues that Mrs Mills was facing?"

219

"Sure – but the kind you'd like to have."

He does not elaborate. Perhaps professional decorum renders him naturally tight-lipped concerning the monetary affairs of others.

"Is that a topic that arose – perhaps with her sister – on the journey to the Lake District?"

"No – I don't recall anything of that nature."

"How about on your return journey – Poppy Lux, I mean?"

"Poppy was very subdued – understandably so. We mainly listened to the radio. I didn't really know how to speak with her or what to talk about." He gives an ironic laugh. "My job's planning for death – not dealing with the aftermath."

"And, as you say – Mrs Mills was well provided for, in that regard."

"Simon's life insurance – our company scheme – it's what you might call 'gold-plated' – what else could it be – we couldn't look our clients in the eye if we didn't buy the Rolls Royce for ourselves. Simon was pretty well off, but he used to joke that dead you could add on a zero to his estate."

Skelgill and DS Leyton exchange another knowing glance; the man is not hiding this particular light under a bushel. Meanwhile DS Jones's questioning continues apace.

"Was it necessary to give Mrs Mills advice in this regard – after her husband's death?"

"Not at all – that's the beauty of this kind of plan. A policyholder dies and a well-oiled machine purrs into motion. It is designed with the feelings of the bereaved in mind."

"And there were no problems – or delays – as regards the verification of Mr Mills' death?"

"But it was by natural causes? Or, at least – "

"Yes, sir?"

"Well – a tragic accident – but as I understood it – it was Simon's underlying heart condition. I mean – I believe I was poisoned myself – but I just felt ill overnight – like I was getting the flu – but it had cleared up by the morning."

DS Jones is about to speak, but the man pre-empts her.

"Wait a minute, Sergeant, are you treating Simon's death as something more sinister?"

She inhales. Her two listeners know what to expect.

"Sir, speaking for Cumbria Police, we are specifically investigating the death of Daisy Mills. While that remains unexplained, inevitably it puts what befell her husband under scrutiny. If we were not alert to any possibility, we would not be doing our job. We shall be submitting a report to the Coroner, who will make a determination if necessary."

Karl Eastwood murmurs what seems to be an acceptance.

"Will that hold up the funeral arrangements, and suchlike?"

"We expect the police pathologist to be finished by tomorrow. Most likely he will give the all-clear as far as your question is concerned."

"Poppy will be relieved if that is the case. I don't think she wants to draw this out any longer than necessary. There are no relatives, you see. Just their father – but he – "

"Yes, sir – we know about that. I take it you will be keeping in touch with Miss Lux?"

"Well – yes – as far as she wants me to be. She can call me any time – she has my number."

"And Mrs Mills – you had one another's contact details?"

A segue of sorts, but there was perhaps no easy way to interpose this question without it striking a discordant note, the scrape of chalk against slate when the schoolteacher's concentration errs. Accordingly, there is some hesitation in the reply.

"Er, yes – I sometimes needed to – when I couldn't raise Simon directly – call her to get hold of him."

"Of course." DS Jones sounds relaxed about the explanation, but her intonation belies a probing follow-up. "Oh, and just something we're trying to bottom out. Can you tell me where you were on the 6th of April this year? It was a Wednesday – in fact the Wednesday before Good Friday."

There is no hiding the nature of the question – but to give the man his due he is neither evasive nor indignant, either of which he might feel entitled to be.

"Most probably at the office and then at home in the evening. These last few months – since I have taken on Simon's clients – my workload has become rather unpredictable – he employed a memory-based system and renewal notices can appear out of the blue. But I would need to check my diary to be sure."

"Is that something I could call your secretary about?"

"I'm afraid not – my diary is in my briefcase on the back seat – I prefer the traditional handwritten format. I could pull off at the next junction and look, if you wish? Although, as I say, there is the possibility that I did something that went unrecorded."

"There's no rush, sir – perhaps if you would get back to me later. As for any uncertainty, if it turns out to be important we can clarify that through your mobile phone data."

Skelgill has sunk back into his seat and has his gaze lowered contemplatively – but now he looks up to see the owner of the voice framed in his doorway – and for a moment DS Jones speaks in stereo, as she simultaneously ends her call with a somewhat disconcerted Karl Eastwood and, in real time, makes her introduction.

'Well – that was a bit unexpected, Guv.'

She enters and puts down a tray of teas upon Skelgill's desk. Skelgill wastes no time in claiming the large mug that is nearest to him.

'Aye – he seems alright. Maybe that's why he showed us a clean pair of heels a couple of times – his wife's got him well trained. When I first clapped eyes on that car of his, I was expecting the type the lads in my local would tell to save himself the money and just get a jacket with "Prat" on the back.'

In fact Skelgill uses a more colourful term. DS Jones and DS Leyton exchange wry grins; their boss can be a bit of an inverted snob at times, albeit a trait borne out of an upbringing that values a man by who he is, not what he has. But now DS Jones corrects another misapprehension on Skelgill's part.

'Oh – I didn't mean Karl Eastwood – although I agree that's a bit of a surprise about his wife. It's the call I've just had with Kenneth Dalbrae.' She looks pointedly at DS Leyton and then back at Skelgill, by way of emphasising there is more salient news to impart. 'They're coming back at the weekend. They have the rental of Rydal Grange until Sunday – they want to hold a kind of memorial service for Daisy Mills at the waterfalls.'

It is DS Leyton who is first to react.

'What – with a vicar?'

DS Jones shakes her head, though she does not appear entirely certain.

'No – I think more of an informal event.'

Skelgill is scowling.

'All of them?'

Now DS Jones nods. 'As I understand it, Guv. I kind of get it, in a way. Especially while there is no funeral in prospect.'

But Skelgill looks no less concerned.

'Whose idea was it?'

DS Jones picks up her electronic tablet from his desk and takes her seat by the window. She regards Skelgill shrewdly. She understands why this could be a significant question.

'I specifically asked him that. He said he got a call yesterday evening from Rik Hannay. He had been speaking with Sarah Rice, who as we know is staying with her brother and Gail Melia. The consensus is that with hindsight they dispersed too hastily – it left them feeling empty – and that they ought to do something out of respect for Daisy Mills. Kenneth Dalbrae pointed out that they'd paid for Rydal Grange and cleared their diaries for this week. So he and Rik Hannay rang round some of the others and it was agreed to go back.'

DS Leyton indicates to his colleague's tablet.

'That sounded like your Eastwood geezer didn't know anything about it.'

DS Jones reflects for a moment.

'That's true – you would think he would have mentioned it – especially when I spoke of the reconstruction.'

'Maybe they won't invite him this time.' DS Leyton shrugs the broad shoulders that inhabit his somewhat ill fitting jacket. 'Mind you – I'd be watching me back – every time this crowd meets, someone dies.'

He looks across at Skelgill – his remark is made in jest – but Skelgill is merely grimacing more severely. He does not comment, and it is DS Jones who picks up the thread.

'At least if we want to speak to anyone after the reconstruction it will be much easier for us.'

This generates nods from her colleagues – and now they all take drinks of tea as if by unspoken agreement to punctuate their discussion with a few moments of contemplation.

DS Jones has with her several sheets of folded paper. When she passes these out, for once she gains Skelgill's attention. The pages unfold to reveal a photocopy of a section of Ordnance Survey map – enlarged and centred upon the hamlet of Rydal. There are various annotations, which she sets out to explain.

'The red crosses are where I would suggest we stop traffic, just after it has passed through the village in each direction. The southerly point would also pick up any motorists turning towards Ambleside from the lane to Rydal Grange.'

Skelgill is scrutinising the map, critically – but DS Jones has anticipated his objection.

'I think we should place an observer out of sight, close to the junction of Church Lane with the A591 – to catch anyone who might be moving on foot within the outer checkpoints.'

She is watching Skelgill – he glances up and nods. He might be volunteering – or indeed commandeering the role. However, she continues.

'Then I suggest we place our stand-in for Daisy Mills at that junction, as though she has just crossed the road to enter Church Lane.'

Skelgill does not respond. In his mind's eye there arrives an unnerving conflation of images; Daisy Mills, limp and diaphanous, slender in the clinging blue dress that she wore to Buckstones Jump; and portrayed in vivid acrylics, the long-haired brunette whose eyes glittered like sapphires, dominating the grand staircase at her home. Rather absently, he poses a question.

'What about timings?'

'See, Guv – bottom left?' DS Jones raises and turns her copy of the map to indicate a column of neatly handwritten notes. 'These are what we have – to the best of our knowledge.'

Skelgill squints at the page before him:

05:30 – Dr Charles Rice left Rydal Grange (on foot to west, cross country) – uncorroborated

07:10 – Kenneth Dalbrae left Rydal Grange (on foot to north, by road) – uncorroborated

07:28 – 999 call from Rydal church public kiosk

07:30 – Karl Eastwood left Rydal Grange (by car to Grasmere) – uncorroborated

07:45 – Karl Eastwood returned to Rydal Grange – uncorroborated

07:55 – Kenneth Dalbrae found Daisy Mills (d.) at Buckstones Jump – uncorroborated

07:58 – Hugo/Jane Grant left Rydal Grange (on foot to west, cross country)

08:10 – DI Skelgill/DS Jones found Daisy Mills (d.)/Kenneth Dalbrae at Buckstones Jump

10:05 – Hugo/Jane Grant returned to Rydal Grange

13:15 – Dr Charles Rice returned to Rydal Grange

Two issues strike Skelgill. The first is the extent to which they are reliant upon individuals' accurate or honest accounts of their movements. Only their own timings are incontestable – and the 999 call was logged automatically. Hugo Grant's cycling app recorded his walk with his wife, and they were also seen returning. Dr Charles Rice's return, he witnessed himself. Skelgill's second concern is the glaring gap in their knowledge – the whereabouts and time of death of Daisy Mills. The pathologist has been unable to improve upon a two-hour window between six and eight a.m. – albeit their own involvement, and the timed distress call, suggest the upper limit is no later than around seven-thirty.

DS Jones can read his frustration.

'Maybe someone will have seen her along the main road, Guv.'

But Skelgill is not optimistic. If Daisy Mills took the path through the meadow and copse, she may have been in sight of passing vehicles for a matter of seconds before crossing into Church Lane and thence the bluebell wood. Skelgill explains his point – but DS Leyton is quick to react.

'Surely, we've got two bites at the cherry, Guv. What about the geezer that followed her?'

And DS Jones chips in.

'Possibly a third – the person who called 999.'

Skelgill nods grimly. He is thinking *if* a "geezer" followed her, and *if* the caller were not Daisy Mills herself, making a futile cry for help (or maybe not even that, but just an ironic courtesy call) – a scenario that they must keep in mind; it is the popular belief, after all, promulgated by them.

But there is a caveat here. If Kenneth Dalbrae's timings are correct, how could Daisy Mills have made the call without finding him too hot on her heels for comfort? There would have been little time to throw herself off Buckstones Jump. He makes a tut of annoyance; such are the ever decreasing circles of conjecture. He looks across at DS Jones.

'Where are we up to on CCTV?'

'DC Watson is over there. She's checking at the shop at Grasmere – probably as we speak. She texted about twenty minutes ago. She's covered the driving route from Rydal Grange to Church Lane – unfortunately no cameras monitor the road.'

Skelgill had not held out any hopes in this regard. He doubts if Rydal comprises more than a dozen properties. He stares past DS Jones. Outside, the weather is changeable; they drove back into heavy rain on their return trip this morning, but now the grey sky is fractured and patches of watery sunlight traverse the landscape; it looks like the kind of northerly that sends breakers barrelling down Bass Lake and renders fishing impossible. But that is neither his problem nor his prospect; until there is some light on the horizon, angling seems a far cry; was it only two days ago that he and DS Jones were false casting on Rydal Water?

They had made an early rendezvous – and he an even earlier start, selecting extra tackle and cobbling together a picnic of sorts (if the ingredients of a fry-up constitute a picnic). It was daylight at five a.m. Daisy Mills could have left as early as that. They will need to set up their watchpoints from dawn. Anyone could have followed her and crept back into bed.

He scowls more darkly – in self-reproach; that his thoughts persist in drifting speculatively.

A shadow falls across the doorway.

Skelgill had only been thinking a day or so ago that DI Alec Smart has been keeping a low profile – at least as far as he, Skelgill, is concerned. There is likely some scheme afoot, although Skelgill has been unable to divine any undercurrents as yet.

DS Jones has her head bowed, reading, and a flare of afternoon sun illuminates peripheral strands of her naturally bronzed fair hair, forming a halo of sorts; she is like a graceful statue, unmoving, her sculpted features in part shadow and her limbs relaxed. It is plain that DI Smart has an eye on the space before her – but DS Leyton gives an exaggerated yawn and slides back in his seat, extending his legs to reach Skelgill's desk and block the path. DI Smart could step over, but it would be too obvious, and undignified.

'Alright, cock.'

The grating Mancunian drawl causes DS Jones to look up – despite that the colloquial greeting is aimed at Skelgill. It is not a salutation that particularly requires a response; various forms of "alright" ("alreet" in Skelgill's more common parlance) are simply everyday English for "hello". True, there is an implied asking after the other person's health – but it is unlikely to apply in DI Smart addressing Skelgill. Thus when there is no reciprocation – about which DI Smart does not seem surprised or deterred – he merely takes a moment to brush the lapels of his latest made-to-measure suit jacket, as if to emphasise its expensive provenance. But he can resist no longer his instinct for one-upmanship.

'I hear you've turned to the spirit world to solve your latest case, Skel.'

He cackles at his own joke.

Skelgill is not one for quick wit and repartee. It is usually afterwards that he thinks of what would have been an excoriating retort – perhaps, in this instance, that a Ouija board would give him about the same strike rate as DI Smart. DS Leyton is having such thoughts – but there is always the risk of being temporarily assigned to work for DI Smart, and thus discretion is the better part of valour in this respect. From his perspective, Skelgill would much rather punch the person who is trying to get the better of him, and take the consequences on the chin, so to speak. His colleagues know him and DI Smart well enough to understand that such underlying tension permeates most of their encounters – and that at times DI Smart can surely only be oblivious to the fate that he is tempting – that the lion he taunts regards him implacably from behind not bars of steely self-control but bendy rubber that may bulge at any second.

Accordingly, Skelgill does not answer.

'The cat's away – the mice can go native.' DI Smart sneers – albeit his confused idiom lacks literary merit. He refers to the fact that the Chief is attending the NPCC conference at Brighton. 'You'll be dancing naked round stone circles, next. Let me know and I'll come and film it for the official Twitter feed – it'll do wonders for recruitment.' He leers at DS Jones, ignoring Skelgill's darkening glare and, having delivered his piece, departs with a lascivious wink at DS Leyton.

It is the latter who looks to Skelgill with some trepidation, but is alarmed in a way that he did not anticipate.

'What is it, Guvnor?'

Skelgill seems to have a glint of triumph in his eye. He regards his subordinate thoughtfully for a second or two.

'Don't tell Smart – but maybe he's just handed us an idea.'

19. POLICE HQ – 2

Wednesday afternoon – DI Skelgill's office

His subordinates back in their regular spots – DS Leyton next to the filing cabinet, DS Jones in front of the window – and priorities accorded their proper place (treacle scones consumed and teas almost so), Skelgill looks inquiringly from one to the other. DS Leyton makes a chivalrous "after you" gesture to his female colleague, although it might be that he suspects he bears the more mediocre news of the pair.

DS Jones smiles obligingly.

'I've got feedback from everyone regarding their whereabouts on the 6th of April.'

She hesitates sufficiently to create a small sense of anticipation – though it is perhaps unintentional and she raises a cautionary hand to temper expectations.

'The top line is we're not suddenly going to haul someone over the coals. The majority require further substantiation if we decide it's necessary.' She glances down at her notes, but she seems to have it off pat, for she begins to recite without reading. 'Firstly, I think we can safely say it's correct that Kenneth Dalbrae, Ben Lomond and Sarah Rice were in London celebrating Kenneth Dalbrae's birthday. Probably the next easiest to corroborate would be Jane Grant, who was lecturing in central Glasgow; meanwhile Hugo Grant states that he was working from his home office – in Milngavie.' (She pauses and her colleagues nod, confirming their recall of their earlier conversation about this location.) 'Separately in London was Rik Hannay – who just says he was "at home" that day. Also describing himself as "at home", you won't be surprised to hear was Harry Badger. Karl Eastwood did get back to me as promised – but he was no more forthcoming – he claims to the best of his knowledge he spent the day mainly at his office in Leamington. Gail Melia – as expected says she attended the beekeepers' fair in Oakham. She replied on behalf of Dr Charles Rice – she says she checked his nature diary and he was birdwatching at Rutland Water. Finally, Poppy Lux was also at home in Shenton Parva.'

DS Leyton is first to respond – and he raises an index finger as one might test the wind direction.

'Perhaps I can shine a light on this.' He waves a sheaf of notes. 'The tracking device from Daisy Mills' motor. I've got the preliminary report.'

He certainly has their attention. He raps the papers with the back of one hand.

'The downside is that most of the data that these things transmit is encrypted – and it's not stored on the SIM. The shortcut would be Simon Mills' laptop or more likely his mobile. With his user name and password we could sign in to his account and interrogate the trip log.'

He looks evenly at his colleagues – but he knows that nothing of this sort was seen at the Mills' property, and may be hard if not impossible to come by. The devices might indeed have been long ago disposed of.

'If we could find which developer's app was used – there's three or four companies sell this service – obviously we could go with a warrant and break into it from their end – but that could take a couple of weeks to organise. It's an option up our sleeve, and I've put those wheels in motion.'

Given these caveats his colleagues would be forgiven for wondering what exactly is the light he proposes to shine; however his voice takes on a more enthusiastic note.

'Our boffins have managed to recover some incomplete data from the SIM card.' DS Leyton frowns at the page. 'Don't ask me to explain this – I can't even pronounce some of these words – but basically they reckon there were two journeys, of exactly 150 miles on both occasions, of unknown dates but with a definite period of separation between them.'

Skelgill wants immediate clarification.

'Is that 150 miles round trip?'

'No, Guv – there's actually four records in two pairs – so it's 150 miles to the destination, and 150 miles back. She must have gone to the same place each time.'

Skelgill shifts his gaze to the map of the British Isles on the wall above DS Leyton's head.

'It's way too far for London. I doubt that's a hundred.'

With some difficulty, DS Leyton cranes around to see.

'That's right, Guv. When we're visiting the outlaws we're in the home straight when we hit the M1 below Leicester. Closer to eighty.'

He reaches up and dips the tip of a stout finger into the pale blue ink of the English Channel.

'What about the Isle of Wight – where Sarah Rice lives?'

These days there is an electronic method of calculating distances that even Skelgill will deign to use – though he is quick to remind anyone that, when he is out on the fells with just a map and compass, neither his thumbs (being an inch wide) nor the earth's magnetic field have yet run out of battery.

His desktop computer provides an answer.

'It's 170 by the most direct route. Twenty too far.'

DS Jones now chips in.

'But, wait – anyway – if one of the trips was on the 6th of April, Sarah Rice was in London – surely we can rule out the Isle of Wight?'

They regard the map in silence. Without needing to measure, it is patently obvious that, in relation to Daisy Mills' home in the Middlemarch area, the majority of the group live much too close – virtually on her doorstep in the case of her sister and Harry Badger; twenty-five miles for Karl Eastwood's office; under forty miles for Gail Melia and Dr Charles Rice; fewer than one hundred to London – while at the other end of the spectrum Glasgow (and the Grants) is twice the distance.

DS Leyton exhales, his rubbery lips vibrating.

'She could have gone anywhere.'

He is correct to bemoan that from the virtual centre of England the permutations are almost unlimited. Deepest Wales, the Essex coast, the North York Moors. None of which and many more like them strike any chords with the detectives.

Skelgill, however, is experimenting online – and DS Jones appears to have had a convergent idea.

'What if she came this way, Guv?'

Skelgill nods. It takes him a moment to get an answer.

'Not as far as Penrith – it's 189.' He types again, changing the name of the destination. But he clicks his tongue in frustration. 'Rydal's 176, by Kendal and Windermere – it's the shortest route.'

He tries once more; this time instead of guessing destinations he simply moves the endpoint flag until the distance calculator winds down to read 150 miles. Now he gives an ironic laugh.

'If you stick to the M6 you get as far as Burton-in-Kendal services.'

Only twenty minutes south of Skelgill's preferred Tebay (where he has a cousin in the kitchen), it is a service station they rarely use. But just as the conversation might become sidetracked by the relative merits of such, DS Jones claps a hand to the top of her head.

'Guv – you said the person that controls the tracker can switch it on. So, if Simon Mills were monitoring his wife's movements – these journeys must have taken place last year.' There is a pause for reflection before she continues. 'That doesn't mean she didn't do the same 150-mile trip on the 6th of April – but it makes it more speculative to join the dots.'

An air of collective frustration infuses Skelgill's office.

But DS Jones is content to march on. She has been marking her notes with a yellow highlighter.

'If we assume she did meet someone on the 6th of April, and we compare that to what we actually know – we can discount the three who were lunching in London – that's Kenneth Dalbrae, Ben Lomond and Sarah Rice – along with Gail Melia who went to the beekeeping event in Oakham. On the assumption that she met a man, then we're down to any one of five. However, given what we know about Harry Badger – and that he lives within a couple of miles – it seems unlikely it was he. Moreover, he has no car.'

'Unless she took him for a nice jaunt to the seaside?'

DS Leyton knows this is unlikely, improbable even – but he says it all the same, his tone flippant.

DS Jones acknowledges his point with a nod, and continues.

'Of the remainder, Karl Eastwood and Hugo Grant have cause to travel for business – they run their own companies, and have clients throughout the country; they can come and go as they please. The fact that Daisy Mills made two identical journeys – and maybe more that went unrecorded – suggests she was meeting someone who had cause to go to a particular location. I mean – the obvious thing would be if the man concerned lodged at a regular hotel.'

Now DS Leyton takes a more serious line.

'But both of these geezers – they're claiming to have been at home that night, right?'

'That's correct.' DS Jones glances at Skelgill. 'But it doesn't have to be an overnight stay.'

Skelgill regards her impassively, but DS Leyton frowns, as if he thinks that would be a little unsatisfactory.

DS Jones clearly wants to push the investigation forward. It is in her nature to tread upon creaking ice, perhaps especially while there is the safety net of Skelgill to haul her back to shore.

'Guv – what Hugo Grant suggested about a long-past relationship – and Harry Badger mentioned it – and that Hugo Grant and Daisy Mills were quite possibly holding hands under the table at the séance? Surely he's the most likely person she was seeing?'

Skelgill blinks a couple of times without actually conveying an opinion. His thoughts are transported back to his encounter with Hugo Grant, who had come openly to cast bluebells on the water at Buckstones Jump.

'Aye. And the least likely to have killed her, eh, lass?'

His softly spoken rejoinder does indeed warn of thin ice. And not only does it flag the risk of jumping to such a conclusion, but also it serves as a reminder that they have not categorically eliminated any of the party.

DS Leyton has DS Jones's map balanced across his thighs, and he refers to the timings.

'Not forgetting that Dr Charles Rice was unaccounted for – he was away from Rydal Grange for the entire morning when she died. What if Gail Melia were covering up for him? What if the regular trip we're looking for was to some bird reserve – with a cosy country hotel nearby?'

Skelgill without any announcement checks on a whim the distance to RSPB Minsmere, Britain's most famous bird reserve, across on the East Anglian coast. The distance is 153 miles. Though he raises an eyebrow he closes the maps application with a flourish.

'Leyton – not forgetting it was Dalbrae we found with the body. I expect he does a good line in crocodile tears.'

They understand he invokes the man's theatrical manner – but DS Jones is prompted by reference to the scene of the tragedy. She extracts a page from her file of notes and raises it as an exhibit.

'The path lab have completed all their tests. No change in opinion concerning the bruising on her wrists – the possibility remains that injury was incurred at the time of drowning, but contusions suffered earlier mask it. However they did find a significant level of Valium in her blood, and it was present in her stomach contents, suggesting she had only recently swallowed some. Dr Herdwick spoke to her GP.' She looks at Skelgill, who had obtained these details during his unofficial search. 'The GP had prescribed benzodiazepine to help Daisy Mills with insomnia – since the death of her husband. But at Rydal Grange there was no trace of any – or even empty packaging in her room or among her personal possessions.'

DS Leyton is looking perplexed.

'What does this mean?'

DS Jones glances at Skelgill, but he seems content that she should speculate.

'The absence of packaging – she could have had the tablets loose in her toiletries bag. Then maybe she woke early and took them. Perhaps she still couldn't sleep and decided to go for a walk. The drug can take up to an hour to kick in – possibly she became drowsy only when she reached Buckstones Jump.'

'Drowsy enough to drown?'

DS Leyton sounds alarmed – as if this is certainly not the outcome they have been striving to uncover. DS Jones looks to Skelgill for advice.

'You would think not – surely it would be cold?'

Skelgill gives a little exclamation accompanied by the sort of face that suggests he imagines plunging in up to the waist.

'Aye – this time of year some becks are still running with meltwater. Brass monkeys.'

He affects a shudder and looks knowingly at DS Leyton, who responds with a small nod of understanding.

DS Jones appears satisfied with his assessment. She speaks in considered tones.

'But I suppose she would be more susceptible to a surprise attack – and more vulnerable – more easily overpowered.'

Skelgill is still grimacing; one of his original thoughts has returned.

'She could have suffered cold shock – it can paralyse the muscles.'

His suggestion adds weight to DS Jones's idea. Not surprisingly a silence ensues, but as a group they are accustomed to these moments, and there is no particular pressure to speak. Skelgill has them schooled in the custom of the fells, "if thou've got sommat to say, mek it wuth sayin'".

DS Leyton finally takes a chance on the rules.

'I keep coming back to that Ouija board malarkey, Guv.' He is looking up at the ceiling, somewhat artlessly, but seems to sense that Skelgill does not entirely disapprove. Besides, there was his boss's cryptic and as yet unexplained comment following DI Smart's incursion of yesterday afternoon. 'Now – I'm not saying a Ouija board couldn't work of its own accord – no one can ever know that – but I'm flippin' well sure the pointer can be moved by one of the players, right?' Now he looks for agreement around the room. 'So, just remind me – which of these geezers that's on our probables list was at the table?'

DS Jones moves to seek out the information from her notes. She finds the page, but compresses her lips before she begins to narrate.

'The trouble is – most of them. Seated clockwise were Kenneth Dalbrae, Gail Melia, Karl Eastwood, Poppy Lux, Dr Charles Rice, Harry Badger, Hugo Grant and Daisy Mills. Not at the table, involved in separate conversations were Rik Hannay and Sarah Rice, and Jane Grant and Ben Lomond.'

DS Leyton nods resignedly. It is of course a ride on the roundabout that they have taken before – and, despite the considerable knowledge they have accumulated since, when stock is taken, they can seem to have made little if any progress.

'Are we there, yet, Guv?'

DS Leyton has blurted out these words – an inappropriate repeat of his joke during their journey south – before he has even realised it. But he receives no answer – for when he looks at Skelgill he sees his boss is staring with a glazed expression at DS Jones. It may be that she is simply in his line of sight, for there is nothing about his expression that suggests appraisal, or admiration, or concern. For his part, DS Leyton is rather relieved that his boss has not comprehended, for the comment was badly judged. And then Skelgill looks at him with unexpected lucidity.

'Aye – we're a sight closer than we think.'

20. CLOSING IN

Saturday evening – Rydal Water

The atmosphere has an ineffable quality after a *pash*, that is the kind of short, sharp shower that descends plumb and heavy in calm conditions, issue from the pregnant underbelly of lowering cloud. Borrowdale hill farmer Arthur Hope introduced Skelgill to the term as a boy, when he and partner-in-crime Jud had been caught napping on Seathwaite Fell, and had burst panting for cover into the byre looking like half-drowned rats that had narrowly escaped a shipwreck. Skelgill was a good minute ahead, upon which his marra's father had remarked.

'How! Young Daniel, thou came down t' fell like t' Helm-wind."

A man of few words; he was the first to predict Skelgill would have a future as an exceptional fell runner. Skelgill had experienced an unaccustomed frisson of pride; the last of four battling brothers, compliments were far from daily fare. But the conversation had reverted to the elements. Arthur Hope exhorted the shivering boys to stand beneath the lintel and fill their lungs with the clean air, scrubbed of dust and impurities.

He has since learned that, far from being 'purified', the curiously stimulating 'just-rained' petrichor has as much to do with a release of microbial chemicals as it does to a dose of disinfecting ozone. But that is equally puzzling – how can there be fungi out here on the lake? He sits watchfully beneath his capacious fishing umbrella – his boat must look like some kind of oriental junk, drifting on a discreet course close to the shoreline beneath Rydal Grange.

He has not – he deems – broken his ascetic custom and come fishing before a case is concluded, precipitately rewarding himself with a treat he does not deserve. No – indeed, he has eschewed the pub and a darts match – and this is not fishing; it just looks like fishing.

There is something to know, and being within sight of Rydal Grange puts him in most danger of knowing it.

He checks his wristwatch. It is just after eight – murky, but there will be protracted twilight. He notices a woodcock roding just above the fringe of trees that skirts part of the lake. The silence is such that even at a distance he can hear the bird's preternatural call, a pixie-like sneeze followed by a thrice-repeated ranine croak. Around him mayflies are laying and random plops of foraging trout have him on tenterhooks – he can tell his head a hundred times to ignore it, but his instincts hold sway; and perhaps it is just as well to have some adrenaline running in the veins.

From the anonymous shadows of his floating hide he has seen occasional movement at Rydal Grange. Lights are now coming on in some of the bedrooms (he notes, not the central one previously occupied by Daisy Mills), and in the garden room that runs the length of the veranda. Once or twice figures have appeared. Two people came out to smoke – to share a cigarette, it seemed. He was too far away to be sure who they were – but pressed he would have nominated Rik Hannay and Gail Melia; an interesting but plausible combination as chief hedonists. A woman emerged to admire the view – possibly Jane Grant – but something distracted her and she retreated within, prematurely it seemed to Skelgill.

He is unable to tell if they have all arrived; the cars will be parked on the far side of the big house. In listening to DS Jones earlier, assessing her final (and typically immaculate) plans for the reconstruction tomorrow morning, they had considered whether Karl Eastwood would come back to Cumbria. There were legitimate reasons why he may not, and perhaps intriguing ones why he might.

There is one way to find out.

*

Skelgill curses under his breath. His approach to within thirty feet of the house has been thus far unproblematic. There is the cover of the trees that run up from the lakeshore on either side, framing the trapezium-shaped meadow. He chose to moor at the Rydal village end and has threaded his way beneath the canopy to the point at which the damp leaf litter underfoot merges into the soft shady lawn, where he and DS Jones had conducted several of their interviews. His fieldcraft has been casual verging on blasé – knowing his adversary is an unsuspecting and in surveillance terms unsophisticated target. But the sudden crunch under his left boot jolts him into alertness. While the Romans had their *lilia*, the best defence against creeping burglars and snooping detectives is to surround a house with gravel. And get a dog, of course.

Were there a dog it would surely have picked up the audible scrape, never mind the ultrasonic notes that are beyond the reach of the human ear. Cleopatra can detect a strand of cooked spaghetti dropped soundlessly into her bowl three rooms away. Strange that none of them has a dog – or maybe they do – these days there are dog-sitters and doggy-day-care and dog knows what – after all, he relies on the saintly patience of his neighbour for such a service. He finds himself speculating upon who would possess what breed – his own accidental acquisition is not the rough and ready cur dog one would expect a fellsman like him to choose for company (although, as Skelgill sees it, at least it is a specimen that other dogs do not want to fight). The Grants he would guess a Scottie, or maybe a Skye Terrier like Greyfriars Bobby. Kenneth Dalbrae and Ben Lomond – it would be a fashion statement, a Weimaraner or a Vizsla, totally impractical in a Soho flat. Rik Hannay – maybe an indolent Old English Sheepdog. Harry Badger – a little snapping Jack Russell. Dr Charles Rice – no, somehow he can't see him with a dog, naturalist or not his manner is cold and offhandish. Perhaps Gail Melia would keep a toy variety in her handbag, much to his displeasure.

Skelgill tuts in self-reproach. Stalled in the shadow of a great oak, he is forced to admit that this idle conjecture is simply a distraction from the plan he does not have. He squints into the gloom. The face of the house is shrouded in shadow; a faint glow shows from a couple of the bedrooms, probably their doors are open and the landing light is on. The downstairs front rooms are in darkness. But he can see enough to recognise the five cars in a neat row facing the building – five cars that include Karl Eastwood's BMW. So he has come – helping out Poppy Lux, perhaps – a comfortable ride when the alternative might have been hitching a lift with Rik Hannay in his battered Volvo smelling of roll-ups. Presumably he stopped by to pick up Harry Badger, as before. There is the trendy Mini that will have carried Kenneth Dalbrae and Ben Lomond from London, Hugo Grant's Range Rover from Glasgow, and Dr Charles Rice's hybrid that he still has not fathomed in which presumably travelled Gail Melia and perhaps Sarah Rice. He counts. That would be all eleven of them.

His mind reverts to the conversation with DS Jones and DS Leyton about the tracking device and he receives a flashback that last night he even dreamed of this. The hallucinated conversation was typically unsatisfactory. They were having a competition, guessing distances and DS Leyton kept getting it right while he was wrong – so accurate were his sergeant's estimates that he suspected him of having some secret source of information – and after DS Leyton had won he admitted he was using not a computer but a Ouija board!

Skelgill's mental meanderings are interrupted now by the crunch of tyres – a vehicle has entered the driveway and is making its way with haste towards the house. It is dark in the wooded grounds and initially he sees just headlights. He steps behind the trunk of the oak and sidles around as the vehicle passes. It is a small car, an old Renault 5 that sounds like it could do with a new silencer.

The Renault slews to a halt – it seems the driver has no intention to park – he nurses the engine while a girl with long straight black hair pushes open the passenger door with the soles of her feet and springs up in a practised manner. Skelgill realises she is cradling a broad, shallow fruit carton stacked with other items. Almost immediately the aroma of fried garlic and chilli assails his nostrils; they have ordered a Chinese takeaway. The girl squeezes between two of the parked cars and mounts the steps beneath the broad porch. It takes her a moment to work out how to attract attention – but she notices a bell push and deftly operates it with her elbow.

In fewer than fifteen seconds the big door swings open and Skelgill sees a figure silhouetted in the frame. At first sight he cannot quite make out who it is, but the mellow stage voice self-identifies as Kenneth Dalbrae. He offers extravagant thanks and reaches into his back pocket. There is an awkward moment as he tries to tip the girl, but she needs both hands to support the not-inconsiderable meal. In the end he reaches over and tucks the note into either a breast pocket or the neckline of her top; from behind, Skelgill cannot tell. The girl however lets out a small squeal of uncertain connotation, which elicits a roguish chuckle from her customer.

When the front door has closed and the car has sped away for its next mission Skelgill stands pensively; it goes without saying that his stomach is protesting – and there could be worse to follow. When he perused the fire escape diagram he had noticed the dining room at the west end of the house, off to the right of the passage and adjoining part of the long garden room, to which it has access. But it also has a large window at the gable end. If the sash is open he might be able to eavesdrop on their conversation.

He chooses to approach and skirt the building, working his way around clockwise from the front door; by keeping close to the wall, ducking beneath the sills, he is less likely to be noticed.

Just as he slips between the same two cars as the delivery girl a light comes on over the front door and there is the sound of the heavy latch being lifted. Instinctively he crouches – but in the second or two available in which to decide to run for it he makes a bolder choice. He drops prone and then rolls in the mode of a motor mechanic, underneath the car to his left. He holds his breath. Footsteps descend the stone steps. He turns his face away as an extra precaution – although surely no one is going to bend and peer under the car. The person passes, just inches from where he lies. There is the squawk of a remote and the crunching feet move on to another of the vehicles. A boot is popped open and then comes the clink of bottles – a case of wine being lifted, by the sound of it. The boot is closed; the person retraces their steps, more judiciously. The front door bangs shut, pushed with a heel, perhaps.

And now a narrow escape, for a text comes through on Skelgill's mobile, and he does not have it switched to silent. Supine, and with just a few inches headroom, he grunts as he raises his hips to extract the handset from his back pocket. With some difficulty he contrives to look at the screen. It is a photograph, a picture of a pint next to a Jennings handpump – his mates taunting him. He relaxes and lets the phone fall face up on his chest. The eerie blue glow of the handset illuminates the gritty, grimy salt-encrusted undercarriage of the car. And suddenly he stiffens. Like an archaeologist deep in the confines of a cave, burrowing for a new species of humanity, Skelgill slowly reaches up into the wheel arch. He has discovered a precious missing link.

He strives to process the implications of his find, but the circumstances are not exactly conducive. Indeed, heaven forbid, someone might decide to shift the car. The outside light has not gone off – evidently it is not on a timer. To avoid detection he would be better served to hotch his way out via the rear of the vehicle. But most efficient is to go forwards – he heaves against the gravel with his feet and hauls on the front axles using the strength of his arms. Once his head is clear he flips onto his stomach and crawls the last yard. Lifting onto all fours, poised like a sprinter in his blocks, he comes face to face with the neat row of wellingtons aligned in size order on the porch.

How! Like a thunderbolt of lightning, like an arc of static electricity that turns the air blue, like a flashing migraine that almost knocks him back to the ground – arrives the brainstorm he has been waiting for. Never mind the missing link, here is the connection.

Almost drunkenly he gets to his feet and reels into the darkness, a lurching dash that, once beneath the cover of the trees, settles into a more practical jog and then an even more pragmatic walk, retracing his route, holding up a hand to ward off stray branches. He reaches his boat; the craft is nosed amidst the great crocodile-skin limbs of an ancient crack willow. He drops aboard, sanctuary gained. As his breathing recovers he sits motionless in the darkness, the calls of the night birds for company. Gradually the maelstrom of his thoughts subsides into something of a navigable whirlpool.

After some time he inhales, and then exhales in the way of a man who has reached some significant decision. He takes out his phone. He glowers at the screen and tilts the handset from side to side, shakes it, then he raises it and draws a figure of eight in the air. This produces the desired effect and he promptly taps out an instruction. There is almost no delay before his call is answered.

'Guv? I was thinking about ringing you.'

DS Jones sounds pleased to hear from him.

'Jones – listen – we don't have much time. I need you to make a couple of calls – I can't trust the signal here.'

Immediately she detects there is something out of ordinary.

'Where are you?'

Now Skelgill hesitates, almost sheepishly it seems.

'I went on Rydal Water – being as I'd left the boat here last Sunday.' His colleague inhales to speak but Skelgill continues. 'Have you got access to your interview notes? I reckon I know what's been going on.'

*

Skelgill realises he has been sitting for a good quarter of an hour. Paradoxically, in the darkness everything suddenly seems clear. His mind has been running on autopilot, scouring the events of the past week, making sense of those that are relevant. Those that were not, that were clouding his vision, have fallen selectively like the proverbial scales from his eyes. He still has some questions, and some doubts, not least about what he has asked DS Jones to do.

The sky has cleared and soft moonlight filters through the intricate matrix of fine fingered lime-green leaves and lemon-yellow male catkins of the willow; one drops on him every so often, like a soft spiny caterpillar that has overreached in search of a meal. His stomach rumbles. He has tinned soup and beans aboard and the means to cook, but the hunger pangs that assailed him when he was tempted by the takeaway have ebbed, if anything he feels a little seasick. But his mouth is dry and he'll always drink tea; he reaches for his flask – not as hot as from the Kelly kettle, but tolerable. Indeed, he shivers. The temperature will drop close to freezing – but stowed in a dry bag are sleeping and bivvy bags.

When he had finished explaining to DS Jones – and they had agreed what she would do – she had suggested that afterwards she could drive over and meet him at a pub in Grasmere. She could make it for last orders. They could fine-tune their plan. Without knowing why, he had declined her offer – he had used the excuse that he didn't want to be seen – what if a couple from the party had come out for a drink – though he knew that was unlikely, surely they were going to get stuck into the wine and nobody would be going anywhere. She had argued that, even if they were spotted, it would just be assumed that the police were staying overnight in the area, to be on the scene for the reconstruction early in the morning. But Skelgill had cautioned that there was no need to take any chances. He told her he might creep back to the mansion house, to keep an eye on things.

He sensed she would protest further – but the task he had given her was pressing, and she dutifully rang off. Anyway – he is on site for the morning – his mooring is barely two hundred yards from the spot where the woodland path emerges onto the highway to cross into Church Lane. He can stand a night in the boat – he's done it many a time; DS Jones would surely not appreciate the discomfort.

But as cold sets into his bones the pub does have a growing appeal; a feeling that is reinforced when he receives another mocking text. This time instead of a pint it is a dartboard with three arrows in the bullseye – a rare checkout that he has only ever once achieved, and that as a drunken teenager in the days before every phone was a camera. Three darts in the bull – how did he do it? One hundred and fifty – inexplicable. *Huh.* Now he thinks he can explain the one hundred and fifty miles that Daisy Mills travelled.

But that must wait until morning.

As he begins to nod off a hazy image forms in his mind: a diaphanous figure draped in a clinging wet gypsy dress; her long dark tresses dripping, her electric eyes frosted and unseeing; she clutches a posy of wilted bluebells as she drifts barefoot through the damp grass of the meadow to pass close by his mooring, stirring the faintest of breezes, sleepwalking to her fate.

A reconstruction of sorts.

21. UNDER THE SPOTLIGHT

Saturday 9.30 p.m. – Rydal Grange

'What is it with you, Clint? How come you're the go-between? Have the rozzers secretly sworn you in as deputy!'

Harry Badger, glass in hand and looking if not sounding inebriated, cackles at his own joke.

But Karl Eastwood feels his cheeks burning, and even in the low light of the dining room he knows he can't hide the discomfiture that marks him out as an outsider. No doubt the likes of Rik or Spike would know how to tell Harry where to go, no punches pulled. But, that aside, Karl has been caught off guard – as he was, his heart in his mouth, when that attractive young police sergeant called him. Now he glances at Kenneth Dalbrae – after all, *he* is the organiser, if not the natural leader of the party (he senses that role falls to Hugo Grant). Karl noticed Kenneth was watching him, jealously it seemed, as he went to take the call in some privacy. At least he announced it was the police before he left his suddenly silenced fellow diners. And now he has faithfully conveyed the message. Harry has nothing to complain about. It is quite simple. The police will be stopping vehicles to interview motorists either side of the village until eight in the morning – and would they all remain at Rydal Grange at least until then.

Not much danger of that, he predicts, going by the amount of alcohol already consumed. Folk are drinking more heavily than last time – perhaps it is the uncertain mood, combined with the salty food. But the phone call has shocked him onto mineral water from now on. Indeed he is breathing rapidly and his stomach is churning as though it would rather not digest the wafer-paper prawns on which he has certainly overindulged.

'I was on CCTV.' He senses the tremor in his voice, it's not like him – this lot think he's normally cool as a cucumber. Isn't that in part why they call him Clint? And isn't a nickname something of a sign of acceptance – he has been content to tolerate it for that reason. Now he feels obliged to provide an explanation. 'I had told them I bought a newspaper last Sunday morning – I went out at about seven-thirty to the little shop in Grasmere. They wanted to let me know that the CCTV in the shop – it – it confirmed what I said, 07:37 hours.'

'*Hah!* He's got an alibi!'

Harry Badger is out of order, true to form.

Karl feels alarm grip his features and tries to fight back the expression. Should he be laughing it off?

Rik Hannay reclines in his seat. 'You mean they've got proof he went out.'

It is hard to tell whether he is gainsaying Harry or adding to his charge. Karl can feel his ears burning. In the momentary hiatus he sees that Kenneth Dalbrae is calculating when he might intervene. Now he can hold back no longer.

'And did you see anything? See anybody, I mean?'

Karl turns down his mouth in an exaggerated manner. But he feels his display is unconvincing – he can detect in the eyes of the others guarded disbelief.

'They don't want me to – well – repeat the drive – especially without warning.' He makes a dismissive gesture with one hand, as if to play down the matter. 'You know how they sometimes do a reconstruction – with their own people.'

The sense of unease, of being surrounded, grows like an invisible weight upon Karl's shoulders. He is trapped when his hormones urge flight upon him. And then Poppy Lux comes to his rescue. She pushes back her chair and rises.

'I'll get the desserts.'

Karl jumps at the chance of escape.

'I'll give you a hand. We'll need fresh bowls.'

When a few minutes later he and Poppy Lux return from the kitchen bearing trays there is a sudden lull in the conversation – he's sure they were discussing him.

But then Spike declaims.

'I propose we play a game of Trivial Pursuit.'

This is met with unanimous groans.

'What about Twister? It's much more fun.'

This contribution, from Gail Melia receives a more mixed reaction; but Kenneth Dalbrae, who would normally be exuberant, seems distracted, and is urgently rotating the ring on the fourth finger of his left hand.

Suddenly, Poppy Lux, standing at the head of the table, drops her tray. They all look at her in astonishment.

'No – we must have a séance.'

She folds her arms, her jaw set defiantly.

Karl feels his heart begin to thump in his chest.

One of the candles gutters violently and creates a diversion. Karl half expects someone to say a spirit just passed through the room. He notices that Jane Grant in particular is staring with a look of fascination at the persistent wraith of rising smoke; she probably knows the equations that describe the behaviour of the particles as they interact with air molecules. Harry Badger, seated opposite, also observes her interest – and like a selfish child spoiling another's enjoyment he leans forward and blows away the smoke and crows with delight. Jane Grant looks at him with bewilderment – he casts about for approbation, but his attention-seeking behaviour seems to please only him.

No one challenges Poppy Lux.

Perhaps it goes unspoken, a mutually understood sentiment – that she must desire some communication with her sister.

It is Kenneth Dalbrae who eventually addresses the issue.

'I didn't bring the Ouija board this time.'

'The spirits don't care about that.' It is Rik Hannay, his tone sarcastic. 'You can do it with a marked-up sheet of paper and a glass.'

Now Harry Badger interjects.

'There's a kiddies' chalkboard on an easel in the games room – we can lay it flat on the table. I can remember the design.'

Karl Eastwood puts down his tray of dishes and they all look at him – perhaps they now think he is volunteering to fetch the chalkboard.

'Excuse me – I'm just going to get a sweatshirt from my car.'

He realises it sounds like a bit of a lame excuse to leave the room – and that they might suspect he will not return. Indeed, Harry calls after him.

'What's up, Clint – the spooks already sending shivers down your spine?'

When Karl returns they have mainly eschewed the dessert of banana fritters and lychees in syrup and have decamped to the drawing room; he finds them crammed around the circular table. Again it is Harry that is quick to goad him.

'*Hah!* Are you going to ask the otherworld which century Coventry will next finish above Leicester?'

A couple of the guys' heads turn – Hugo Grant, he knows, is a Foxes fan; he was talking to him about football last weekend. What Harry refers to is the pale blue hoodie that Karl has donned. Embroidered across the front is the Coventry F.C. nickname, 'The Sky Blues'. But at least it shows he's no gloryseeker that follows Manchester or Chelsea. The only available chair is next to Hugo Grant, who shifts to make space and grins sympathetically.

'Every dog has its day, Harry.'

'Every fox, you mean, Hugo!'

Hugo Grant nods pensively.

'Aye – we did – and who'd have thought it.'

But now Harry Badger shifts his point of attack to Hugo Grant. He jabs at the air with an accusing finger. Hugo has let his guard down. The Midlands equivalent to the north British "aye" is more of an "ar".

'You're starting to sound Scotch. You'll be saying "Hoots, mon" next and wearing a tartan skirt with no underpants.' Then Harry turns to make a fawning face at Jane Grant. 'No offence,

Jane. I'm sure you keep your knickers on, despite Hugo's best efforts.'

Karl notes that she politely indulges Harry's crass humour. And Hugo seems unperturbed. He wonders if he would be so tolerant if it were his wife – but then again she is probably made of sterner stuff than Jane Grant – and she's more outgoing, never short of a keen riposte. She'd have a belittling retort, perhaps that Harry wouldn't know female underwear if he woke up wearing it. Or she might invoke her role in the police, and subtly threaten him. But as for garments, Karl is now wishing he could take off the hoodie. Apart from it being a red rag to the Leicester City supporters in the room, he is suddenly far too warm. But to do so will just draw attention back to it. Best to suffer in silence. Besides, a start is imminent.

Harry Badger seems to have usurped Kenneth Dalbrae's role as master of ceremonies; indeed Kenneth is subdued. Karl wonders if much of Kenneth's eccentricities and histrionics were contrived for Daisy's benefit. And Harry, despite being obviously the worse for wear, has made a good job of chalking out the makeshift Ouija board, the alphabet in an arc, two rows of letters, the numbers one to zero across the bottom, 'goodbye' beneath, and 'yes' and 'no' in the upper corners. There are symbols, pentagrams, skeletal hands, and a goat at the top. Perhaps he has some latent artistic talent. Perhaps he'll cut off an ear if he keeps drinking like this.

But now it is Poppy Lux that takes control.

She gets to her feet and switches off the main light. It seems to Karl that they are plunged into complete darkness and will never be able to see, but there are candles lit around the drawing room and gradually his eyes adjust. However, they could do with a candle actually on the table, though it would impede the physical process in which they are all about to partake. Poppy squeezes back into her place, she is between Sarah Rice and Gail Melia; Harry makes no protest this time about the lack of a 'girl-boy-girl' arrangement; perhaps even he recognises that Poppy might wish for moral support of a sorority nature. Along with Hugo, Karl has Spike on his other side. They are both confident types, in their own ways; Hugo reserved, more of a listener who speaks thriftily, but when he does his contemporaries pay heed; Spike, on the other hand, looks at you as though he is not interested, and doesn't even pretend to be – but he's done well for himself, he's the famous one in the room.

'I want us to be serious.' Poppy's voice brings Karl out of his musings. 'None of the Elvis business.'

Karl sneaks a glance at Rik Hannay. Last time he was sniping contemptuously from the sidelines, mocking the concept of the spirit world, but now his expression seems foreboding, almost funereal. Of course, he was famous, too, once – Karl remembers the TV series – although to Rik's credit he doesn't bang on about being an actor. But no doubt Harry would be quick to remind him that his stage career went downhill thereafter.

'I want to ask directly for Daisy.'

It seems to Karl that no matter how credulous or cynical they each are, collectively they respect her wishes; she is the bereaved sister after all. Poppy reaches forward and places a finger on the inverted whisky tumbler that Harry has procured for the purpose of planchette.

'You must touch it lightly. And no one must move it.'

Poppy seems to be speaking through gritted teeth. Karl regards Kenneth Dalbrae – he was all over the last séance, in his element, Karl had thought. Now he looks like he has already seen a ghost, his face seems aged and pallid in the flickering candlelight. He is tight-lipped and clearly is not about to speak.

Karl reaches forward with all the rest. There is an awkward moment when Spike seems to want to get a better position and presses against the side of Karl's own finger, but Karl holds his ground and he relents.

'We must all think of Daisy.'

Poppy closes her eyes and so do several of the others; they certainly seem to be taking it seriously. Karl suffers a sudden pang of doubt, a flash of imposter syndrome, perhaps – should he go through with this? *Can* he go through with it? His pulse is rising once again and the queasiness welling up in his stomach. Is he scared? His hand is shaking and surely the others will notice. He curses the hoodie as sweat trickles uncomfortably from his armpits.

And, then, without any verbal request for the spirit of Daisy Mills to come to them, or any announcement of its arrival, the glass begins to move. He feels it glide easily across the smooth surface of the chalkboard and come to a stop over the number 4.

Nobody speaks.

Even the sound of breathing is silenced – perhaps they have all stopped breathing!

After a pause – Karl is counting in his head, one Mississippi, two Mississippi – of ten seconds the glass moves again.

This time it shifts up the board to the double arch of letters – to the upper arch, left of centre.

'F'

And then only a two-second gap. It edges one space to the left.

'E'

And now another short pause before the glass seems to jerk but not move. And another two seconds before it drops to the lower row, dead centre.

'T'

Karl drags his gaze away from the glass – he sees that Kenneth Dalbrae is mouthing the letters and frowning – clearly they make no sense.

But the word seems to be complete. Karl counts another ten seconds before the glass abruptly slides across from 'T' onto 'W'.

And now it keeps moving, with short pauses.

'A'
'T'
'E'
'R'

And it stops.

Karl hears Gail Melia inhale sharply and under her breath she says, "Water".

But everyone is waiting.

Will another word come?

Suddenly, 'D'.

And then, 'A'.

And then nothing more.

They wait. The 'convention' – bizarre as it may be to say it – seems to be a short gap between letters and a longer gap between words. But now there is just a long gap – a very long gap, which ends to Karl's consternation when the glass suddenly accelerates towards him and participants let go and he finds it cupped in his hands. His forehead and palms are damp with perspiration and he looks around – almost in panic, it must seem to the others.

'She wants you to fetch her a drink!'

Of course the quip is Harry Badger's – but for once his remark is not so ill judged and there is a ripple of nervous laughter.

Gail Melia is agog.

Sarah Rice, who has been unobtrusive throughout, holds up a tentative hand.

'What did it mean – what's F-E-T?'

Karl is about to respond and has to check himself – when to his surprise Jane Grant pronounces; the professional scientist in their midst, she has paid close attention.

'It wasn't F-E-T. It spelled out two e's. F-E-E-T.'

'Feet?' Sarah Rice sounds perplexed.

Now, perhaps feeling one-upped by Jane Grant, rather pompously Spike interposes.

'It said 4 FEET WATER – she drowned.' He looks pointedly at Kenneth Dalbrae. 'She drowned in four feet of water, didn't she?'

Kenneth Dalbrae recoils.

'I don't know? Four feet? I should think it was much deeper than that. Ten. Twenty. I don't know. Ask the police, not me.'

Sarah Rice persists in a manner that is almost childlike.

'Do you really think that was Daisy?'

She addresses this query to her elder brother – but before he can knock down her suggestion Rik Hannay interjects.

'It could have been D-A for Dalbrae.'

He smirks sardonically. Kenneth Dalbrae makes a strangled sound of protest. Karl sees that Ben Lomond is watching his partner with a look of disquiet.

All eyes turn upon Kenneth.

He raises his hands in a gesture of fending off the others.

'Don't look at me!' There is a note of desperation in his normally so assured voice. 'For all I know she fell and bashed her head on the rocks.'

There is a moment's reflection – but it is clear that Rik is working up to another jibe. Karl notices that Sarah is glaring at him censoriously; a long-time ally of Kenneth, maybe she has an inside line too on Rik and is signalling he should retract his insinuation. And, indeed, perhaps he tempers what he was about to say.

'Why are we being told something we already know?'

Harry Badger leans forward.

'Maybe there's more to come?' He produces a Machiavellian leer. 'Let's try again – Daisy might get a second wind – *name somebody.*'

'No!'

It is Poppy Lux that exclaims. And she rises and grabs up the chalkboard and backs away, clutching it proprietorially. She switches on the main light, rendering them all suddenly blinking.

Rik Hannay seems unperturbed by her rather drastic reaction.

'Get what you wanted?'

She looks at him, alarm in her eyes.

'I – I don't know what I wanted. To know that Daisy is – I don't know.' She flounders for a response. 'But I know I want to stop.'

'*Ha-hah!*' It is Harry. However, he is pointing not at Poppy but – to Karl's dismay – at him. 'Clint looks like someone's walked over his grave!'

Now attention switches to Karl. But if he appears pale and shocked he feels only like he is overheating. He pulls self-consciously at the neck of his hoodie.

'What is it, Karl?'

It is Poppy Lux that seems to perceive something that perhaps the others do not. But when he provides no immediate answer and appears tongue-tied the intrigue is almost palpable. Poppy's voice takes on a strained note.

'Karl, if you've remembered something, you ought to tell the police. Like you said, they'll be outside the village in the morning.'

Karl realises he must look like he is wrestling with his conscience.

'No – it's – it's nothing. Nothing to speak of.' He mops his brow with the sleeve of his hoodie. Then he strives to regain a semblance of his customary composure; he holds up the empty glass, recalling the finale of the séance. 'But – maybe that drink?'

Harry Badger needs no further encouragement. He rises inelegantly and yaws for the cluster of wine bottles that have been moved to a sideboard. It seems to Karl that a wave of relief washes around the room, that the tightly knit group may disembark from the tempestuous little voyage.

Karl meets Poppy's gaze – she gives a faint smile.

22.
RECONSTRUCTION

Sunday, 5.45 a.m. – Rydal Grange

When Karl Eastwood peers out of the kitchen door he is struck by the severity of the early-morning chill. He is glad of his much-maligned 'Sky Blues' top and pulls up the hood. It endows upon him a superficial sense of reassurance, anonymity of a kind – maybe that's why youths bent on trouble wear these things; although given last night's ribbing there could be no doubt of his identity were he spotted leaving by one of the party.

He has a kind of strained caffeine-craving headache. He slept badly; he could swear he saw every hour on the bedside clock. But if there was a silver lining he did not need his alarm. He has dressed and left his room as noiselessly as the old house permits. Being at the end of the landing involved tiptoeing past several doors, and the floorboards betrayed him more than once. Now he opts to leave the back door ajar rather than gamble on the scrape of its iron latch.

On the veranda there is a further booby trap, a scattering of dry kindling. Harry Badger was all for a barbecue and had unilaterally begun making preparations until outvoted and the takeaway ordered. Harry was probably irked to have to cough up his share of the cost, and had simply abandoned his handiwork. The small axe is embedded in the chopping block and sticks lie where they splintered. Karl picks his way over them to the head of the stone steps.

He edges through each of the rusted paddock gates in turn. Beyond, the long meadow-grass is sodden with last evening's rain and the night's dew. There is no obvious path; the cold wetness immediately seeps into his trainers.

Over to his left the lake extends; mirror-like, it captures an inverted image of the hillside beyond, every detail sharp and crisp, walls and trees and sheep in perfect fidelity. Melodic birdsong swells the resonant air; it seems to come from all around; perhaps there are larks high overhead. Invigorating scents from herbs bruised underfoot rise to complement the zesty morning smell. These are stimuli that would normally lift the spirits. Instead there is just the obstinate queasiness that has plagued him since dinner.

If only he can get safely across the meadow and into the wood.

Halfway, he experiences an unaccountable sensation that he is being watched. Should he dare turn around? Would it betray his motives to do so – that he is feeling guilty, that his mission is clandestine? If it were simply that he could not sleep and had come for a walk, would he stop and look back at the house? They all know he conveyed the police message to remain at Rydal Grange – and yet here he is, making a beeline for the village. Better not look back. He should have brought binoculars – that little pair he keeps in the car. It would seem more natural to raise them and scan around, follow an imaginary bird along the horizon, over the house.

But what if someone has seen him? What if they follow him? What would that mean?

*

As the figure in the sky-blue hoodie disappears into the copse down by the lake a second emerges onto the veranda of Rydal Grange. Clad in dark outdoor clothing and a close-fitting hat and gloves, stooping briefly to pick up something, almost without breaking stride, the person quickly descends the zigzag of steps, fastening and pulling on a small backpack, and passes through the gates into the meadow. Moving swiftly, they follow precisely the track freshly pressed into the long grass. Just once, they glance back at the big house, an apprehensive act, and hurry on apace.

There can be little doubt that the second figure intends not to be seen, either by an onlooker or by the person ahead. But the delay in allowing the first to enter the wood risks the hunter losing their quarry. It is essential to re-establish visual contact before the road, where there is a choice of three directions. Passing beneath the trees they quicken their pace along the winding path – to the left there is a glimpse of a rowing boat on the water. It drifts gently away from the bank, its occupant motionless, all that is visible from the rear is a weather-beaten waxed jacket and a shabby wide-brimmed hat, and a fishing rod held in angled concentration. In response the figure in black swoops erratically from trunk to trunk.

Here is the footbridge, the Rothay rushing softly beneath, and the cover of shrubs just short of a stile. Beyond is the road that connects Keswick to Windermere, passing through Grasmere, Rydal and Ambleside. To emerge would court exposure. And, indeed, the sky-blue hoodie is suddenly close at hand – the distinctive colour discernible through the foliage, the tallish figure standing in the middle of the junction, facing away up Church Lane. He has his hands tucked in the belly pockets of his top and the hood still raised. Halted, he seems indecisive, and shivering a little in the shade of the trees. He tilts his head to left and right without actually turning – as if trying to make a decision about which way to go, or whether to wait. He stamps his feet a couple of times. He raises his right arm and checks his watch, and then listens to it – as if he thinks it might have stopped. He shrugs – and looks more pointedly ahead, inclining forward on his toes. And then, reaching a decision, he sets off up the lane.

He passes the red phone box – glancing at it – and the church, without looking. Indeed his stride becomes more purposeful now, lengthened and loping, his back arched when before he was upright as he descended through the meadow; it must be the adverse gradient of the lane. And, his choice made, he wants to get on with it. He shows no concern that he could be followed. Besides, he would not have stood so openly in the road.

The lane is a dead end – at least, as far as the short metalled section goes. It terminates with a gate; thence there is only one route, the footpath that climbs first through the oak woodland and then onto the open fellside, tracking the course of Rydal Beck up to the waterfalls and pool at Buckstones Jump. The follower can bide their time – for there can be little doubt where the man in the sky-blue hoodie is heading.

There has been no traffic so far, and it seems unlikely in this quiet hamlet at such an early hour. No one is at work on a Sunday, hardly anyone stirs – and fishermen, like the angler on Rydal Water, are already at their stations. In due course the dark figure crosses the road into the lane. Like the first, they glance at the telephone kiosk; maybe there is a faint hesitation before they continue, pulling down their hat and readjusting the straps of the backpack for comfort, as though the contents are heavy or awkward in shape and have shifted a little.

*

Almost in the manner of Rodin's *The Thinker* the figure in the sky-blue hoodie crouches pensively on the ledge above Buckstones Jump, where plucky children launch themselves on sunny days.

He seems resigned to wait it out. Again he checks his watch, but shows no discernible reaction. If there is some rendezvous the other party has yet to show up – still time, perhaps, for him to change his mind. But changing his mind does not change his knowledge.

And his destination can be no accident.

It is a spot not without danger. Though the face is sheer and the mountain pool deep, rocks jut beneath which must be navigated. It takes a decent leap to clear them, ideally a running jump. A careless slip on the dewy turf could result in a head injury, unconsciousness, and drowning.

An accident waiting to happen.

*

The hooded top ranks high in the garment industry's hit parade of successes. In recent decades it must sit alongside leggings for its ubiquity, perhaps even a notch or two above, given its unisex appeal. But the hoodie's great innovation – the hood – is also its Achilles' heel; it shuts off the wearer from the outside world; in particular it impairs the hearing. Skelgill, fishing, will only ever wear a hat – how else would he detect the fine movements of trout and pike? The detachable hood of his ancient Barbour is exactly that, detached, in a drawer in his garage, as good as new (but for patches cannibalised for repairs to the jacket). In Skelgill's case there is a further impediment: the suggestion that a hoodie might be worn for reasons of fashion – and, as he has therefore put it, he "wouldn't be seen dead in one".

*

In a direct line behind the hunched, preoccupied 'thinker' the pursuer makes a steady approach. Reaching to within twenty feet they drop to one knee and swing off the little rucksack. They unfasten the flap. They pull out a yellow-handled hatchet. They leave the bag and rise. They move forward once more, steady now giving way to stealthy. At six feet they raise the axe, the heavy flat back of its steel head in the forward position.

At three feet the black figure seems to relax. They have the other at their mercy. There is nothing he can do now. Poised to strike, the black figure takes advantage of the moment to switch to a two-handed grip.

'NOW!'

What could have been a sheep suddenly exhaling but surely was a hissed human voice – of indeterminate origin but unambiguous urgency – is the catalyst for an extraordinary cameo.

The figure in the sky-blue hoodie leaps from the precipice.

With the hatchet, a swing and a miss.

Behind, the crackle of bracken.
Exploding from a foxhole, a short burly blur.
The hatchet raised in vain.
A collision.
Momentum beats inertia.
They both sail over the edge.

Instantly another, slender and athletic, springs from cover, rips away and discards some kind of radio headset and without hesitation dives elegantly.

And finally one more person emerges from the vegetation, stout and stoic, wielding a video camera and striding to film what more ensues.

Through the lens the normally placid pool beneath Buckstones Jump appears in a state of tidal flux – but what is captured for the record can roughly be described as – first – that the figure in the sky-blue hoodie has wrestled the figure in black to the shallows and indeed has them face down on the shingle with an arm up their back, while – second – in the deeper waters the athletic one is supporting the stocky one who, despite having chosen to barge the axe-wielding would-be assailant over the edge, looks a fish out of water and is plainly relieved to be in receipt of competent assistance. The prism of the camera is non-judgemental, and at a distance this little stramash could be mistaken for a bunch of drunken revellers daring one another to make the leap and fighting afterwards. Although there are recorded no corresponding cries of exuberance or combat; the microphone picks up just one spluttered sentence, revealing to the discerning ear.

'Aargh! Struth! Cor blimey! You were right about those flamin' brass monkeys, Guvnor!'

23.
DECONSTRUCTION

Wednesday, 11 a.m. – Police HQ, interview room

The man, elbows on the table and head in hands, looks up forlornly as DS Jones enters, followed a moment later by Skelgill.

Their faces are stern – but it is a sternness that could not fairly be read as reproachful.

'Mr Grant – would you like a tea or a coffee?'

'What – oh, no – thank you – I was running early – I stopped at Southwaite.'

That he refers to a motorway service station causes a reaction in both detectives. In Skelgill's case it is probably a conjuring of some olfactory memory. For DS Jones it appears to be something of a more professional nature; however, it diverts her only fleetingly.

Hugo Grant, evidently out of good manners, perhaps a little old fashioned, rises. DS Jones holds out a downturned palm, to indicate he should not take the trouble.

'Please, sir – have a seat.'

He does as she bids, and watches rather numbly as they settle opposite and DS Jones puts down and separates her notes into piles.

Skelgill is empty handed.

He observes Hugo Grant with the same enigmatic expression as when he entered; it might be a kind of grudging appreciation of his predicament.

The man is first to speak.

'May I ask – how is Jane?'

He looks from one police officer to the other. Skelgill now stares rather balefully. DS Jones is conscious of potential hyperbole, given the circumstances, and has to resort instead to platitudes.

'She seems calm and collected. She will be carefully monitored. Her well-being is our priority.'

'Is she here?'

'No – she was transferred to the custody suite at Carlisle. She has a court appearance this afternoon. After that we would expect her to be remanded to a women's prison until the trial. Most likely Low Newton.'

Hugo Grant makes a choking sound, as if he cannot quite believe he is hearing these words.

'Is she – is she – cooperating?'

DS Jones glances at Skelgill – but she reads no sign that she should prevaricate.

'If you mean is she answering our questions I am afraid the answer is no. She has opted to remain silent.'

Hugo Grant seems to wince – as though he personally feels what is the final nail driven into the coffin of his wife's guilt.

'That's a pity.' His voice sounds distant, like he has spoken his thoughts. 'I wonder if she would talk to me?'

DS Jones folds her hands on the table, though her tone remains courteous.

'Unfortunately, sir, that's not possible at this juncture. You will have visiting rights in due course. But you must consider that you will certainly be cited as a witness for the Crown.'

He maintains steady eye contact, though his expression is pained.

DS Jones frowns in a sympathetic way, but now she gets down to business.

'Sir. First of all, thank you for coming today – you have saved us a journey. That is much appreciated.' (Hugo Grant turns up his palms, almost apologetically – what else could he do?) 'We would like primarily to fill in some gaps in our knowledge. Not, I emphasise, to make the charges against your wife more damning – but complete information may save embarrassment at a later date.'

'I see.'

'And, secondly, we would hope to answer any queries that you may have. Within the bounds of confidentiality and the protocols to which we must adhere.'

'Thank you.'

DS Jones continues in a matter of fact manner.

'You might find some of the questions intrusive.'

She pauses. Hugo Grant nods compliantly.

'Were you having an affair with Daisy Mills?'

Skelgill cannot suppress a sideways look at his colleague. Talk about shooting from the hip.

'No.'

'*No?*'

Hugo Grant smiles ruefully.

'We just used to meet for lunch and go for a walk – a chat.'

Though DS Jones has difficulty hiding her surprise, there can be no doubt that he sounds entirely candid.

'Could you elaborate on that, sir?'

'Look – I realise I should have mentioned it. And – well – in a way, though it was platonic it is disingenuous of me to say we weren't having an affair. We fell in love at school and never fell out. You could say it's been a lifelong affair. To this day I can't explain why we didn't end up together, and Daisy always said neither could she. Have you ever got on the wrong side of an arête from a friend when you've been skiing? One minute you're arguing over which is the piste, the next you're in different valleys. We kept in touch over the years – in some more than others – we occasionally met with mutual friends.' He glances from one officer to the other. 'You'll recall I said I saw Daisy and Sarah and Kenneth in London quite a few times. But we've always lived so far apart that we've never been able to meet casually, like you might, for a coffee. Daisy's mother died a couple of years ago and I think it changed her perspective. She phoned me in a terrible state. Simon wasn't the sympathetic sort and I think at the time she had fallen out with Kenneth. I'd known her Mum pretty well – I think she had me lined up for Daisy – and although I couldn't go to the funeral for diplomatic reasons Daisy made me promise that I'd make some effort to see her. So that was the catalyst.'

DS Jones pens a note on a blank pad to her right. Skelgill peers at it – but it is in shorthand and not intended for him. She considers the point for a moment, but then picks up where Hugo Grant left off.

'So you began to see one another about two years ago?'

He nods.

'That's right, her Mum passed away in the spring. I think it was in July that we first met.'

'And how often did you get together?'

'It wasn't a regular arrangement. We said we'd try to make it roughly every quarter – but we didn't manage that. I think it has been maybe five or six times.'

'Did you meet at Burton-in-Kendal services, sir?'

It is Skelgill who has interrupted.

Hugo Grant looks flabbergasted.

'Yes?'

Skelgill grins smugly – although this is clearly a reaction aimed not at the bewildered man but at DS Jones. His colleague flashes him a generous smile. He leans back in his seat to indicate she should be the one to elucidate.

'Did you know your wife was tracking your and Daisy Mills' movements?'

Hugo Grant is rendered speechless. He shakes his head.

'On Saturday night we found a tracking device underneath your Range Rover. It is identical to one we discovered earlier hidden on Daisy Mills' Fiat. Interrogation of your wife's computer and mobile phone reveal that she purchased two such items in December last year. We are awaiting the detailed data – but it is clear she has been using the online app to monitor your respective journeys.'

Hugo Grant appears stunned by the revelation – but he is an intelligent man. He looks at Skelgill, and now returns to his question.

265

'Burton-in-Kendal – it was the halfway point. It meant we each only had to drive for a couple of hours. Two-and-a-half at most. Instead of five hours for one of us – which becomes ten in a day and is impossible.' He looks penetratingly at Skelgill. 'I guess if you were tracking both cars, it wouldn't take Sherlock Holmes to put two and two together when they converged. That's really smart.'

DS Jones regards him reflectively – perhaps that even in this devastating moment he can express admiration for his wife. She is about to continue when he raises a question of his own.

'But – how did she fit a tracker onto Daisy's car? Did she follow me one time?'

'The tracker on Mrs Mills' car was first activated just after you and your wife attended the Mills' Christmas cocktail party.'

Hugo Grant folds his arms and nods introspectively, as if a penny is gradually dropping.

'You know – Jane's not into cars – she's very Scottish when it comes to conspicuous consumption – it's not done to flaunt wealth or be impressed by it. I wondered at the time why she wanted to go and see Simon's legendary Ferrari –'

He tails off. The detectives briefly make eye contact. Another little piece in the jigsaw.

DS Jones now places a carefully manicured forefinger on the note she had made.

'Sir, you said a few moments ago that you were unable to attend Mrs Mills' mother's funeral for "diplomatic reasons" – could you please explain that?'

Hugo Grant grimaces – she has touched upon a raw nerve.

'I probably made the mistake – a long, long time ago – of saying too much about Daisy. When I first started going out with Jane – you know, how you share stories of your past relationships – it's part of getting to know one another? I described Daisy as – well – Rod Stewart was playing on the juke box and I said, that's her – *the first cut is the deepest.*'

Suddenly tears well up in his eyes.

Clearly, Daisy was that cut.

The detectives wait patiently, both perfectly still.

'Sorry.' Hugo Grant gathers himself and wipes his eyes and grins sheepishly. 'He was a pop singer in the Seventies, long before your time.'

DS Jones flashes a mischievous glance at Skelgill. There was a drunken police karaoke night – a mutual colleague's leaving do – when he performed a creditable rendition, in style if not tunefulness. But that is another story. And now Hugo Grant has something more to say.

'Anyway. Look – I've never been one for having affairs – everything has been fine between Jane and me – but I'm away quite a lot – and, as I said, from time to time I've met up with old friends and Jane was aware of that – I never concealed anything. And Jane seemed okay about things. But I did become conscious that Daisy was a special case.'

'In what respect, sir?'

Now he frowns.

'It's hard to put a finger on it. If I give you an example: about ten years back a bunch of us went camping for a weekend in Savernake Forest – that's in down Wiltshire. It was Rik, Harry, Spike and I – for Rik's fiftieth. When I got back Jane said something like, "and that Daisy, what's her name, was she there?" I mean, it was unashamedly a blokes' drinking trip in primitive conditions, and I'd made that clear. But she'd obviously been thinking about it.'

'And did you ever indicate that you might be meeting with Mrs Mills?'

He shakes his head.

'I decided it was simpler to keep any communications with Daisy secret.'

Now there is a long pause. Hugo Grant eventually swallows.

'I was right about that, wasn't I?'

This is clearly a debatable point. If the 'relationship' had been in the open maybe there would have been a different resolution, however unsatisfactory, and not the drastic outcome they are now faced with. But, yes, perhaps he was right about his wife's stance.

267

'So I got a cheap phone from Tesco – just to call Daisy and make arrangements.'

His rather naïve explanation sounds so much less sinister than DS Jones's original assessment of a stranger with a 'burner' phone.

She is content to wait for Hugo Grant to continue.

'Of course, Daisy was in a similar situation with Simon. He wouldn't have approved.'

'She didn't tell him she was seeing you?'

Hugo Grant shakes his head decisively.

'She went to some lengths to cover her tracks. I think Gail Melia suspected, but had it been common knowledge, I would have heard. I mean – you've met Harry Badger.'

Enough said.

But now they have referenced Simon Mills, and there is the reminder that this hangs in the air. A silence ensues until Hugo Grant speaks again. And it seems he seeks their approbation.

'It was a ludicrous situation, when you think about it. There we both were – neither of us wishing to get out of our marriages, neither of us trying to have an affair – and so close as friends that we were more like brother and sister. I remember Daisy saying – when she phoned me about her Mum – *is this it* – will we never be allowed to meet? We were prisoners of our past.'

DS Jones takes a leaf from Skelgill's book and waits in silence. And eventually Hugo Grant continues. Suddenly there is a note of tentative optimism in his voice.

'Surely Jane didn't intend to kill Daisy – surely she went to remonstrate with her? There must have been an accident, and then she panicked?'

DS Jones and Skelgill have agreed that, if necessary, they will outline something of their case.

'She may well claim this in her defence. But we have video footage from Sunday morning of your wife approaching with a raised axe an unwitting man she believed to be Mr Karl Eastwood. She intended to harm him – perhaps to inflict a head injury that could have led to death by drowning. And taken with what we know – about the tracking devices, about your wife's movements on the previous Sunday morning, and forensic evidence that suggests Daisy Mills was held under water – it appears that what took place was at least in part premeditated.'

Confronted with these stark images Hugo Grant's expression is one of conflicted horror. Yet still he grasps at a straw of what might be mitigation.

'Sergeant Jones – you say last Sunday morning – but Jane made me tea and we went out for a walk.'

'Sir, what were you doing before she brought you tea?'

'Well – I suppose – I was asleep.'

'Did you wake when your wife got up to make tea?'

Now he hesitates.

'No, I don't think I did.'

He answers in a way that accepts DS Jones might rest her case. But now she offers a caveat of sorts.

'What could not have been planned was the séance. Out of the blue came the suggestion that Simon Mills was murdered and the inference that Daisy Mills knew by whom. However contrived that was – even if it were a prank – it made her a potential target. If someone present had killed Simon, now they might kill Daisy to silence her. We believe that your wife capitalised on that opportunity.'

Hugo Grant has the startled look of one knowing they are about to witness a car crash.

'Sir, the séance clearly disturbed Daisy Mills. Probably she could not sleep, despite taking some tablets, and decided to walk to the waterfalls. You all heard her mention to Kenneth Dalbrae that she might do such a thing when he announced the itinerary. We think early on Sunday morning Mrs Grant heard Daisy Mills leaving – or perhaps saw her crossing the meadow from your bedroom window – and followed her.'

Now DS Jones looks pointedly at Skelgill – but he simply inclines his head to indicate she should continue.

'Our reconstruction identified an eyewitness – an elderly man who had gone to tend his wife's grave in the churchyard in Rydal. From a kneeling position, between the headstones he observed a woman that matched your wife's description hurrying down the lane from the direction of Rydal Fell. This woman saw someone approaching and took refuge in the telephone kiosk. A man that met the description of Kenneth Dalbrae, in a distinctive pink shirt then passed in the uphill direction, apparently unaware of the woman in the phone box. At the same time the emergency services received an anonymous call mentioning a female casualty at Buckstones Jump.'

Hugo Grant is plainly riding a rollercoaster of emotions. He puts both hands to his face and rubs his eyes, and shakes his head rapidly as though he has just woken from a bad dream.

'Jane intended to frame Kenneth?'

His tone is incredulous.

'It certainly seems to be a possibility, sir. Responding to the distress call, we duly discovered Mr Dalbrae at the scene of the tragedy.'

Hugo Grant looks disbelievingly at DS Jones.

'But, Kenneth – he loved Daisy, too.'

His words are sincere, but perhaps DS Jones feels obliged to defend the detectives' right to have harboured suspicions.

'It would not be the first time that love has been the motive for a murder, sir.'

The man has lowered his gaze, but now he suddenly looks up, first at DS Jones and then at Skelgill.

'Did you suspect me?'

Skelgill emits an involuntary chuckle. And, though he does not answer, he glances at DS Jones in a manner that suggests had his team thought such a thing they would have had him to deal with first.

Hugo Grant seems to understand something of this unspoken exchange, and he nods appreciatively.

'But what about Saturday night – I mean the one just past? Karl Eastwood knowing about all this – I don't understand.'

DS Jones gives a shake of her head.

'Sir, Mr Eastwood did not know what was going on. But his wife holds a senior position in the police force. Following consultation, Mr Eastwood, and indeed Poppy Lux, were asked to put on a small act. For Ms Lux it was to suggest a second séance, and for Mr Eastwood to spell out a message on the Ouija board. Then he would pretend that message had jogged a memory, something that might be useful to the police. Your wife tried to stop him passing on that information.'

'You set a trap.'

Hugo Grant does not sound censorious – simply accepting; they did what they had to do.

'Mr Eastwood went to find us, knowing we would be somewhere in the vicinity early on Sunday morning. A logical place to look would have been Buckstones Jump. We had observers along the route in radio contact and we filmed what took place.'

'Was – Karl Eastwood – was he not in danger?'

'Within a few minutes of leaving Rydal Grange Mr Eastwood exchanged places and outfits with Inspector Skelgill.' (Hugo Grant looks sharply at Skelgill, who affects indifference to bravery in the line of duty.) 'We had asked him to wear a distinctive hooded top. As a precaution overnight he had locked his room. And an officer was stationed close by.'

That DS Jones does not this time refer to her superior is perhaps indicative of a certain amount of post-rationalisation as regards the safety of Karl Eastwood. Skelgill snoring in a boat a quarter of a mile away was not the most alert of sentries.

Despite his evident shock, Hugo Grant demonstrates that he is thinking through the events as they had unfolded.

'The séance, then – that Poppy initiated. What was it that so prompted Jane?'

DS Jones nods.

'When Karl Eastwood earlier announced he had been out to buy a newspaper, your wife would have calculated that they each must have returned at the same time. Perhaps she even saw him, or at least heard his car on the driveway. We guessed that in her haste she left wet footprints leading to your bedroom – or, at least, she could be persuaded that she had done. You were in Room 4. Mr Eastwood was in Room 5.'

'You mean *four* wasn't the depth – it was the room number? And *wet feet.*'

271

'That's correct, sir.'

He gazes at the part-shaded windows beyond the detectives, unblinking, as if he is imagining what lies beyond. After a moment he snaps out of the little daydream.

'We're not really outdoor types. For our walk we borrowed wellingtons from the porch. Remember I told you that Jane wanted to come back because her feet were hurting? She had waded out of her depth and her boots had overflowed. I thought it was a bit foolhardy – not like her at all. She was covering it up, wasn't she?'

Skelgill is nodding, just perceptibly. He glances at DS Jones and raises an eyebrow. She might be about to respond, but Hugo Grant has moved on.

'And the D.A. – not Daisy, not Dalbrae – but Jane's maiden name, Dalmellington?'

'Yes. That was the idea, sir.'

'But – how would Karl have known that?'

'Mr Eastwood told us that at the Mills' cocktail party he'd had a conversation with your wife. They discussed their family origins. He has ancestors from the west of Scotland and they got on to the subject of surnames. So he did in fact know, although I don't believe it hinged on that. I imagine your wife was repressing an immense burden of stress, and it would not have taken much to trigger a response. Quite likely she was not thinking clearly about the backstory – just that her secret was under threat.'

Hugo Grant lowers his gaze and abstractedly turns the gold band on his ring finger.

'I can't believe it. Jane – killing someone. Almost two people.'

Then he looks sharply from one police officer to the other.

'What about Simon Mills?'

DS Jones makes a placatory gesture with her left hand.

'We don't believe your wife was connected in any way, other than she took the opportunity of the Mills' Christmas gathering to plant the tracking device. A thorough investigation by South Mercia Police concluded that Mr Mills' death was accidental. We reviewed the evidence, and could not identify any new leads. But there remain unexplained elements, and there is a reasonable case to be made that tampering took place. The motives for such may lie elsewhere.'

Hugo Grant nods broodingly. Although her words might come as a small relief, something seems to be troubling him. DS Jones detects his hesitancy.

'What is it, sir?'

He seems to start – he regards her with surprise, as though he has noticed something for the first time – indeed his eyes seem to wander in fascination over her hair, which she has not tied back and which is catching in its natural highlights glints of sun that penetrate the venetian blinds.

'I've never told anyone about this. In fact I haven't thought about it for a long time. I met Jane through her roommate at university – she was called Sally, whom I'd been out with for a drink once or twice. Sally invited me to the end-of-term ball. When I called round to their flat to collect her, Jane came to the door wearing Sally's dress, all done up to the nines. She said Sally had suffered a calamity with her hair – she had this great mass of strawberry blonde locks, really striking. Jane said she had agreed with Sally that she would come in her place – to save wasting the cost of the tickets. I didn't even see Sally; I was probably late getting there and Jane hustled me away. And it wasn't as if Sally and me were an item – although I think we could have been, given time. But the dance was a success and before I realised it, Jane and I *were* dating.'

Hugo Grant pauses to press his fingertips to his temples, as though prising these details from some crevice of his memory requires more than mental effort alone. Both detectives listen with bated breath, for there must surely be some corollary.

'It was the following academic year. Jane had a flat of her own, and I'd never really seen anything more of Sally. But one evening we were in a pub on Byres Road – it was packed with students, I think it was Burns Night – and Sally was there with a bunch of her girlfriends, I remember she looked fantastic, with her amazing hair like a great headdress. I was conscious of some sort of tension – not that anything kicked off, just dirty looks across the room – but later on one of Sally's friends pushed in next to me while I was in the scrum at the bar. She was pretty drunk and she just came out with something like, "you know Jane sabotaged Sally's hair that night, don't you?" I had no idea at first what she meant, but she told me that Sally's leave-in conditioner had been tampered with – it wrecked her hair and gave it a green tinge like you can get from a swimming pool.'

He looks questioningly at DS Jones, hoping she will understand. She responds accordingly.

'It takes chlorine to cause that effect. The chemicals could have been hazardous.'

Hugo Grant shudders, as if it had been his own misdeed.

Skelgill interjects.

'Did you ask her if she did it?'

He nods.

'Yes. She kind of laughed, and said something like, "it's a dog-eat-dog world" – except I think it was about cats, you know?'

The detectives ponder his explanation in silence. Certainly he has provided an insight into his wife's character that is not apparent from the reserved and reticent impression she gives. And now he has something to add.

'I think on the night of the first séance she might have seen Daisy holding my hand at the table. I can't help feeling responsible for all this.'

DS Jones regards him penetratingly.

'Sir, there comes a point beyond which you cannot hold yourself responsible for someone else's actions. And what you did at the table, it would have been a supportive gesture, under the circumstances.'

Hugo Grant does not look entirely convinced. He sighs reflectively.

'My mates all expected me to have married someone glamorous, someone with a big personality; not someone dour and plain.'

It is a peculiar confession, albeit the strain of the situation must be telling upon him. DS Jones seems to realise that he is regarding her almost forsakenly – but she becomes conscious that Skelgill too is looking at her. A smudge of burgundy forms upon the Mediterranean complexion of her prominent cheekbones.

'Someone more like Daisy.'

She has said this before she has realised it; but Hugo Grant does not appear offended that she has engaged with the rather intimate tangent he has taken. And, now, a little paradoxically, he shrugs his shoulders.

'You know – I don't think it would have worked out. Okay – Daisy and I had some sort of enduring bond – but she, well – how can I put it? I would say that while she was popular and good company – most of the others perceived her as childish, selfish, spoiled – she wasn't quite adored. Maybe that made it all the more infuriating for Jane.'

24. RYDAL WATER

Sunday, 7.00 a.m. – mid May

'It's hard to imagine a more beautiful place than this.'

Skelgill does a kind of exaggerated double take. DS Jones is grinning; she understands she is tempting fate, issuing a challenge to the god of Murphy's Law. She raises a palm apologetically.

'I know – last time I said that, the mountain rescue rang.'

Now it is Skelgill's turn to grin.

'This time, lass, my mobile's in the car.'

DS Jones shrugs languidly, in the way of *que sera, sera*. She turns her gaze across the lake and up towards Rydal Grange.

Skelgill squints at her from beneath the brim of his Tilley hat. He has insisted that she don his spare midge hat, and wear eye protection, for they have graduated to fly-casting with a team of three hooks.

'If your phone had been in your car a fortnight ago – if we hadn't intervened when we did, I mean, so early, so soon after Daisy Mills died – say a walker had found the body later in the day – I think the whole sinister side of it could have been overlooked. Jane Grant might have faded into the background.'

Skelgill nods pensively.

'Aye. She dropped a clanger making that phone call.'

'It must have been a spur-of-the-moment decision. But probably it seemed irresistible to put Kenneth Dalbrae in the frame. She couldn't have known for sure that Daisy Mills would go to see the waterfalls that morning. She would have had to improvise when she realised the opportunity was unfolding.' DS Jones turns to look at Skelgill. 'She *did* improvise – and trust you to notice the wellies, Guv!'

Skelgill grimaces, despite what is intended as a compliment.

'Thing is, I didn't.' He waves a hand as if midges are troubling him. 'Well – I did, but I didn't. Dalbrae saw some boots were missing and so he guessed Daisy Mills had gone to the pools. We found no footwear. We weren't even thinking about it. When I got down to Rydal Grange I noticed two gaps in the row on the porch, a small pair and a big pair – and later they were back. The Grants had used them. It was staring us in the face that it wasn't Daisy Mills but Jane Grant that had taken the first pair. Like you say – she improvised.'

DS Jones nods.

'I don't see how we could have put two and two together. We had so little information at that stage. And Kenneth Dalbrae was a glaring distraction.'

But Skelgill remains dissatisfied.

'I'll tell you what else was bugging me – when I had a deek about the Mills' place? In Daisy Mills' wardrobe – all these fancy shoes – she had big feet – size six or seven, I'd say. Dalbrae told you it was a small pair that had gone. I should have listened harder to my instincts.'

DS Jones nods and has to readjust the too-large hat as it threatens to slip over her eyes.

'Jane Grant was probably soaked, Guv – I mean, her jeans and top. I bet she left a trail of water to their bedroom, not just footprints. There must have been a bundle of sodden clothes to be discovered, if only we had known it.'

Skelgill rubs a knuckle against the stubble on his chin, his jaw set determinedly.

'She'd have been just about the last person we'd have suspected.'

DS Jones reflects upon his assessment; her gaze drifts across the milky surface of Rydal Water.

'I suppose she was banking on the insinuation that Simon Mills was murdered. Any investigating team would be bound to link the two deaths. That immediately made her an outside bet – how could Jane Grant have possibly engineered the poisoning incident? Why would she, even? So, in a way, she did succeed – she sent us off on a wild-goose chase.'

Skelgill suddenly laughs, a rumble of ironic triumph in his throat. DS Jones plies him with a look that demands clarification.

'Aye – but what she didn't bank on was us daft country coppers – wild-goose chases a speciality.'

DS Jones chuckles – he takes the mickey out of himself but it is a disguised warning to anyone who might try to escape justice on his beat. *Don't.*

And he is right. Had they not set off for the Midlands with an open mind they would not have discovered the tracking device on Daisy Mills' car. DS Leyton would not have confirmed DS Jones's hypothesis that Daisy Mills was secretly meeting someone. Pieced together with a pinch of serendipity – itself borne out of Skelgill's incorrigible habit to follow his nose, however irrational it might seem at the time – these facts and many other small contextual learnings came together into a coherent, compelling pattern that fitted the motives of one person and one person alone, Jane Grant.

'But it did feel like we were making progress – that there was something in the offing.' DS Jones's tone is constructive, and she points beyond the bow, as if to emphasize her nautical metaphor. 'It wasn't like we were drifting aimlessly.'

Skelgill gives an ironic laugh.

'Like we are now!'

He affects offence, as though she is castigating him for the dearth of bites and apparently rudderless progress about the lake.

'No, Guv!' She protests the innocence of her remark. 'You made us wait. For example, the tracker on the Fiat – it would have been easy to jump to the conclusion that Simon Mills planted it.'

Skelgill looks a little perplexed.

'I thought we did.'

But DS Jones is determined. She shakes her head vehemently, again almost dislodging the hat.

'I can see what you do. You notice all the signs.' Again she gestures, more sweepingly now. 'A heron over there. A swarm of flies over there. A splosh over there.' (Skelgill cannot suppress a grin at her description of a rise, but he allows her to continue.) 'But you don't go flailing at the oars to chase one thing and then the next. You wait, wait, wait.'

Now Skelgill makes a face of genuine resignation. He looks inclined to say what else is there to do in the absence of understanding. As he has reiterated more than once, seek motives in a tight-knit group of friends and they will come spilling out of the first closet you open. But he settles for a halfway house explanation. He develops his companion's angling analogy.

'I find the longer I fish, the luckier I get.'

DS Jones grins wryly.

'Now I'm not sure that's going to apply to me. I feel there's a certain threshold of skill required in order for luck to kick in.'

She makes a cast. It is not entirely clear whether she refers to catching criminals or fish. Skelgill watches acutely where the flies have settled. That he does not say anything might suggest he is satisfied with her efforts on both fronts.

DS Jones begins to retrieve, using the figure-of-eight method he has shown her. Skelgill's gaze is drawn to the motion of her slender fingers, she does it with a natural dexterity; she is a quick learner and for all her analytical skills she has intuition in spades; perhaps she just doesn't know it.

After a moment's silence she brings the subject back to the loose ends of the case. They have each made telephone calls, and have not yet entirely apprised one another of the outcomes.

'What did Harry Badger say, by the way?'

Skelgill scoffs disparagingly – his disdain plainly aimed at the man and not at DS Jones for conjuring his spectre.

'He's in no hurry to admit to owt. I put it to him, straight – gave him a chance to come clean and look good. I said whoever made up the "Simon Murder" business did us a favour. Jane Grant was gunning for Daisy Mills, whatever – it just gave her an angle. But it also gave *us* an angle. If there'd been no séance – no flippin' palaver, as Leyton puts it – just a woman drowned in a dangerous pool – we'd have thought a lot less about it. Just like you say.'

DS Jones nods.

'I see now why you were right to insist that the two deaths were connected. I mean, technically they weren't – but the way you just put it – *they were*. The first séance was the fulcrum, the middle of the merry-go-round. It kept us spinning.'

Skelgill growls again.

'Spinning? There were times I felt reet nickt int' head.' He borrows from hill-farmer Arthur Hope's stock of colloquialisms. Discombobulated, perhaps. His attention is drawn to some item of minutiae, an invisible zephyr that mimics a fish cresting the surface. Without altering his gaze or his expression he speaks evenly. 'Did you ever consider a supernatural explanation?'

DS Jones regards him with a look that expects a punchline – but there are times when it is impossible to tell if Skelgill is joking. He hails from a clan that has its roots embedded deep in fell country, where reality and superstition are not always clearly delineated. She gives a nervous laugh.

'I couldn't ever see you proposing that to the Chief, Guv.'

'I'd have said it was Smart's idea.'

To her relief, he has a mischievous glint in his eye. He casually pulls up a leg and rests his boot on the middle thwart on which he sits, and then crooks an arm around his knee and grabs his wrist to lock the pose. He gazes calmly across the water; beyond, under the oaks is a wash of bluebells. Relaxation does not come easily to Skelgill, but DS Jones sees it now. She chuckles more confidently. He turns his head.

'What is it?'

'Oh. When I spoke with Karl Eastwood – actually, I recorded a conference call with him and his wife for the CPS. Something he said made me laugh. When he was moving the glass – right at the end of the séance – he felt another person pulling at it! He had to yank it away to avoid a conflicting message. He said his heart was in his mouth.'

Skelgill raises a sardonic eyebrow.

'I bet that was Badger, an' all. Darth *blank* Vader.' Skelgill inserts a colourful expletive that would not win the acclaim of George Lucas, but its comic timing makes DS Jones laugh.

'That's another thing you won't have to explain to the Chief.'

Skelgill nods wryly, but his thoughts may have moved on. After a moment he responds, his tone strangely introspective.

'Harry Badger did say one thing. Surprised me a bit. Said he pitied Hugo Grant – having to go through life loving Daisy Mills and her loving him. Reckoned there was no actual reason to stop them getting together.'

Perhaps Skelgill's uncharacteristic sentimentality prompts DS Jones to play devil's advocate.

'Just that they were married to other people, maybe?'

Skelgill looks like he disagrees, and remains curiously discomfited.

In silence, he watches her cast.

'Strike!'

DS Jones has not quite been paying attention and she misses the silent swirl that sinks the black feathery *Bibio* that Skelgill has tied onto the top dropper.

She strikes correctly and firmly, but a split second too late – any trout worth its salt knows stainless steel from a soft-bodied hawthorn.

'*Ow!*'

It is DS Jones who exclaims and Skelgill responds with an oath – intoned not in reproach but with concern – for, while he instinctively swayed away from the rapidly returning team of flies, DS Jones rather more naively sat in the line of fire – and the said *Bibio* has embedded itself into the ball of her right thumb where she grasps the cork butt.

Skelgill takes the rod and lays it aside.

'That's sore!' DS Jones pulls off her sunglasses. A hint of panic enters her voice. 'It's right in. How will we get it out?'

Skelgill takes her wrist in a firm grip, as though she is in danger of exacerbating the situation. He has pliers attached to a zinger on his vest and with a deft twist he removes the hook.

DS Jones winces retrospectively and Skelgill grins broadly. He holds the fly for inspection like a slightly manic dentist after a successful extraction.

'Don't fret lass – see – it's barbless.'

When it would be easier to let go he keeps hold of her wrist and reaches one-handed for a wicker trug in the stern. He fishes out a first-aid kit and now needs both hands. He lays her wrist, palm upwards on his knee. The wound is tiny but bleeding nevertheless. Skelgill presses for half a minute with an antiseptic wipe, his lips compressed in concentration and breathing through flared nostrils, as if the near-catch and subsequent injury has raised his heart rate. DS Jones sits in entranced compliance.

Next he selects a plaster and bites open its wrapper before laying it carefully over the sterile puncture mark. As he applies pressure with his palm, in a smoothing movement, DS Jones's fingers, like one half of a Venus fly trap, close over his. It is a moment reminiscent of their reconstruction of Daisy Mills' clasp on Hugo Grant – and indeed DS Jones squeezes hard and digs in her nails between Skelgill's knuckles. She feels him flinch and she laughs, but does not let up. Her dark eyes are sparkling.

'The first cut is the deepest.'

Skelgill grimaces in a show of defiance, but beneath the shadows of the battered hat brim there is vulnerability in the grey-green eyes.

'Aye – but surely there's no hard and fast rule about that, lass?'

***

POST SCRIPT

Two months later – article in the Middlemarch Mercury

Edition Friday 23rd July:

'POISONER' ON LIFE SUPPORT

There has been an extraordinary development in the case of the 'Christmas Gin Poisonings', which was reported extensively in the *Mercury* at the turn of the year.

'Extraordinary' since a suspect has been named as Dr Gemma Amanita, 41 of Daventry University – whom attentive readers will recall, contributed an article to the *Mercury* on the very subject. She put forward an expert opinion that the harvesting of berries was the source of contamination. It is now believed that this was an attempt to throw the police off the scent.

DC Mary Garth of South Mercia Constabulary spoke exclusively to the *Mercury*:

"On Wednesday evening Dr Amanita's husband George, 53, returned home to find his wife in a state of unconsciousness. What is believed to be the missing sixth bottle of poisoned gin was found beside her, half-empty, along with a suicide note. Dr Amanita was conveyed to Middlemarch County Hospital, but so far has remained in a coma."

Meanwhile, a confidential source at Daventry University has told the *Mercury* that it was an 'open secret' that until recently Dr Amanita was conducting an affair with a married colleague. Our own inquiries have revealed that her lover's household was one of those five involved in the Christmas poisoning incident, and the man's wife, along with Dr Amanita's husband, were the persons most seriously affected among eight people present for a dinner party.

Dr Amanita, as a Senior Research Fellow of the Department of Botanical Sciences, would have had access to the deadly compound atropine in its synthetic state. While it is too early to divine exactly what might have taken place in December, and what the motives and modus operandi of the poisoner were, it is tempting for the amateur sleuth to jump to a melodramatic conclusion.

Pressed on this matter, DC Garth was a little taciturn:

"In collaboration with our colleagues in Cumbria Constabulary, we have eliminated all other possible suspects. We would hope in due course to question Dr Amanita in connection with the death of Mr Simon Mills, which may now be considered a case of manslaughter. In the meantime it would appear that some people had a narrow escape."

In the light of these astonishing revelations the *Mercury* contacted the The Rutland Gin-Trap Gin Co., which has suffered much adverse publicity during this period of uncertainty. On hearing the breaking news, proprietor Mr Jack Battlingbrook sounded surprisingly phlegmatic, and would only comment, *"Multum in Parvo!"*

Answers to this little mystery on a postcard, please.

Next in the series ...

A BLIND EYE TURNED, AN INJUSTICE DONE

High in lonely Swinesdale, notorious burglars Jake and Boris Baddun perish in a burnt-out stolen Mercedes. Known associate Dale Spooner leaves his biological signature and the predatory DI Alec Smart moves in for the kill. Spooner is convicted, and now languishes in jail.

A rumour reaches Skelgill: *Spooner is innocent and can prove it* – a cast-iron alibi, a video on a hidden mobile phone. But Spooner will not talk. At stake is the safety of his girlfriend Jade Nelson and their young child.

While Spooner remains the fall guy, the real killer walks free – and organised crime pulls the strings. Realising the jeopardy, unable officially to re-open the case, Skelgill and his team walk a tightrope. Their challenge: to penetrate a mystifying wall of silence, and 'unsolve' a murder – while nobody notices.

Printed in Great Britain
by Amazon